THE UNDEAD DAY SEVENTEEN

RR HAYWOOD

Copyright © R. R. Haywood 2015

R. R. Haywood asserts his moral right under the Copyright, Designs and Patents Act, 1988, to be identified as the author of this work.

All Rights reserved.

Disclaimer: This is a work of fiction. All characters and events, unless those clearly in the public domain, are fictitious, and any resemblance to actual persons, living, dead (or undead), is purely coincidental.

No part of this publication may be reproduced, copied, stored in a retrieval system, or transmitted, in any form or by any means, without the prior written consent of the copyright holder, nor be otherwise circulated in any form of binding or cover other than that in which it is published and without a similar condition being imposed on the subsequent purchaser.

Design, Cover and Illustration by Mark Swan

The story so far

The battle at the munitions factory was won but Lani was torn. Her body made weak by the incessant and relentless purge of the undead seeking to destroy Howie and all he loves.

Lani was strong and her body fought the infection but the mind is a powerful thing. On hearing a static filled radio transmission between Howie and Marcy she believed he had betrayed her.

Her mind broke and with it her body lost the ability to fight the infection.

Howie and the team were imprisoned but escaped by an old tunnel leading from the fort.

With the help of Marcy they fought their way back inside to rescue Lani only to find the fort held hostage and Lani on a killing spree.

With tensions running at breaking point, Maddox and his crews watched while Howie tried to reason with the woman he thought he loved.

Lani led Howie into the old armoury where the weapons and grenades were stored. They were together and alone.
Base emotions took over, the fear of death and an act of sex with a woman holding a grenade.
She pulled the pin. They fought and Howie only just escaped

as the grenade detonated, taken off his feet and blacking out on the hard earth as the armoury exploded.

The Undead Day Seventeen continues the story....

CHAPTER ONE

I'm out for a few seconds at most. The pressure wave of the detonation takes me off my feet and the overwhelming assault to my senses shuts my mind down as my eyes fill with flame and my head fills with noise. One single detonation as the first grenade goes off followed a split second by more explosions as the rest of the grenades follow, then rounds in the weapons and the flames scorch the night air as bullets ricochet off the solid walls of the fort.

My eyes open and I gain full sight of the roaring devastation unfolding just metres from me. Lani inside and there is no way she could have survived that. Nothing could survive something like that. Not even Dave.

I twist round on the ground to see the rest have dropped to the ground in fear and supplication. Almost as though in prayer to the gods of fire and destruction as the old armoury dissipates and blows apart. Rolling thunder claps boom for miles and I scrabble further back from the wall of heat beating at my face as scorching chunks of wall are turned into missiles that fly through the air.

With my hands covering my head I glance round and

up at the rest and spot a youth torn in half by a spinning fragment of debris that hits him with an explosion of blood and guts. More rain down on the heads and above the noise of the inferno I can hear screams of pain and agony as limbs are broken and skulls are fractured by the pressure wave sending the deadly lumps across the ground. At the far end the previously terrified and mute survivors are either up and running hell for leather in every direction or hugging the ground. The distance seems vast but the spinning chunks cross that ground seemingly with ease and more people are taken off their feet. I want to shout and roar for them to get down and stay down but the cacophony of sound threatens to burst my eardrums.

It goes on and on with an ever increasing ferocity as the walls of the rooms to the old armoury are blown asunder in every direction.

Tears pour down my face from shock, terror and pain of seeing Lani turn so viciously and the emotions burn through my heart and mind that everything we have done has been wrong. We were given a chance at redemption. Given immunity and a chance to make something good amidst the brutality of civilisation collapsing but look what we've done. A fort on an island with high walls that gave refuge but our own folly has destroyed it and brought more death. The incessant ability of mankind to cause pain and suffering and at the point I felt I could have changed something, done something or made it better I dropped my trousers and had sex instead.

Base emotions of pleasure and lust. I couldn't perform with Lani before because I was tired, worn out and exhausted but right there, in that room, I wanted to have sex as the pressure of the life and death struggle awoke something within me.

Hate consumes me with a sudden ferocity that has me on my feet and stalking towards the crews of youths lying pissing themselves in fear on the ground. Missiles screech past me like comets with flaming tails but I pay no heed and every step has my blood boiling hotter in my veins. Bodies torn and shredded lie in my way and the air is filled with the agonised screams of the dying.

'MOVE AWAY,' I grab at the first child and launch her further away from the area of danger, 'MOVE BACK... MOVE...' I grab and heave at them, dragging the children further back.

'DAVE...GET THESE KIDS MOVED.'

'MOVE BACK NOW...'

That voice booms louder than the raging fire and the explosions still detonating with percussive force that shakes the ground. Clarence lurches up shaking his head and grabbing a child in each hand he wades away to dump them and come back for more. Nick follows him a second later and grabbing a child he runs back then stops, stares at the broiling flames and looks over the expanse of ground to the survivors at the far side. With Lilly on his mind he looks to me and finds me waving to go and he runs flat out as heedless as I from the chunks of rock and brick splattering the ground.

'BLOWERS...COOKEY...GO WITH NICK.'

They're up and running as Nick leaps a flaming chunk that lands feet in front of his path. His arm waving at the survivors to move up the vehicle ramp and away from the missiles. To stay where they are is a lottery of death as the burning fragments work like shotgun pellets that take grown men and women off their feet.

Roy is up and working, dragging screaming children away. Paula too. Marcy clutching a little girl and shielding her with her body as a chunk of wall scorches right past them. Dave doesn't grab anyone but his voice does the work of five of us put together. Leaning low he bellows with such power that whole groups of kids are sent scuttling away from him.

I'm taken from my feet with a rugby tackle to the legs and I land hard with the air ripped from my lungs. Maddox on top of me and the chunk of wall sailing over our heads misses us by inches. His face is a mask of pure energy, both terrified and focussed with the job at hand. With the missile passed he rolls off and surges back to his feet as agile as a cat and grabs my wrist to pull me up. The second my feet gain the ground he's off and running to usher, badger, shepherd and push his children away from the immediate vicinity.

Several are dead or dying with bodies inflicted with varying degrees of injuries. The one I saw being torn in half is spread across a distance of several metres and so badly mangled there's no way of knowing if it was a boy or a girl. More scream and clutch at broken arms or legs pulverised by heavy fragments. Others lie still and seemingly asleep and there's no way of knowing if they're dead or unconscious.

With the majority of the youths now away and safe we set to work running from body to body. Fingers to necks and ears to chests trying to detect heartbeats and pulses but the noise is so bad and the vibrations of the fire so harsh we can't tell anything. I scoop a black clad boy up with blood running free from his ears and run towards the medical bay with him draped in my arms. He feels so light and frail. Just a small child with thin limbs and pain etched on his face. He doesn't cry out or say anything but stares at me with wide eyes filled with terror.

'DOCTORS...DOCTORS...' I boot the door open, run

in and lay the child on the first bed as the four doctors run from the back. Two of them with fresh cuts and bruises to their faces that can only have come from Lani. 'More coming in,' I rush back out and almost collide with Clarence coming through the entrance carrying a young girl with a mangled right leg. Roy behind him, Paula behind Roy and there are still more to come.

As I get out I spot Nick and Blowers shouting for Clarence as they struggle to carry a heavy man between them. Clarence runs out and I grab his thick arm and wave at the lads. He nods and runs over to scoop the screaming man from them then runs back as though he is carrying a child.

'FIRE.'

The word strike a chord. Not an order to open fire but a warning and I spin to see Dave pointing to the tents and hastily erected structures put up by the survivors now flaming from the scorching hot fragments of grenade metal and burning rock landing amongst them. Bone dry from the hot sun and they go up with a whumph as the hungry flames find new fuel to eat.

I can't match Dave's voice to shout and anything uttered by me will be swallowed by the incredible noise already in the fort. I sprint towards the fire knowing the new armoury is only protected by double wooden doors set metres away from the edge of the tents and structures. If those doors go then the inside goes and we'll be missing a whole lot more than one section of wall. I know there are water pipes set in the wall with hoses attached used for everything from washing to drinking. The heat is immense. From my right where the old armoury is and my left from the new fire spreading at an alarming rate.

I get to the wall and follow it along to the first hose with my hand shielding my face from the wall of super-hot air wafting at me. Grimacing I clutch at the spokes of the tap and twist it hard until the length of thick rubber stiffens with the fast flow of water sent charging through.

Hand over hand I pull the hose to me until the end comes into my hands. I turn it round and quickly blast myself with cooling water with my eyes screwed shut then I drag it over and lay the end so the spray is aimed towards the first row of tents.

I run along the wall towards the rear gate and the next hose I know is set there and suddenly the fort feels so huge and it takes seconds to run the distance. The fire is closer here and the heat steams to dry the water I sprayed down my body. The spokes are turned, the hose stiffens and I get the end angled towards the fire. The flames are huge. Well over my head height and they roar with a noise that makes me think it's a living creature fighting to stay alive.

These tents have to be moved. If they catch alight these two hoses will do nothing to stop the flames getting to the wooden doors of the new armoury. With the hose held in front like a sword I dive forward and stay low from the raging heat threatening to sear my skin. Grabbing pegs I try and heave them free from the rock hard ground but they've been beaten down with hammers and I lack the strength to pull them out. I grab the material and try to rip it away but the ropes are strong and refuse to yield from their grip on the pegs.

I move back from the fire and look round frantic to find something as Dave runs towards me.

'KNIFE...CUT THE ROPES...'

He nods and a split second later a blade appears in his hand. With his lightning speed he surges along the row flicking at the ropes and lines that snap as the tension is cut. Tents fall inwards sagging from the lack of support.

I grab the first one and start ripping it up and away from the ground and heave it towards the fire. Someone at my side working with me and I catch the swish of long hair that is suddenly gripped, twisted and tied back from Marcy's face.

'GET THE HOSE,' I go for the next tent while she darts back and aims the spray towards the flames. 'ON ME,' I drop and wait for the cooling water to rush over my skin then I'm up and grabbing at the flimsy material to rip it from the ground to be thrown at the flames. Let them be burnt now in a controlled way rather than burnt so close to the doors.

Marcy runs sideways to grab the second hose and holding both she showers me and Dave who passes me a knife to cut the lines and tear the material apart. Soaked but burning hot we work with faces flushed red. This is hell. Fire and fumes. Noises of explosions. People screaming. Dead bodies. Blood and innards strewn everywhere. We died when the infection started and this is where we have been sent for nothing man made can be this terrible and frightening.

The lads sprint into the fray and within a split second have processed the work so desperately needed to be done. Marcy sprays them and they set to work. Hands are singed and we cry out at the flames getting closer and closer like a monster that grows higher with every passing second.

I catch glimpse of a body within the flames. Someone who didn't move fast enough or cowered down to hide from the devastation with a flawed instinct that the walls of the flimsy tent would protect them. Eaten by fire and I pray they suffocated quickly as the flames ate the oxygen from around them. My team come one by one. Out of breath and already exhausted from lack of sleep and constant motion but they dive in to keep the flames from the wooden doors but they grow bigger and hungrier and edge closer to prove our pathetic efforts are in vain.

Nick runs behind Marcy and grabs the hose in his hands then works back to follow it to the wall. He finds the tap and drops to a crouch as he feels along the pipe fixed to the wall and traces it back to the doors of the new armoury. I catch his train his thought and realise the pipe runs over the top of the doors. He turns and I nod at him, 'DO IT...'

He shows me an open handed gesture, showing that he's got nothing to sever it with.

'CLARENCE...'

'HERE,' he runs towards me with his bald head shining red from the heat. I and the big man turns to see Nick pointing frantically at the pipe above the doors. A confused look crosses Clarence face until he traces the pipe down to the tap then along the hose to Marcy still spraying the lads at work. The realisation hits and he runs to Nick and reaches up to grab the pipe above the door with two hands. He pauses and bunches his muscles before the explosion of power wrenches the pipe free from the fixings that ping the brackets off into the air. Another pause and this time he roars as he pulls the pipe down and snaps it clean in half with a strength that still makes my mouth drop open.

That he can snap a pipe is one thing but that pipe is feeding two hoses that are both spraying water with high pressure. As that flow is broken so the water comes powering from the fractured pipe with double the flow that came from one hose. A jet of water like that from a fire hose and it gushes metres before it sails down into the flames.

Marcy stares dumbly at the hoses and turns with a

worried look before noticing the broken pipe being held and angled by Clarence as he directs the spray towards the edge of the fire.

'THE GROUND,' Nick shouts and waves at the ground immediately in front of us. Clarence dips the pipe and instantly the water is sluicing on the hard compacted earth. Puddles form and streams are created as we make a desperate bid to stop the flames getting any closer. They do get closer and for a few charged minutes we watch the battle play out as the flames lap at the water that evaporates in clouds of steam. The sustained flow replaces that taken and for a while it could go either way. The fire roars with fury at being denied a path and for the final few seconds we're all beaten back and making ready to flee with the belief the fire will get the doors.

Relief sags every single one of us on the spot when the flames dwindle to a less terrifying blaze and I spot Marcy still clutching the inert hoses and staring with her mouth hanging open and the fire casting an orange glow on her reddened features. It starts raining and the ground spatters with a million droplets of water. Every one of us looks up into the clear sky and then round to see Clarence holding the pipe straight up so the water shoots high to spread and fall back down. I step forward and stand quietly in the deluge soaking through my clothes and plastering my hair to my scalp. It's hot right here and the water is cool. The contrast sends shivers down my spine and I know there is a million things I should be doing but I don't want to move. A sensation of movement and I look to see I'm not the only one doing it. Cookey, Blowers, Paula, Nick. All of us are there within that false rain and I'm taken back to Tower Bridge in London when we stopped to face Darren. It rained then and the liquid seemed to cleanse us somehow.

Christ, it feels like months ago, years even. When did that happen?

'When were we at Tower Bridge?' I ask out loud.

'Sixth day,' someone answers, maybe Blowers, 'I was thinking the same thing.'

'What we doing with that?' Clarence asks from next to me. I open my eyes and slowly turn to see he's wedged the pipe in place to keep the water spraying up.

'With what?' I reply.

'With the pipe? It'll keep spraying.'

'There'll be a shut off valve somewhere,' Nick says.

'Let it run for a bit,' I say with a nod to the flames. I look round like a mother hen counting my brood, 'where's Roy?'

'Helping the doctors,' Paula says.

'And Reginald?'

'Cowering with the children,' Marcy says and finally releases her grip on the hoses.

'Is that safe?' I ask her.

'Reggie?' She reaches up and sweeps her soaking wet hair back from her forehead so it lies flat and glistening down her back, 'he wouldn't hurt a fly.'

'Sure?'

'I'm sure. He hates blood and he's the most squeamish man I've ever known.'

'But...'

'He's not a vampire, Howie,' she cuts me off with a warning look, 'he's the same as me.'

'Fair enough.'

'What now?' She asks and gives voice to the question no doubt running through everyone's head.

'Now?' I lift my face to the glorious rain pattering down and the image of Lani rushes into my head. The image of her smiling and I can almost hear the way she laughs when

Cookey gets her going. That changes to the snarling beast that was in the old armoury and the look of pure hatred she had for me. Except it wasn't her. It was the thing inside. The infection. The hive mind at work as it saw me. But then Lani was still there and it was Lani I had sex with. The thought of it appals me. That we had sex while she clutched a live grenade. We tried to have sex before but I was too tired, too exhausted and didn't perform. It grated on me when I heard Roy and Paula had done it five times in one night and like a cheap idiot I felt like I needed to prove something and right there, at that precise moment when my life was at stake I felt horny and took the chance. What the fuck was that about?

'You okay?' I feel a hand on my arm and look down to see slender fingers smudged with dirt and attached to tanned hands and slim arms. Marcy looking at me with what appears to be genuine care but she withdraws her gentle touch when the snarl touches my top lip. Blanching she looks away as though both hurt and ashamed.

The intense hatred rears back up. Not at Marcy or at what she is or the fact she touched my arm but for everything we have become. I look over to the old armoury and the flames licking at the sky. The dead bodies on the ground offend me. The screams of the dying bring insult to the injury of our failures. We are but men and we are flawed but I always thought those flaws were what made us human. That the perfection lay in the imperfections. We fucked up but we meant well but then the road to hell is paved with good intentions. Isn't that what they say? They? Who the fuck are they? *They* are the same fucking idiots that failed to stop bad things happening and right now bad things are happening. People are crying in fear. Real people who just a short time ago were leading lives so wrapped up in the day to day drudgery they had no concept of real life and death struggles. People who have fled, run, hidden and finally got to the place they were told was safe.

Mr Howie and his army. They run the fort and it's safe there. It's the last bastion of the living and outside those gates we fought to protect this place and so many have fallen and given their lives so we few can remain. Big Chris gave his life. My sister, Sarah gave hers. Ted, Sergeant Hopewell. Terri. Steven and Tom. They fought and died and they did so that life can keep going and what have we done with it?

Doing something wrong makes you human. Making mistakes is part of life. Making the same mistakes again and again makes you a dumb cunt.

A spark of realisation brought by a memory of the safari park and the awful sight of the gorilla fighting the lion. Both wanted to survive. Both wanted to live. Both were willing to give the ultimate so their kind could continue and they did it with everything they had. There was no holding back.

The fort has to remain and it has to be a place free from persecution or force otherwise all we're doing is creating the same environment for mankind to fuck themselves over with again.

Children with guns? What the fuck was I thinking? How did that happen? We poured scorn on news bulletins of African children forced into being soldiers and I've done the same thing here. How? I stare at Clarence and see the failure in his eyes. I look to Blowers and see it in him. All of them have failed but only because I have. I lead and they do as I do.

The abhorrence sends a cataclysmic feeling of doom sinking in my gut only to rear up with the same stubborn refusal to be quietened that has kept me alive so far and a nagging voice pulls at the back of my head.

Why would Lani kill herself? Why would the infection kill the one person who knows more about us than anyone else turned so far?

'Shit! We're putting the wrong fire out…'

I burst away towards the old armoury and the fierce blaze roaring into the night sky. She wouldn't kill herself. The infection prizes survival too much to simply let one of our team be blown up like that.

I head to the closest section of wall near the raging fire and starting hunting for hoses and taps. The pipes are visible and it doesn't take long to trace the pipe to the nearest tap and I'm suddenly very aware this is the tap we used so much to clean up from our fights and work. I grab the tap and twist the spokes but nothing happens. I twist and twist and stare about failing to understand why the water won't flow.

'The pipe runs above the armoury,' Nick gets to my side, 'it would have burst when the wall blew out.'

We run down and past the scorching heat until we find the wall on the other side of the old armoury and the pipe that runs along and disappears into the ruined mess.

'GET MORE HOSES,' I shout the order at the team and repeat it several times for the noise here is incredible. They run off as Nick finds the tap and twists it fully on. A new sound joins the cacophony, of water instantly turning to hissing with evaporation as the jet sprays from the unseen broken pipe directly into the blaze. I grab at the pipe and heave like Clarence did. It takes me longer but Nick helps and we ping the rusted brackets from the wall to free the pipe that we drag out until the red glowing end is in view. The broken section has already melted away but the spray of water now coming out cools the metal as fast as the heat tries to warp it. We can't touch anywhere near the end for fear of the heat but we get it pulled out and working together we aim the jet at the wide section of missing wall.

It isn't enough. Not by far. The fire is so fierce that it seems the water is having no effect at all. Another hose is dragged up and already flowing it too is turned onto the blaze. The gap between the inner and outer wall only runs across the front and partially into the sides of the fort. This far round and there is only one outer wall separating the fort from the sea. It's thick but no doubt the force of the blast has blown it out and given an escape route for Lani.

Looking at it now and it seems impossible that anything, let alone a human being, could survive that blast but within my mind I recall there was the initial explosion then a slight pause before the rest went up. Lani would not kill herself and the infection would not kill a member of the team after trying so hard to get us.

A third hose finally joins in but a botched job has been done connecting two lengths of hose together and the flow is far less than the other two. It does work but it's painfully slow and the constant flow of water works to cool the closest section and the flames are beaten back inside the rooms and as my eyes adjust, so I start to see glimpses of the interior. The walls inside have been blown apart with huge gaping holes but enough remains to have given some cover. I was right too, the outer wall is blown and here and there I catch a fleeting view of the sea beyond. It's ironic that just feet away is enough water to douse these flames instantly but we're in here relying on things that are only marginally more powerful than garden hoses.

Inch by inch we claw back the section from the fire. The water does part of the work but also the lack of fuel.

With everything burnt away within the old rooms the fire has only brick, stone and plaster to eat. The wooden frames are gone. The furniture too. The fire is tamed but the heat remains too high for an entry to be gained and with only three hoses it renders us useless and impotent. We pace up and down. Nick hands cigarettes round and we smoke. We don't speak other than to give commands or pass observations. Maddox joins us and we wait, we bloody wait for what feels like eternity until we can start inching closer to peer inside.

'Soak me and Dave,' I call out and wait for the hoses to be turned on us. Once drenched we start inching towards the ruined entrance and gain the first foothold inside the rooms. The smell is disgusting. Wet burnt chemicals like rubber and oil. It reeks and brings tears to my eyes and I have to clamp my hand over my mouth. Dave doesn't seem as affected and gets further in than me. In the main room and the floor is covered with lumps of blackened slag that are totally unrecognisable of any form. The interior walls are broken and fractured and the humidity is awful. Water pouring in to an area of such high heat that it feels like a steam room.

We use torches to shine down and round the floor of the main room. Into the corners of the wall that still stand and we toe the sodden steaming disgusting black heaps on the ground and search for anything that might resemble a human form.

In truth the devastation within is so total that she could have melted into any one of the unrecognisable lumps or have been blown apart. It doesn't feel right though. It feels empty.

Dave turns slowly shining his torch round the walls, 'where was she?' He asks.

'There,' I point to a spot a couple of feet to the side of him.

'Here?'

'Er,' I turn and look back at the entrance, 'yeah...I think so...it looks so different in here now.'

'The grenades were on the floor?'

'Yeah, there I think,' I point to the ground between us, 'she wouldn't have killed herself. The infection wants us too much to have let that happened. She got out that hole,' I shine my torch through the gap in the broken interior wall and out through the ruined outer wall to the dark surface of the sea beyond.

Dave holds the torch in front and motions as though pulling something from it and I realise he's using it like a grenade. He holds it firm and turns to look at the doorway to the trapdoor room where the broken outer wall is. He nods and holds the hand holding the torch out.

'Dropped...One...' He pace quickly away to the door of the trapdoor room, 'two...' He disappears from view into the room then his head reappears as I look through the broken chunks. 'Three....if she got down into that corner the blast would have gone past and...'

'And what? She got out? Dave? And what?'

He stands completely still shining his torch into the corner of the room where he indicated Lani was hiding before she got out.

'Come in here.'

The tone of his voice sends a river of ice through my veins. The command so gently given that it's quite possibly the worst thing I have ever heard.

'Dave?' I croak the word out and cross the short distance to the doorway, 'what?'

He doesn't say anything but steps aside and shines the

torch into the corner. Within a split second I have taken it in. All of it. The whole of it. My gut flips, twists and sinks down with such a wrench I stagger and lean against the still hot wall.

'Fuck...'

Lani dead. The knife still in her hand that was used to tear a slit in her guts. Blackened from the fire. All of her hair burnt away and the skin blistered and already peeling away from the bone. The innards scooped out by her other hand are cooked and smoke like burnt offal and the smell hits me at the same time as I my mind processes the view. I drop down and puke on the floor with hot bile that retches from the stomach. My eyes fill with tears and my throat burns but I make myself stare up and over at the corpse.

That she ruined her own body in the last seconds of death is obvious. Was it her doing it to prevent the infection taking control or was it the infection doing it as a message?

'She could have got out,' I rasp and glance the few feet to the gaping hole in the outer wall, 'it's right there...she could have...' I puke again and this time only acid comes out.

'She disembowelled herself, Mr Howie.'

'I can fucking see that.'

He looks down quickly at the harsh rebuke, 'I'm not fucking blind, Dave. I can see it. I can her guts have been ripped out by her own fucking hand.'

'I'm sorry.'

'What else has she done? Go on...tell me....what else has she done?' My anger vents at him and a rare look of misery crosses his face. He shuffles position and looks first at me then away from my demanding gaze.

'I can't tell if you are asking a real question or not,' he

says so quietly and so wretched it rips the vehemence from my mind.

'Sorry,' I say in a whisper. Swallowing the bile I force myself to look at Lani and slowly get back to my feet. I aim the torch and slowly take in the horrible details. She got to the corner as the blast swept past and enough of the wall remains to have given enough shelter from the blast and initial debris. She would have been singed and possibly battered but there was a way out. A safe exit.

'Why?'

'Why what, Mr Howie?'

'She's ripped her own guts out...'

'And slit her wrists.'

Another lurch of pain shoots through my heart but my wavering torch picks out the ends of her arms and the blackened pools beneath each wrist. They are dried out now from the intense blaze but I've seen enough pools of blood now to recognise what they were.

Her left hand holds the knife and in the midst of the misery the abstract memory of Lani being right handed comes to mind. Not that it matters now. She's dead. Either she took her own life in such a way to make sure she could never come back or the infection did it to prove something. Either way she is dead. Lani is dead.

'Mr Howie.'

'What?'

'Up there.'

I look at him as though in a dream. That none of this is real. Lani isn't dead. Was that my wishful thinking that she got out? Was it a carefully disguised hope that she was out there alive and somehow we'd find her and she would be okay? That she would be like Marcy and come back to normal. All the energy has gone from me. All the fight and the need to keep going and do something worthy. I feel drained and exhausted to the bone. So bloody tired.

'Mr Howie,' he looks at me and motions with his head back to Lani.

'I've seen enough, mate.' I say the words wearily and slowly blink as the stress and tension finally all play out.

'Look.'

'At what?' I turn and glance at the body then shrug, 'what?'

'Up there.'

I glance up and that stress and tension ramp through the fucking ceiling and suddenly it all makes sense. The guts were opened as a message. *Look what I can do.* The wrists were slit so enough blood pooled out. The knife is in her left hand because *she is* right handed and the right hand was needed to write the message on the wall above her head where the plaster is still mostly clean and free from the fire.

There, upon the wall and in thick letters of blood are the words that make me know Lani was fully turned.

One race

The e at the end is smeared as her body dropped lower from the exertion of holding herself up while her vital life blood pumped from her wrist. The spray from the arterial bleed is obvious across the wall. Underneath those words are three more. Three words that tell me this is not over.

He is coming

CHAPTER TWO

Day Six

The body is dragged across the blood stained lawn by one ankle gripped and pulled with ease. The entrails stink and the air is filled with the stench of shit, urine, undigested food, stomach acids, blood and vomit. Rotten flesh left in the sun too long so it blisters and cooks. Boils that burst with puss that dribbles down and the flies swarm like a cloud above the cadavers lying strewn about.

The boy heaves and pulls. He stops and grips harder then pulls again. His face bright red from the exertion. Leaning back and the body shifts position so he takes a step and tries dragging it but the bloated corpse is too heavy. Finally, and with a huff, he drops the leg and scouts about for a smaller body. A young woman, thin framed with her ribs showing through the thin skin of her abdomen proves an easier weight to handle. He scoops to grab a wrist and heaves back with all of his might. The arm detaches with a soft tearing noise. The boy staggers back and falls to his arse. Anger flares on his tanned face. In an instant he's up and charging at the dead woman. The arm is lifted and slammed down so the torn end slaps at her face. A tantrum explodes and the anger unleashed is fed until rage builds and vents. Again and again he uses the woman's arm to beat her with.

'What you do?' Gregori shouts from the far side of the front lawn.

Ignoring him the boy continues to thrash the woman. Beating the arm down again and again until the ragged stump flays and spills goo down over her exposed abdomen.

'BOY!'

'What?'

'Stop this now.'

'NO.' He gets angrier and beats harder as Gregori drops the ankle and marches back across the blood stained lawn. The arm is dropped and the boy starts using his feet to slam into the woman. He kicks the ribs, hearing them break. He stamps down on the head and aims for the nose. When it breaks and splinters he retains enough sense to shift his aim and drive his heels into the eye sockets.

Gregori wrenches him away to send him spinning off to the side. The boy is up the second he gains his wits and charges back with blind fury etched on his face.

'Stop,' Gregori orders and is ignored as the boy runs past to continue his beating of the already dead woman.

'I count...'

The boy continues unabated, slamming and kicking to hear the bones break and render the corpse as bloodied and broken as possible.

'One...two...'

Heedless of the words being uttered the boy carries on the destruction. As Gregori sounds the start of the next word he stops suddenly and spins round to glare up at the pock-marked face of the Albanian.

'I stopped,' the boy sneers.

Gregori's nose flares and his eyes narrow at the impudence of the tone. Never would he have dared speak in such a way to his trainers. The temptation to strike the boy is strong and as if feeling it, the boy lifts his head and offers himself to be hit. Defiance in his eyes. Goading and provoking. Anger is an emotion to be used not wasted. Gregori bites it down and shakes his head slowly before turning to walk off.

The boy blinks then blanches. The anger draining instantly from his face.

'Her arm came off,' he says quickly as though trying to explain. Gregori ignores him and walks to another body. Without glancing at the boy he grabs the ankle and starts dragging it across the lawn towards the growing mound at the far side.

'Her arm came off,' the boy repeats, 'Gregori... Gregoreeee....her arm came off.'

The Albanian shows no reaction but stares ahead with a face devoid of expression.

'Sorry, Gregoreee....' The boy runs to the side of the adult and tries grabbing the other ankle.

'What I say?'

'What?' The boy asks while trying to help by clutching ineffectually at the other leg.

'What I say about anger?'

'Her arm came off,' the boy huffs.

'And this make you angry?' Gregori asks, 'you waste energy. You waste time. You gain nothing from this.'

'But...'

'You no listen. You no learn. You...'

'I am learning, Gregoreee. Honestly I am.'

'Why you do this then?'

'Her arm came off and I fell down and...and...'

'And and and...' Gregori mocks the tone, 'and nothing. You let anger win. You waste it.'

'Sorry,' the boy drops his head and stays quiet while they drag the body to the mound and heave it to the top.

'No,' Gregori slaps the boy's hand as he goes to wipe his face, 'what I tell you about this? You no listen.'

'Sorry,' the boy says again and drops his hands to his sides.

'They have disease. Disease get in you and you are like they.'

'Sorry.'

'No be sorry. Don't do these things.'

'Okay.'

'Go wash and rest.'

'I don't need to rest.'

Gregori looks down at the red face shining with sweat. Working all morning and the bodies used as practise kills were left littering the ground to create obstacles the boy had to navigate while bludgeoning, hacking, stabbing and killing the infected brought back in the van. Now the ground is being cleared and a funeral pyre created to burn off the ones killed to make room for the next.

'Wash. Rest,' Gregori knows the boy will work. He also knows the boy will rub his face and touch his mouth. He also knows the boy has already rubbed his face and touched his mouth and was stood-by waiting to kill him should the change come. When the boy didn't change Gregori put it down to either pure chance or something else. The something else would be that the boy is immune and given the fact the infected people didn't show any reaction to the boy made Gregori even more resolute to watch him closely.

Gregori had noticed it yesterday. The boy was practising using a wooden baseball bat while weaving in and out of the staggering men and women. They groaned and made noises. They drooled and held their hands clawed and ready but not once did they try and lunge for the boy.

It was Gregori they wanted. The Albanian saw time and again the openings the unskilled boy left and watched as the undead should have lunged there, clawed there, bitten there but they didn't. Gregori moved round the killing field, watching as the undead followed and tracked his movements.

The boy appeared heedless to this knowledge and whipped in and around them to strike and batter with the bat.

'Knees,' Gregori said again and again. Eventually the boy got it and the strikes began to gain direction and aim. The boy would strike with all his strength into the stomach or sides to virtually no effect. With much less force but with greater control the strike delivered to the leg joint would cause the body to fall. Once the boy learnt this he went faster from male to female striking to make them fall. When the last one dropped he whooped and jumped up and down excitedly then waited for them to get back up so he could do it again.

The killing blows were harder. Taking a body down with a bat is easy. Making it stay down was far more difficult.

A hard strike to the head sent a jarring shockwave from the thick skull up the bat and into the arms of the boy. Gregori let this happened several times before stepping in.

THE UNDEAD DAY SEVENTEEN

'Skull thick,' he said after taking the bat from the boy and tapping it dully to the side of an adult woman's head, 'neck soft,' he poked the end of the bat into the soft flesh of the groaning woman's neck.

'This...this is spine,' Gregori felt the back of the boy's neck and tapped lightly at the hard ridge of bones, 'break this and the body no move...it die...watch...'

Like a golfer taking a swing Gregori aimed and swooshed the bat in a wide arc to connect with the side of the woman's head snapping it over to the side with an audible crack.

'Is she dead?' The boy peered down.

'She dead. I break spine not head. Understand?'

It took several more before the boy began to grasp the complexities of striking *through* the target instead of hitting at it. The angle of strike had to be right too. Too low and the head wouldn't snap over. Too high and you risked cuffing the scalp. Above the ear with a firm swing and a follow through and the head snapped over to break the spine.

With a furrowed expression of complete concentration the boy practised and practised. The day wore on. The sun was hot and they sweated freely. The boy paid no heed and stayed relentless and sustained as he struck head after head until the first one snapped over with an obvious killing blow.

'I did it! Gregoreeee...I did it...'

'You did?' Gregori was in the shade at the side of the house drinking water. He strode over and looked down at the corpse. Toeing the side of the head he could tell the neck was broken.

'Good. This good.'

'Are you happy with me?' The boy asked earnestly.

'Yes. I happy. Now do rest.'

'Okay.'

Gregori watched as the boy applied himself and went from body to body. Some had to be struck several times before he got it right but with practise and focus the boy narrowed it down and the last two were done in succession.

It was enough for that day and they spent the evening eating, drinking water and resting before another early start this morning.

'Wash. Drink water,' Gregori repeats the words and watches as the boy slips off to the shade at the side of the house. The hose is turned on and the boy uses the brushes and soaps to cleanse his hands and arm thoroughly before rinsing his face off. Only then does he take the jug and carefully pour water into a cup before sitting on the ground to drink it down.

Gregori gets the next body and starts dragging it towards the mound enjoying the sensation of his leg muscles being taxed. Last night when the boy went to sleep, Gregori stayed awake and felt a growing sense of unease that bordered on panic at not knowing what he was doing. Gregori always knew what he was doing. He was collected from one place and taken to another place. He killed who he was supposed to kill and was taken to the next place. It was ordered. Structured. Disciplined. Last night he paced and fretted with his mind racing to understand emotions he had no experience of.

Now there was no order or structure. There was no mission and no pick-up and no next job to do. He could go home to Albania and that was his first instinct but meeting the boy had changed that. He had fooled himself into thinking that he would find the boy a group of survivors and hand him over. That evolved into a plan that he would stay with the boy as a man with a child was less threatening than a man alone. That plan was completely flawed as well Gregori knew. He didn't need other survivors. If he was hungry he got food. If he was tired he would make a safe place and sleep.

Why then? Why keep the boy? His tantrums and temper were hard work. His incessant questions and never ending supply of energy and every hour felt like an added weight as he became more and more responsible for the boy. He didn't know his name. He didn't really know how old the boy was or what his life was like before this. He didn't want to know. He wanted to be rid of the boy and go on alone like he always had except he couldn't.

With a resigned sigh he heaves the body up and stares down at the twisted gruesome limbs splayed out and the dead faces staring up into the clear blue sky.

Why was it so hot? England wasn't a hot country. It rained and had grey skies. This was like Med heat.

The boy had no regard of death. He understood it, Gregori was sure of that much as he had seen his own mother die. He thought back to a few minutes ago and the sight of the child using the arm to beat the dead body. It wasn't that it was disrespectful. Gregori had respect, his job was a profession and one that he took great pride in but the boy had a complete lack of regard that the thing being beaten was once a person. They were things that the boy viewed as objects. He didn't fear them either. There was something else there too but it was too fleeting a thought or instinct for Gregori to grasp.

He looks round at the surrounding land. Setting fire to these bodies will create smoke that will be seen for miles. Gregori had already scouted the area and knew they were isolated but with these clear skies the plume would still show for a great distance but they had to be burnt or otherwise they will soon be overrun with rats and vermin.

The last body is dragged and stacked and while the boy rests in the shade, so the Albanian unscrews the cap off the fuel can and starts splashing the pungent liquid over the bodies.

Once emptied he walks back to the van and puts the fuel can inside the back then closes the sliding door. He crosses to the side of the house and uses the hose and soap to thoroughly clean his arms, hands, torso and head. He drinks water and watches the boy staring intently at a line of ants marching past his small feet.

'Come, we go,' he downs the last of the water and heads to the van as the boy springs to his feet and runs after him.

'Come,' the boy mocks with a deep voice, 'we go...come we go...are we going to the park?' He asks with a sudden hopeful tone.

'No,' Gregori says instantly then thinks for a minute, 'maybe...if we see park...maybe...'

'Yay!' The boy clambers into the passenger seat and slams the door closed, 'we're going to the park...do you like the park, Gregoreee?'

'No. I hate the park.'

'Do you like the slide?'

'I hate the slide. What is slide?'

The boy laughs as Gregoi starts the engine and swings the van round. With the window wound down he lights a match while holding the wheel steady with his knees.

'Don't you know what the slide is?'

'No,' Gregori holds his hands outside the window and stuffs the ignited match back in the box that flares bright with a small plume of sulphuric smoke. As they draw level to the mound he flicks his wrist and sends the flaming box up and onto the top. The van pulls away and with a dull whump the mound ignites as the petrol soaked bodies burst into flame.

'What is slide?'

CHAPTER THREE

Day Seventeen.

A day wasted. I spent yesterday scribing notes and making observations within my notebooks. I told myself it was important and everything had to be recorded. In truth, and despite the inner turmoil of self-reflection and observing a negative character flaw I will admit freely that I was too fearful to go back out.

There. I said it. I am terrified beyond words. It has been only a few days since I left the safety of my hideaway and nothing is really that far beyond what I expected. But predicting a thing is not the same as experiencing a thing. I am a scientist not a soldier and I now long for the safety of my hideaway. Jess and I could go back and resume our simple existence. The chickens will still be there and I can grow crops. I will be like Robinson Crusoe. Carving out an existence in a fertile land of plenty. The infected will be the same as the cannibals Crusoe faced and with the precautions I took it is highly unlikely they will find my place.

But I cannot go back. To go back is to undo everything I have planned and prepared for. It is twelve months and more of work and dedication wasted by a few days of fear.

I knew the infected would mutate. I knew that. I had seen it and we had worked out the rate of spread of the infection and the likely percentages of those who would suffer the mutations but still, they are utterly bloody frightening.

The evolution is completely different to what we predicted too, but then we always knew the predictions were mostly guess work as we had no previous event to measure it by.

It feels futile and there is something else inside me. The futility grows from the knowledge that finding any of those on my list will be met with peril and disaster. The chances of finding just one immune survivor are very slim.

The other thing that I feel started as a reaction, a throw-away thought that has since seeded within my mind and now grows roots through my beliefs. It is the contrast between the world and the people within it.

Right now I am sitting on an old chair dragged out from the barn used as a day room at these stables we have used to hide in. The sun is gloriously warm and the morning is breath-taking in her beauty. I saw the sunrise this morning. I saw it. I watched mesmerised as the rays penetrated the *blackness of night and I heard the world around me awake. Birds singing, chirruping, bleating and calling out. Rabbits that run within the fields nearby eating grass. Butterflies floating wondrously past my head. Bees hovering and working from flower to flower. I can see these things right now. This world is alive and functioning in almost perfect harmony. We are the only negative thing within it. Do we even deserve the chance to survive? Since mankind has walked the earth we have killed and slaughtered. We have made species extinct for food and pleasure. We have raped, murdered, stolen, damaged and ruined everything we have touched.*

Within arm's reach is my assault rifle. It is loaded and ready to fire. I have a pistol on my belt and other weapons within my baggage. Tools designed for the purpose of killing but without mankind they are useless and redundant.

If I die right now... that is to say if I shoot myself dead the initial retort of the weapon would silence those animals within hearing. Startled they would run and flee but they would return and the cycle of their lives would continue. IF... if no person were to ever come here again that cycle of life could continue for evermore. The stables would eventually fall apart and the land would become forest once again. Life would not only survive but it would thrive.

This feeling of nihilism grips me hard. It makes me not want to go back out there. The last few survivors will fight and eventually die out. The infected will cease to be and...

. . .

THE UNDEAD DAY SEVENTEEN

I have to stop this train of thought that gathers speed within my heart. *I WILL CONTINUE. I MUST*.

I must focus and bring my mind to the here and now. Not a few miles away is the town I entered with the massed infected. Hundreds of them in one place. What for? For what reason do they gather and remain? I am between a dozen to twenty miles away by my reckoning and able to flee a greater distance should the need arise.

For what purpose do they gather?

Do I continue my quest to find those that should be immune or do I try and find out the reason for the gathering, and in so doing, perhaps divert a greater catastrophe?

My mission must come first for only by finding the immune can one hope to bring a final solution.

Onwards I must go then. With great fear in my bones I must remain true to my objective.

I am a scientist and not a soldier. I am not cut out for this.

I will continue.

. . .

I *am scared.*

N*B*

CHAPTER FOUR

'Lani is dead.'

I say the words as we walk from the old armoury and meet with the team. They crowd in, all of them. Cookey's eyes fill with tears that he tries to blink away but they tumble and fall to streak clean rivers through the grime on his face. Nick looks away with a sharp intake of breath and Clarence sags on the spot. Blowers stiffens with that hard look I've seen now so many times that tells me his emotions are threatening to take over.

'How?' Paula asks the question quietly, almost whispered for the desire to know the very last few seconds.

I take a deep breath and swallow the hurt down, 'she got into the corner…she could have got out but…but she took her own life instead…'

'Oh my god,' Cookey's voice breaks as the tears flow faster down his cheeks.

'Not like that, mate,' I force the emotion from my own voice, 'she had turned fully.'

'But…' he stammers with a look of confusion mingled in with the obvious pain on his face.

'She cut her own stomach open and pulled the insides out...then she slit her wrists and used the blood to write a message on the wall...'

Cookey drops to a crouch as his chest heaves with the sobs that come thick and fast.

'Get up,' I tell him soft but firmly, 'you need to hear this...this is what we're dealing with now.'

He shoots up and forces his face to show a mask of anger, 'go on.'

'The message was one race then underneath it says he is coming.'

'Fuck,' Nick says.

'That wasn't Lani that did that. That was the infection. It did that to show us it is in control. It cut her guts open to taunt us. It sacrificed the one who knew more about us than anyone else turned or infected and it did it to prove a point. If Lani had got out she could have come back and wiped this fort from the earth. She was faster than most of us, Christ only Dave was faster than Lani in a fight but it knew. The infection knew that even as good as Lani was she wouldn't get through us. So it did that instead. Do you understand?' I glare from face to face, forcing them to look me in the eye. Mo Mo looks heartbroken but he holds that look as I continue. 'This is what we are dealing with. This is the enemy we face. If one of us turns we make a vow now they will be killed instantly and without mercy or hesitation. Dave, if I turn you will kill me. Do you understand?'

'I understand.'

'If you turn then it means we can all turn,' Clarence says heavily, 'if one turns then we should all be killed.'

'Agreed?' I ask the group.

'Agreed,' Blowers says instantly.

'Agreed,' Cookey nods as Nick repeats it.

'Paula?'

'Agreed,' she says softly.

'Roy?'

He nods but stays quiet.

'Mo Mo?'

'Course,' he says so softly.

'Dave, these are your instructions. If one turns you will kill all of us.'

'I understand. Then I will kill myself.'

'Yeah,' I say slowly with a sigh, 'yeah you probably should.'

'Knife or gun?'

'Do what?'

'Do you want to be shot or stabbed?'

'Fucking hell, Dave!'

'You might have a preference.'

'Fucking preference! Shit mate. I don't think I'll be that bothered if it comes to it.'

'I would like a knife used on me,' he says.

'How? I mean…' I stop and think for a minute, 'if you've just killed all of us how the hell are you going to kill yourself with a knife?'

'Slit my throat.'

'Slit your own throat? Jesus, Dave! Just shoot yourself in the head like a normal person.'

'Bloody hell, Dave,' Clarence shakes his head in distaste.

'What if I don't have a gun?'

'Fuck me. Use the knife then if you don't have a gun.'

'Would you like me to slit your throat or stab you through the heart?'

'Personally I want to be stabbed through the ear mate. Right through the ear. The right ear.'

'Okay.'

'I was joking. I do not want to be stabbed through the ear.'

'Blowers wants to be stabbed in the arse,' Cookey says weakly, 'he told me earlier...fact.'

'Dave, do not stab Blowers in the arse,' I say quickly.

'Can I be shot please,' Paula says meekly.

'Shot. Okay,' Dave nods.

'Shot,' Clarence says.

'Shot. Okay. Paula and Clarence to be shot.'

'This is so fucked up,' I say loudly.

'Nick?'

'Shot please, Dave. Or stabbed through the heart quickly if you don't have a gun and if you don't have a knife either then break my neck.'

'Okay,' Dave says.

'Actually can I change mine to what Nick just said,' Paula says.

'Yeah, good thinking, Nick,' Clarence says, 'I'll do what Nick said.'

'Actually,' Paula says, 'I think it would be easier if we all went for the same thing? Everyone up for that? Shot through the head or stabbed through the heart or neck broken. Yes? Everyone agreed?'

'Seems fair,' Mo Mo says with a thoughtful look.

'Blowers still wants to be stabbed in the arse.'

'I'll go with everyone else,' Blowers says with a glare at Cookey.

'Okay. Shot or stabbed or broken neck. Got it. Marcy?'

'Me?'

'Yes. What would you like?'

'Oh....I didn't think I was included.'

'Of course you are,' Paula says, 'do you want to do what everyone else is doing or something else?'

'Well I'm not sure if I will turn again...but er...yes, yes I think I will go with the shot to the head or stabbed through the heart or neck broken please, I mean if that's okay?'

'Course it is,' Paula says, 'Dave, Marcy is the same as everyone else.'

'He's right there,' I point stupidly at Dave, 'he heard it.'

'Well I was just saying,' Paula points out huffily.

'Reginald?' Dave asks and looks round for him.

'He's still hiding with the children but put him down for the same as me.'

'Understood. Mr Howie?'

'I don't fucking care! Jesus I cannot believe we are having this actual discussion.'

'You brought it up,' Paula says.

'Yeah that if one turns we should all be killed but not an actual discussion on the merits of an individually tailored death. It's fucking morbid.'

'Plan ahead,' Paula says, 'seven P's and all that.'

'Jesus!'

'What?' Cookey asks.

'What?' Paula asks Cookey.

'Seven P's? What's that then?'

'Proper Pre Planning Prevents Piss Poor Performance,' she explains.

'Wow,' Cookey mouths, 'that is so cool...that should be our motto.'

'Crap motto,' Nick sneers, 'sorry Paula, I didn't mean *it* was crap just not suitable for a motto.'

'Oh I agree,' Paula says, 'too long for a motto.'

'Dave, can you shoot a bow?' Roy asks suddenly, 'that's how I would like to go.'

'Might be a bit time consuming,' Clarence says politely.

'I probably can,' Dave says, 'if you let me try first.'

'I'll show you,' Roy says, 'you'd be very good with a bow. However, in the meantime should I turn then maybe consider stabbing me with an arrow through the eye?'

'Like the battle of Hastings?' Cookey asks, 'we did that at school.'

'Urban myth,' Roy replies, 'there are no accounts of King Harold being shot through the eye.'

'It's on that wallpaper isn't it?' Blowers says.

'Wallpaper? You mean the tapestry?' Nick asks.

'Yeah,' Blowers nods.

'Fucking wallpaper?' Cookey tuts, 'thick cunt.'

'It goes on the fucking wall doesn't it?' Blowers asks.

'Through the eye then? With an arrow, please,' Roy says to Dave.

'Got it. If I don't have an arrow will being shot or stabbed or neck broken be okay with you?'

'I guess so, but I would prefer an arrow. You know, a fitting end and all that.'

'Trust you to be awkward,' Blowers says testily.

'He asked and I am simply pointing out my preferred method,' Roy says with a lift of his chin.

'Dave did ask,' Paula points out.

'Maddox?' Dave asks, 'do you have a preference?'

'Me?' Maddox says calmly, 'yes. My preference is for all of you to fuck off.'

'Eh?' I ask with a blink, 'bit harsh mate.'

'You lot are messed up,' he says looking round at them all one by one, 'even Mo Mo has become like you now. You should go.'

THE UNDEAD DAY SEVENTEEN

'We *are* going,' I reply.

'Good. Leave and make a point of being seen somewhere else so whoever that person is doesn't want to come here.'

'What person? Have I missed something?' Cookey asks.

'The message,' Nick says, *'he is coming...'*

'Oh that, yeah...yeah good point, Maddox,' Cookey says seriously.

'How have you stayed alive this long?' Maddox asks, 'all of you? How?'

'Well, we haven't all stayed alive,' I say, 'seeing as Lani is dead.'

'Go,' Maddox says bluntly, 'you should go. All of you.'

'I already said we are,' I say.

'Where are we going?' Clarence asks.

'Stop!' Maddox holds a trembling hand out and I remember with a smidgen of satisfaction that he was tazered eight times by Lani. Fuck him. He deserved it. 'I don't want to know. Just go.'

'Maddox has a point there,' Clarence says, 'if we attacked them and get seen doing it then they won't come here.'

'What like guerrilla warfare?' I ask.

'Eh? Are we going back to the safari park?' Cookey asks, 'gorilla? Get it? Fuck off I know what guerrilla means.'

'Thick cunt,' Blowers says.

'You are,' Cookey coughs into his hand.

'Dave?' I ask the small man now happy and quiet with his orders of execution.

'Yes, Mr Howie?'

'Is that a good idea? Guerrilla tactics against them.'

'Hang on, I just suggested it,' Clarence says.

'Yeah I know, I was asking Dave what he thinks.'

'I was in the army too,' he says with a growl, 'in the Parachute regiment...for a long time...'

'Yeah I know,' I say again, 'but...I...fine! We'll do that.'

'Don't do that, boss,' Clarence groans, 'now I feel guilty.'

'No it's fine. We'll go with your suggestion.'

'Oh bloody hell, Dave? What do you think of *the* suggestion?' Clarence asks.

'Good idea,' Dave replies, 'we are outnumbered vastly but we are a small unit that can move fast so we can use hit and run tactics to inflict losses and harass the enemy. Our advantage is also our perceived disadvantage. We can draw them into one place while bugging out to attack another location then come back when they start to disband.'

Silence. Nick coughs. Cookey looks down. Maddox shakes his head in disdain.

'That,' Clarence says slowly through gritted teeth, 'is exactly what I meant when I said guerrilla tactics.'

'Of course,' Dave says.

'But I didn't feel the need to explain it like that.'

'Of course,' Dave says again.

'It's what guerrilla tactics are,' Clarence says.

'I know.'

'So you don't need to actually point them out when saying it...you just say guerrilla tactics...You don't say a combustible engine mounted on a chassis with a steering mechanism...you just say car.'

'I know.'

'Stop saying I know!'

'Of course.'

'You little...'

'Enough,' I snap, 'we're all tired. Get ammunition and we'll go.'

'Go where?' Cookey asks, 'aren't we sleeping here? I'm fucked.'

'No chance,' I say, 'we'll find somewhere else to sleep. The quicker we're out of here the better. Load as much as you can carry and we'll head back to the Saxon.'

'We can stay in the house Reggie and I used,' Marcy suggests.

'Ssshhh,' I press my finger to my lips, 'don't let Maddox know where we're going.'

'Grow up,' Maddox snaps and walks off.

We all stare after him as Marcy shuffles on the spot and clears her throat, 'he has a point.'

'What?'

'You lot are messed up. I mean...Lani just died and... you're making jokes and...'

'What we supposed to do?' I ask with the hardness creeping back into my eyes, 'fall down and cry? Will it bring her back or stop it happening again? Will it bring Sarah back or big Chris? What about Jagger? Will it stop the fact that Lani shot him?'

'Howie?' Marcy blanches in hurt shock at the barrage.

'We deal with it and move on. It's done. Don't for one second think we ain't dying on our feet because we are.'

'Okay...I'm sorry, it was stupid and...I should have thought it through...my apologies.'

'It's okay,' Cookey says after an awkward pause, 'it's like the time Dave cut April's head off. I was devastated but valiantly I struggled on...'

'You will clean everyone's weapons today, Alex.'

'What?'

'I told you that I did not cut her head off and I warned you what would happen if you said it again.'

'Weapon cleaning? I always get made to make the brews!'

'You're already on brew duty. Weapons cleaning is the next punishment.'

'So unfair.'

'Pardon?'

'Nothing, sorry, Dave.'

'My rifle is fucking filthy,' Nick points out, 'and my pistol…'

'I'm going to shit on my rifle,' Blowers says.

'What when you pull it out your fat backside?'

'Fuck you I don't have a fat arse.'

'Fat arsed fucker.'

'Fuck off, Cookey.'

'Lads, enough. Get ammunition and we're going. As much as you can carry.'

We move out heading back towards the new armoury.

'Do I have a fat arse?'

'No, Simon.'

'Thanks, Paula. Fuck you, Cookey. Paula says I don't have a fat arse.'

'She's being polite.'

'Fuck you, Nick. Marcy? I don't have a fat arse do I?'

'You have a lovely backside,' she says with a smile as she recovers from the harsh words I said.

'Who has the best arse?' Cookey asks immediately, 'bet it's mine.'

'Paula,' Marcy says with a grin as Paula turns to give a quick smile back, 'Howie? Can I speak with you please?'

I nod and ease up to let the others go ahead and watch as Dave takes a wider angle to keep me in his peripheral vision.

'I'm sorry about what I said,' she says in a low voice.

'Forget it. I shouldn't have snapped at you but you pointed out the bad thing we were all ignoring.'

'I realised as soon as I said it. It won't happen again.'

'Fair enough.'

She goes to say something then stops and frankly I am too tired and drained to prompt her.

'Am I coming with you? I mean, Reginald and I?'

'I think it's best,' I say.

'Because of Maddox here or...?'

'Both. Yes because Maddox will try and detain you or lock you up or something and yes because I...I don't know...I just know that you need to be with us until we figure this out.'

'How will we figure it out if we're not here?'

'We'll have to figure that out too but being here isn't an option now. So yeah, you and Reginald should stay with us.'

'Not tied up or anything?'

'See that dog?' I point ahead to Meredith running amidst the group.

'Meredith?'

'She knew the second she saw Lani that Lani was turned. She's only a dog but she's proven many times to be our best detection against them. She's fine with you and if you turn then so will she. Plus we have Dave.' I add as a side.

'A dog's sense of smell is something like ten thousand times more powerful than a human's,' Marcy says, 'she must able to smell the virus within the blood.'

'Maybe...probably.'

'I am so sorry about Lani,' she blurts as she gets to the point of what she really wanted to say.

'Okay.'

'It's not okay...I feel...'

'Not now, Marcy. I can't...just not now, please?'

'Sorry,' she winces.

'You don't have to keep saying sorry. It is what it is.'

We walk in silence to the opened doors of the freshly stacked crates of ammunition we brought back just a short time ago. Bags are found and filled with magazines. Belt pouches too. Clarence gets the heavy machine gun and stacks it to the side with boxes of the bigger belt fed rounds. Once our bags are all filled we pick crates up and start heading back down to the gates. A rifle and a pistol each and a few more as spares. It's hard work and we're already running on empty. The banter stops and I can tell we all drop into pain filled silences made worse by the gap of Lani not being with us.

We load the boats up and Maddox sends Reginald out with some older youths to bring the boats back and with the night sky only just breaking for the new dawn we start the chugging engines to sail across the bay.

On the beach we unload and Nick remembers to tell Maddox's lads where the crew from the beach are locked up. They go off as we ferry our supplies to the Saxon and load her up but being back with the vehicle only seems to make it worse. Lani was always with us. Working with the lads, chatting to Paula and smiling at me. The hurt threatens to pull me down several times and I curse and grunt and smoke cigarettes to try and avert the feeling.

Nick drives the Saxon slowly behind while the rest of us walk the short distance to the beachside houses. Marcy and Reginald lead the way to the house they used as though somehow that is the chosen home for the night. Familiarity I guess. It's a big detached house with lots of bedrooms. Space is found and rooms claimed before we all drift back to the kitchen to strip and clean weapons. Nobody mentions that it was Cookey's punishment today.

We drink water to hydrate. We scrub our faces, arms and wash the worst of the grime from our bodies before finally, and with the new day just starting, we sink into the soft mattresses. As my heads comes to rest I fear the pain will take over and have me sobbing into the pillow. Instead there is only the darkness of forgiving sleep.

CHAPTER FIVE

Day Six

The boy laughs and claps his hands, 'get him, Gregoreee...get the duckie...' That's what the boy called them. Duckies. Catch a duck on a pole and win a prize. A game played in school or on a computer, maybe something he had seen on television or at the fair. Gregori didn't know but he knew he should be irritated at the word.

The dog pole was taken from the police station in the town. A long thick metal shaft with a loop of wire at one end and a handle to pull the wire taut at the other. It was perfect for catching people, loop the wire over the head, yank it tight and use the pole to shove and guide them into the van. Getting the pole was easy and that was something that did irritate Gregori.

They were meant to protect people. They had taken an

THE UNDEAD DAY SEVENTEEN

oath and took the money so why did they hide in the police station? He knew they were in there. He could smell them the second he smashed the rear glass on the back door in. That was another thing that irritated him, police stations should have thick safety glass in their external doors, not normal glass that could be broken by the butt of a pistol.

'GO OUT NOW. WE ARE ARMED AND WILL FIRE ON YOU.'

That was the greeting shouted down from the end of the corridor when he got in and Gregori knew they didn't have guns. Only a few English police carried guns and the weapons were kept in secure armouries in the main division stations, not these little stations.

Figures scuttled into view before him. Six foot high riot shields and people wearing NATO helmets and leg guards. He walked slowly down the long tiled corridor as they formed up and listened to the orders being shouted. They were nervous, terrified even. Men that shouted angrily which only served to reveal the fear. Women too. Women in riot gear. Five of them formed up and sealed the end of the corridor and all five of them shouted for him to get out.

That also irritated Gregori. There was no need for all five of them to shout at the same time. It was amateurish and confusing. They shuffled feet and knocked into each other. Their hands were shaking. One of them had a Tazer that was pointed down the corridor with a red dot that was meant to rest solidly on Gregori's chest but instead it wavered all over the place.

'Stick for the dog,' Gregori said, his accent thick but the words clear enough to understand, 'I need stick for the dog.'

'GET OUT,' a woman screamed, an older woman at the point of hysteria. Her eyes were wide behind the visor of the helmet and Gregori noticed the three stripes on her body armour. A child cried out. A woman crying. Voices from further in the station. These people had brought their families to hide and stay safe while everyone out there was struggling and dying. It wasn't done right though. The door should have been barricaded. The access yard should have been blocked and sealed. Signs should have been put up warning people to stay away. Instead they'd gone on the basis of making it look like no one was here which made them fools and cowards.

'Stick for the dog,' Gregori said again, 'I need this.'

'YOU WILL LEAVE NOW.'

How many warnings were they going to give? How many times did they have to tell him they would fire if he didn't leave? He was getting closer now, closer to the shield wall.

'I'm bored,' the boy walked into the corridor behind him, 'can we go now?'

'I say to you wait,' Gregori said turning round to chastise the boy, 'I say I get stick for dog and you wait. You no wait.'

'I'm bored,' the boy whined.

'IS THAT YOUR SON?'

Gregori turned back with a scowl on his face. Why shout that question? They had seen the boy and could be using it as a means of negotiation but instead they were injecting the same near hysterical force into their voices.

'Gregoreeeee,' the boy whined, 'can we just go now?'

'I need stick,' Gregori said to the shield wall, 'give me stick.'

'GET OUT...LEAVE NOW OR WE WILL FIRE ON...'

'What with?' Gregori asked with the first sign of irritation in his voice, 'fire what with?'

THE UNDEAD DAY SEVENTEEN

'Tazer him, Ian.'

A crackle, a fizz and the barbs flew past Gregori to sink down onto the floor.

'With this?' Gregori asked pointing at the wires, 'you fire with toy?'

'I'm bored!'

'Give me stick.'

'Reloading,' Ian shouted fumbling to do the job with his big riot gloves still on his hands.

'Gregoreeeee, I'm bored...'

Knife out in his right hand, the left hand gripped the top of the nearest shield and yanked it from the grip of the person meant to be holding it properly. An explosion of action as batons were lifted to strike but the knife was already plunging into the tiny gap between the helmet and the shoulders. Blood pumping out. Confusion and everyone screaming but they were all too close together in the corridor and were banging into each other. A backstab, a step and another stab, step right and slice a wrist open, step left and pull the helmet back to expose the throat that gets cut open.

One by one they fell and the tiled floor ran thick with the blood of the fools and cowards.

The dog stick was on a hook right behind them and he took it while the people upstairs screamed in terror and the boy tutted and crossed his arms in a huff of impatience.

'Get the duckie,' the boy claps his hands and dances about as Gregori loops the wire over the neck of the man and yanks the handle down. A gargling sound from the throat and the infected man claws ineffectually at the air.

Gregori smiles. He was changing and felt it but couldn't stop it. He'd never got irritated before. He'd never smiled either. Unless he needed to appear harmless when approaching a guard at a gate. Now he smiles at the boy laughing and clapping his hands at the *duckie* being caught.

He shoves the male hard forcing the back of his legs to hit the low edge and letting gravity and inertia do the rest. The man being pushed further into the side of the van and held in place.

'Go,' Gergori says and watches the boy clamber up into the side of the vehicle and pull down the dog collar fastened to a wire bolted to the roof. This was the last one needed to be taken and the van was full. The boy moves between their legs, pushing them aside so he can get the collar.

'Okay,' the boy says and works his fingers under the loop to pull it free from the males neck and over his head. The infected do nothing. None of them doing anything other than staring out the side of the van to Gregori. The boy moves through and around them, pushing against legs and letting the back of his hands brush the males face as he pulls the wire up.

Gregori slides the pole out and watches carefully as the boy leans forward and works to get the collar round the infected man's neck and in so doing, the boy leans in with his own face inches from the mouth of the infected.

'Poo,' the boy says, 'he smells soooo bad...done it.'

Why aren't they going for him? Gregori steps closer to the side of the van and watches the reaction from the captured infected straining against the collars as they track his movements.

'Why they no bite you?' He asks.

'Are we going to the park today?'

It was infuriating. The boy had no fear but couldn't answer a straight question.

'You want park?' Gregori was learning though, 'you want go park?'

'Yes!' The boy replies.

'We go park...but...tell me...why they no bite you?'

'Can we go on the swings?'

'No. No swings. No park. You tell me why?'

'Oh but you said...'

'I said you tell me *and then* we go park...you no tell we no go park.'

'But but...'

'Why, Boy? Why they not bite you?'

'They like me,' the boy shrugs and turns to look up at the drooling faces.

'Why they like you?'

'That's two questions,' the boy says accusingly, 'you said one question.'

'One question...two question...many question...why they like you?'

'You said one question and we can go to the park.'

'You want candy?'

The boy's eyes widen in surprise, 'sweets?' He asks as though hardly daring to believe it was even possible.

'Yes. You want the...*sweets*?'

'Yeah,' the boy says with excitement.

'Why they like you?'

'Because I'm nice,' the boy laughs.

Gregori sighs, this was about as much sense as he was likely to get and he was fast learning that asking a small child to account for something serious was like teaching rocket science to a dog.

CHAPTER SIX

A few hours but it's enough and this time I don't sit bolt upright sweating from some fleeting nightmare but wake up slowly with eyes blinking against the glare of the sun pouring in through the window.

Sadness weighs heavy on my heart as the caustic memory of Lani charred and burnt and mangled from self-abuse swims through my head. I squeeze my eyes shut and sit up. Everything hurts. My legs are stiff, my shoulders are tight but the pain of moving alleviates the memory so I get up and stretch with audible winces and groans just to do something other than think about Lani.

Another feeling is there too and one that is stronger than my feelings of loss. Something else that pushes to the forefront of my thoughts and makes itself known with every sense I have.

I am bloody hungry. Not just hungry but starving. Ravenous. I need to eat. My mind and body are urging me to eat, to find food and take in nourishment. When did we last have food? I can't even remember. I get dressed and turn my nose up at the shit clothes we pilfered from these houses. After days of wearing combat gear these feel flimsy and stupid. Jeans, t shirt and trainers. Food and clothes. That's what we need. And a toothbrush as my mouth feels like a furry cesspit.

Movement from outside the small top floor room tells me others have woken up too. I step out onto the landing and watch Clarence stretching like a bear.

'I'm starving, mate,' I say with a voice still gruff from sleep.

'Same,' he stops stretching and scratches his stomach.

'Everyone else up?'

'Dunno,' he yawns and stretches again, 'what's the plan?'

'Food and clothes.'

'Good plan,' he says then sniffs the air at the same time as the aroma reaches me.

'Coffee,' we both say at the same time and like the infected we turn and shuffle down the landing and navigate the stairs on stiff legs and red bleary eyes. This must be what it's like to be infected. Drawn by a scent but unable to fully compute the intricacies of fine motor skills.

The kitchen is full of more infected zombies. One stands outside the open rear door smoking. Two yawn and groan while stretching. Another blinks slowly. Marcy sits at the table with her head propped up by one hand while Paula sits down heavily next to her. Mo Mo shuffles in and he too stops to stretch and groan. I snort laughter at the sight which spreads as they all seem to get the visual joke.

Only Reginald seems awake and alert and like Dave, he doesn't look any different than he did yesterday. Dressed in a clean shirt with a tie perfectly knotted he busies himself boiling water from a gas stove as he pours another boiling pan of water into waiting mugs. Sugar sits in a fine china tea cup with a teaspoon sticking out the top.

'Is that milk?' I ask staring stupidly at the box of individually sealed milk portions.

'Not in the true sense of the word I am afraid,' Reginald replies, 'it is a milk derivative heated to a super high temperature and no doubt all the taste and goodness has gone but yes, it will serve to give lightness to the bitterness of the coffee.'

'Milk,' I say and stare at the box.

'I could only find sugar,' he says busily, 'I was not sure if any of you took sweeteners or not.'

'Yeah,' I say slowly, 'we're watching our waistlines.'

'Blowers,' Cookey goes to say then coughs his throat clear and tries again, 'Blowers needs to fat his...fuck it!'

'Cocked that one up,' Nick points out.

'Too early,' Cookey groans.

'It is past ten o'clock, the morning has almost left us,' Reginald says.

'Ten? So we've had what...five hours sleep? Better than for a...cheers,' I cut off when Reginald hangs me a mug. He serves them up and we dive into the box of milk tearing the film lids off to pour the minuscule portions into our coffee. Heavy on the sugar and with an actual mug of real coffee I head outside to join Nick in the garden.

'Nice,' I look round the garden so carefully designed. Being so close to the shore and the outside space is minimal but the previous owners did what they could to make their second home as habitable as possible. It grates me which is an unfair reaction to people who had done well in life. A big glass topped table with heavy wooden chairs around it and a big sun shield umbrella in the down position pokes through the carefully made hole in the table. Nick's cigarettes already wait on the dark frosted glass so I help myself as Cookey and Blowers join me. Paula drifts out and slides one from the packet. We sit down as the others feel the need to stay together and come outside to sit under the hot sun so we can drink coffee and be like normal people.

'What's the plan?' Paula asks.

'Food and clothes.'

'Food. I'm fucking starving,' Nick says.

'You're always starving,' Paula reminds him, 'what I'd give for a full English,' she adds.

'What would you give?' Clarence asks.

She thinks for a minute, 'a little toe? Maybe a little finger if it was freshly cooked and worth it. You know, I lived on bloody muesli and yoghurts before this. Bloody yoghurt,' she shakes her head at the memory.

'Low carbs, low fat…' Marcy says with a snort of air from her nose.

'Are you hungry?' Mo Mo asks her.

'Starving,' she says.

'So, like…are you not infected anymore or what?'

'Truthfully I have no idea,' she says.

'You don't look infected…apart from your eyes,' Mo Mo says.

'Your hair is gorgeous,' Paula says, 'are you tanning? I mean, is your skin taking the sun?'

'It is,' Marcy looks down at her bare arms, 'I don't know. I lost everything I had before and just became normal again. I eat and…drink…I get tired and all the normal things. Reggie is the same.'

'Reginald,' Reginald calls out from the kitchen.

'But if…I mean, your blood, does it have the bad shit in it?' Mo Mo asks.

'Maybe,' she says with a shrug and I notice she doesn't look uncomfortable at the attention from everyone.

'So's like, if you get cut we should not touch you then.'

'I can,' Cookey says, 'me and Blowers will render first aid if you get hurt, Marcy.'

'Thanks, lads,' she smiles.

'I'll do the kiss of life on you and...yeah,' he grins while linking his hands behind his head, 'Blowers can do Reginald.'

'Twat,' Blowers doesn't bother putting any effort into the insult but sips at his coffee.

'Or Mr Howie,' Nick says, 'he's immune so he can do mouth to mouth on...fuck...shit...sorry!'

'Awkward!' Cookey laughs with delight.

'Just slightly embarrassing,' Marcy blushes and looks down.

'Are we all immune?' Mo Mo asks still following his serious train of thought.

'No idea,' I reply.

'Kiss Reginald and find out,' Cookey says.

'Nah thanks,' Mo Mo says.

'What's that? Oh she's done it right there,' Paula grimaces at the smell of shit wafting over and the grinning face of Meredith as she squats next to the table to crap on the patio.

'Well it is outside,' Nick laughs.

'I can't sit here next to that,' she says.

'Come on, drink up...we'll move out and find something to eat.'

'What else we doing today?' Cookey asks as we all start standing up and draining our mugs of coffee.

'I said, food and clothes.'

'Is that all? Like....no massive battle then or...find some neurosurgeons or a fighter jet?'

'No mate,' I smile over at him, 'just food and clothes.'

'Day off then?' He asks hopefully.

'Day off? Yeah, yeah I guess it is.'

'Fucking awesome! Can we go up the coast?'

'We can go wherever you want, mate. We need to be seen though, all of us...'

'So,' Cookey narrows his eyes, 'let me get this right? We're going for food and new clothes and the only thing we have to do today is be seen? Is that right?'

'It is but the way you say it makes it sound like a bad thing.'

'No no, just checking,' he rubs his hand together and grins evilly.

'Cookey...don't be a dick today,' Clarence says quickly.

'Roger, not being a dick,' Cookey nods.

'Right, everyone sod off and get loaded up...Mo Mo, wait here a minute please mate.' He looks at me startled while everyone heads back through the house.

'You okay?' I ask once the rest are gone.

'Fine,' he says too quickly.

'Mate, we've all lost people and it hurts like fuck but...'

'Why is Marcy with us? He asks suddenly.

'You know what happened with Marcy? Before I mean?'

'Yeah, the others said...Why we keeping someone like that with us?'

'Because we need to find out what's going on.'

'How we gonna do that?'

'No idea mate, I need time to think but between us we'll come up with something.'

'But…can I ask you this stuff? Like, you's the bossman and…'

'I'm not the bossman and you can ask what you want. You're part of this team now, mate. As much as anyone else.'

'So how does having Marcy and Reginald with us help find out what…like, what we need to find out?'

I think of the draw I felt that pulled me to find Marcy again and then think how I can verbalise that without sounding like a complete weirdo.

'Something connects us all,' I say slowly while still thinking of what to say, 'like a bond but deeper, does that make sense?'

He nods and stares intently at me.

'Marcy is part of that, I can't explain how I know but just that I do.'

'I get it,' he says quietly, 'like me and Jag had a…'

'Bond?'

'Yeah, you get me?'

'Course, he was a good friend to you.'

'Fucking hurts,' he blurts, 'more than like losing anyone else and…fucking Lani just shot him. Sorry, I know she was your girlfriend but she just shot him…like he didn't matter to anything and she didn't care and I was too slow I could have shot back and stopped her but…I couldn't do anything cos Jagger was down and I was crying, you get me? S'fucked up innit? Like he's just dead and never coming back.'

'Fucked up, mate,' I say gravely, 'and it doesn't get easier either. The lads make jokes and piss about but they do it to mask the feelings otherwise we'd all fall apart. Mo Mo, I know this is harder than anything you've ever done before but look at the world around us. There is no help coming or no one else to dig us out the shit now. We've only got each other and we need to rely on each other. You're in a bad place and I get that, but I need to know you're going to jump in if anything happens.'

He nods firmly and locks eyes on me, 'I will, I promise.'

'Take it easy today, mate. Join in with the lads or stay quiet or sleep or whatever. My advice is join in otherwise you start brooding and it's fucking hard to pull out of that. You get me?'

He looks at me sharply at the words as though gauging if I'm taking the piss.

'Bro? You get me? Innit?' I say and hold my fist out towards him.

'What's that?'

'Don't we fist bump or something?'

'We can if you want,' he stares at the fist then grins and laughs with an expression that changes his features completely. 'S'fucked up,' he pushes his fist against mine.

'Innit blood, but seriously…don't people do fist bumps?'

'In America they do, Mr Howie. Not where I came from.'

'Oh okay, so we can't do fist bumps then?'

'Er, not really.'

'High fives? How about that high five thing that goes on for like ten minutes and ends with a hug or something?'

He stares at me deadpan, 'hug? You want to hug?'

'Awkward,' I laugh, 'come on, that shit stinks.'

We head through the house and out the front to the waiting Saxon.

'Hey she's back,' I call out at the sight of Clarence jammed in the hole while fitting the GPMG.

'She is,' he calls out then looks at Mo Mo, 'you alright?'

'Yeah fine, cheers,' Mo Mo nods as he heads towards the lads smoking at the back.

A minute later and we're back where we have always

been. Me in the driving seat with Clarence up front and the rear filled with the chatting team. Eleven of us plus the dog which is why Clarence is up the front as he wouldn't fit in the back.

'We need a bigger Saxon,' Nick calls out, 'and it's fucking hot in here.'

'Leave the back doors open,' I call back.

'Is that safe?' Reginald asks, 'and where are the seatbelts?'

The chat is lost to me as the big engines sputter to life and the heavy vehicle vibrates as though awakening from a deep sleep. It feels strange having no direction and no vital objective to undertake. A free day within which we can do whatever we want, and not just today but from now on. The fort was our promised land and it still stands. Maddox can fix the outer wall and get it back running as it should be but that's not our concern now. We got the doctors, and as valued as they are with giving medical aid, they can't help with the infection or tell us why some of us are immune and why Marcy and Reginald are no longer what they were.

So many questions. So much to find out and understand and no bloody clue with where to start but the pressing urgency is to find food and eat.

I navigate the roads full of the debris from the storm and soon we're out and on the open coast road with rolling fields bordering one side and the glorious sweeping bays on the other. It's stunning. Truly beyond words and the contrast to the carnage we have seen staggers me to the core. It's hot, it must be the end of July and August will soon be here and if the world hadn't of ended the news stations would be full of the amazing summer that no doubt would be the hottest since records began. Or is it *because* of the end of the world that this weather is so good?

THE UNDEAD DAY SEVENTEEN

Today will be a down day. Food and clothes. After that we'll start trying to work out where to look for answers and where to go.

We pass signs for towns indicated as being a few miles from the coast but I head further along the coast road and away from the area we've come to know so well and somehow, putting distance between us and the fort feels right.

An hour of quiet driving, lost in my own thoughts and as I glance to Clarence I can see him dozing with his head resting against the back of the seat and his long legs stretched out as far as the gap allows. We crest a long hill and there, stretched out beneath us is a glorious seaside town complete with a pier stretching into the sea. It looks white and beautiful with a sandy beach adorning the long sweeping bay. The pier isn't particularly long but it's distinctive and even from here the thick black stilts are visible.

A place like that must have cafes, restaurants and places to find food and with hope the residents would have been the ones sent against us in the days before and the place will be empty.

I head down the hill that snakes through the winding countryside bordering the town. Rock walls start to show and detached cottage farm houses that once serviced the land. We hit the bigger houses on the outskirts a few minutes later and even I can hear the chat has dwindled in the back as everyone stares either out the front or the open back doors.

'Hang on,' Nick shouts, 'can you go back?'

'What for?' I slow down as we pass a petrol station on the edge of a small industrial section filled with the standard shitty looking units.

'Sign back there said there was an outdoors unit.'

'Well spotted, Nicholas,' Clarence goes from dozing to wide awake. He rubs his face and yawns noisily while I come to a stop and consider trying to turn this huge beast in a normal street or simply reverse back. I go for the turn and knock out a garden fence and a low wall in the process, much to the delight of those in the back.

'Down there,' Clarence points to a side road. I turn in and we stare at the passing units still boarded and locked up. Within the town now and the storm damage is obvious with fallen trees and even a chimney stack lying across the road but for once we don't see any bodies.

'Goodmans,' Clarence reads the sign above the shuttered front. Goodmans outdoor store.

'Shutters,' I point through the windscreen, 'drag 'em off?'

'Might as well,' he says and opens the door to drop down. Everyone gets out to stretch legs while I turn round to bring the back up against the metal shutters.

'It's open,' Nick shouts, 'no padlock.'

'Eh?' I lean out of the open driver's door.

'I said it's already open,' Nick says as he drops down and heaves the shutter up. It rolls easily on well-oiled hinges with a loud clacking noise like a train going past.

I look at the sign above the door and the graffiti spray painted on there, it looks weird, like a road sign. A red circle with a vertical white line across the middle.

'SHIT...no!'

'What?' Nick spins at my warning, the shutter clatters to the top and they come spilling out. Meredith, squatting on the floor taking a piss whips round with lightning speed to charge at the thick horde coming from the doorway. Totally unprepared and only pistols on our belts with the assault rifles and axes in the Saxon.

'Blowers...Cookey....' I charge forward and barrel into the horde, aiming for one and I punch him back into the doorway while he bends forward at the waist trying to bite me. The team scatter back from the ones already free from the door. Dave with knives in his hands rips through them with ease. Meredith takes two down within seconds while Clarence sends a huge fist into the head of another.

Blowers and Cookey join me pushing at the one in the doorway to prevent the others getting out. A thin built adult male with teeth gnashing and snarling with drool flying about. Blowers punches his head while Cookey draws his knife and stabs repeatedly into his stomach and chest.

'Throat....duck...'

Blowers and I turn away as Cookey whispers the blade across the throat. Blood spurts thick down his chest and he gets ripped downwards and out of our grip by Meredith seizing his ankle between her teeth and pulling him back.

'No,' I gasp and try to pull him back but she digs her paws in and yanks her head side to side with a vicious ragging motion that throws him clear from us.

'Move!' Mo Mo bellows and we dive down to the sides as he lets rip with the rifle on automatic. Bullets fly over our heads and into the dense bodies of the undead still trying to get back out.

'CEASEFIRE,' Dave roars. Mo Mo complies and quickly drops to one knee to change magazine, 'let them out,' Dave adds with a knife in each hand.

The three of us by the door scrabble away to avoid the mass charge spewing out. The first one is taken out by Meredith launching from the side and probably having the time of her life. I run to the Saxon, vault the back steps and get to the front to draw my axe. By the time I free the double head from being jammed under the seat, turn round and jump down they're pretty much all dead save for one crawler that gets her throat cut by Dave.

'Oh,' I stand impotently and stare round at the dead bodies, 'did Dave get them all?'

'Him, Mo Mo and the dog,' Clarence says, ' I think I punched one and Cookey did that one in the doorway.'

'Fuck,' I say with a big sigh, 'that was a shower of shit. Not one of us had a weapon ready.'

'I did.'

'Apart from Dave none of us had a weapon ready and who the fuck puts zombies in an outdoor supply shop?...and who the fucks paints a sodding no entry sign above the door but doesn't write the words or put a sign up saying there are zombies in here....who does that?'

'We had our pistols,' Nick says defensively.

'Complacency is a killer,' I say reproachfully, 'we need to switch on.'

'Seven P's,' Cookey says.

'Seriously though, why are there zombies in that shop? Marcy?'

'How would I know?'

'You were a zombie once.'

'Not funny,' she says with a scowl at me.

'Explains the lack of bodies,' Paula says.

'Eh?' Blowers asks.

'No bodies,' she motions round at the ground nearby, 'none on the way in either. Didn't you notice that?'

'Like I said,' I say after a few seconds of awkward silence, 'complacency is a killer. Anything left in there?' Stepping over the bloody bodies and I have to stop as Meredith trots past with an arm dangling from her mouth and runs back to where she was pissing before to once again squat down and finish the job.

'She does that,' Mo Mo says to Reginald staring aghast at the sight.

'You were quick mate, well done,' I say over my shoulder to the youngest member of our team.

'Nicely done, Mo,' Clarence says.

'Urgh it fucking stinks,' into the doorway I pause and take a breath from outside before stepping fully in to see the shelves and racks are empty, 'cleared out,' I add as I get outside wafting my hand under my nose to rid the smell.

'All of it?' Marcy asks and pokes her head in only to pull it back within a second, 'I'll take your word for it,' she grimaces and walks further away.

'Mr Howie, that's got the same sign on it,' Nick points across the service road to a bigger unit sealed up with the same shuttered front. A sign above the shutters proudly states that they are the cheapest sign makers in the town and blazoned across the front is another hand painted no entry sign.

'Sign on a sign on a sign makers,' Roy chuckles, 'are we doing it?'

'Doing what?' I ask him.

'Opening it?'

'Er...dunno, do you want it opened?' I ask him.

'Well,' he says thoughtfully, 'we're a nice distance away, Dave could try the bow out...for if he has to kill me...later...if one of us turns.'

'Fair point, yeah alright then...Clarence, do you want to show Marcy and Reginald how to shoot? I'll go let them out.'

'I beg your pardon?' Reginald asks with a look of absolute fright on his face.

'Shoot mate, fire the rifles...'

'Good god no! I cannot think of anything worse than...*shooting* a firearm. Oh my word, is this the plan? To bolster your ranks with foot soldiers? Using us as cannon fodder to cull the living challenged...oh I cannot fire a weapon surely I cannot.'

'Okay okay,' I wave my hand at him to stop the rising panic.

'Marcy?' Clarence asks.

'Are you being serious?' She looks at Clarence then over at me, 'I was infected...both Reggie and I were infected.'

'Yeah, we know.'

'So why the hell are you giving us guns? Maddox was right, how the hell have you stayed alive?'

'We got a Dave and a Clarence,' Cookey says, 'and a Meredith.'

'What if I turn the gun on all of you? How can you trust me?'

We all look at each other blankly.

'You just said complacency kills,' she says with a voice rising in volume, 'I was one of them,' she points to the bodies on the floor, 'I am with you to find out what this...this...*this*...' She waves her hand to motion between us all, 'all means...'

We all carry on looking at each other blankly.

'So you want to shoot or not?' Clarence asks as Marcy's mouth hangs open.

'You do get used to it,' Paula says, 'the way they act I mean. You do adjust.'

'I was infected,' Marcy says again, 'Darren turned me and...'

'They'd kill you instantly if they didn't trust you,' Paula says quietly, 'and even with a machine gun in your hands you won't be faster than Dave.'

'What if I shoot him first?'

'Here,' Clarence ejects the magazine from his assault

rifle and racks the bolt to eject the round in the chamber before holding it out for Marcy, 'take it, it's not loaded.'

'What for?'

'Take it and point it at Dave. Do it as fast as you can.'

She looks to the side at Dave standing with his arms hanging casually at his sides and not a flicker of expression on his face, 'Dave,' Clarence says, 'just to prove a point okay?'

Dave doesn't reply but just stands mute and watchful. Marcy hesitates then slowly reaches out to take the rifle, as her hand touches the stock she turns to look at Dave and not seeing any movement she frowns and gently lifts the weapon away from Clarence's grip. Still he doesn't move. She lowers the barrel to aim the weapon at the ground then slowly turns to face the small man.

'And?' She asks with a glance round at Paula and Clarence.

'You haven't pointed it at him yet,' Clarence says quietly.

'Its inches,' Marcy breathes, 'I can lift it inches before...' She lifts the rifle and whereas Dave was not holding a pistol he simply is holding a pistol now and aimed perfectly and unwaveringly at Marcy. With her barrel still pointing down she pauses, freezing mid swing then blinks several times. 'Okay,' she nods a shallow nod, 'I understand.'

'Now turn round,' Clarence says.

'Why? Oh...' She stares at the weapons all aimed perfectly and unwaveringly at her head. Not a sound made or a motion given away but every pair of hands holds a weapon. The joking is gone. The humour vanished and the eyes of killers stare her into the ground. Every single one of them stares with dark brooding eyes. Mo Mo is not a child right now and the lads show the eyes of men much older than their true years. She smiles nervously but not a mouth twitches in response.

She looks over at me. I'm the only one not holding an assault rifle, just my axe resting over my shoulder and I see the understanding in her eyes. She's seen us fight before and knows perfectly well what we can do. She was with Darren when we slaughtered their hordes and this serves to remind her exactly who we are.

'Relax,' I call out in a low voice and as one the weapons are lowered and the tension evaporates instantly. 'I'll go let them out...Nick hold the dog back if Marcy is going to practise shooting.'

'Will do,' he says cheerily and makes a lunge for the dog who growls at the thought of the arm being taken from her.

We do come across like a bunch of idiots, I muse as I cross the road. It feels weird having Marcy so close. Like she *has* to be close. That it's ordained or pre-ordained or whatever the saying is, and I know I'm not the only one that feels like that. The team treat her normally despite everything that's happened. We all feel it. This connection. This bond. What the hell does it mean? Even Meredith treats her like normal and the weariness she showed Reginald before is gone and now she just plain ignores him. I think she could sense his fear of her and in turn that made her nervous of him.

Now here we are, in a seaside town about to kill more undead while Clarence hands her a fully loaded military assault rifle to aim in my direction. Yeah, suddenly this doesn't feel such a good idea. I glance back as though to smile and offer a prayer of thanks at the subtle nod Dave gives me while he positions himself behind Marcy being shown how to handle the weapon by Clarence.

The shutter is the same as before and pushed down

with a clasp but not locked. I look up at the sign and take in the precision of the lines of the circle and the neatness of it. Good paint has been used too. The red is bright and obvious and the white line stark and crisp. Someone has taken time and effort to do this and manhandling bunches of zombies into enclosed spaces isn't easy either. Come to think of it, how would you do that? Unless you lured them and had an exit out the back with someone else ready to pull the shutters down.

I turn back to the team and see them spread out in a long line and Nick firmly holding Meredith back. Marcy holds the weapon somewhat awkwardly and Dave now holds Roy's bow with an arrow notched ready to be drawn back. Roy stands at his side seemingly talking about archery stuff. I bloody hope Dave can ditch that bow and get a pistol up if Marcy does decide to kill me. Mind you, she's had plenty of chances by now.

Oh well, in for a penny in for a pound, 'ready?' I call out and get the affirmations both verbal and nodding in return. Then, just for the hell of it I bang a few times on the shutter to get them pumped up. In response I hear an audible groaning rising from within. I lower the axe ready and flick the clasp free with my toes then after one quick glance back I bend over and yank the shutter up before legging it off to the side.

A few clear steps and the lack of firing has me stopping to turn and see the shutter has rolled back down. Sheepishly I go back, grasp the bottom and heave it properly this time before legging it away. It clatters up and the entrance is thick with undead, starved, emaciated and looking ready to fall down. They must have been in there for bloody ages but they come flying out as fast as ever with wild red bloodshot eyes, clawed hands and mouths drooling with saliva. A rancid stench precedes their arrival. An intense smell of decay and rotting flesh, of putrid breath and shit all mingled with stale body odour. Meredith gives voice and strains to be let go.

Keeping my axe held ready I move steadily back to be well away from any missed shots. One out front. A big woman that would have once had a mane of red hair. Now it hangs limp and greasy with great bald patches showing on her mottled scalp. These undead have been in that place for days, maybe weeks. Paler and thin but they're still alive and it makes me wonder how long they'll stay alive. A normal living person couldn't survive that long without food or water. Their skin is sucked tight over their bones showing that every last drop of moisture has been drawn to keep them functioning but still they produce saliva that hangs like that from an old dog.

The force of the arrow striking the big red haired woman makes me blink in surprise. Soundless and it sinks into her side causing her to veer off but she stays on her feet. I glance over to see Dave already pulling the next one back. The distance isn't great but still, for a first shot with a bow the accuracy is stunning. The next one strikes her shoulder. The third hits her thigh. The fourth is dead centre in her back and like a porcupine she keeps coming. I've never known Dave to miss at anything and I look over wondering what how he's handling not being perfect at killing something and I can't help but laugh when he passes the bow back to Roy, pulls his pistol and shoots her with a perfect head shot. Her brains fly out to the side and this time she slumps dead on the ground.

An assault rifle booms with the louder more distinctive retort. Marcy aiming and firing single shots under the careful watch of Clarence. A look of intense focus on her

THE UNDEAD DAY SEVENTEEN

face as she aims and fires. Feet planted apart and the weapon held ready but I can see the tension in her stance and Clarence speaking softly to help her relax. I take in the team from an offset angle. The four lads ranged out to the side look incredibly competent and much older than their true years and with a jolt the absence of Lani hits me hard again.

A true death, total and complete and no coming back. I'll never see her again. Never hear her voice or be able to hold hands while we sleep. I've known her for about nine days. Just nine days but it feels like months and years. We didn't even bury her, didn't even stop to offer a prayer or deal with her body but moved on going forever forward. She deserved a funeral pyre that blazed into the sky. She deserved a day of mourning, of words spoken to honour her passing but instead we fucked off to get some sleep and that was my responsibility. Yeah so we only knew her for a few days but everything now is magnified, time is compressed or the feeling of longevity is lengthened. I can't explain it but this hasn't been seventeen days. I've known these people my entire life. We've always done this and been together. What I was before is gone, eradicated from history.

We are all that we are now and always have been and always will be. There is no past. No future. Now. Just the now and the second we are in at this point and what we do with this second will define us forever more. The loss bubbles with nihilism that mingles with despair yet there is hope and worth. We *are* worthy and what we do is worthy too. We've been given a gift and we're only just scraping at the basic understanding of what it means.

Here they come and I don't run back now. I don't scuttle or flee to gain room but I watch and stare as they come staggering towards me with anger that builds clearly in their red bloodshot eyes. Static I wait. Fuelled with lust for blood they come then a sudden recognition in their eyes, like a focus or intelligence coming into their eyes. That's it. An intelligence that wasn't there before. I saw it. The switch from fetid wild beast to an organised hive mind that quickly gains pin point accuracy and the horde cease the full on frontal charge to spin and change into a horseshoe line with the recessed mid-point aimed at me and the long lines at the sides trying for my flanks.

It happens quickly with fluid motion and they charge coordinated with an almost graceful synchronisation. My axe comes up into a two handed grip and rather than letting them gain the full momentum I run at the middle then off to the left at the last minute and spin my axe round to cleave into the neck of the closest male. The power of the swing drives clean through, detaching his head that plops down with a dull thud and the follow through is so strong it digs deep into the shoulder of the one next to him. A back step and I swing round keeping the axe held mid height and a stomach is ripped open to let the sticky innards spill out. As I went into them and they charged at me so I become faster and move with greater precision. Being where I need to be and taking advantage of the gaps created by the massed execution of their manoeuvre. An uppercut drives one side of the double headed axe deep into a groin that opens an artery and the blood pumps down like gushing piss onto the concrete road. I boot that one hard into two more then spin and remove a leg at the knee joint. The firing starts again, single shots no doubt and I hear it well enough to keep my position and not risk running into the line of fire. Instead I ease back to draw them with me.

They come and they die a second death but one that is permanent. The virus is spilled again and again onto the ground. A ripple of energy goes through them so palpable I am aware of it rather than seeing it. Like a feeling or a sense and I'm ready for the harder, chemical fuelled charge a split second before they do it. Slicing left and right, up and down. Stepping back then lunging forward and the trail of broken bodies grow thick in my wake and suddenly I turn and run, bored, hungry, wanting it over and done with.

'Shoot the buggers,' I shout over my shoulder and wait for the weapons to open up and feel the pulse of excitement at hearing the GPMG burst to life with the more distinct thudding fire rate. Cut down in seconds and it's over nearly as quickly as it began.

'How was it?' I call out to Marcy while walking back.

'Strange,' she says while handing the rifle back to Clarence, 'I thought it would hurt more and have more… what's the word again?'

'Recoil?'

'More recoil,' she says, 'I think I'll need a bit more practise before I'm any good.'

'I need food before we do anything,' I head back towards the vehicle as Nick finally lets Meredith go bounding over to sniff at the bodies littering the ground. She finds one still alive and rags it senseless with a vicious snarl that snaps the beast's neck.

'Same sign over there…and down that road,' Paula points at the next unit along then down the next side road leading to the next row of shuttered businesses.

'Weirdoes,' Blowers snorts with disdain, 'we doing 'em?'

'Food,' I say with a shake of my head.

'Thank fuck for that,' he says. They load up and we drive smoothly from the industrial section and back onto the main avenue leading towards the town. Tree lined with big Victorian houses on both sides. Garden walls, picket fences and litter bins everywhere. The signs of damage are as evident as anywhere else. Windows smashed and some of the houses are burnt out. Front doors hanging off but still no bodies and the rain from the storm has washed most of the blood stains away.

The avenue leads to a mini roundabout with four junctions leading off. One goes into the High Street, one goes off towards more houses and the other two lead down onto the seafront. With a nice touch of irony I go through the red circled sign indicating no entry and head onto the seafront with the idea of finding a café or restaurant.

From the roundabout we get onto the straight road bordering the beach and see tourist England in its finest glory of shit souvenir shops and shit fast food next to the gaudy signs of local cafes and more shit souvenir shops. It looks rundown, broken, faded, old and bloody awful. Two big hotels dominate the seafront. Vast white fronted buildings with huge plate glass windows on the ground floor and the many levels above show the balconies of the rooms. It looks communistic, formulaic and dreadful. A complete lack of character and done to cram as many old people into one place to squeeze every penny from them.

This town looked gorgeous from the hill above, but here, driving through it and seeing it up close shows the cracks and rot. The pier stretches out from the shore on thick stilt like legs. A huge white building sits on the first half and the latter part is given over to what looks like a walkway and fishing area. It's dirty. The white façade is streaked with filth. The whole place is dirty and if it wasn't for the gnawing hunger I would happily drive straight through and out the other side.

'Hotel kitchen?' I ask Clarence while pointing lazily at one of the two communist leisure blocks.

'Worth a go,' he grunts with the same look of disdain that must be showing on my face.

With the Saxon stopped we pile out and this time we're all armed to the teeth with rifles up and aiming out. Blowers leads the lads out into the road with an order to secure the sides and front.

'Quiet now,' I say in a hushed tone, 'Dave and Roy, you two take front.'

They mount the broad steps and start up towards the front doors that are already smashed in with glass littering the ground. Roy stops and sweeps his foot over a pile of glittering fragments before calling back quietly that it's safety glass. Paula was holding Meredith and on being let go the dog bounds the steps with her nose held down and sniffing.

We all watch to see if she takes a scent of anything but she veers side to side and round the big lobby area without a growl or a hackle raised. Dave threads behind her into the lobby and stops to stare at each exit while listening for sounds from within. Treading carefully, Roy heads over to the reception counter and views behind it then disappears from sight into the office at the back, giving a thumbs up when he comes back.

To the left is the double entrance to the dining hall, the doors are wedged open and it looks like a riot took place inside. Every table is overturned, every chair is on its side or back. Table cloths strewn everywhere and table condiments lie broken on the floor.

Ahead of us is the main corridor leading into the accommodation room where no doubt the patrons had to surrender their passports to the Gestapo officer on duty.

'Fucking dump,' I mutter and earn a glance of agreement from Marcy.

'I used to work in places like this,' she says in a whisper.

'Yeah? Any good?' I ask while waiting for Dave to proceed.

'Awful, like cattle farming,' she says with distaste, 'I hated it.'

'Ahead and to the left,' Dave says pointedly, 'two points of danger. We can split and check both or...'

'Stay together, we'll go for the dining room first. I'm not wasting a day checking hundreds of hotel rooms.'

'After the units though?' Paula asks, 'they could be stacked up in there.'

'Could be,' I reply with a shrug, 'if they come out we'll deal with it, Dave go left through the dining room, Blowers?'

'Yes, boss?'

'Two of you in here to keep the reception secure, two out front watching in line of sight.'

'Got it, Mo Mo and Nick inside, Cookey out here with me.'

We wait for the two to get into the lobby then proceed carefully into the mess of the dining room.

A vast room. Square with white walls and cheap prints adorning the walls. Blood everywhere. Thick smears across the floor and splashes dried on the walls. Flies and insects buzz happily. The windows magnify the heat and within seconds the sweat is sliding down my neck. It stinks too.

'No bodies,' Marcy says as we reach halfway into the room, 'this is giving me the willies. Reggie, are you okay?'

'I am not okay,' he says with a strained voice, 'I am decidedly not okay. I am the opposite of okay. I am terrified and I do not wish to be here. Mr Howie, may I wait outside with your esteemed colleagues?'

'Go for it,' I reply, 'Nick? Reginald is coming out.'

'Okay,' he calls back.

'He is squeamish then,' I remark once the little man has almost run from the room.

'Very.'

'Did he not have that issue when…you know…when you were killings thousands of innocent people and generally ruining as many lives as possible?'

'Howie,' Paula snaps at me as though I said something dreadful.

'What? She did,' I reply.

'Still,' she says with a huff, 'that was rude.'

'Rude? Fuck rude. You didn't see…'

'No he didn't,' Marcy interrupts my flow that was building to a rant.

'Eh?'

'Reggie, he never turned anyone. He couldn't face it.'

'Oh…oh fair enough. He's just gone up in my estimations then.'

'I take it I'm still at the bottom of your estimations then?'

'Bottom? There is no bottom for what you did.'

'Kitchens,' Dave says dully from ahead of us.

'Go through mate.'

We keep going, stepping over the debris while ranged out in a line.

'I *was* infected,' Marcy says after a few second of silence after Dave and Roy have pushed through the swing doors into the kitchens.

'So?'

'So it was the virus that did it. Not me.'

'Not you? But you knew what was happening.'

'I was aware but…'

'Should have killed yourself,' I say bluntly, 'as soon as you turned you should have killed yourself. Where was it?'

'Where was what?' She asks in a curt tone.

'Where did you get turned?'

'The hotel on the seafront, the one that Darren set on fire...'

'Yeah, I remember it.'

'Outside of there. He bit me and waited for me to come back.'

'Sounds romantic.'

'I was terrified,' she glares across the room angrily, 'this monster had bitten me and was cradling my head while I died...does that sound romantic?'

'Oh I don't know, the flames in the background, the night sky above...you and Darren spooning on the pavement...'

'Fuck you,' she hisses.

'Nah thanks, save that for your infected boyfriends.'

'How dare you!'

'Enough,' Paula snaps.

'I know what I did and I will do anything to help put it right.'

'Right?' I stop walking and stare past Paula to Marcy, 'how the fuck you gonna do that? You killed hundreds of innocent people. You fucking ate them...you cannibalised them and...'

'I am here aren't I,' she turns to face me, 'and I saved you twice after that.'

'Fuck off,' I scoff, 'saved us so you could fucking trick us later.'

'I had no idea what was going on. The infection did that. NOT ME!'

'That's what Hitler said.'

'Howie!'

'Boss,' Clarence looks at me with a grimace.

THE UNDEAD DAY SEVENTEEN

'Did you just compare me to Adolf Hitler?' She demands.

'I don't know. Did I? Was he infected too when he committed genocide?'

'She did save us,' Clarence says.

'Save us? She got us into that fucking mess in the first place!'

'Did I? Did I make that prisoner come after you?'

'Probably. You probably did it *so* you could save us and then be the hero and lure us into a false sense of security so you could try and infect us with sex and...'

'Oh now hang on,' she walks towards me with a dangerous look in her eyes, 'you said that I was aware when Darren turned me...'

'You knew exactly what...'

'Did you say that? Did you say I was aware when Darren turned me and I did those terrible things?'

'Yes. Yes I fucking said that.'

'Don't swear at me.'

'I'm not swearing *at* you I'm swearing generally.'

'You were swearing at me.'

'Grow up.'

'You said I was aware and I should have killed myself. Is that right?'

'Yes. Yes and yes. How many times do I have to say it? Yes you were perfectly aware and you should have killed yourself.'

'And in the fort that night?'

'What about it?'

'Were you aware?'

'Aware of what? What are you getting at?'

'Were you aware you were getting horny and wanted to have sex with me?'

'Oh God,' Clarence moans, 'sod this...you coming?' He asks Paula.

'Behind you,' Paula says.

'I did not want to have sex with you,' I snap back, 'that was chemicals doing that.'

'Why didn't you kill yourself then? Go on? You were aware you were horny and wanted to have sex with me...'

'That is not the same thing and I did not want to have sex with you...'

'You had a bloody great big erection and were dry humping my leg!'

'We heard that,' Paula calls back.

'That was chemicals.'

'So you should have killed yourself. You knew what you were going to do and knew it could have made you infected.'

'I'm immune.'

'You know that *now* but not then. Mr Howie...righteous and perfect in everything he does. You would have had sex...we were about this far away from kissing if I remember rightly,' she says holding her thumb and forefinger a fraction of distance apart.

'That,' I growl with my eyes locked on hers, 'is not the same as killing hundreds of people.'

'If you had turned...and there was a very real risk you would have turned...you would have done the same as me except worse...you turned would be a thousand times more dangerous than Darren and all the rest put together...you knew that mister bloody Howie...'

'Fuck...'

'Stop swearing at me! Judge me. Fine go ahead and judge me. I know what I did but you aren't so innocent.'

'I would have killed myself,' I turn away muttering.

'Would you? The same chemicals that made you want to have sex would have flooded your body and made you do the things I did.'

'Fucking stupid.'

'Oh good come-back.'

'You still killed loads of people, all I did was get horny and that was your fault too.'

'Oh for the love of God. I am here. Reginald and I are here to do whatever it takes to make this stop. If a scientist walked in this room right now and said this would end but it would mean shooting me dead I would do it...'

'We all would,' I turn back to her, 'anyone would.'

'You know what I mean!'

'No food, it's all gone off,' Roy walks past with the others behind him.

'I suppose that's my fault too is it?' Marcy scowls at me.

'Know what,' I say her with a nasty smile, 'probably fucking is.'

'Grow up.'

'You grow up,' I stomp after the rest kicking chairs from my path.

'Does that make you feel better?'

'This?' I boot a chair and send it flying across the room, 'not really.'

'Imagining it's me? I cannot believe you just said all that.'

'It was the bloody truth and no, I am not imagining it is you. *I* wouldn't do that. *I* wouldn't hurt you for the hell of it.'

About to retort and she blinks and stares at me. Her face red and flushed and the anger is evident.

'Cat got your tongue?'

'You're an idiot,' she says and looks away. We get to the

double doors at the same time but both hold back to avoid walking through at the same time. We hesitate, not looking at each other then both tut as we both try and walk through at the same time which makes our shoulders brush.

'Oh excuse me,' I say sarcastically.

'Gonna dry hump me again?'

'I did not dry hump your bloody leg!'

'You so did,' she shoots me a look of hatred, 'you know you did.'

I snort and roll my eyes, 'I wouldn't do it now.'

'Good!' She recoils with malicious pleasure, 'I wouldn't want you to. Do you think I even liked it having you leching all over me?'

'Leching? I was not fucking leching? That's bloody awful thing to say.'

'And accusing me of genocide and being like Hitler is okay is it?'

'That was below the belt.'

'Lech.'

'Murderer.'

Outside we get down the steps side by side and split directions as I head to the front of the Saxon and she goes for the back.

'Dry humper,' she shouts and pulls herself into the back.

I get into the front and slam the door closed, 'where next?' I ask out loud.

'Er,' Clarence hesitates and turns round in his chair to face the back.

'Marcy? Where would you like to go?' I ask without turning, 'maybe we can find some people to eat. Would you like that?'

'No I would not like that. Maybe we can find someone for you to lech over.'

'Great. Fine by me. I'll lech over anyone apart from you.'

'So you do lech then.'

'No I do not bloody lech. Paula, do I lech?'

'Not getting involved.'

'I don't lech. This is stupid. I'm hungry.'

'Well go then.'

I twist round to stare down past the others to Marcy sat by the open back doors, 'where? Where then?'

'Try a supermarket? Shop? Another café? What's up? Your first idea failed so you dry up?'

'Oh fuck off with the dry comments you murderer.'

'Nicely done though.'

'Alex!'

'Sorry, Mr Howie.'

'We're trying a supermarket,' I announce and start the engine but the anger flows from my mind into my brain and the signals sent to my limbs make my movements harsher than they should be. The vehicle starts. I slam my right foot down and it stalls to tick over and a soundless interior remains within the Saxon.

'Dry humper.'

'Murderer,' I start the engine and force my movements to remain calm.

'Want me to drive?' Clarence asks brightly.

'No, thank you, Clarence.'

'Okay,' he says with the same light tone.

We go along the seafront and up an incline to the junction with the main High Street hard on the right side. Another no entry from this position and the turn is too tight to make in one go so I go forward, select reverse and edge back while turning the wheel the other way. I stop, engage a forward gear and turn the wheel back the other way and edge forward but the angle is still too tight so I once again stop, select reverse and pull back while turning the wheel back the other way.

'You hit something,' Marcy calls out at the dull thud followed by a distinct clang of metal from the lamppost falling over, 'lamppost. You knocked a lamppost over.'

'Yes, I am aware but thank you for pointing that out.'

'You're welcome.'

'It's good you have such awareness for danger…'

'Screw you.'

'Pity you didn't have such awareness once before.'

'The lamppost is on the ground if you want to dry hump it.'

'That,' I say through gritted teeth while forcing the wheel back over, 'would be better than dry humping you.'

With the wheel over I edge forward then throw caution to the wind and instead of doing another shuttling back and forth I simply push on and take out a huge chunk of wall.

'Brute force,' I nod happily to myself and gain the main road down. Shops on both sides broken and looted but the damage here doesn't seem as bad as it could have been and again no bodies.

'Co-op,' Clarence points ahead to the supermarket sign.

Once again we come to a stop and spill out with eyes up. Blowers taking the lads to form a perimeter guard while Dave and Roy head to the door. Reginald scoots past me with a look of fright and heads straight to Clarence and Paula waiting a few feet off leaving Marcy and I trying to not to look at each other.

'It's open,' Dave says after a few minutes of standing next to the wide open doors.

THE UNDEAD DAY SEVENTEEN

'And empty,' Roy adds.

Empty shelves stripped of everything. I head past them into the store and realise someone took time and effort to empty this place. Meredith runs past me with her nose to the ground.

'I'll check the back,' I call out and stomp down the first aisle towards the rear. Meredith sniffs but doesn't show reaction. I hold my assault rifle ready and find the rear double doors leading to the back storerooms.

'Here,' I click my tongue and shove the door open with my foot as Meredith comes running over with her claws skittering on the tiled linoleum floor.

'Fuck it,' one look tells me this place has been stripped empty. Dave gets to the doors behind me while I peer round into the vast storeroom.

'Anything, Mr Howie?' He asks.

'Nope. Fuck all,' I walk back and we head down the aisle back to the front.

'Nothing?' Paula calls out.

'Nothing,' I confirm and fix my eyes on Marcy who glares back. Neither of us look away so I scowl and she returns the gesture.

'Sainsbury's down the road a bit,' Mo Mo calls out from his position on the other side of the road.

'Dave, would you and Roy mind checking it out?'

They head down side by side. Paula, Clarence and Reginald drift down to speak with Blowers while I pat my pockets looking for a smoke.

'Nick, Mr Howie would like a cigarette,' Marcy says.

'Sure thing,' Nick jogs over while I shoot another scowl at Marcy who looks back at me with a look of minor victory on her face, 'boss?' He hands me a packet and I start wriggling one out while he jogs back to the others, 'keep it,' he says.

'Thanks, Nick,' I say and get one into my mouth then immediately groan at not having a lighter. Now I look stupid. More stupid than normal.

'Nick,' Marcy calls out with delight in her voice that makes me wince, 'Mr Howie doesn't have a lighter.'

'Sure thing,' Nick jogs back and hands it to her before running back to the others.

'Thanks, Nick,' I call out again and glance over to see Marcy holding the lighter but making no effort to pass it to me.

'Can I have the lighter please,' I ask while rolling my eyes.

'Are you going to apologise?'

'Apologise? What for!?'

'For saying what you said,' she says quickly.

'Fucking no way.'

'No lighter then.'

'Grow up and give me that fucking lighter.'

'Stop swearing at me.'

'I'm not swearing at you! I'm hungry and I want a cigarette.'

'Apologise and you can have one.'

'Oh my fucking God, Marcy. Give me that lighter.'

'Apologise.'

'Lighter.'

'Apologise.'

I could get a lighter from one of the others but suddenly that doesn't feel right, like it would be cheating. The point would only be scored by getting the lighter from Marcy.

'Give me the lighter,' I hold my hand out.

'Give me an apology.'

'Marcy, give me that lighter,' I step closer while holding my hand out.

'Apologise,' she demands angrily.

'Okay,' I say with a big fake smile, 'you apologise for calling me a lech and I'll say sorry for mentioning the fact you killed lots of innocent people.'

'Here,' Paula at my side thumbing the wheel on a disposable lighter and shooting foul looks at both of us, 'if it shuts you two up.'

'Thank you, Paula,' I light the end and smile again at Marcy.

'You still owe me an apology.'

'Tell you what, you write a letter of apology to all the people you killed then I'll...'

'Infection. It. Was. The. Infection. Not. Me.'

'You knew.'

'I did not.'

'You knew.'

'I did not.'

'All day long, you knew.'

'Oh trust me I can keep going forever and I did not.'

'Empty,' Roy says heavily.

'Right,' I step back and stare up and down the street, 'have we got radios?'

'Nope,' Clarence says.

'Cock it, right...load up we'll keep looking.'

Huffing to myself I head back to the Saxon and quickly puff on the cigarette before pulling myself up halfway into the driver's seat and pull off down the High Street. We stop at the next café, get out and search it only to find it stripped empty and get back in. The next one is the same. The one after that is just Dave, Roy and Meredith and so it goes. Every food outlet and café has been stripped. From the

High Street we go back down onto the seafront and start trying the other outlets.

'I don't think I've ever been this hungry,' I say to Clarence as Dave and Roy get back in from checking the last place.

'We all are,' Paula says from behind me, 'pier? It's the last place.'

'Pier it is.'

The short drive along the front brings us to a concrete hardstanding in front of yet another fast food kiosk resting amongst a sea of cheap town centre style benches.

'Movement inside,' Clarence says, 'eyes up.'

'Lads, on me,' Blowers jumps from the back as I get out the driver's door and pull my assault rifle out to hold up and aimed.

'What did you see?'

'Someone inside, running back away from the doors.'

'Away from the doors? Like a normal person?'

'Dunno,' he says.

'Fortified,' Dave joins me behind the big bonnet of the Saxon. Three sets of double doors to the front of the pier that would no doubt be wedged open during the summer months to entice people inside. Adverts and signs for a bar, café and amusement arcade inside but two of the sets of double doors have been secured with thick wooden boards fastened on the inside. The remaining set of doors have boards across the bottom three quarters leaving the top section unobstructed to view out. The windows to the sides are boarded too. Someone has taken time and effort to do this and now it makes sense why the town has been stripped. The survivors have retreated to the pier and stashed the food.

'Paula, you and I will go to the doors. Everyone else stay alert but try not to look too threatening.'

'How do we do that?' I hear Mo Mo ask Blowers.

'Widen your stance a bit and hold the weapon down… yeah like that…and smile if we see anyone…unless they shoot at us in which case don't smile…or smile and then shoot them…'

'Got it,' Mo Mo says.

We sling our assault rifles and head to the door, Paula and I so we appear less threatening. Marcy keeps to the side and puts sunglasses on and I think Reginald is still hiding in the Saxon.

'Hello?' I call out in what I hope is a friendly voice, 'anyone there? We're not a danger to you…we will not enter or use force…'

We stand listening, straining to hear anything while Paula peers through the glass to the inside.

'Anything?' I ask.

'No, HELLO?' She call out, 'I'm Paula and this is Mr Howie…we're from Fort Spitbank down the coast. Is anyone there?'

'Movement,' Dave says in a low voice.

'How can you tell?' I ask him knowing full well he can't see anything from his position.

'The dog,' he says simply.

I look down to see Meredith peering intently at the bottom of the door with her head cocked to one side. Ears pricked, and her tail wags slowly but giving no indication of the infected.

'Someone's coming,' Paula says, 'two men…one has a… er…shotgun, is that a shotgun?'

'Let me see,' she moves over so I can peep through, 'yeah, shotgun. Double barrelled.'

Two men walking down the side of the interior hugging the wall. One is huge with thick arms and a thick neck, like a body builder or a nightclub bouncer. The other one is older with greying hair, thickset and clutching the shotgun in his hands.

'Hi,' I call out so they can see me clearly, 'I'm Howie...'

'Howie? Mr Howie?' The thickset man asks as they stop a few feet back from the door.

'Yeah, from Fort Spitbank. We were looking for food but...'

'We've got it all in here,' the body builder says in a surprisingly high pitched voice. I stop myself from rolling my eyes at the information given so freely.

'We heard about you,' the thickset man says, 'and Dave and your soldiers from the government.'

'Right, yeah that's us but we're not...'

'What's happening?' The thickset man asks quickly with a step forward and I can see the worry clear on his face, 'is it getting better yet?'

'Better? No mate...it's...er...have you been in there since it began?'

He nods and glances at the body builder, 'I own it... James here was the bouncer on duty when...you know... when it happened.'

'How many people you got in there?'

'Fifty or so,' the pier owner says, 'we figured the government would get a grip and send people. What's happening? Is the vaccine ready yet?'

'Vaccine? What vaccine?'

'Everyone here says the government will get a vaccine and send it out with the army. Someone else arrived a week or so ago and said they'd heard about you...and the fort and...we talked about coming down to you but voted to stay here and wait.'

'Oh right, listen I don't think there is a...'

'We got all the food,' he steps closer as though in desperation, 'and a couple of shotguns....but we didn't hurt anyone did we, James?'

'I hit that bloke Mr Wheeler, when he took the beer.'

'Yeah but we haven't done anything else though,' Mr Wheeler says quickly, 'we haven't killed anyone and...I'm one of the town councillors.'

'Oh right,' I say with a nod, 'it's good that you've er...got everyone safe in there...how much food did you say you have?'

'Enough to last a few months,' Mr Wheeler says, 'we've rationed it...fairly...James wanted a bit more protein but...he fishes, don't you, James.'

'Got a rod,' James says, 'you can fish from the end when the tide is in.'

'Great, er...'

'And we got them into the units too...'

'Pardon?'

'For the vaccine,' Mr Wheeler says, 'we got as many as we could into the units...sorry, the industrial units by the petrol station, that's where you should start with the vaccine.'

'Oh the units, yeah...with the shutters and the no entry...'

'We did that,' James nods eagerly, 'we thought it would let anyone know there was people inside...'

'We voted on it,' Mr Wheeler adds.

'Okay, listen about this vaccine...I don't think...'

'Our families are in there,' Mr Wheeler blinks and swallows with emotion, 'my wife and one of my kids...James's mother is in there too. We managed to er...sort of lure them in and shut the doors...they're still alive though, we check them every day and...you know...for when the vaccine comes...'

'Your families? In those units?'

'Everyone we could find,' James says, 'I think we filled up like four units...like we couldn't get everyone but we did our families...like all the people in here did it...'

'Families?' I ask meekly.

'For the vaccine,' Mr Wheeler says.

'Shit,' I say from the corner of my mouth to Paula stood to the side with an obvious wince on her face.

'We killed them all,' she whispers.

'I know...' I whisper back.

'What's happened?' Clarence steps in closer.

'They've got fifty people in there...' I nod at the door while whispering quietly, 'and they put their families on those units...'

'The ones we killed?'

'Yeah.'

'Shit.'

'Yeah.'

'Er, Mr Wheeler...I am afraid to say there is no vaccine,' I blurt the words out and grimace while waiting for the reply.

'Hang on,' he rattles some keys and starts unlocking the door before swinging it open, 'oh....there's a few of you,' he looks round at the team ranged about and seems to stand taller at the sight of the army vehicle and the lads holding assault rifles and looking every inch like soldiers.

'There is no vaccine,' I say again gently.

'Oh, not yet?'

'Er...'

'They'll get one,' he nods quickly, 'it will happen. The government won't just let it happen and not...you know, like do anything about it...What about NATO? You heard anything from them?'

'NATO?' I ask in surprise, 'mate, there's nothing. Everything is gone. Governments, police...army...everything...'

'But you're here,' he says looking at me, 'we heard about you. Didn't we James?'

'We did, really we did.'

'No, I believe you but we're not from the army and... listen there is no help coming and...'

'But you're here and you're soldiers.'

'Okay, listen. We're not soldiers...'

'He looks like one,' James points at Clarence, 'and he does,' he points at Dave then at Roy, 'and they do,' he nods over at the lads, 'and that's a military dog,' he looks down at Meredith, 'and everyone said you're Mr Howie which means you're like an officer and you've got an army truck and those guns are army guns and...'

'We are from the army,' Paula says quickly, 'we just er....we say we're not as people expect too much from us. We are...just a small unit and we're strictly on observation only...'

'Knew it,' James says eagerly, 'they're from the army, Mr Wheeler.'

I wince inwardly at the lie knowing the consequences and false hope it could bring, but truth be told it was on the tip of my tongue just before Paula said it.

'We're here to tell you there is no vaccine and no formal help is coming,' Paula says, 'isn't that right, Mr Howie.'

'That's right,' I say seriously, 'I'm sorry to say it chaps, but you're on your own.'

'What about our families? We've got 'em all locked up in the units.'

'Have you?' I ask too lightly while Clarence coughs and turns away and Paula suddenly finds something on her fingernails to pick at.

'Should we leave them there?' James asks, 'do we feed them? What about water?'

'Feed them? No...no don't feed them...' I take a breath and exhale slowly, 'there is no hope I'm afraid.'

'Oh there will be,' Mr Wheeler says as though giving me encouragement, 'you must have seen some terrible things out there....but don't lose hope, Mr Howie. The government are amazing people and they will get a vaccine. Are the other towns storing their infected families too?'

'Not sure,' I say with a shallow non-committal shrug, 'er...to be honest er...most towns have er...killed them? Yes killed them...er...that's the chosen thing and one that we er... advocate and suggest is the er...right course of action.'

'Kill them?' Mr Wheeler asks in horror, 'but they're no harm to anyone where they are. I mean only a bloody idiot would not see the signs we've put up. We can show you if you want.'

'God no! I mean no, we've got a lot to do.'

'It's not far, James and I can take you down.'

'Really, no need,' I hold my hand out, 'Sergeant Clarence, can we load everyone up please to er...get ready to move out.'

'Sir,' Clarence salutes and strides away, 'you heard the officer, load up and get ready.'

'So do we feed them? We did try but they don't seem to want to eat anything,' James says, 'I even threw in a few live fish but they just flapped about.'

'The fish or...'

'Yeah the fish.'

'Yeah don't feed them...just er...best to just leave them.'

'Of course,' Mr Wheeler says, 'didn't you say you were looking for food? Do you want to take some of our supplies?'

'No, we meant...I meant we are making a list of the food storage places. Er, Paula they can be put down on the list,' I nod at Paula.

'Sir,' she nods.

'Right,' I say brightly, 'we'd better get back on the road, got a lot to check and...yeah so...stay locked up and don't let anyone in if you're not sure about them. No lights at night, er...Fort Spitbank is down the coast and can offer you a safe...maybe a safe place to stay.'

'We'd better call a meeting,' Mr Wheeler says to James as I beat a hasty retreat from the entrance to the Saxon.

'Keep us in mind when that vaccine comes,' Mr Wheeler shouts, 'even if it's experimental. Anything that helps.'

'Will do, er...over and out,' I climb up into Saxon and start the engine.

'Over and out?' Clarence ask while offering a smart salute from his window.

'Arse,' I mutter and pull away with a calm sedate pace as we go back up the hill and away from the pier, 'did you fucking hear what he said?' I ask once we're safely away.

'I feel so bad,' Paula calls out.

'Was that their families in those units?' Marcy says in a shout to be heard over the engine.

'It was, they put them there for safekeeping,' Clarence replies.

'I was shooting them!'

'We all were,' Clarence says, 'we didn't know.'

'They're still infected and dangerous,' I say as though to

alleviate the guilt. They sink into animated chat while I focus on the road and the emotions of guilt from slaughtering some poor sod's infected family and the growing unease of being so bloody hungry.

'We should have eaten before we left,' I say more to myself than anyone else.

'We had to get out,' Clarence says darkly and a feeling of being selfish sweeps through me that although I am hungry, the others must be too and Clarence is twice our size.

I put my foot down and feel the engine rise in pitch as we gain the exit road and barrel into the glorious rolling countryside.

CHAPTER SEVEN

As the understanding of the human physical form increases, so too does understanding that the human mind and brain are far more complex. Lani was taken then she was no longer part of the hive mind. That was days ago. She was one then lost. The infection saw Lani in the places where the losses were taken.

Lani came back. She did not turn or die to return in the true state of living but she was simply there. Her body was made weak by the injuries sustained but her body had also adapted and changed to the virus within. It was part of Lani now and that change to her DNA made her heal faster and increased her pain threshold. The cell structure was different. The way her body responded to trauma and injury was changed. Her blood clotted faster. Her natural health blended with the virus to keep Lani functioning far beyond the level she was before.

The injuries were dealt with. Clotted and sealed. The pain signals from the damaged nerve endings were muted and pain reducing endorphins were released.

Lani would have healed and continued to function perfectly but it was the mind that enabled the virus to take over.

Shock. A dangerous thing. On hearing the conversation between Marcy and Howie her heart rate increased at the same time as her blood sugar plummeted. Such an instant reaction and her body's natural reaction was to fight the change but her shock continued as she grew to believe Howie loved Marcy. She fought for him. She risked her whole life for him. She adored, worshipped, idolised and above all else she loved him. For being the leader she loved him. For being the one who can fix this she loved him. For being the man he is she loved him and to have that love given to another was more than her mind could handle.

Fractured and broken she sunk down deeper into a world of pain and betrayal and as her weakened body tried to react to mend the damage so the virus outgrew the anti-body that kept it at bay. It wasn't instant. Her body had learnt to fight the virus and work with it so when the virus increased it did so in order to repair and contain the damage done. The antibodies retaliated but they were stretched too far and over minutes of the night, and as her mind descended into the madness of lunacy so the virus was finally able to sweep through and take that which it had once dominated.

Lani became the true state of being and the infection saw through her eyes at the fort laid out with children kneeling in supplication. It waited. It knew what Lani knew, that Howie would come back.

The infection watched as Howie did return and it became aware that Howie could see through the host to the pure entity within. It lead Howie into the old armoury and away from Dave who it knew would slaughter Lani the host faster than Lani could react.

THE UNDEAD DAY SEVENTEEN

The infection felt as Lani the person reacted to the presence of Howie. It felt the love and it retreated enough to let that love show. Then it watched as Howie copulated with Lani. In control but allowing Lani enough of her natural reactions so Howie made love to the infection.

Then, at the pinnacle moment of copulating the infection saw Howie's pupils dilating and read his signs as his own body flooded with sleep inducing hormones. So it struck. This was the moment, timed to perfection with Howie embraced, alone and unable to defend himself. Away from the dog. Away from the giant. Away from the mocking young men and away from Dave.

A mistake. A belief that Howie alone with Lani would render him weak but he wasn't and his reactions were far faster than even the infection thought possible. The pin was pulled. Howie ran out. Lani took cover. The blast swept through. The escape was possible and the infection sought to use that escape but the calculations were done. Lani sent back would be Lani killed for Howie and his team are too strong to be taken.

The mind is powerful and it was shock that brought Lani down. So the infection took the knife and opened her stomach then cut her wrists and as the blaze took the hair from her head so the infection left the message.

Plant a seed. Water it. Nurture the seed so it grows to take hold and spread roots. The seed is planted. It will take hold.

The infection knows Howie leads his team away from the fort. It knows they are moving. It saw through the hive mind of many eyes on the industrial estate.

Now it waits. Waiting. Watching. Expectant.

CHAPTER EIGHT

Day Six

'Where? Show me.'

The boy touches the sides of his neck with his hands, 'in the neck...'

'Where in neck?'

'Here,' the boy points to the position of the artery, 'and then here,' he puts his right hand on the inside of his left wrist, 'and here,' he slouches to touch the tops of his legs where the thighs meet.

'Good, you small...you no reach neck...you do this one,' Gregori touches his own groin.

'Okay,' the boy nods seriously but doesn't take his eyes off the shiny blade of the knife held by Gregori, 'can I have it now, please.'

Gregori holds the knife out blade first to the boy who

goes to take it then stops and giggles, 'wrong way, Gregoreeee.'

'Good,' Gregori says and flips the knife over to offer the handle to the boy instead of the blade.

'Yay,' the boy takes the knife and holds it the way Gregori showed him, with the blade out and his arm away from his body. He paces away to the horde shuffling slowly across the garden in front of the house. Three van loads taken today. Each load brought back and set free while they returned to the nearby towns and villages to get more. The infected stayed nearby, shuffling and groaning dully in the blazing sun.

Thirty of them now. Groaning and shuffling quietly with drool hanging from their mouths and every single one of them heading towards Gregori who skirts the group in an effort to keep them turning.

The boy gets to the closest one, aims and stabs into the big thigh muscles of the adult woman. He pulls the knife out, re-adjusts the aim and stabs again aiming for the groin. Blood seeps out but slowly and it clots quickly. The boy works hard, stabbing and hacking with grunts of exertion.

'Up,' Gregori calls out.

'I'm trying,' the boy shouts back and stabs harder up into the groin and yanks back hard as a gush of blood pours from the severed artery, 'I did it...Gregoreee look, all her blood is coming out now...'

'Which way she fall?'

'Er...' the boy steps back and ponders this weighty issue as the woman shuffles and starts to wobble as the blood drains from her body, 'that way,' the boy picks a side at random and watches as the woman falls the other way to slump on the ground.

'Again,' Gregori calls and moves round to keep the infected turning.

It takes time but the boy, given the fact that he wants to play and make jokes, learns fast and applies himself to the task at hand. With grim determination the boy moves from body to body. Stabbing into groins and legs as his aim slowly improves. The way he grips the knife, the force applied, the angle of attack and the thrust and slicing motion.

They bleed and get stuck with the blade again and again but not one flicker of reaction do they show the boy.

It's hard work and the boy struggles to get the direction needed and knowing if to strike from the back or the front. A big male with huge thighs and no gap between them. The boy darts in and stops dead at the sight of the meaty muscles. He backs up and angles the attack then runs round the back of the male trying to find a way into the groin. At the front he stabs into the pelvis and tries to work the blade lower but the muscles and flesh are too dense to penetrate. His face flushes with temper that Gregori has already come to recognise as the pre-cursor to a tantrum and he waits expecting the boy to start kicking and hitting the male.

Instead the boy steps back and looks up at the male, 'sit,' he shouts like giving a command to a dog. Gregori tuts and shakes his head then stops as the male does as bid and slumps down onto his backside, 'lie down,' the boy gives the command, 'open your legs.' On his back the male spreads his legs and waits patiently as the boy gets between the thighs and finally gets access to the groin that he stabs down into, 'got it!' He turns grinning as the man bleeds out from the severed artery on the grass behind him.

The unease that Gregori felt before only increases, doubling, trebling, soaring with a creeping sensation that makes the hairs on the back of his neck stand up. The boy moves to the next one and carries on like nothing happened. Gregori's heart races, his chest tightening and a sick feeling spreads through his stomach. He bites it down, forcing the emotions away as he watches mesmerised at the boy dominating the infected adults and now he's learnt that trick he uses it again. Telling them to open their legs, stand still, bend over, bend down, lean forward, hold their arms out. They do it. He cuts throats and wrists and nods happily at the blood spraying into the air as Gregori turns and strides away with his own throat feeling like it's closing up.

CHAPTER NINE

He is coming.

What the fuck does that mean? Who is coming? For about five seconds I ponder this weighty issue before my stomach gurgles and I go back to thinking about food. I'm craving junk. I want pizza. Kebab. Burgers. Ice cream. Roast dinners. Crumbs, I want everything. My entire focus is on filling the hole within my stomach.

Purposefully I drive deeper into the countryside and away from the immediate coast trying to find a rural town or village. Somewhere off the main road that will have resources. Resources? Sod that. I mean food. Lots of food. And a comfortable sofa so I can digest and maybe read an old newspaper or flick through a book. The image seems lovely. A big meal and then a quiet afternoon of relaxation. Maybe even heat some water and have a bubble bath. Suddenly my head extrapolates the image and includes Marcy in the bath with me.

I blink and shake the image away. I hate her. I hate what she was and the fact she's still here instead of Lani. Christ,

Lani only died a few hours ago and I'm thinking of Marcy being in a bath with me. Selfish. Disgusting. I am a hateful disgusting man. I am a very hungry hateful disgusting man.

I could kill her. Marcy I mean. Just shoot her in the head and be done with it. But I couldn't kill Marcy any more than I could kill anyone else in the team.

I am so hungry.

Hungry.

Hungry.

'Town.'

Hungry.

'Eh?'

'Town, boss...'

'At last,' I blink again and focus on the job in hand. Perfect. A village in the middle of nowhere.

Houses that look a bit more intact and less damaged. Bodies here and there, old and decomposing. Storm damage. A few cars left at rakish angles but really far less than most place we've seen.

An old fashioned petrol station comes into view. One of the really old ones outside a repair garage and without the enormous flat roof overhead or the stale sandwich selling shop nearby. I glance down at the fuel gauge. Just below half.

'Fuel,' I pull in and bring the Saxon to a gradual halt beside the pump. Houses on the other side of the street and the village centre just a stone throw up the road. 'Nick, work your magic mate.'

'Will do.'

Disembarking we stretch and feel the heat of the sun beaming down.

'It's quiet,' Paula says from a few feet away.

'I know right,' I smile at her, 'perfect for a day off.'

'Our day off has been pretty shit so far,' she says with a slow grin, 'you feeling okay?'

'Yeah fine, you?'

'Hungry and getting grouchy,' she says with a pointed look that I choose to ignore and instead follow Nick as he waits for Clarence to break into the garage with much huffing, grunting and cursing.

'Boss.'

I turn to see Mo Mo standing next to a flatbed recovery truck, 'this is diesel,' he says and draws a knife which he skilfully wedges into the gap of the fuel cap and with a ping it pops open.

'You done that a few times then,' I laugh as he gets to work on the locking fuel cap.

'Few times,' he says, 'done it,' he stands back with the screw fuel cap in hand.

'Fuck me, mate,' I can't help but grin, 'good skills.'

'Did you just get that off?' Clarence strides over to stare first at the fuel cap then the flatbed.

'Yeah.'

'Well done, Mo Mo,' a huge hand almost crushes the youth to the ground.

'Pipe,' Nick gets to work slicing a length of hosepipe left at the side of the garage, 'we'll need a bottle or something.'

'Why?' I ask while watching him scout round.

'The Saxon is higher than the flatbed,' he says while toeing an old rusty metal tray, 'the fuel won't flow up.'

'So we siphon it down into something then pour it into the Saxon?'

'Yes, boss,' he says.

A metal bucket with a pouring spout is found at the back and is quickly put to use as Mo Mo sucks the pipe to force the fuel to flow out then spits the diesel from his mouth and shoves the end into the bucket.

'Cheeky fuckers,' Nick laughs, 'you see that?' He asks Mo Mo.

'Lot of tax on fuel,' Mo Mo chuckles, 'we used to get red from the farm machines out of town.'

'What?' I ask and walk closer to see the bucket filling with red liquid, 'is that not diesel?'

'Red diesel,' Nick says, 'tax exempt or fucking low tax or something, it's meant for farm machinery and plant stuff, these buggers were using it for their recovery vehicle.'

'And that's not allowed?'

'No, tax man would go nuts,' Nick laughs, 'like really heavy fines and shit.'

'Customs people came to the estate once,' Mo Mo says with a grin, 'they wanted to dip some tanks.'

'Did they?' Nick asks.

'Nah,' Mo Mo laughs, 'their van got stoned and they called the police who said they were too busy to come so they's fucked off.'

'Will it still work in the Saxon?' I ask with concern.

'It's normal diesel,' Marcy says from behind me, 'just with dye in it.'

'Is that right?' I ask Nick.

'Really?' Marcy says.

'Well I don't know,' I say hotly.

'You've never heard of red diesel before?' She asks.

'No, Marcy. I haven't. I worked in Tesco and didn't have a car.'

'I worked in a hotel and I didn't have a car but I've heard of red diesel.'

'Good for you. Well done.'

'Oh here we go, Mr Howie getting snappy again.'

THE UNDEAD DAY SEVENTEEN

'Only with you.'

'Hungry!' Paula says in a curt tone.

'Sorry, Paula,' Marcy says before I can apologise.

The bucket is filled then carried over and poured carefully into the fuel opening of the Saxon.

'Mr Howie, can you check the gauge please?' Nick asks.

'Aye, on it,' I head round and clamber up to see the dials, 'yeah almost full. Load up, we'll go for the main square.'

They climb in. I pull off. A minute later we stop and they all get back out again into the bog standard village square complete with a nice big monument in the middle and some benches. Boutique shops border the edges. A florist. Pharmacy. Cake shop. Newsagents and a few antique style things, oh and the hairdressers.

'Doesn't look too bad,' I turn round to see only the newsagents window has been smashed through. The rest look mostly intact and the bodies lying about are actually reassuring as it means the infection hit this place instead of them all being locked up in someone's garage or shed.

Dave heads to the obvious start point of the newsagents and sticks his head through the broken window.

'Empty,' he says walking back.

'Right, houses then. Listen, we might as well split up. It seems safe here...anyone got any objections? We stay within the square and check the flats above the shops and the houses for food in kitchens. I know we said we're not splitting up but we'll be within earshot of each other. Everyone okay with that?'

Nods all round and I rub my stomach at the audible gurgling sounding from it.

'Blowers, you take the lads. Paula and Roy...er... Clarence you take Dave and Reginald and...shit...'

'Messed that one up,' Marcy smiles nastily, 'go on, change your mind.'

'No. That's the teams,' I say stubbornly but feeling like a complete prick for putting myself with Marcy.'

'I'll go with Clarence and Dave can stay with you,' she says.

'I will stay with Clarence,' Dave says which makes everyone turn to stare at him. He shows no reaction and doesn't offer an explanation but the sting is there.

'Okay,' I say while Clarence raises his eyebrows in surprise, 'er...any reason, Dave?' I ask carefully.

'Yes, Mr Howie.'

'...Right, and that reason is what?'

'You are bickering and that is not good for moral. You should work together to resolve your conflict.'

'Ask a question,' I blush at his rebuke, 'that's er...sorry, everyone. Sorry about that. I'm hungry and...'

'We're all hungry,' Dave says forcing the point even further.

'Yep, very true. Anyway,' I pause at noticing the smile on Paula's face and the lads avoiding eye contact with me, 'Marcy? Okay with you?'

'Of course,' she says politely, 'and I'm sorry too,' she adds quietly.

'Er...any issues and just shout...um...off you go then,' I add a shooing motion with my hands which just makes me want to fall down and die from shame.

'Lads,' Paula says as they start to walk off, 'you do that side, we'll do this one...Clarence you okay doing that side and er...Mr Howie, the side behind you? Is that okay?'

'All good,' I say quickly and watch as they break away, 'oh god that was awful,' I groan once they're out of earshot.

'Even Dave is blowing you out now,' she says quickly then holds a hand up, 'sorry, bad joke...'

'Fuck's sake, Marcy. We just got told off for doing that.'

'Couldn't help it,' she says defensively, 'you were wide open.'

'Yeah like....'

'Stop it.'

'But you said one so I should be able to say one back.'

'We're not in a playground, Howie.'

'Feels like it.'

'Fine. Go on then.'

'What?'

'Say your joke so we're even and then we can both be mature.'

'...'

'Well go on then.'

'No. It won't be funny now.'

'It wouldn't have been funny anyway.'

'Would have,' I state confidently, 'with timing and delivery.'

'Would you like me to laugh when you say it? Would that make you feel better?'

'I'm hungry,' I say with my chin out before I turn and head off.

'Wrong way.'

'What?'

'That's Clarence's side...we're this side.'

'Oh for fuck's sake!'

'Seriously, Howie. How have you stayed alive this long?'

'Dunno...' I walk past then stop to look at her, 'longer than you lasted though,' I add spitefully and instantly regret it.

She blanches and goes to retort but stops herself and walks past me, which just makes me feel even worse.

We walk in silence. Marcy empty handed and me with the assault rifle in one hand and my axe in the other.

'Marcy.'

'What?' She stops and turns.

'You're not armed.'

'You are,' she says bluntly.

'You should be armed,' I put the assault rifle and axe down before undoing the belt holding the pistol.

'What are you doing?'

'What does it look like?' I say fumbling with the buckle.

'I don't want your gun.'

'You should be armed.'

'You're armed,' she replies.

'Yes and if something happens to me how you going to defend yourself?'

'I...'

'And then stop the bad thing from getting to the others? What if they get in trouble and I can't respond?'

'Fine,' she holds a hand out to take the belt as I hand it over. She tugs it round her hips and goes to fasten the buckle at the front, 'it's too big,' she drops down to adjust the size while I tap my foot and sigh, 'it's too big!'

'I heard you.'

'Stop tapping and sighing then.'

'I sighed once.'

'Once is enough.'

'Done now?'

She pulls it back on and fastens the buckle in place, 'happy now?'

'Not really.'

'Why?'

'How you going to pull the gun out?'

'What?' She looks down at her right hip then twists round trying to see the pistol hanging down her backside. She tuts and starts trying to pull it round but the angle makes the belt bunch up instead.

'Oh for God's sake,' she says between gritted teeth.

'Come here.'

'I can do it!'

'You'll be there all day, let me pull it round.'

'I said I can do it.'

'I'm hungry and want to eat.'

'Fine.'

'Thank you,' I snap and move in to grasp the holster and start trying to tug it round, 'it's all caught up now,' I say testily, 'fuck's sake,' I take the pistol out and hand it to Marcy, 'hold that,' she takes the gun while I work at the holster and start inching it round to her side, 'don't shoot me,' I add.

'Thought never crossed my mind.'

'Yeah right, done it.'

'Thanks, how does it work?'

'I thought Clarence showed you.'

'Only the rifle. Forget it, I'll ask him later.'

'No we'll do it now, here,' I take the pistol from her hand and eject the magazine before sliding the top back to make sure no rounds are in the chamber.

'Safety is here...see it...'

'Yes.'

'Magazine goes in and pushed home, slide the top back and that takes the top bullet into the chamber for firing.'

'The chamber?'

'This bit, the long bit...where the bullet is held before it comes out the pointy end.'

'I was only asking.'

'And I was only saying. Just point and shoot. It recoils a bit so hold it firm and away from your face.'

'Okay.'

'And don't shoot yourself.'

'You'd love that wouldn't you?'

'Mind you, if you didn't do it before then why would you now?' I ram the magazine in and slide the top back before handing the pistol over, 'it's ready to fire and the safety is on.'

'On?'

'Yes on. The safety is on. Push the safety off and you can shoot things.'

'Tempting,' she says with a quick narrowing of her eyes.

'You had that chance,' I narrow my own eyes and stare back.

'When was that again?' She asks, 'remind me? Oh was that when you dry humped my leg?'

'I did not...you know what...I'm hungry and...'

'So let's go then,' she goes to push the pistol into the holster, misses and drops it to the floor. I sigh and manage a quick foot tap before she grabs it and gets it into the holster.

A quick glare at me and we start off towards our side while I listen to the bangs and smashes of doors being kicked and windows being broken from the other sides.

'Start at the end,' I point to the first house in the row of terraced cottages.

'As you say, Mr Howie.'

'Don't start.'

'It's not a start it's a continuation of before and I wasn't doing anything, I was being polite.'

'Whatever.'

'Is it locked?'

'Oh let me try my x-ray vision,' I stop and make a point of staring at the front door still a few feet away.

'Such a child,' she huffs and strides past me and grabs the handle.

'No!' Dropping my axe I rush forward and pull her to the side as she pushes the door open. She turns at being grabbed and we end up face to face with me glaring angrily.

'I'm sorry,' she says quickly and genuinely, 'I didn't think.'

'Switch on,' I snap, 'anything could have been behind that door.'

'You're right, sorry,' she looks deep into my eyes then blinks and looks away which makes me realise I'm still stood pretty much pressing against her. I pull back and aim the weapon into the doorway and the empty hall beyond.

'I'll get your axe,' she brushes past me, 'sorry.'

'You said sorry already.'

'For brushing past you.'

'Oh...wait here,' I push the door open fully and step inside. A door to the right into the front room. I step in and scan quickly, 'clear,' through the front room to the dining room at the back then through the connecting door into the kitchen and back down the hallway, 'ground floor is clear, I'll check upstairs.'

'Okay,' she nods and hesitates, 'can I come in now or...'

'Best wait until I've checked upstairs...the front door was unlocked so...'

'I er, I should imagine that's pretty normal for a little village like this.'

'Probably,' I mount the stairs and head up to check the two bedrooms and bathroom at the top, 'clear,' I call down.

'I'll check the kitchen,' I hear her footsteps head down the corridor. The cottage is immaculately clean. Some dust from over two weeks of being empty but other than that it looks so nice and homely. The bedrooms have a double bed in each with white sheets and blankets instead of duvets and the sheets are folded back smartly with crisp clean pillows. The bathroom is the same and only one toothbrush in the holder.

'Anything?' I head down the stairs and into the kitchen to find the small table in the centre being stacked with tins from the cupboards.

'I love old people,' she says, 'they keep everything.'

'Fuck yes!' I rifle through the tins finding tinned fruit, baked beans, corned beef, spam, mushy peas, ravioli and all manner of goodies.

'Pasta,' she plonks a sealed bag down on the table, 'ketchup...salad cream...oh my god!'

'What?'

'Penguins,' she turns with a big grin holding a multipack of the chocolate bars.

'Seriously?' I ask stupidly at the sight.

'Hang on,' she rips open the outer pack and pulls one free to hand over, 'eat something.'

'We'll take them all back for the others...'

'Howie, eat,' she says with a firm nod.

'Okay, you have one too.'

'I can wait...'

'No both of us,' I say as firmly as she told me.

We open the little bars and stare longingly at the chocolate, 'fast or slow?' She says then looks up to see I've shoved mine in whole and already munching away.

'Howie!'

'What?' I try and say but my mouth explodes with the taste and texture of real food and the word comes out muffled.

THE UNDEAD DAY SEVENTEEN

She shrugs and bites hers in half. With her eyes closed she moans softly, 'couldn't find any chocolate before.'

'None?' I ask somewhat mesmerised at the sight of her eating with her eyes closed. Seemingly aware and she opens them quickly to catch me looking so I turn away and start going through the tins again.

'Why do you hate me?'

'You know why.'

'Why were you looking at me like that?'

I shrug and wipe my mouth. The biscuit was lovely but it's only made the hunger worse, 'I'm hungry,' I say without looking at her, 'I was just staring…that's all.'

'Oh, I thought I had chocolate on my mouth,' she says in such a way that it makes me realise she *really* did think she had food on her mouth and now I've just admitted to staring at her.

'Any bags?'

'Mr Howie?'

'In here,' I drop the tin and charge towards the door as Mo Mo comes running in, 'what's up?'

'We've found loads,' he says with a grin, 'everyone has…'

'Nice, mate,' I say with relief at thinking something had happened, 'we've got loads in here. Tell everyone to eat what they can now then meet back in the middle…Mo Mo!'

'Sorry,' he turns back from already having started to run off.

'Tell them to leave their doors open so we know which house they're in and we meet back at the Saxon in one hour. Got it?'

'Got it.'

'You can go now, Mo Mo.'

'Okay,' he grins and runs off as I turn back to the kitchen and let a deep sigh of air out.

'You moved so fast then,' Marcy says.

'I thought something had happened.'

'No, the way you moved…from there,' she points at the table, 'to there in a split second.'

I shrug and move to the gas stove in the vain hope the gas will still be on, 'did you find any coffee?'

'Coffee? I wasn't looking for coffee.'

I stare down at the gas rings and offer a prayer to the God of coffee that this place will have a special supply of gas from a sealed system that hasn't been fucked up or broken for the last seventeen days.

'What are you doing?'

'Nothing,' with a hopeful grimace I twist the knob and blink in surprise at the hiss of gas coming out, 'fuck me!'

'No thanks.'

'There's gas.'

'Gas?'

'The gas is on…' I press the ignition switch and offer a second prayer to the God of ignition switches that this one is battery operated and not run from the mains. It clicks and forms a spark which ignites the gas ring in a perfect circle of blue flame.

'FUCK YES! Did you find coffee?'

'You already asked me that,' she steps to my side and pulls the three metal tins over from the side of the kettle, 'sugar, tea…and coffee.'

'Oh my god…this is the best day ever.'

'You sound like Cookey.'

'Right….tin opener…'

'Here, what do you want first?'

'Don't care,' I say while I twist the cold tap on to let it pour for a while.

'Spaghetti hoops?'

'Anything, really...'

She opens the can, finds a spoon from the drawer and stuffs it in the top, 'here you go.'

'Cheers, what you having?'

'Er...'

'Share this,' I grab a spoon from the drawer and hand it over, 'they're so nice,' I say with wide eyes and a mouthful of cold spaghetti hoops.

'Share?' She asks holding the spoon while the water thunders into the sink bowl behind me.

'Mmmm,' I hold the tin towards her, 'have some.'

'Howie, I might be infected,' she says quietly, 'we can't...'

I shake my head quickly, 'I'm immune...' I say and wave the tin, 'really, they're so nice.'

'Maybe I shouldn't,' she says with a tight smile, 'I'll have the ravioli.'

'Hands off that ravioli. I want that ravioli...I want all of it so we'll have to share.'

'Howie, it's a big risk.'

'I've been bitten,' I say after swallowing the mouthful, 'and had a human heart shoved in my mouth and...'

'What?' She stares at me in shock.

'And I bit a blokes throat out,' I nod and delve the spoon back into the tin, 'and had eye juice drip in my mouth from an eye I popped and...'

'Urgh stop it.'

'I'm immune. You're...fuck knows what you are but whatever you are can't hurt me so...' I waggle the spaghetti hoops at her, 'we share otherwise I'll shoot you if you touch the ravioli.'

'You'll shoot me?' She asks and steps closer to push her spoon into the tin.

'Sorry,' I pull my spoon out to give her room, 'yeah I'll shoot you...they're so nice.'

'Are they?'

'Like really nice.'

She tilts her head and opens her mouth to receive the spoon. I can't help but watch and I much as I hate her, right now I want her to enjoy the taste I was enjoying.

'Oh my,' she chews then stops and closes her eyes.

'Nice?'

'Better than nice. You wouldn't really shoot me.'

I take another mouthful and chew the little squidgy hoops so all the tomato sauce bursts out into my cheeks and tongue.

She goes for another spoon and has to step closer to see down into the tin, I wait and our hands brush as she lifts and I descend.

'Still good? And yes I would shoot you.'

'Amazing,' she says with a mouthful, 'yours?'

'Same.'

'You had a human heart put in your mouth?'

I nod and wait for her hand to come out so I can get another spoonful, 'still beating.'

'No way?'

'Yeah,' I close my eyes and chew the hoops before swallowing them down and still the water thunders into the bowl behind us. 'That's what the baddies do,' I add pointing my spoon at her, 'they do bad things...but I guess you know that.'

'All gone?' She asks, 'and yes I was a baddie that did bad things.'

'One left, go on.'

'You have it.'

'I've had more,' I push the tin at her.

'Oops,' she goes to push the spoon in and misses.

'You keep on doing that.'

'Clumsy and I've done it twice,' she gets the last few hoops on her spoon and wolfs them down.

'Did you ever put a human heart in someone's mouth when you were a genocidal maniac?'

'Not that I recall. Were you a complete prick before becoming a hero or did it just happen recently?'

'Always been a prick.'

'I figured.'

'Murderer.'

'Dry humping prick.'

'Next?' She asks turning back to the table, 'ravioli?'

'Definitely.'

Using the opener she cuts the top off and lifts the tin up to offer it over so I can see the fat squares of goodness within the rich sauce.

'Hang on,' she turns and grabs a plate from the cupboard and spoons them out before grabbing a fork from the drawer. She stabs a meaty parcel and offers me the fork. I take it and push the ravioli into my mouth and bite down to burst the parcel apart. Chewing contentedly I stab the next one and hold it out. She leans forward and without thinking I lift the fork to her mouth. Her lips part showing her white teeth and the tip of her pink tongue that darts out to lick her lips. She closes her mouth over the fork and slides back to pull the ravioli off. I swallow at the sight and stab the next one for myself. She chews. I chew. I stab another and hold it up for her. She takes it in the same way and this time while watching me. I blink and clear my throat. She chews. I chew. One for one we stab and eat while I feed both her and me. The food is delicious. The taste is amazing but I want more.

With the last one gone and Marcy holding the plate I reach my hand up and run my forefinger through the juice left on the surface.

'Good idea,' her finger joins mine as we trace swirls through the sauce to lick off and the sight of her finger going into her mouth makes me sigh audibly.

'If only your boyfriend could see you now.'

'Darren? He wasn't my boyfriend.'

'No? What was he?'

'Oh he was the man that murdered me,' she says pulling a sauce laden finger from the plate to suck dry.

'Yeah but you made it up for since.'

'Next?' Her voice is deeper, lower, huskier.

'Anything.'

'First one I touch, okay?'

'Do it,' I nod eagerly and with our eyes locked she reaches down and fumbles through the table top knocking several over in the process.

'Clumsy,' I say in more of a whisper than I intended.

'Very,' she pulls her hand back up and flicks her eyes over to read the label, 'peaches,' she says with a look back at me and one eyebrow raised, 'want peaches?'

I nod and this time the tin opener isn't needed as she peels the top back. I take the plate from her and put it on the side so I can get closer and smell the fruit as the lid comes back.

'Slippery,' she pushes her fingers into the juice and tries to grab a segment of peach, 'got it.'

The opening is there. Her fingers holding the prized peach above the tin. I'm inches away and leaning in. She lifts it higher and the peach touches my lips, 'careful,' she says. I open my mouth and suck the peach in and her fingers brush my lips as she guides it safely in.

'Oh fuck...fuck that's good...'

'Sweet?'

'So sweet,' I say and watch as she fishes for the next one and scoops it up and into her own mouth. I can smell her. I'm so close I can smell her hair and the air is full of peaches and tomato sauce. Her left shoulder brushes against my right side.

'Ready?' clutching the next segment between thumb and forefinger she lifts it out but it slips and plops back in. She grabs it again and this time it lands in the palm of her hand, 'still want it?'

'Fuck yes...' I lean in as she palms the peach into my mouth and the tip of my tongue touches her palm. She blinks and blushes.

'You licked my hand.'

'Sorry,' I shrug, 'I still hate you.'

'Hate you too.'

I don't care for the insults because the peach is making my mouth have an orgasm and still the water thunders into the bowl behind us. We get gooey and messy eating peaches and it seems right and proper that she feeds us both.

'Spam,' we repeat the same thing and stand face to face and eye to eye as she fumbles through the tins for the next one, 'meat,' she says with a flash of a smile.

This one takes longer to open and the wait makes it all the better.

'Need a knife,' she says as the pink meat slides noisily from the tin onto the plate we used for the ravioli.

'No we don't,' I grab the slab of meat and hold it up for her to take a bite. This isn't fruit or ravioli. This is meat and teeth are needed. She bites down and takes a chunk away from the corner. I tilt it back and bite down on the same spot she did and her focus sharpens intently as my mouth touches the part her mouth touched. Her saliva in my mouth. Her hand comes up and covers mine to tilt the meat back to her. She leans in and bites down on the same spot again as though competing with the challenge. My saliva in her mouth now. Like wolves we share the spoil. Edging closer until we're but inches apart so the tilting only has to move the least amount of distance. Her hand still covers mine in an almost dominant action of control as she pulls it gently towards her then pushes it just as gently towards me.

Sauce from the peaches glistens on her chin so I take it the next level and reach out with my clean hand to slide my finger up and over her soft skin to remove the juice then suck the juice into my own mouth. She breathes heavily at the action with a look of determination and a crimson blush that starts flowering up from the base of her neck.

'Tomato sauce,' she runs a finger down the side of my mouth and pushes the finger into her own mouth while staring straight at me.

The last chunk of meat and it comes my way with a covering of gelatine fat glistening across the surface. I open and she feeds me, pushing the meat into my mouth and I spot the bits of fat and meat stuck to the end of her finger. I hold her hand and pull it closer to my mouth and I take that too. Her finger. In my mouth. I suck the meat and gelatine as she slides it free. Breathing heavy she glares at me defiantly, 'you missed some,' she says without looking at her finger still extended. She pulls her hand to her own mouth and slides the same finger between her lips. My hand still on hers and my knuckles brush the tip of her nose.

Now I breathe heavy and glare defiantly.

'Next?' I ask while flicking my eyes from hers to her finger sliding out from her mouth. My hand still covers hers. She twists so hers goes on top. I pull back and twist so mine covers hers again. We don't blink. Gentle movements. Dominance being tested. With her other hand she fumbles through the table and pulls the next tin up.

We both read the label and dare the other to laugh or show reaction. Neither of us do.

I turn to grab the spoon while she gets the lid off and this time I feed. The spoon dipping into the thick yellow custard and pulled out to be lifted to her mouth. She takes it in and the custard dribbles down her chin. I use the edge of the spoon and scoop it back up and aim it towards her mouth but her hand comes up to cover mine and the aim is reversed towards me and I take it without blinking. My turn next and while her hand clasps over mine I spoon the custard into my mouth and this time the dribble is taken away by a soft finger that traces a stroke over my chin and the spillage goes between her lips. Messier than the peaches and every spoonful seems to be dribbled. Her fingers clear mine and the edge of the spoon clears hers.

With her hand on mine she operates the aim as I go for the next one and at the last second she deliberately veers it away so it smears across the side of my face and plops down onto my t shirt.

'That's for being so mean,' she whispers and her eyes are challenging.

I delve the spoon in and lift it out towards her mouth. Her eyes narrow with suspicion at the lack of messing about. I lift an eyebrow as though to suggest the time for playing is over and there is eating to be done. She pauses, shrugs and goes for the spoon which is twisted over so the contents in the cradle fall down over the front of her t shirt. We both stop and stare down at the big yellow dollops landing on the top of her cleavage. She lifts her head slowly and fixes me with a look.

'That's for saying I dry humped your leg.'

Eyes fixed on mine and she pushes a finger into the custard, lifts it out and flicks the dollops on my face.

'You did dry hump my leg.'

I take it without flinching and push the spoon in then lift it out and smear it gently across the side of her face.

'I did not.'

'No?' Her head tilts as she asks and a new idea forms in her eyes. Her hand tenses over mine holding the spoon which she guides towards her chest. The tremble is evident but she tightens her grip and glares as though daring me to pull away. I meet that gaze and aim the edge of the spoon to gently brush the biggest dollop of custard from the top of her breasts. Safely on the spoon she pushes it back towards me with a slow mischievous grin forming on her face. I could refuse but the rules of the game have been set and to back out now would be a sign of weakness. So I take it. The custard that fell on the tops of her breasts is taken into my mouth and the spoon comes away clean.

A look of small victory in her eyes and the game continues as the tension builds and the water from the tap thunders into the bowl. Her hand still on mine as we go for the next spoonful of custard and the back of her index finger brushes against the rim of the tin which she pulls away quickly with a sharp intake of breath. A bead of blood forms quickly on the cut, crimson and stark on her skin.

'You okay?'

'It's tiny,' she says as we stare at the small bubble of blood. Her eyes flick to mine and with understanding I stare back. Blood on her finger and a desire to know the limit in her eyes. I nod, almost imperceptibly and gently I start pulling her finger towards my mouth as the breath catches in her throat and her eyes widen as I get ready to take the victory of the challenge. The tip of her nail touches my lips and we pause, the last fraction of distance for the bead of blood to be taken into my mouth.

'No,' she pulls it away quickly and pushes the finger into her own mouth, 'enough.'

I exhale and close my eyes for a second, releasing the tension. 'You bleed,' I say for lack of anything else to say.

She nods with her finger still in her mouth. She pulls it out and stares at the tiny cut, 'clotting already.'

'Is that normal?'

'For a small cut,' she nods then laughs softly, 'want to stab me and see if I clot?'

I snort a dry laugh, 'can I,' I ask, 'nah...listen, sorry for what I said...'

'Ah at last he apologises.'

'Blood sugar? Hungry, tired...stressed...'

'I know,' she says knowingly, 'but you were still really mean.'

'Really mean?'

'Really mean,' she nods.

'Really really mean?'

'Very funny,' she rolls her eyes.

'Your turn.'

'What for?'

'To say sorry.'

'So you apologised to get an apology in return?'

'No, I apologised because some of the things I said were out of order.'

'Some? Try all.'

'Some, and yeah you owe me an apology too.'

'For what?'

'Dry humping?'

'But you did.'

'Marcy, I did not dry hump your leg.'

'I was there,' she says innocently, 'I remember it. I remember thinking this is Howie dry humping my leg.'

'You did not!'

'So did.'

'You were busy making faces at me and taking your clothes off.'

'Oh you remember that bit then,' she says, 'just not the dry humping.'

'I remember it very well,' I say with a blink, 'it's scarred into my mind.'

'Oh,' she pulls a sad face, 'was it that bad?'

'Which bit?'

'Seeing me naked.'

'Eh? No that was fine...er, you know...yeah that bit...oh fuck off.'

'What?' She laughs, 'you've gone red.'

'Well, you were making those faces anyway.'

'What faces?'

'Pouty faces...like all serious...like a porn star,' I pull a mock serious lustful face and make fish lips while widening my eyes, 'like that.'

She bursts out laughing and covers her mouth, 'I was not doing that.'

'Were.'

'Probably in response to you dry humping me.'

'I wasn't even horny,' I say with a nod.

'You were,' she says, 'you bloody were. I saw it.'

'Marcy!'

'What?' She laughs, 'I did see it.'

'Well, you don't actually *say* that to someone.'

'You said you weren't even horny and I was simply

pointing out the evidence to the contrary...that I saw your erection.'

'Marcy!'

'You saw me naked,' she grins evilly, 'and I saw you naked...except you still had your trousers round your ankles.'

'True,' I admit ruefully, 'was it the chemicals?'

'Pardon?' She asks with real shock.

'Forget it,' I turn to get another tin.

'Hang on,' she turns me back to face her, 'what did you say?'

'Forget it.'

'Howie, say that again.'

I go to speak but the water still thunders in the bowl behind me and for a second I think it's that noise that I can hear but Marcy knows that sound as well as I do and her eyes widen as the blood drains from her face and we freeze stock still.

CHAPTER TEN

The scientist was wrong.

The gathered horde are not between a dozen and twenty miles away. They are twenty five miles away.

Twenty five miles to the south to be exact and that town, filled and waiting, snaps as one with eyes right as the small man gives death to a host and as one they start walking. As one they start jogging and with bodies warmed they run.

From the local knowledge contained within the hosts, the infection calculates the distance, the route, the weather, the heat, the terrain and it sends them as one. From the fittest to the fastest they run as one to cover the five miles.

CHAPTER ELEVEN

'Oh this is most frightening.'

'What is?' Clarence looks down to the bespectacled man adjusting his tie knot.

'Everything,' Reginald wails.

'Dave, nice touch back there,' Clarence says to the other small man.

'What was?'

'What you said to the boss.'

'I didn't touch Mr Howie.'

'No, I meant...forget it,' Clarence gives up instantly, knowing he lacks the patience of Mr Howie in his ever pressing need to understand Dave. Instead he focuses on the door of the first house in the row on their allocated side. He takes the lead and gently tests the door handle to see if it yields to the touch.

'Locked,' he sighs, 'check the back?' He turns round to spot Reginald staring over the square to Howie and Marcy arguing visibly as Howie hands his pistol over.

'Where's Dave?'

'Oh dear,' Reginald says, 'they hate each other so.'

'Reggie, where's Dave?'

'Back is locked,' Dave says walking from the side.

'Right,' Clarence replies tightly, 'of course it is.' He steps to the side to peer in through the window to the tidy interior of the cottage.

'Done it,' Dave says dully, 'looks clear.'

'Of course you have,' Clarence turns back and catches Marcy kneeling down next to Howie, 'what are they doing?'

'Mr Howie is giving Marcy his pistol,' Dave says.

They watch as Howie stands over Marcy adjusting the belt before standing and both of the gesturing angrily as she tries to reach the pistol round her back.

'Dave,' Clarence warns as Howie's bodyguard lifts his rifle at the sight of Howie handing Marcy the pistol while he moves the holster. 'Dave!' Clarence snaps when he doesn't lower the assault rifle.

'Oh dear,' Reginald says fretfully twitching his gaze between Dave and the two in the middle of the square, 'oh good lord she didn't shoot him,' he says with relief as they start heading off.

Clarence sizes the door up while the two small men track their beloveds as they argue and bicker towards the house.

'Will they be okay?' Reginald asks.

'Yes,' Dave replies.

'Are you sure?'

'Yes.'

'How can you be so sure? I am not sure. Really I don't know how you can be so sure.'

Dave stares at Reginald devoid of expression. Reginald stares back full of expressions, his face morphing from a

THE UNDEAD DAY SEVENTEEN

grimace into a smile into worry then finally deep concern at being stared at so blankly.

Behind the door explodes inwards from the huge foot aimed to perfection at the main lock, 'ha!' Clarence nods and turns so they can stare in awe at his perfect kick. 'You two okay?' He asks at seeing them staring at each other strangely.

'Yes,' Dave says without looking away from Reginald.

'I...' Reginald goes to say. 'Do you have to stare at me in that way? It is most disconcerting.'

Dave stares.

'Dave, leave him alone. Come on,' Clarence says shaking his head he walks through the broken doorway and into the house. 'Anyone home?' He calls out and waits with the rifle held ready. He stiffens as Dave walks in behind him and heads straight up the stairs without a word spoken, 'Dave, you check upstairs.'

'I am.'

'I was being sarcastic.'

Dave doesn't reply but clears the upper floor with his usual lightning speed before heading down the stairs and waiting behind Clarence.

'Clear?'

'Yes,' Dave says.

The big man takes a deep breath, 'you could have said.'

'I did.'

'Only when I asked.'

'By the fact I came back down should be signal the upper floor is clear and we can proceed.'

Clarence goes to retort then snaps it off at the perfectly logical answer laid out.

'Oh dear,' Reginald mutters from behind them both. He turns to see Howie pushing Marcy from the door to their house then back to see Clarence glowering at Dave and Dave staring blankly up at the red face of Clarence, 'oh dear, conflict everywhere. May I go with another team?' He asks, 'Paula seems nice. Perhaps I should be with Paula and Roy?'

'Mr Howie said you're with us,' Dave says without breaking eye contact from Clarence.

Reginald frets and adjusts his tie knot. The previous world was not kind to Reginald. The base acts of modern society appalled him. He was polite but somewhat patronising as those with greater intellect often are. He fretted day to day in the same way he still frets day to day. When the world fell and his intellect failed to protect him he came back as a minion to be bid by the hive mind controlled by Marcy. When that ended, so too did the power Marcy yielded over him but he stayed with her simply because being away from her was not an option.

He felt, deep down inside, that Marcy acted with honest intent when she went to the fort. There was no trickery or deceit and what happened later, with the pheromones, was something he had no knowledge off. The days spent in the houses while Marcy recovered were fretful but she recovered and soon they were both showing signs that the infection had left them. They ate food. Slept. Drank water. Defecated. They did as humans do. He wanted to leave and go somewhere quiet where they could hide out, and when she refused so the fretting began again. Now there was just conflict. Last night was terrifying. Fighting. Shooting. Shouting. Explosions. Dead bodies. Young people injured and screaming. Fires.

When they left with Howie and his team at dawn he felt glad to be away from the fort but conflicted at being with such an obviously violent group of people who seemed to attract trouble at every corner of every street.

He vowed to stay hidden, stay small and stay quiet. Fret quietly and go along with it until he could talk some sense into Marcy but then she started arguing with Howie and he felt lost within the team. They were all strong characters with strong voices. Tough people with guns and knives and axes who had killed time and again. They responded so perfectly to Howie's commands and worked fluidly as a team, and with Marcy bickering with Howie so he felt even more isolated.

Looking back into the house he stares worriedly at Clarence and Dave glaring at each other. No, he muses to himself, Dave doesn't glare. Dave just stares and his face is unreadable. Reginald liked Clarence. There was something warm and human about the big man, like a protective bear that worried about his brood.

'Er,' he clears his throat, 'perhaps you gentleman would like some food now?' he enquires politely, 'in the kitchen, which is er…down there I believe,' he goes to point then remembers that pointing is rude so sort of waves in that general direction instead.

Dave walks into the kitchen and casually looks round, 'clear,' he says clearly, 'crawler in the garden.'

'A what what?' Reginald stops in the doorway to the kitchen and tries to peer round Clarence's huge girth.

'Crawler,' Dave says.

'You mean a living challenged? In the garden?' Reginald edges forward and looks through the glass of the back door to the old lady slowly clawing herself across the sun parched lawn, 'oh gosh. What do we do?'

'Dave?' Clarence asks looking through the cupboards, 'you mind?'

Dave unlocks the back door and steps out as Reginald balks and backs away to watch the other small man walk casually over, drop down and swipe the blade of his knife deftly across the old ladies throat. She gargles noisily, pumping blood onto the grass before slumping down as Dave wipes his blade on her knitted cardigan.

'Loads here,' Clarence says, 'you hungry, Reggie?'

'Reginald,' Reginald says automatically.

'Baked beans, macaroni...meatballs...some pasta, rice, rice cakes...bloody hell, she's only got a four pack of tuna in here.'

'Any cheese?' Reginald asks, 'we could make a tuna and pasta bake...are there tinned tomatoes?'

'We'll be eating it all cold im afraid,' Clarence says almost apologetically. He knew he shouldn't like Reginald as Reginald was on the enemy's side. But he did like Reginald. He liked the way the man was always so neat and tidy and the way he fussed and fretted over Marcy. 'Unless the gas is still on,' he adds.

'Gas? Oh I see, the gas stove...let's see shall we...yes... yes it appears the gas is most certainly on. May I see what we have? Oh okay, yes...the macaroni will certainly make a cheese dish which could be blended with the tuna and...'

'Clarence?'

'Mo Mo?' Clarence strides away into the hallway leaving Reginald to mutter and sort through the food tins.

'We found loads, Paula and Roy has too.'

'Good, check with the boss and see what he wants to do. I suggest we eat first then meet back in the middle after...'

'Got it.'

'Mo Mo!'

'Yeah?' Mo Mo turns back from starting to run off, 'can

you politely suggest to Mr Howie that they sort their shit out.'

'I'm not saying that,' Mo Mo says.

'Fair enough,' Clarence shrugs. He turns back to the kitchen and stops at the sight of Reginald pulling saucepans and plates from cupboards. 'Everyone has got loads of food,' he says, 'I think we'll eat in here then meet after.'

'Uh huh,' Reginald says, 'right,' he turns grinning first at Dave then Clarence, 'you two sit down and I shall rustle us up something in no time.'

'You cooking then?' Clarence asks with a bemused grin, 'we could just open the tins and eat it cold.'

'And we could also defecate on the floor but we are not animals,' Reginald promptly replies, 'we are civilised and shall eat like civilised people.'

'Okay,' Clarence chuckles and crosses to the table where he eases his considerable weight into a groaning wooden chair and looks across at Dave. 'Think they'll be okay?'

'Yes,' Dave says.

'You're hard work you are, Dave.'

'Yes.'

'Glad we got that sorted, need a hand, Reggie?'

'Gosh no, I am more than capable here. I suggest with start with a light aperitif of grilled pilchards, tinned unfortunately but that shall be followed by a tuna and pasta medley based in a rich tomato sauce and finished off with a light fruit salad.'

'Right,' Clarence blinks and stares.

'I will boil some water for tea while we wait, would you care to wash your hands now or...?'

Dave and Clarence look at each other and both recognise an order subtly disguised as a request.

'Now?' Clarence asks Dave.

'Yes, now,' Dave says.

'Mr Clarence?'

'In here and it's just Clarence, I'm not mister...'

'Soz,' Mo Mo pants, 'head's fucked innit...Mr Howie said we can eat in our houses and meet back in an hour,' he goes to run off, stops and turns back, 'anything else?'

'No,' Clarence says.

'Not in there!' Reginald exclaims in horror at Dave starting to wash his hands in the kitchen sink, 'upstairs please, gentlemen. That is not hygienic at all. Really! That is exactly the sort of thing Marcy would do.'

They head upstairs and Clarence stares silently at the dead body in the bath while Dave washes his hands before they swap over and Dave stares at the body while Clarence scrubs up.

'Suicide?' Clarence leans over to look at the congealed and dried pool of blood at the bottom of the bath.

'Yes,' Dave says.

'Can't blame him I suppose,' Clarence shakes the water from his hands.

'No,' Dave says.

Back in the kitchen they resume their places at the table while Reginald rushes hither and thither opening tins and unscrewing tubes of puree. He slides the grill open and turns the pilchards as the room fills with the heavenly scent of cooked fish.

'So,' Clarence says to fill the silence, 'you like cooking then, Reggie.'

'One might say I enjoy the culinary arts,' Reginald says while stirring a pan, 'it is the mark of a civilisation to take the basic ingredients to enhance the flavours and compliments of each food. Of course, so much more attention is paid these days to the correct nutritional values and I do pride myself on finding the right balance between proteins, carbohydrates and fats but alas, with such a limited menu I am restricted with what I can do.'

'Oh,' Clarence says and stretches his legs out, 'so you think you and Marcy are not infected now?'

'Truly I do not know,' Reginald says with a glance at Clarence, 'really I wish I was able to provide a more succinct answer. Oh I say, is it wise for me to be cooking for you?'

'Just don't spit in it,' Clarence smiles.

'I certainly would not! I have scrubbed my hands thoroughly and...'

'I was joking.'

'Oh, of course. Forgive me, my humour does not match the soldier humour you all display.'

'You worried then?'

'Worried?'

'About being with us?'

'I am not worried,' Reginald says with a firm shake of his head, 'I am terrified and completely out of my depth. I cannot fight or wield a weapon and I feel faint at the sight of blood. Marcy and Mr Howie are bickering and truly that worries me greatly.'

'They'll sort it out,' Clarence replies, 'one way or another,' he adds in a low mutter that earns a glance from Dave.

The pilchards are served. On plates and with knives and forks. Fresh water in glasses and the three men eat seated at the table with Reginald glaring at Dave's elbows on the table until Dave takes his elbows off the table.

They are gone within a few seconds. Wolfed down with lips being licked and eyes turning towards the amazing smells coming from the pots on the gas hobs. The middle course is served. Pasta mixed with macaroni, tinned tuna and blended with tinned tomatoes, baked beans, meatballs and puree.

The taste is incredible. While Marcy and Howie feed each other within their charged room so the three eat from clean bowls using clean spoons and pardoning themselves from the belches given from the empty stomachs taking food. Fruit salad follows. Several tins opened and spread with two larger portions for Clarence and Dave and a more modest portion for Reginald. Water comes to the boil while they eat and the three coffee mugs rest on the side waiting to be filled.

'Reginald,' Clarence leans back and sighs as the last of the fruit is swallowed down, 'that was perfect, mate.'

'Oh I hardly think so,' Reginald says with a fretful shake of his head, 'meatballs with tuna? Oh no, but the proteins were there to ensure your muscles are replenished and I can only apologise for the mixed flavourings but...'

'It was lovely!' Clarence laughs, 'stop fretting, want coffee?'

'Oh gosh sit back down and let me do it.'

'You cooked,' Clarence says happily now his blood sugar is rising back to more safer levels and the world is suddenly looking not quite so shit, 'I'll brew up. Dave, you clearing?'

'Yes,' Dave clears the table while Reginald frets back and forth at the sight of the two toughest men he has ever seen doing domestic chores.

'I reckon,' Clarence says contentedly after stirring the last mug, 'that we are probably the most civilised ones here. Mr Howie and Marcy will be glaring at each other across their table. Roy is probably getting Paula to check all his new lumps and the lads are probably sitting amongst a pile of empty cans while talking about boobs and each other's mothers.'

He freezes with the mug held to his lips. Dave snapping his head up. Reginald's eyes widening like saucers as a hundred voices and more pierce the air with the howling screams of the undead.

'Shit,' the mug falls as Dave rises and Reginald panics.

CHAPTER TWELVE

Forty five minutes for a regular.

Thirty five minutes for someone who trains hard.

Five miles to be covered but with the heart rate monitored perfectly and the exact doses of chemicals, endorphins and energy releases controlled from the nervous system, the horde can do it in thirty.

Old. Young. Infirm. Diseased. Fat. Obese. Anorexic. The sick, lame, weary and normal run at the same pace with a motion that would put an Olympic distance runner to shame. Perfectly fluid and every movement is controlled.

They do not lurch or stagger and they do not waste precious fluid by drooling.

The infection has learnt. It has evolved.

. . .

THE UNDEAD DAY SEVENTEEN

It has retained resources to be deployed.

It will not give in.

It will not stop.

One race.

CHAPTER THIRTEEN

'Now Roy?'

He nods with so much worry etched into every line in his face that the irritation disappears instantly, 'okay,' she says softly, 'where?'

'My neck,' he tilts his chin up to stretch his neck out.

'Your neck,' Paula asks staring at his neck, 'er, where am I looking?'

'On the right side,' he says brushing his fingertips over the right side of his neck, 'it feels all...' he holds his hand away from his neck as though it's being pushed by something big, 'all like...' his hand opens and closes quickly, 'like pulsing and growing...'

'Here?' She asks gently touching his neck.

'Oh god,' he whimpers with his eyes screwed shut, 'can you see it? How big is it? Oh god oh god...'

'Roy, I was checking I had the right place,' she says soothingly, 'hang on,' she puts the assault rifle down on the floor of the hallway to the cottage so identical in layout and design to the others. With both hands free she grips him as though to strangle but gently, softly, massaging with the touch of a lover, 'I can't feel anything.'

'It feels swollen and...stiff on one side...and...here,' he motions again to the right side.

With his eyes closed she stares at him with genuine care. The man is so fit with not an ounce of fat on his lean frame and he's worked so well with the others and seemed to make a real effort not to say things that would offend them. She hardly knows him but they were together when they met the others so a team within a team they remain. A loyalty and deep respect that grows with every passing hour.

'There's nothing there, honey,' she says using a term of endearment now they're alone and away from the others.

'Sure?'

'Really, I can't feel anything different...' she feels again, slightly harder knowing there is nothing there but also knowing the torment within his mind, 'honestly, Roy. I promise I would never lie.'

'Okay,' he exhales slowly and opens his eyes, 'thank you.'

'Anytime.'

'I get it when I'm stressed,' he says with her hands still holding his neck.

'In your neck?'

'Always have,' he replies and covers her hands gently with his, 'the doctors got so fed up with me,' he says while stroking his thumbs over the backs of her hands.

'I won't,' she says.

'One day you will.'

'No.'

'It'll get tiresome and...'

'Not to me.'

'I don't want to stay with them,' he says while staring into her eyes.

'I know, I told Howie we were thinking of leaving...'

'What did he say?'

'Not much, everything that's happened...I couldn't push it again...not after...'

'Lani, of course,' Roy says, 'I do like them but...and if you want to stay I'll stay with you.'

'Roy,' she smiles sadly, 'I wish I knew you before this.'

'You wouldn't look twice at me,' he says kindly without any trace of venom.

'I would.'

'A weird hypochondriac?'

'Definitely. You are handsome, you know that. What?'

'Im not.'

'You are, I think you are.'

'You are beautiful.'

'I didn't say it so you'd say it back.'

'Okay, I take it back then.'

'Oh no you don't buster!'

'Come here,' he pulls her in close.

'I'm hungry,' she says with her lips hovering close to his.

'Me too.'

'Paula?'

'Mo Mo, in here...what's happened?'

'Nothing, Blowers said to tell you we found loads of food and should we eat now or take it somewhere? You get me?'

'Hang on,' with a smile at Roy she walks into the kitchen and starts rooting through the cupboards, 'yeah loads in here too. Go and see Clarence and Mr Howie, suggest we eat here and then meet back in the middle later.'

'Got it.'

'Mo Mo!'

'Yeah?' He says running back.

'Suggest it politely.'

'I will,' he shouts running off.

'What do you fancy?' Paula asks facing the open cupboard. She smiles at the feel of his arms enveloping her round the waist and the soft touch of his lips on the back of her neck. She drops her hands to hold his and they stand clasped together enjoying the warm embrace of human touch. She sighs heavily and nestles her head back as his brushes the side of her cheek.

'Do you really want to leave them?' She asks.

'I just…' he pauses, 'yes, yes I do but I'll do what you want. I'm not good round people, I say things that…wind them up and…I've got no tact or…'

'Telling me,' she chuckles and reaches back to slide her fingers through his hair, 'I don't know, I feel like a sense of responsibility to them. Like we belong together. Does that make sense?'

'Yes.'

'It's not about being safe,' she says quietly while enjoying the cuddle, 'I know I'd be safe with you and…'

'You underestimate yourself,' he murmurs, 'you survived on your own.'

'I did,' she agrees, 'and I would do again, but surviving and living are two different things. I could *survive* on my own but I can *live* with you or the team.'

'I understand.'

'And I don't mean for you to protect me either although I know nothing would ever get through you…'

'I'm not Howie or Dave or Clarence.'

'You're not far off, Roy,' she says firmly, 'you can fight as well as any of them.'

'Not those three. You've seen them...all of them...even the lads, they're so fast.'

'They've been doing it non-stop for days.'

'And Lani? My word she could fight.'

'She could,' Paula sighs.

'I think it's right she died like that.'

'Really?'

'Imagine if she came back.'

'Oh I see, sorry...I thought you meant...yeah you don't have much tact, Roy.'

'We'll stay with them then.'

'No. If it makes you feel uncomfortable then we can leave.'

'That wouldn't be fair to you,' he says, 'and Howie relies on you now. He made you a manager in the tunnel.'

'Urgh that tunnel,' she shivers.

'You looked so sexy in that tunnel.'

'Roy!'

'You did,' he tightens his grip round her waist and commences the kisses to the back of her neck again.

'Paula?'

'Here,' Paula calls back as Roy steps back from the embrace.

'Mr Howie...' Mo Mo pants to get breath, 'said everyone got food so eat...eat now and meet back in an hour...'

'Okay, Mo. You okay?'

'Fine!'

'Make sure you all eat lots.'

'Will do.'

'See what I mean?'

'What?'

'How can you leave them?'

'I will,' she says, 'for you.'

'We'll see,' he says, 'now I have a pressing issue that I need to discuss with the personnel manager.'

'Okay,' she laughs and adopts a serious expression, 'how can I help?'

'It's a personal issue,' Roy says gravely, 'and one that needs to be discussed in private,' he adds taking her hand and gently pulling her towards the stairs.

'Oh,' she says, 'now?'

'Oh,' he stops with a look of worry, 'we don't have to I was...'

'Get up there, you,' she rushes into him and starts pushing him towards the stairs, 'you got me going kissing my neck like that.'

'I think we should eat first,' he says switching sides and letting himself be pushed up the stairs.

'Yep,' she pulls her top up and over her head.

'We've only got an hour,' he pulls his own top off and drops it on the floor.

'Yep,' they reach the top of the stairs and come together with lips meeting hungrily. Roy walking backwards and being guided to the main bedroom and the double bed within.

Shoes are tugged off, belts undone, trousers pulled down and the floor litters with clothes as they fall back onto the soft mattress and take delight in the exploration of each other's bodies.

What was frantic lust slows to a deep care as they take time and kiss deeply. Hands holding. Skin touching. Breathing heavy and they sink into a bliss so rarely taken amongst the desperation to survive.

Later, with sweat beading on their bodies they stay naked on the bed while working their way through tinned food brought giggling upstairs with a tin opener and cutlery.

While Reginald creates civilised society and Howie and Marcy edge closer with the fierce challenge of dominance so evident in their manner, so they lounge and make a mess on the bed and eat cold baked beans.

'Where would we live?' She asks just before spooning another mouthful.

'Wherever you want,' he says, 'we could get a big van and kit it out like my old one.'

'Oh yeah, I remember your van. It was really nice. What did you have in it?'

'Generator, batteries, weapons, books...well I had a kindle that I kept charged up...'

'Oh really,' she pulls a face, 'are you sad you lost it?'

'Find books anywhere,' he says.

'True,' she looks round for a bookshelf.

'In the hall,' Roy says, 'but it's all Mills and Boon.'

'Oh, no fifty shades then?'

'I didn't see one. We could put a big bed in there, maybe get a converted coach or something like that and just move from site to site.'

'Oh sounds bliss,' she sighs with the post coital warm sensation and her stomach slowly being re-fuelled, 'soft sheets,' she sighs again, 'you think we'd get bored?'

'We could visit places.'

'Like where?'

'Scotland, Wales...Cornwall...anywhere...'

'We could find an old castle somewhere!'

'We could,' he says between munches, 'bit cold and draughty though.'

'You could teach me how to shoot a bow.'

'You could teach me to be less annoying.'

'You're not annoying.'

'I am.'

THE UNDEAD DAY SEVENTEEN

'Yeah, you are but not to me. What if I got pregnant?'

He stops and stares with the spoon held in front of his mouth, 'are you?'

'Might be,' she says too casually, 'we didn't use protection and...'

'Oh of course, I suppose you can't get any now.'

'Birth control? We could get some but I hadn't taken it for ages. No point.'

'Oh. I see.'

'Yes.'

'So you could well be pregnant.'

'Who knows? Would that bother you?'

'Nope, not at all.'

'Really?'

'Really. We could raise a child.'

'Shit,' she stops eating for a second, 'when you say it like that.'

'I'd abandon you and run away.'

'Would you?'

'Yes. And not pay maintenance.'

'I'd come after you.'

'Okay,' he carries on eating, 'I'll stay with you then.'

'We don't know if I am pregnant. I'm just saying it's a possibility. I'm due on in a few days...I think,' she stops to think for a second, 'am I?'

'I don't know, are you?'

'Er...yes, yes I am,' she nods suddenly and carries on eating.

'They'd never let you leave if they thought you were pregnant,' he says after a few minutes.

'On the contrary, I think they would want me to leave...'

'Less danger?'

'Exactly.'

'Makes sense, could you imagine that lot with a baby?'

'It'd be the safest baby in the world.'

'Very true,' Roy nods in agreement and starts flicking the empty cans off the bed.

'What you doing?'

'Making room.'

'What for?'

'More sex.'

'We've just eaten. I can't jump around now.'

'Er, I can jump and you can…'

'Okay,' she says and starts clearing the bed, 'but I am full so don't go crazy.'

'I won't. Should we use a condom?'

'Do you have any?' She stops clearing the bed to look at him.

'No. You?'

'No.'

'Oh well,' he reaches out for her.

'Maybe we shouldn't then,' she says biting her bottom lip, 'if it worries you.'

'It doesn't worry me,' he says gently.

'Sure?'

'Very.'

Gently this time. Slow and gentle and the conversation brings a new sensuality to their touches and the longing looks they share.

She lies on her side with Roy behind. His left arm underneath her neck to cradle her head. His other hand on her hip that snakes round to stroke the soft skin on her stomach. Motion together. Back and forth. It builds slow but grows until the groans fill the room. In pitch and volume they rise as they lose themselves in the intimacy of togetherness and towards climax they journey.

So close together and their heads fill with the sound of the other. Minds numb to all else other than the now. Hands touching. Senses alive. She pushes back and in so doing they only hear each other and not the first noise from outside and as they reach climax so the noise of a hundred undead and more finally reaches them as the infected give voice in a howl that pierces the air.

CHAPTER FOURTEEN

From the eyes of the crawler left for days in the garden of the cottage the infection saw Dave coming to deliver death. But it saw past Dave and it saw Reginald in the kitchen with Clarence.

Reginald was with Marcy. Marcy was a host of great importance for she retained some of her own intelligence but could hold the hive mind as if it were her own.

Marcy left the hive mind. She was an intrinsic part but then she was no longer there and with her went Reginald.

Marcy is with Howie. Howie is in the village. Lani is dead. The infection understands psychology and knows Howie will be distracted with grief and loss. He will be mourning the passing of his own comrade and lover.

Marcy cannot be with Howie. That cannot be allowed. This must be stopped.

. . .

THE UNDEAD DAY SEVENTEEN

From the mind of the crawler the infection gains the knowledge of the village square and calculates the best form of attack is go for the middle at the same time as the rear of each section. Engulf them. Flank and out-manoeuvre. Swarm them with ranks that drain their energy and hold the strongest and fastest hosts back for the end.

Howie is strongest when they are together so the infection must divide the enemy forces.

Divide and conquer.

Make them weaker.

End this. End Marcy.

One race.

CHAPTER FIFTEEN

'Buttmunchingarsemonkeytwatmcgee,' Cookey says with a nod at Blowers, 'been working on that one all morning.'

'Nice,' Blowers says with a nod of admiration.

'What the fuck is going on?' Nick asks with a look back at Howie and Marcy arguing in the middle of the square, 'they're going for each other's throats.'

'Fuck,' Cookey spins with his rifle lifting to aim.

'Not literally you fucking twat,' Nick says, 'd'you think I'd stand here watching if they were actually doing that?'

'Dunno,' Cookey says, 'probably.'

'We get the flats then,' Blowers says with a look at the newsagents and then across to the recessed front door, 'that it?'

'Front door?' Asks Nick, 'must be.'

'Clearance,' Blowers says as they walk towards it, 'me in front, Cookey behind me then Nick and Mo Mo, you hold the door to give us a safe exit.'

'Roger roger rubber ducky,' Cookey says.

THE UNDEAD DAY SEVENTEEN

'I am so hungry,' Nick complains, 'you hungry?' He asks Mo Mo.

'Starvin',' Mo Mo says and watches the fluidity of movement from the other three young men as Blowers assumes a natural command. Not bossy. Not in charge like Mr Howie or Clarence or even Paula, but just that he knows what he is doing and the idea of *not* doing what he says just doesn't form.

The loss of Jagger hit Mo Mo hard. The two of them had been inseparable for years, closer than brothers. They'd done everything together and rejection from their family lives only pushed them closer to a wild, almost feral existence. They hung out, committed crime, ran from the police, got arrested, bailed and everything was funny, it was a game as they had each other.

Now he's gone. Shot down and killed just like that. A blink of an eye and he's dead. A part of Mo Mo died right there. Like a piece of his soul was torn away and the emptiness inside will never be filled but Mr Howie was right. This is a new world and there ain't no help coming and no one else to sort this out. They's got each other and that's it and as much as Mo Mo feels like dropping down to weep and die he won't as the thirst for revenge grows stronger than the desire to give in. He wants them. He wants to kill and slaughter them. He wants the skills Mr Howie and Dave have. He wants the speed the lads possess and the instinct of Clarence.

Mo Mo isn't thick. Not by a long stretch and his lack of formal education means nothing now. From the streets he came and scrabbled to live day in and day out. Finding food. Somewhere to stay. Avoiding the bad guys and the police. Running. Hiding. Fighting. Skills that he now thrives on and for Jagger he will get better until he can do to them what they have done to him.

So he listens and watches the way the lads move, the way they hold their weapons and scan, always watching, forever watchful, always looking up to the distance then back down to the close vicinity. Always mindful of what is left and right and where the points of attack might come from.

At the door they pause and Blowers gently eases the door handle down.

'Locked,' he says quietly.

'Window?' Nick asks, 'we can reach down.'

'Do it,' Blowers steps back as Nick steps in and using the butt of his rifle he smashes the glass pane above the door lock. Mo Mo holds position behind them, scanning the area and watching with interest as Howie passes something to Marcy who then drops down to kneel in front of him.

'In,' Nick says and pushes the door open, 'you first?' He looks to Blowers then down at his legs as Meredith chooses her team and pushes through the legs to get inside the door.

'Doesn't look like it,' Blowers says and steps in after the dog. A flight of stairs going up and with the rifle raised he goes carefully as the dog crests the top and disappears from view.

'Smell anything?' Cookey asks quietly from behind him.

'Nope, you?'

'Musty, like stale air,' Cookey says.

'Good sign,' Blowers replies as Meredith runs past the top of the stairs and disappears again. 'Doors...'

'How many?'

'Four, left, ahead and two on the right. Going left, you hold there.'

'On it,' Cookey moves up as Blowers heads to the internal door on the left. He goes through quickly.

'Clear,' he calls out, 'lounge.'

'Cool,' Cookey waits as Blowers comes back and gets through into the next room.

'Clear, bathroom....'

'Two cleared,' Cookey calls down to Nick who passes it on to Mo Mo outside.

'Bedroom, clear,' Blowers walks back and pushes the last door, 'dining room...leads to the kitchen and...fuck me!'

'What?' Cookey's body tenses as his finger instinctively lifts away from the trigger to prevent any risk of firing towards Blowers who reappears grinning from ear to ear.

'Nick, get Mo Mo and come up,' Blowers calls out, 'have a look,' he motions to Cookey.

'What?' Cookey asks with a big smile at seeing Blowers grinning so widely. The room is much bigger than he expected and stretches back with enough space to allow the six seat dining table and the large open plan kitchen at the far end.

'Fucking jackpot,' Cookey laughs with delight at the contents of the newsagents stacked up against the wall. Trays of tinned food. Cigarettes in long sealed packets. Drinks, cans, bottles, spirits, beers, wines, snack food, chocolate bars. The whole shop scavenged and brought up into the flat.

'What...Fuck!' Nick stops dead at the sight, 'nobody here then?'

'Nope,' Blowers says still staring at the hoard of food, 'seen this, Mo,' he says to Mo Mo walking in behind Nick.

'Nice,' Mo Mo says, 'that from the shop?'

'Looks like it,' Blowers says, 'maybe whoever lived here owned it?'

'No one here then?' Mo Mo asks.

'No, must have gone out,' Blowers says.

'And never come back,' Cookey adds.

'She thirsty?' Nick looks down at Meredith sniffing through the piles of goodies, 'when did she last drink?'

Not waiting for a reply he turns the cold tap on and swills the plastic washing bowl out before filling it up. She comes to his side, panting and wagging her tail.

'I'll go see what the rest want to do,' Blowers says moving towards the door.

'I'll go,' Mo Mo says.

'Nah,' Blowers replies, 'get stuck in,' he nods towards the food.

'I'm there,' Mo Mo beats him to the door, 'I'll see what they want to do right?'

'You sure?' Blowers asks, 'I don't mind going.'

'I'm younger,' Mo Mo says with a quick smile, 'fitter... you get me.'

'Cheeky twat,' Blowers laughs, 'go on then.'

He turns back to see the dog lapping greedily at the bowl and Nick taking a cigarette from his packet, 'want one?'

'Go on,' Cookey catches the pack before passing it to Blowers, 'he gone?'

'Yeah,' Blowers says checking the door behind him.

'He's quiet,' Cookey observes in a low voice.

'Hit him hard,' Nick says, 'they were good mates.'

'We'll keep an eye,' Blowers lights the cigarette and drifts over to the stacks of food.

'You think they'll be alright?' Cookey asks.

'Who?' Blowers asks in return.

'Your mum and the fucking postman, Mr Howie and Marcy you dumb fuck,' Cookey says.

'Yeah, they'll be alright.'

'They really going at each other,' Cookey says drawing on his smoke, 'd'you think Mr Howie really hates her?'

'Why? Do you?' Nick asks.

'Me? Nah, like...I think she's nice...like...I shouldn't like her but I do, and Reggie...'

'Same,' Nick leans against the kitchen side, 'you think she's still infected?'

'Fuck knows, Blowers?' Cookey asks.

'Asking me for?' Blowers says, 'how would I know?'

'I don't think Mr Howie really hates her,' Nick says after a silent pause.

'No?' Cookey asks, 'you think he likes her? Like *likes* her?'

'Yeah,' Nick snorts, 'don't you?'

'Dunno,' Cookey says, 'I miss Lani.'

'Fucking stop it,' Blowers shoots him a dark look, 'don't do that.'

'Sorry,' Cookey mutters, 'what's gonna happen now? I mean, what we gonna do?'

'Again,' Blowers says, 'what the fuck you asking me for?'

'Just asking you touchy cunt.'

'Fuck you.'

'Get bent.'

'You wish.'

'Wish what?'

'That I was bent.'

'You are bent.'

'You are.'

'Your mum is.'

'My mum is bent?'

'So bent.'

'Fuck me,' Nick groans.

'Blowers, Nick wants to be fucked.'

'Twat,' Blowers sighs.

'Did you see the way Mr Howie spoke to Lani last night,' Cookey finally gets to the thing on his mind, 'that was...I don't know but...'

'Weird,' Nick picks up the train of thought, 'he knew, straight away...fucking knew she was turned and he was right at it...at the infection I mean.'

'Yeah,' Cookey says, 'I've never met anyone like that before, have you?'

'Like who?' Nick asks, 'Lani?'

'Mr Howie.'

'No, not by a fucking mile. Or Dave, or Clarence either...'

'Blowers, did you meet people when you were in the army before?'

'Did I meet people?' Blowers asks, 'no I was on my own...they gave me an instruction book and a gun and said to train myself.'

'Funny cunt, I meant did you meet people like them?'

'I was in for a few weeks,' Blowers says, 'and no I didn't...I don't think even *they* met people like them before this.'

'We're doing something,' Cookey says seriously.

'Do what?' Blowers asks after a pause and bursting out laughing.

'Yeah we're in here,' Nick laughs.

'Fuck off,' Cookey groans, 'I meant we're doing something...like a real something.'

'What?' Blowers asks still laughing.

'Something special, like...it means something...you both know that right?'

'Yeah,' Nick's laugh dies down to a low chuckle, 'you're a twat for saying it like that but yeah.'

'Blowers!'

'In here,' the laughter is gone and three men grab weapons and make for the door as Mo Mo charges up the stairs, 'what?'

'They's all got loads too,' he stops for breath, 'and Mr Howie said to eat now and meet back in an hour.

'Fuck yes!' Cookey is gone, moving back to the food and ripping through the plastic coverings to pull tins and packets out, 'who is being mum? Shall I be mum? You'd like that you dirty fuckers,' he adds at the other two laughing.

'We going all in or being civilised?' Blowers asks picking up a tin of baked beans.

'FUCK!'

'What?' Blowers turns quickly to Nick standing over the gas hob.

'Gas is on,' Nick says, 'fucking gas is still on...actually on...look...' he steps aside to show the blue flames of the hob burning bright.

'Right you heathen motherfuckers,' Cookey says, 'we're doing this civilised...with plates and forks and shit.'

'We could just eat from the tins,' Nick says with a worried look at Cookey's air of determination. 'What you doing?'

'Gonna heat this up and have a meal,' Cookey announces, 'a hot meal and we'll sit at the table and say Grace and everything.'

'I don't say Grace,' Mo Mo says suddenly, 'I'm Muslim.'

'Shit, sorry Mo,' Cookey blurts, 'we can say what you do...say...or like...you cunt,' he laughs at the grin splitting Mo Mo's face. 'Thought I'd offended you then.'

'Do Muslim's say Grace?' Nick asks.

'They pray,' Mo Mo says, 'like before and after the food, like giving thanks to Allah...You're meant to do it before and after everything.'

'Really? Do you do it?'

'Me? No.'

'Why not?'

'Do you?'

'Do what?'

'Pray.'

'Pray? Fuck that, I don't pray.'

'I'm no different to you. I don't pray,' Mo Mo says.

Nick thinks while moving across to the table. Sitting down heavily he stretches his legs out, 'so like, your name is Mohammed then?'

'Yeah.'

'Were you parents Muslim?'

'No they called me Mohammed for fun.'

'Really?'

'Nick, you thick cunt,' Blowers laughs as he sits down at the table.

'Oh,' Nick looks at the grin on Mo's face, 'sorry.'

'Yeah they's Muslim but fucked up, like...' he trails off.

'What?' Nick presses.

'Nuffin' It ain't interesting.'

'Yeah it is, go on.'

'My grandparents were like fucking proper devout, you get me? Like full on...my mum and dad were raised strict but they's were here, in England so they'd didn't wanna be so strict but my mum had to be cos they'd hurt her but my dad didn't...and he was drinking and gamblin' and fightin' and getting nicked...and like, my mum was disowned cos she got with him.'

'Shit,' Blowers says, 'but they still called you Mohammed though.'

'My dad wanted to call me Mark,' Mo laughs, 'but my mum said I had to be Mohammed. Dad hated it, hated what people thought of it...hated the terrorist stuff and...'

'Did anyone give you shit for that?' Nick asks.

'What for people blowing shit up? No, not ever...not on the estate. It weren't like that...like *everyone* was from somewhere else...'

'Makes sense,' Nick says.

'Mo is what my dad called me cos he wouldn't say Mohammed.'

'So do you eat pork?' Nick asks.

'Like yeah I do but...like it feels wrong and...like on my own I won't eat it and...but like when I was with the crew and they were eating it then I'd eat it but...s'fucked up innit,' he says with a laugh.

'You don't have to eat it now,' Cookey says listening from the kitchen.

'Eat what I can now,' Mo says.

'Fact,' Nick says.

'You don't want the beans with pork sausages in them then?' Cookey asks, 'what about Macaroni?'

'Anything,' Mo finally sits down at the table, 'so what we doing now? Like after this I mean?'

'Dunno,' Blowers says, 'the boss'll get an idea and we'll do something...probably attack London or something fucking nuts.'

'London? What like proper?'

'He would,' Nick chuckles, 'and we would too,' he adds ruefully.

'He'd do it on his own,' Cookey calls out, 'with just the axe...like fucking charge head on and take them all out.'

'Dave'd be with him,' Nick says.

'And us,' Mo Mo says quickly.

'Fuck yes,' Nick laughs again, 'give Meredith some food, Cookey.'

'I'm busy, you do it.'

'I thought you were being Gordon Ramsay.'

'Yeah but not the fucking dog feederer too for fuck's sake…what do I give her?'

'No beans,' Blowers shouts, 'use that tuna…she loves tuna.'

'How many tins do I give her?'

'Fucking hell, Cookey…' Blowers huffs, 'shall I do it?'

'I don't know, shall you? Shall you like to get off your fat arse?'

'I don't have a fat arse, Paula and Marcy said so.'

'Marcy has a lovely arse,' Cookey says with a firm nod, 'and great…'

'Alex!' Nick says imitating Dave.

'Fuck off,' Cookey laughs, 'oh poor April.'

'Don't start that,' Blowers groans.

'What we need,' Cookey says between spooning the contents of a tin into a saucepan, 'is a load of women…like a netball or hockey team or something…all hiding and we find them and rescue them and they're like *oh boys you're all so handsome and strong* and we're like *it's okay ladies we're just doing our job* and they're like *oh how can we ever repay you* and we're like *we don't need payment* and they'd be like *oh but boys surely you must be rewarded for your bravery…but alas it is our moisturising time and we must moisturise but our hands are so soft and we need strong hands to do the moisturising* and we'd be like *oh we can help you with the moisturising* and they'd be like *oh boys come with us so you can moisturise our bodies* and we'd be like FUCK YES!' He pauses to watch the others laughing hard, 'and then Blowers would be like *but I don't moisturise ladies...do you have any men netball players I can moisturise* and they'd be like *only old Bert who drives our coach* and Blowers would be like *I shall moisturise Bert I shall for shalling and moisturising men is what I like to do* and the women would be like *oh but Nick is with Lilly and that only leaves two of you to moisturise so many of us beautiful ladies...* and then while you two,' Cookey points at Nick and Blowers, 'are playing with Bert me and Mo would be in a room with a load of naked hockey players and...and...yeah so fucking chew on that fact. You up for that Mo Mo?'

'Fuck yes!'

'Have fun with Bert, Blowers.'

'I will,' Blowers says wiping the tears from his eyes.

'Nick can film you seeing as he's married now.'

'I'm not married.'

'Good as. Can you mix macaroni with beans?'

'No,' Blowers says.

'Too late, done it.'

'What the fuck, what are you doing?'

'Putting it in together...in pans...cooking and shit.'

'Cookey, you can't just put everything in a pan and call it cooking.'

'Fuck you and yes I can...because, Simon, I have already done it.'

'Don't call me Simon, Alex. What have you put in so far?'

'Don't call me Alex, Simon er....everything?'

'What's everything?'

'Everything, Nicholas, is baked beans, some tins of tuna, er...pasta...macaroni cheese and ravioli, then I threw some pot noodles in but not the fruit…I can put the fruit in now if you want?'

'Pot noodles? You've put them in the pan?'

'Yes, Nicholas I have put them in the pan.'

'What dry?'

'No I spat on them first.'

'Cock.'

'Fuck you,' Nick says, 'Mo, can you cook?'

'Nah mate.'

'Oi, I'm cooking and doing a good job of it.'

'That isn't cooking, Cookey…that's…'

'Plates?…Actually I think bowls will be better…ooh I've got an idea how about we go French and have the big pan in the middle and everyone can dig in.'

'That's not French,' Nick says, 'that's fucked up.'

'WATCH OUT,' Cookey shouts while hefting the big steaming pan across the kitchen, 'hot stuff coming through…hot stuff…coming through…carrying a hot pan…gonna drop it…fuck it's too hot!'

'Such a cunt,' Blowers snaps as the pan slams onto the table.

'Bowls,' Cookey comes back carrying four big bowls and a huge ladle, 'right, don't be shy.'

The other three stare down into the pan, at the gooey mess steaming away.

'Is it safe?' Mo Mo asks quietly, 'we's gonna be poisoned.'

'Definitely,' Blowers says.

'Fact,' Nick adds, 'fuck it, food's food,' he ladles a generous portion into a bowl and sits down to take the first mouthful.

The other two stare, waiting, watching, expectant to see Nick keel over clutching his throat or vomit to the side. He doesn't. Instead he nods and takes another mouthful.

Blowers goes next, a small spoonful taken cautiously. Mo Mo follows suit with an equally small amount wobbling on his spoon.

'Twats,' Cookey tuts and helps himself, filling his bowl before sitting down and looking at his own serving. He starts to load his spoon and stops. Baked beans squashed with tuna and cheesy pasta with all manner of other things stuffed in there. Over to the kitchen he looks and the serving heaped into a bowl on the floor for Meredith who edges closer with neck stretched out to sniff the contents.

'S'nice,' Nick says.

'Is actually,' Blowers takes a bigger spoonful and shovels into his mouth. An explosion of taste and texture. Soft food that releases tangy juice. Warm and filling.

'S'good,' Mo Mo says between mouthfuls, 'really good.'

'No faith,' Cookey sighs and starts eating as Meredith finally licks the top of her mound then decides that it is edible and tucks in with big snapping bites.

In silence they eat, bowls emptied and re-filled. Meredith gets a second portion. Nick takes a third bowl and feels his stomach starting to expand. Holes are filled. The gnawing hunger abates. Blood sugar rises and the here and now suddenly isn't so bleak.

Mo Mo looks up at the lads. Young but so old and experienced. Blowers glances at Mo as the youngest member takes another mouthful. Cookey dreams of netball girls while Nick simply eats and the dog snuffles the floor around her bowl.

'Fuck,' Nick sighs heavily and pushes his bowl away, 'nice, Cookey...very nice. Mind if I smoke?'

'I'm still eating,' Cookey says.

'Oh well,' Nick lights up anyway and flicks a finger to the scornful look from Cookey.

'Done,' Cookey burps, 'chuck one over.'

'Blowers?' Nick asks.

'Go on then. You don't smoke then Mo?'

'Just weed.'

'Fair one,' Blowers lights his and inhales contentedly, 'bother you if we smoke?'

'Yeah, like...can you's stop.'

'Seriously?' Nick asks.

'Yeah,' Mo Mo grins slyly.

'Dick,' Nick smiles.

An air of content. A period of relaxation. To digest and talk quietly with mild jokes and mild rebukes. Time off from the relentless action of fighting, running, killing and trying to survive.

Meredith lies down and starts cleaning herself. Cookey sits back in his chair and sighs. Nick blinks heavily. Blowers scrapes his chair back to lift his legs to rest on the corner of the table. Mo Mo freezes. His face going from an expression of being satiated to one of intense concern.

'What?' Blowers drops his legs at catching the sight of the young lad.

'Fuck,' Mo Mo's nostrils flare.

'What?' Cookey sits up.

Meredith lifts her head and cocks it to one side. Ears up, eyes focused and slowly the hackles on her back rise as she lifts from the ground to stand square and solid.

Blowers flicks eyes wide to Meredith then to Nick and on to Cookey and Mo Mo. Slowly he reaches down to lift his assault rifle. Nick copies the motion. Cookey stands from the chair and moves the few feet to collect his and the air pierces with a hundred and more voices of the undead screaming a deathly howl into the air. Feet drumming on the ground and the place is alive with noise.

'STAND TO…'

'Dave,' Blowers whispers and even from this great distance the sound of his voice carries faint but clear.

Seconds it takes to check magazines, pull bolts back and make ready, seconds more to cross the floor to the door and out into the hallway and in that time the square is filled and already they pour through the still open door at the bottom of the stairs.

CHAPTER SIXTEEN

A four sided village square. Four rows of buildings of equal length and height. Three are rows of cottages. One is a row of shops with flats above. Behind them are countryside gardens divided by hedges. Long and narrow three of the rows back onto the open countryside that envelopes the village. The rear of the fourth backs onto the village and the clusters of houses and winding streets.

A half mile from the square they divided and move seamlessly to gain the correct angles of attack. The main force to be sent into the middle where they can push out to drive the team into the rear gardens. Other forces are sent to the rears, ready to meet them on the egress.

More are sent into the village and yet more are held back in the cover of the trees to wait and respond as the need arises.

. . .

THE UNDEAD DAY SEVENTEEN

A silent approach and the hard surface of the road was avoided to prevent the sound of so many running feet preceding the attack.

Not a cough or a wheeze was emitted. Not a stagger or trip. Not a voice given to sound other than that required to draw breath.

At the last second, and as they breach the corner and charge equally to all four sides so they draw in air and let rip with a spine tingling howl that rips through the peace and quiet, and the instruction is clear. Find her. Kill her. End Marcy.

Organised.

Ruthless.

One race.

CHAPTER SEVENTEEN

The water from the tap thunders into the bowl and the tension built between us diverts to all out shock at the piercing sound ripping through the air. Feet drumming. Many feet. Voices howling. Many voices. Multi-directional and before I can even turn to face the open front door I know they are vast in number and coming from every direction at once.

'STAND TO…'

Dave's voice, faint but clear. My heart ramps to beat with a thunderous rate. Blood pumps to surge past my ears and my focus sharpens as the expectation of the fight prepares my body.

Separated from each other but the Saxon is in the middle with the GPMG on top. If I can get to that…but Marcy…Marcy can't fight. I can fight. Fuck it, I'd charge out there now and take the lot on but Marcy has no experience. I race down the hallway to the open front door and see them streaming into the square sprinting flat out as they aim to cover all four sides. Hundreds of them and pumped up too.

THE UNDEAD DAY SEVENTEEN

Wild and filled with rage and already the route to the Saxon is blocked.

The wild noise of their howling ends abruptly and what comes next sends shivers down my spine and I turn slowly to see the creeping look of horror on Marcy's face.

Her name said by every undead at the same time.

'*MARCYYYYYYYYY…*'

I slam the door, grab Marcy and start pushing her down the hallway but they're already coming lithely over the garden fence to drop onto the lawn. So many of them and the rear is cut off. I pull Marcy to a stop and drag her back down the hallway and up the stairs as the front door crashes open. I throw my axe to the top of the stairs, twist and take aim as they come surging through the doorway. Fully automatic and I spray down with a hail of bullets and at such close range the effect should be devastating. They get blown back but they take those shots without a flicker of reaction and still they keep coming.

Scrabbling backwards up the stairs I yank the rifle off and chuck it up then reach for the axe. Marcy stands there wide eyed and seeing them from a whole new angle roots her to the spot in fear. They are coming for her. They want her. Every pair of eyes is not on me but staring at Marcy.

A hand grabs my left ankle as I grasp the axe and I'm pulled down with such force it lifts me from the stairs. I manage to get my right foot out and push hard to launch myself higher into the air and I sail backwards with teeth gritted and slam into them as they start coming up.

We land in a tangle of bodies and limbs from which I thrash to break free. One gets past me so I grab *his* ankle and yank him down. He lands face first on the step with a sickening crunch that snaps the bone in his nose.

Hands clawing me. Teeth digging into my shoulder as I

try to get up. I'm facing up the stairs, flat on my back and managing to block them from getting past but it can't hold. The axe still in my hand but no room to swing it so I jam the sharp double headed blades up and start swishing them side to side as hard as I can. The damage is low but it's enough to open their skin and remove a few fingers. One of the blades bites deep into a neck and forces the body off to the side against the wall creating enough space for me to lurch up and forward.

'Howie...' Marcy starts coming down the stairs to help.

'NO!' I scream and with a strangled yell I break up and free and get up two steps which is enough room to swing the axe back round and drive hard and deep into the pressed crowd. The first blow takes a head clean from the shoulders and it drops down to be lost amongst the bodies. The follow through takes the blade into a shoulder and renders one arm useless. Still screaming I slice the other direction and again the blade bites deep through them. They show no reaction so I slice left and slice right in desperation to keep the two steps I have gained.

More coming in through the door and I'm beaten backwards, going up one step at a time until some clever fucker decides to remove the bannister rail from the stairs so he can reach up from the sides. A pistol retort behind me and Marcy firing down. The first few shots miss but finally one strikes the head and blows the back of the skull off but the idea has been passed and more start gripping the spokes of the safety rail to snap and rip them free.

'UP,' I push into Marcy, driving her to the top of the stairs and they charge right behind us. I gain the top step and have a second spare to plant my feet and face down while they face up.

Then they hit. Two abreast with an unrelenting surge

that chokes them on the stairs for only the top two can get at us and they are chopped back down the stairs to fall and stagger into those behind. Their energy ramps and for the first time I see them using hands to wrench the ruined corpse aside. Actually grabbing and pulling them with such strength it sends a shiver of fear through me. They detect it and all eyes snap on me and with a screaming howl they charge harder.

A swing up deep into the groin of one and the cut opens an artery so it pisses blood out in a gush like a waterfall. The one behind her slips on the stairs so I kick out to send the cut one back down. A lunge and a small female dressed in torn and bloodied sports gear gets past me by ducking low. I lash out and grip her rancid greasy ponytail to rip her off her feet and back down the stairs she goes like a bowling ball scattering the pins of the undead.

I see him at the bottom. A big man. Not tall but wide with no neck and his shoulders are like an Olympic weightlifter. He dominates the space around him and waits patiently while those in front of him get cut down. As they fall he reaches out to grasp the bodies and fling them casually over the side of the stairs. He looks immense with slabs of muscle and thighs the like of which I have never seen before. His arms are as thick as Clarence's but without the height it makes him look ridiculously strong and squat. His head doesn't loll but remains fixed and staring. His red bloodshot eyes are fixed on Marcy then he flicks to stare at me. I grasp the axe handle tighter and adjust my stance.

'Shoot him,' I say quietly and watch with horror as he smiles. His lips stretch out to form a smile. Wicked and macabre and his skin is mottled with death but the rate of decay looks less on him than the others.

Rising panic in my voice, 'Marcy...shoot him...'

She fires and the first bullet goes past him and into one behind that is killed outright. She fires again and again she misses. He doesn't charge but waits patiently and that awful smile grows wider. I hear her take a steadying breath and aim before the next shot takes him dead centre in the chest and he doesn't flinch, doesn't move and doesn't even look down at the dribble of blood.

'His head,' I force calmness into my voice then hear the dry click of the gun as it clicks empty.

Stand-off.

Face off.

I could go for my pistol but I know that movement will prompt him to charge. Same with the assault rifle but the magazine is empty and I won't have enough time to change it.

He moves up onto the next step that creaks under his weight. Those behind him wait silent and watchful. I swallow and lower my weight and my movement makes him freeze. We lock eyes. Mine dark and brooding. His red and full of the hive mind of the infection and projecting a confidence that unnerves me. That fear makes the blood in my veins run cold and it hits me that we could die here. The undead are different. They've been ramped up before but not like this. They seem more cohesive and determined. Then it hits me what the difference is. They're more human now. The way they stand and move. The way they don't loll heads or drool but remain focussed and watchful.

Oh well. Fuck it. We've had a good run and even if I get ripped limb from limb they'll still have to face Dave, Clarence and Meredith and with an audible exhalation of breath so the fear goes and I'm left with a sensation of utter calm radiating out from my core. I smile down at him and lower the axe like a benevolent God taking in his mortal subjects.

'All of you,' I say and I was going to finish off with something cool but he's charging with a speed that defies his size and I just have time to lift and swing. He snatches a hand out and catches the shaft. It gets twisted over like a bar between us that I grip two handed. His hands planted on the shaft next to mine and he takes me off my feet and back through the bathroom door and it's like being hit by a truck. He slams me into the toilet and my head smashes through the vanity cupboard above the cistern. Glass breaks and the flimsy wooden thing splinters from the hard impact of my skull. He lifts me up bodily by the axe shaft then slams me down so I strike the cistern and that too gets ripped from the wall then down harder onto the ceramic toilet bowl. Water sprays from a ruptured pipe and the speed is so fast I don't think to let go of the shaft that he still grips.

I'm wrenched up off my feet and he twists his upper body round to slam me through the glass pane of the shower cubicle. Water gushing out onto the floor. I'm screaming but still too stupid to let go of the shaft. With the glass side of the shower cubicle smashed he pushes me into the corner and I slide down as he pushes me to into the tray. I get my feet up and start slamming them into his legs and knees but it's like kicking a tree and that smile still adorns his face as he decides being down is boring and up we go. The top of my head hits the bottom of the electrical shower box with a loud thud that sends a searing pain down through my neck.

Then he rags me. Like Meredith when she grips a neck and wrenches her head side to side so he does it now but using his body weight and strength. I bounce into the tiled walls left to right in a speed that gets faster and harder. The wind is driven from my lungs. My head spinning with a pain that makes me feel sick and dizzy. Marcy's face appears beside his. On his broad back and she slams her fists into his ears with a look of terrified fury on her face.

The thought permeates my head that if the rest come up then we're done. Finished. But I'll be buggered if this sod is getting away with it. I drop my right hand to my hip and scrabble to tug my knife out from the scabbard which isn't easy when you're getting slammed side to side by a huge weightlifter with a screaming woman on his back pounding on his ears. I want to tell her to go for his eyes but for some reason I can't summon the air to talk and I put that down to him bench pressing me into the walls with the axe shaft.

As I go right so my hand is trapped between my side and the wall and I have to wait to go left before trying to tug the knife free. Not enough time so I wait to go right again and give it a desperate tug when we go the other way. It comes free but before I can draw my arm up we're going back to the right and I'm slammed into the hard tiles again. Marcy looks furious and stops pummelling his ears to rake his skin open with her nails and livid welts that seep with blood are soon gauged across his face and head.

To the left and I manage to point the knife out and jab it into his leg. He doesn't flinch so I aim higher and stab him in the stomach. Still he doesn't stop and on the next switch of direction I lunge up and get the point to drive deep into his chest but it only seems to aggravate him so he drops the axe and grips those meaty hands round my throat. Instantly the air and blood flow is cut off and the booming rush of panic fills my mind as crimson dots appear in my vision.

I get the knife up under his chin and stab up. Blood pumps from his mouth but still he squeezes and rags me while screaming with demented rage that sends the blood flying from his mouth. The point of the knife is driven further into his neck under his chin and I stab again and again until I get through the thick skin and sinew to cut into the artery. The blood sprays thick and fast and coats Marcy as she sinks back from the incredible noise and mess.

He slumps forward. An immense weight that crushes me down into the shower tray and with much heaving we get him free and I slide out. A thunderous pounding as the rest come charging up the stairs and I just about get my foot to slam the door closed and wedge my feet against it with my shoulders pressing into the base of the toilet bowl.

Panting hard I glance up to see Marcy drenched in blood and bits of gore. She looks wild and in that second I notice the red bloodshot look of her eyes are nowhere near as bad as they were.

'Your eyes...' I say stupidly.

'Oh God,' she sinks down at my side and gets sprayed full in the face by the broken water pipe. She coughs and splutters then sinks back as I burst out laughing. The sight of her looking so worried and so serious only to get blasted by the water. The hysteria of being choked and almost dying at the hands of a single undead in the bathroom of a cottage. Panic and fear mingle with the comedy of it all and I can't stifle the laughs as she coughs, wipes her eyes and shoots me a filthy look.

'Get your feet on the door...'

She turns, nods and dives down to get tight into my side as her legs stretch out and her feet wedge against the inside of the door. Four legs pinned straight. Knee joints locked and thank fuck the door is an old solid wood thing instead of a modern cheap ply door. They get the other side but the pressure they can exert is not enough to force the door open.

'You okay?' She grunts.

'Yep, you?'

'Broke a nail,' she holds her hand up to show me the snapped nail of her index finger, 'bastard.'

'Me?'

'No him.'

'Go for the eyes next time.'

She looks at me for a long second then nods, 'didn't think of it.'

'No worries,' I tense harder as the pressure of the door increases.

'Are you hurt?' She asks.

'Nah...yeah...fucking hurts like a bitch...'

'Don't make me laugh,' she snorts through her nose.

'I don't think they like you,' I turn my head to look at her, 'fucking hell, Marcy!' I groan and turn away.

'What?' She demands.

'Your top.'

'What about my top? Oh...oh yeah...'

'Oh yeah she says...'

'Well, that's what happens when water sprays on a t shirt.'

'Yeah but...you can see everything.'

I turn back to see her staring down at her own chest and the perfect outline of her breasts showing through the soaking material, 'they look really good,' she says quietly, 'I love my boobs.'

'Uh huh.'

'Don't you think they look good?'

'Er...'

'No but seriously, look...Howie...look....'

'I'm not looking.'

'Why not?'

'Cos it's not exactly appropriate is it?'

'They're gonna get through and rip us apart in a second,' she says as though talking about the weather.

'So?'

'So treat yourself and give a girl a compliment.'

'Seriously? You want the last thing I ever see to be your tits?'

'I was....'

I turn and look. She's right. They do look amazing, 'they look amazing,' I say with a sigh.

'Thanks,' she says brightly with a big grin.

'No worries,' my eyes stay fixed on the off white top.

'You're still looking,' she points out.

'Aye, they haven't come through yet.'

'Yeah, bit weird now.'

'Really? Want me to stop?'

'Can you stop ogling me please?'

'You asked me to.'

'I'm not just a piece of meat you know.'

I look up into her eyes, 'they'll come.'

'Where are they?' She asks in a whisper.

'They'll come...'

She stares at me for a long second as the door rattles and thumps against our feet, 'they would have got here by now,' she says softly, gently, almost apologetically, 'but we can hold on,' she adds quickly at seeing the look of loss and worry form on my face, 'Howie...I was wrong, they'll come.'

'Yeah,' suddenly I don't feel so confident. They would have been here by now and I can't help the growing sensation that something has gone wrong.

'We can hold,' she says again, more quickly this time.

'Not for long...my legs are shaking.'

'You just took a beating, relax and let me hold them.'

'Marcy...'

'I've got strong legs, rest and let me do it,' she says with an arrogance that sets me off.

'Oh wonderful boobs and strong legs yeah?'

'What? I do have great boobs and I do have strong legs.'

'You are so vain.'

'I am not.'

'So vain...I bet you were bloody horrible before this.'

'I beg your pardon? What does that mean?'

'You know exactly what I mean.'

'No. Explain.'

'Vain.'

'Horrible before this? In what way?'

'You're so beautiful. Like...perfect...'

'I bloody am not perfect,' she scoffs but casts me a sideways look while saying it.

'You so are and you know it. Your body is like...just incredible and you look like a fucking super model or something and...your hair...it's like just fucking amazing...I bet you were a right bitch.'

'Howie! Stop it. I was not a bitch.'

'So vain.'

'Stop saying that.'

'Were you?'

'Vain? No I was not vain.'

'Seriously, were you though?'

'No!'

'But be honest...were you vain?'

'No...not vain...vain isn't the right word.'

'Yes it is. You were vain.'

'I was not vain.'

'Conceited then.'

'No,' she whines but looks away when she says it, 'I wasn't conceited and like...full of myself but...'

'Ha! Knew it. You were so vain.'

'Yes alright I was vain. Happy now?'

'Blissfully.'

'Thanks,' she says scornfully, 'but I wasn't a bitch.'

'How can you be vain and not be a bitch?'

'Like I wasn't a bitch to girls that weren't as pre...'

'Not as pretty?'

'I didn't mean it like that.'

'Not as pretty?'

'Stop saying it like that...'

'You said it. You said other girls that weren't as pretty. Give me your pistol,' I grunt.

'Here, I didn't mean it like to say girls weren't *as* pretty as me but...just that I wasn't a bitch if a girl *wasn't* as pretty as me.'

'So vain,' I eject the magazine from her pistol and pull a fresh one from my pocket.

'You are horrible. You know that?'

'Vain.'

'Horrible.'

'Here, safety is off.'

'Thanks.'

'Try aiming better next time.'

'Oh sorry I haven't had as much practise as you.'

'No worries, you preferred your teeth when you were murdering.'

'Howie!'

'What? You did.'

'Pack it in.'

'Vain.'

'What is your problem with me?'

'My problem? Seriously, Marcy? You killed like...'

'Yes I know full well what I did but that isn't it.'

'Isn't it? Yes it bloody is. It so is,' she stares at me so knowingly I have to get angrier to enforce the point, 'it is,' I exclaim, 'really is.'

'Okay,' she looks away with a roll of her eyes.

'It is,' I say again.

'You were eating spam off my bloody finger five minutes ago,' she snaps, 'now you're back to being a dick.'

'What?' I say incredulously.

'I said,' she says through gritted teeth, 'that you were eating spam from my finger five minutes ago...remember that? Sucking my finger?'

'Was hungry.'

'Yeah right.'

'I don't fancy you.'

'Who said you fancied me?'

'You did.'

'I didn't.'

'You did.'

'You mentioned it. I never said it.'

'I don't fancy you...I don't!'

'Okay, you haven't got to keep saying it.'

'Good. As long as we are clear.'

'Clear as day.'

'Good.'

'You don't fancy me.'

'No.'

'So why do you keep glancing down then?'

'Oh fuck off, Marcy. They're bouncing about and...'

'And what?'

'Stop laughing at me.'

'I'm not laughing at you. I'm just laughing.'

'They're bloody massive and bouncing about and soaking wet...I can't *not* look.'

'But you don't fancy me.'
'No!'
'Just my boobs.'
'Yes! No...fuck off.'
'It's okay, Howie. You can look if you want.'
'Piss off. I won't look again.'
'You would have kissed me if they hadn't come.'
'WHAT?'
'You so would,' she shoots me an accusing look, 'you were going to kiss me.'
'I was not. You were going to kiss me.'
'Oh no, no no no...'
'You were puckering up.'
'Puckering up?'
'Puckering up. Like...like you did before.'
'When you dry humped my leg?'
'Oh for the love of...please...please...I did not dry hump your fucking leg.'
'Stop swearing at me!'
'I am not fucking swearing *at* you. I am fucking swearing generally and because some massive fucking bloke just beat the shit out of me and now I'm trapped in a fucking bathroom with a vain cow and her massive boobs who is accusing me of dry humping her leg and saying I was about to kiss her after she jammed her finger in my mouth...'
'Howie...'
'So swearing is being done to alleviate the pressure of the situation and not being done to offend you but fuck me if it isn't the end of the world and I think you should be able to cope with someone fucking swearing and..'
'Howie, stop ranting.'
'But fucking...' I was going to keep ranting but the look

she gives me reminds me of Dave when he says I was ranting. 'Sorry,' I apologise with a huff.

'Don't be.'

'Dave says I rant sometimes.'

'Does he?'

'Yeah and sometimes, like…and this is going to sound really stupid but…'

'But what?'

'Nothing.'

'No what?'

'It'll sound stupid.'

'We'll be dead in a minute.'

'Fair one. Sometimes I think Dave can hear my thoughts.'

She stares at me for long seconds then blinks just once, 'yeah,' she says, 'that does sound stupid.'

'Thanks for the support.'

'Hear your thoughts?'

'Marcy, you had a fucking hive mind with a shit ton of zombies.'

'I did but Dave? Really, Howie?'

'Sometimes,' I try and shrug but being wedged against the toilet prevents the full effect of the motion. We're getting drenched from the burst pipe and my legs are burning with pain.

'I know I'm thinking shit and he hears it. Like, he comments on what I was thinking when I didn't say it loud but…'

'Maybe you did say it loud.'

'No…the first…maybe the first few times but then I know I was thinking other times and he…'

'You must have been talking out loud,' she decides.

'I hadn't finished saying what I was going to say,' I say pointedly.

'Go on then,' she says after a pause when I don't continue.

'I did finish but you still cut me off.'

'My god you are so touchy.'

'I am not touchy.'

'I never thought you were like this, really I didn't.'

'Like what?'

'Touchy and abusive.'

'Abusive? I am not abusive.'

'You've been abusing me all day.'

'Yeah but don't say it like that. I am not an abuser.'

'I never said you were an abuser...'

'Saying I am abusive is saying I am an abuser.'

'Okay, wrong word. You're not an abuser. Sorry, I didn't mean that way.'

'Honestly, I'm not an abuser...I'd never be like that...' My voice trails off as a fresh burst of pain shoots through my legs, up my spine and into my neck.

She looks at me with worry then suddenly grits her teeth as though in pain too.

'What? You okay?' I ask quickly.

'Yeah just...bit of cramp.'

'Where?'

'Left leg.'

'Thigh or calf?'

'Thigh.'

'Can I do anything?' I reach down and get my hands onto the solid muscle of her upper left leg and start rubbing it, 'any good?'

'Yeah...' she winces again, 'harder...'

'Here?' I drive the points of my thumbs into the muscles

and rub back and forth as the clamouring from outside only gets louder and the pressure increases by the minute.

'That's good,' she groans in pleasure, 'you've got strong hands.'

'Does it still hurt?'

'If I say no will you stop rubbing?'

'Er...'

'No then...really hurts so keep rubbing.'

My legs tremble and shake and the pain brings tears to my eyes.

'Hey,' she says imploring me to look, 'don't bloody stop... it's cramping again.'

'Sorry.'

'Ah that's better...bit higher.'

'Here?'

'Yeah, bit higher...that's it...keep going up.'

'Where?' I wince and grit my teeth but focus on rubbing the front of her thigh that feels so warm beneath my hands.

'In a bit...'

'In?' I ask and try to work my hands towards her inner thigh.

'And up...go up,' she urges, 'up a bit more.'

I work the muscle round to the inside leg and then start up. I can't move to look down so can only feel where I'm going.

'Bit more, really hurts,' she winces.

My knuckles graze the crutch of her jeans.

'Yep, just a bit more up,' she says.

'Marcy!'

'What? It's so nice...' She says with a sudden evil grin and mocking eyes, 'go on,' she whispers, 'just go up a bit more.'

'I am not rubbing your...'

'My what?' She asks innocently.

'Your...lady parts.'

'My darling,' she mock purrs, 'you already are...hey, Howie...Hey, look at me...come on, look at me, Howie.'

'What?' I growl through the pain and forcibly work to lock my shaking legs in place. The pain is incredible. My head spins and I glare to rid the dizziness sweeping through me. My hands lock on her thigh, squeezing hard as though to force the energy back into my weakening body.

'I can't hold them,' I say through a desperate exhalation of air, 'I can't hold...'

'They will come,' she says, 'Howie, look at me...they will come.'

'Marcy,' I swallow and look back into her eyes.

'I am sorry,' she cuts me off, 'I am so sorry...'

'What...'

'No, listen,' she says urgently, 'I deserve everything you said and...I shouldn't have said anything back at you.'

'Marcy, stop...'

'Howie, listen! I did all the things you said I did and...' tears break from her eyes to roll fat down her cheeks, 'I can't take it back,' she sobs, 'I can't ever make it not have happened...'

'Marcy...'

'Please, just listen. I want you to go.'

'What?'

'The window, go out the window...I can hold them for a few seconds and buy you time to get away.'

'No way.'

'Howie, you have to finish this,' she says emphatically.

'No fucking way,' my teeth show from the exertion of keeping my legs locked against the almighty pressure coming against the door.

'You know what I did. Everything you said...I did it...I shouldn't have argued back but...'

'Stop...please stop...'

Her mouth copies mine with a humourless grin and the veins in her neck start to bulge as she takes a greater strain to hold the door closed as my own body weakens by the second. Her face just inches from mine and she weeps silently.

'I wanted to fix it....with you,' she pants and draws breath, 'I am so sorry...'

'Please, stop, Marcy,' tears prickle at my eyes at the pain in my legs and the sadness of it all. That her heart is breaking in front of me is beyond doubt and remorse isn't the word to describe the hurt in her eyes.

'But please know...it wasn't me...' she grimaces and for a second I think she'll give up there and then but she rallies and forces her legs to remain locked, 'not me...not me...I would never do that...'

'Marcy...'

'Tell me you believe me,' she demands with fresh tears falling down her cheeks, 'I need to hear it, please...I don't deserve it but...please...'

'I believe you.'

'Oh don't cry, Howie...you can live...go...get out and...'

'No,' the pain is too much, the sheer burning of lactic acid and only pure stubbornness holds me in place, 'won't do it...we're team...we stay together.'

'Team?'

'Team...' I cry out from the agony and glare unflinching into her eyes, 'we stay together...oh god it hurts.'

'Go,' she begs, 'please go...get out and finish this.'

'NO,' I roar into the air, 'we are team...the team stay together...' I choke off with a sob.

THE UNDEAD DAY SEVENTEEN

'Don't cry,' a gentle hand reaches out to stroke my cheek so tenderly. My own rises to cover hers, 'go,' she begs again, 'Howie...get out...I can hold them...don't cry my Howie...'

'You don't cry then,' I reach out to wipe the tears from her face as we get shoved another centimetre into the base of the toilet.

'I am so sorry,' her sob breaks my heart, 'I can't...I can't take it back...'

'I shouldn't have said those things to you,' I say softly.

'You should...I did...I can't ever make it not happen and I remember it...I remember what I did, Howie...'

'Marcy, stop...we'll...' I cup her face and tilt it to look at me and my thumb traces a swirl as it brushes across her cheek.

'Argh,' she grunts and we both hold tight, clinging to each other as the door gives another tiny distance and crimson dots form behind my eyes at the pain radiating from every inch of my form. Her hand reaches round my neck to grip hard. Mine remains gentle upon her face, 'go,' she whispers with her eyes squeezed closed from the pain, 'they need you...*not me*...go...finish this and...'

'No...fucking...way...'

'Just go.'

'No...I won't...' I grimace and draw breath and pain of the like I have never felt seems to pulse through every bone in my body, 'won't leave you,' the words rush out and the finality is clear in my tone.

Her eyes snap open, fixed on mine. I nod to show the intent of my words and her hand grips my neck harder still as though using me to cling on to.

'I didn't...' I hiss and stare at her, 'I didn't...dry hump...you...'

She smiles and the pain in her eyes only grows deeper,

the sadness of existence and living only to die and be taken and turned to come back as something she had no control over and now to die again.

My hand moves from her cheek to the back of her neck and I apply pressure to drive us closer. The risk of an inch of movement and it makes us both cry out with the pain but our foreheads touch and that pain was worth it. I can feel the heat from her body as the water pours into the room. Her hand moves us between us, the hand holding the pistol. She looks up to make me know it's there.

'I'm not coming back again,' she whispers the words and I nod as she pushes the point under her own chin and again we give a tiny increment and the howls from the other side tell us they know they are slowly gaining. 'Kill me when they come...'

'I will,' I promise the whisper gently.

I close my eyes. She closes hers. I pull her closer and she comes. Cheek to cheek and the water pours over us as the undead pummel the door that gives a fraction at a time and each jolt sends searing pain through our bodies and fresh tears that mingle as one.

CHAPTER EIGHTEEN

Hundreds of them and still they stream into the square from all four corners and the swirling motion they performed atop the car park a few days ago is being repeated only faster and harder than before. From the right the dense ranks come flowing with near perfect precision into dense ranks coming from the left and the contraflow is only doubled by the ranks from the other corners. Two, three, four and five abreast and the circles within circles rotate and spin like a plethora of spinning tops that swirl dizzyingly across the open ground.

Sounds of attack and defence coming from the other sides and the violence offered is far beyond anything they have seen before. A wild energy unleashed with feral abandon yet orchestrated and fluid to the point of perfection. Units within units. Teams within teams. No single infected working alone but everything done together.

A split second on gaining the front door and yelling the warning and Dave takes it in as the closest rank break free to charge full on towards him with an incredible speed.

Clarence right behind him. A look of awe on his face at the changes seen and the ferocity being shown.

'Too many...DAVE TOO MANY,' he shouts the warning and reaches out to yank Dave back in the house. He slams the door and braces it with his shoulder as the almighty impact from the other side sends him reeling back down the corridor. They pour through, snarling with utter hatred as Dave draws knives and whirls into the space in front of Clarence. He cuts and spins to slice throats and stab into groins. Arteries opened that gush blood high up the walls or out onto the wooden floor of the hallway.

They compress from behind with a solid mass of human form that pushes on with ever increasing force to get inside.

Clarence gets to his feet and runs back into the kitchen and past a terrified Reginald to wrench the back door open. Infected dropping from the fences onto the lawn. He spins round, grabs the assault rifle, aims and fires into the charging bodies. Burst spray aimed at each with the intent to drop them down and buy time. They weave and buck but each gets struck with the bullets that rip them from their feet to spin them round. The soldier counts the rounds in his head knowing when the magazine will be hitting empty. He spins again, dropping the first rifle to snatch Dave's up, turns, kneels and continues the firing. Aiming for head shots this time at the ones cut down from the first hail of bullets. Most are killed outright with skulls blown away.

'CLEAR,' he shouts and plucks the magazine from the rifle to slam a new one home, 'DAVE,' he roars without turning, 'BACK IS CLEAR...'

'TOO MANY,' Dave's words make him turn with a speed that defies his great size and the sight makes his heart lurch in his chest. Dave fighting at speed with arms that blur and bodies that stack on the floor but still they charge and push even Dave back with a sheer crazed lunacy. Dave cannot retreat without them charging instantly. A few more seconds like this and they'll be pouring into the back garden again.

Eyes wide, mouth open and he thinks of a way to slow them down enough to get Dave away and safely out the rear.

He grabs the first rifle and changes the magazine while constantly checking the rear garden.

'Hold these,' thrusting the weapons into Reginald's trembling hands he grabs the gas stove and rips it free from the fittings with a grunt, 'DUCK,' he shouts and launches the heavy oven as Dave drops instantly to the ground. The solid metal appliance ploughs through the double fronted rank ripping them from their feet.

'OUT,' he barks and snatches the rifles back. Two rifles. Thirty rounds to a magazine. Sixty rounds. Fully automatic and he lets rip with both and lets the power of the weapons rip them apart. At such close range the bullets rip through the first body, into the second and out into the third behind. As the first ones are blown back so the bullets can hit the ones behind until the hallway is filled with the bodies being slaughtered.

'Cut the gas pipe,' he orders Dave, 'Reggie, out the back...now....NOW,' he roars when the little man doesn't respond. Reginald yelps and scampers away as Dave grabs the thick rubber pipe above the safety shut off valve and cuts it clean through. Gas hisses into the room as the weapons click empty. Out into the back garden they go with Clarence slinging one rifle while changing the magazine in the other.

'Ready?' Dave draws his pistol and glances at Clarence.

'Do it,' Clarence hands the loaded rifle to Reginald and

starts reloading the second one. The pistol fires. A single shot that strikes the metallic valve cut from the rubber pipe. The single spark ignites the gas filled air which bursts with a dull roar and fills the kitchen with a burning blue flame.

'Dave, on point...Reggie stay between Dave and me...GO.'

Dave heads off with his pistol held one handed. He twitches and fires into the head of a female vaulting the fence. The skull implodes as the body slumps down into the flower bed. To the end of the garden they race and only pause for Clarence to beat the fence down and open a path out into the open countryside. Dave falters, hesitating with conflict at going the opposite direction to Mr Howie.

Clarence spots the worry and turns round with the same thought in mind as the first flaming bodies burst through the open back door to charge alight down the garden. One after the other they pour out. Hair ablaze. Those with clothing are on fire. Those naked are burnt but still they come.

'We can lead them away from the others,' Clarence says urgently, 'move out.'

The order given and for a second, Clarence thinks Dave will refuse and go back but the small man turns, nods and starts moving.

They run out, directly out. In a straight line intending to draw as many with them as possible. Dave in the front keeping pace. Clarence in the rear with his full stomach churning from the recent food and the sweat already beading on his head. Reginald in the middle whimpering with yelps as he fixes his eyes on Dave's back and runs too terrified to look at anything else.

CHAPTER NINETEEN

'Was that you?'

'No,' she freezes mid-motion and feels his hand tighten the grip on her thigh. Behind her he lies, spooning as they build to climax, 'Roy...'

The howls fill the air and the thunderous voice soon rip through the square as the feet march in a rampage toward the open doors of the houses.

They clinch with an instinctive desire to be closer at the point of peril. This cannot happen now. Naked upon the bed with food in their bellies and the promise of a peaceful day ahead.

Roy moves first, rolling back and dropping off the edge of the bed to his feet and over to the net curtain covered window. Paula watches him. The contours of his wide shoulders tapering down to the natural v of his waist and in that second she gains the true measure of the man. A man so tormented by his own irrational fears that he shunned mainstream life and gave in to the conditions that controlled him. He is naked but shows not a flicker of fear as he turns and gently says, 'they're here,' his tone even, his face a mask of utter competence.

Her stomach flips and her heart lurches to miss several beats as it ramps from sexually charged to terrified in an instant. She scrabbles over the bed dislodging empty tins of food and dodging the plates and cutlery left scattered on the carpet.

At the window she joins him. Shoulder to shoulder as they watch the undead swarm from all four corners in a dazzling display of pure coordination. Lines of men, women and children that swirl with flow and contraflow. The ranks double and triple and staring at them from above becomes sickening. Something awful and beyond the capability of man. A display that would take communist armies months to prepare and drill so they could display their power to the world. Here it is done without warning, without planning and executed instantly and without mistake.

They watch mesmerised as the first ranks peel off to charge towards the block containing Howie and Marcy. As they spin and trace the nausea giving motion so another rank separates and another and another. An all-out attack driven towards Dave and Clarence. More towards the block containing the lads and yet more coming towards them.

'GO,' Roy bursts to life and runs naked from the room into the hallway knowing he won't have the time to get down and lock the door before they reach the threshold. A plan already in mind and he shoves a foot on the end bannister post and heaves himself up to thump the wooden hatch to the loft away.

'Paula...up here...'

'Yep,' she grunts and thrusts the assault rifles at him to throw up, 'clothes,'

'NOW PAULA,' he hears the thumping feet pounding

closer across the ground outside. He jumps down and takes the bundle of clothing from her hands as she runs still naked from the bedroom, 'up…go…' he urges her onto the bannister post and grabs an ankle to roughly push her up into the hole. Looking up and instinctively he averts his eyes from the nakedness on display as she heaves and wriggles herself up and into the loft.

At the door now. Voices snarling and feet reach the stairs as Roy vaults onto the post and jumps straight up through the hole. His hands grip the edge, his legs dangle for a second as the effect of gravity takes over from the jump up and with a yelp he gets in and rolls away as Paula plops the hatch cover back down.

'Did they see you?' She whispers into the perfect pitch black of the loft.

He shakes his head then realises she can't see him, 'don't know,' he whispers in reply, 'did you get my shoes?'

'No…I don't know what I got…hang on…I got a shoe…I think it's mine.'

'Oh, are mine still down there?'

'Where do you think they are?'

'Okay,' he says with a nod, 'I'm nodding,' he adds.

'Ssshhh.'

The sounds beneath them make it clear the undead have gained the upper floor and with the loft covering the width and depth of the house working out directional sound is near on impossible.

Hearts hammering. Tension mounts. Breathing low and shallow. Blood thundering in their eyes. The sounds of attack from somewhere else. Gunshots from an assault rifle. She wants to shift position as the joists under her naked body are hard and digging in. She wants to clear her throat and get dressed and check the weapon is ready for firing.

Just one day. That's all they wanted. Just one day away from the constant danger of dying, from running and fighting and hiding. From being too hot, too hungry, too thirsty and so bone weary tired it makes you want to cry. They were naked and talking about babies just a few minutes ago. Normal stuff that normal people do. Not hiding naked in lofts waiting to find out if the undead have locked onto the pheromone trail and are now staring hungrily up at the wooden hatch.

With a start she realises they have no hand weapons. Roy's sword and bow are in the Saxon. She has her knife but that is a last resort thing. Two rifles and a couple of spare magazines and there were so many of them. So many. How did they find them here? Why are they swirling like that again? Thoughts race through her sharp mind as she works the problem to gain a solution.

In a loft of a terraced house. That means one end will be the outside wall and the other will be a fire wall to the next house. She thinks back to running through lofts before and finding the weird man hiding out with his stash of batteries. The sudden memories flood her mind. Of the time she spent alone in her home town culling them group by group until the last one fell. The traps she set. The tests and learning and she did it alone with brains over brawn. Now it's about direct combat and fighting in a group and constantly being protected by Roy and the others. She loves them for doing it but being protected is not the Paula that walked away from the rapist bastard Clarke in her office on the first night.

Brains over brawn and there is more than one way to skin a cat or slaughter a big horde of infected.

Moving gently she feels through the clothes and starts dressing. Pushing her legs into the jeans and fastening her bra before tugging her top down over her head. Decisive movements that settle her heart rate and bring focus back to the game.

She gropes the air and feels for Roy. Sinking down over his body she holds her mouth close to his ear, 'keep them busy here.'

'Why?'

'I have a cunning plan,' she kisses his cheek and moves away before he can say anything else. She doesn't have to wait to be rescued or rely on Roy to protect her. She can take the fight to them.

Feeling the joists she works along to the water tank and round to where the firewall should be. Step after step and her hands grope the air in front of her face. Nothing. She heads further and keeps going until she knows she is past the point where the firewall would be. No firewall then, old cottages built a long time ago and they must have been kept in the family to have avoided modern fire regulations.

Too dark though and not a hope in hell of finding the next hatch. She needs light. There might be electric lights fitted but the power is off. No matches, no lighter and no torch. Everything is in the Saxon.

Seven P's, she winces the rebuke silently at herself vowing to carry a bag from now on. A small rucksack that should be with her at all times. They should have one. A personal survival bag containing a torch, batteries, first aid kit, water and a multi-tool.

She has to have light so instead of going forward she crabs sideways and feels for the sloping roof and the beams supporting it. Hard going and she bumps her knuckles and bangs her forehead before finally touching the inner membrane of the roof. She draws the knife from the scabbard and starts slicing through the thick taut material. Valuable seconds go by but the blade has been sharpened by Dave and does the job with ease. Chunks come away to be lowered to the ground and placed instead of being allowed to fall and make noise.

Fingering the roof she detects the rough underside surface of the tiles and starts working to ease it away from the fastening. Pushing it out then side to side before it clicks free and almost falls away before she grabs it and eases it back through to be laid down.

Light pours into the loft. A ray of pure sunlight that dazzles her eyes so adjusted to the pitch dark. She looks round and spots Roy lying still naked next to loft hatch watching her. She gives a thumbs up and motions towards the clothing at his side, *get dressed*.

The loft hatch to the second house is but yards away but she also notices there is no firewall until the second to last house. Boxes are stacked. Old carpets and rugs rolled up. Small wooden crates and the trust these residents must have had with each other harks to a time gone by.

With speed now she can see, Paula heads down the joists to thread a route through the boxes and stacked goods until she reaches the far end and the last loft hatch. A new firewall only a few feet away and it must have been constructed when that house was sold.

She drops down and listens with her ear close to the hatch. The air is filled with noise but nothing immediate that indicates they are beneath her. Slowly she cracks the slab of wood and gains a view down into the hallway. The open bathroom door, she moves round and spots a bedroom door also open. Carpeted floor and the walls are neutral in colour. With a last glance over at Roy she eases the hatch off and lowers herself down through the opening to drop lightly onto the carpeted floor.

She holds still with her heart booming and cranes her body to look down the stairs to the front door that's still locked. Into the bedroom first and she just manages to supress the yelp at the corpse lying on the bed. An empty bottle of pills lying on its side on the bedside table. The shock of seeing a normal dead body still gets her. Not a rotten infected corpse or the mangled remains from a fight but a real person who died naturally and something about the choice of the act taken gives a sense of pride, of virtue and dignity. That this person could see what was happening and decided, of their own free will, not to be a part of it.

A pair of sensible shoes put neatly to the side reminds her of her own bare feet. She nods her head as though giving a minute bow of respect and starts opening drawers to find a pair of cotton socks she can use. Wearing someone else's shoes is weird and wrong. The folds and creases are different. The dips for the heel and ball are slightly off and the ridges made by the toes are offset but protection is a far greater need than discomfort.

Shoes on she moves downstairs and into the kitchen, going straight to the gas stove. A quick turn of a dial and the hiss of gas coming out brings a tight smile to her face. She turns all the dials and opens all the doors to the appliance so the gas can pour out into the room.

A gunshot from next door followed by a spray of burst fire and she runs back up the stairs and uses the bannister post to clamber up into the loft to find Roy standing dressed over the loft hatch holding an assault rifle pointing down.

'They found us,' he calls out, 'how long do you need?'

'Few minutes, can you hold them?' She replies running along the joists to the next hatch.

'Yep,' he says confidently, 'if you see any shoes anywhere…'

'Size?'

'Nine, well nine and a half to be precise but I can do nines or ten at a push.'

The next hatch is opened and she drops down with a smile forming at the casual manner of her lover. That he doesn't ask *what* she is doing shows the implicit trust he has. No questions or wild panic about him.

She lands and listens, head cocked to the side and again edges round the top of the stairs to see down to the front door that's slightly ajar. A dark stain smeared across the downstairs hall and round splodges of footprints that walked through the wet blood over two weeks ago. They were in here when it happened but not now.

Shoes for Roy. She checks the bedrooms, opening wardrobes and cupboards but finding only shoes for an old lady and nothing for a man. With time pressing, Paula heads downstairs and gently pushes the door closed while listening to the incredible noises coming from the other side. Into the kitchen and she flips dials and open doors to the oven before racing upstairs and climbing back into the loft where she pauses to get her breath back.

'Any shoes?'

'Nope,' she pants and watches him fire a single shot down into the house, 'you okay?'

'They're different,' he says in a voice that catches her undivided attention.

'Different how?'

'I don't know...charged up and...more switched on? Yes, more switched on.'

'Not good, one more and we'll have to go.'

Further along and she flings the loft hatch aside, sticks her head down to listen then swings confidently down to land on the floor. A quick check down the stairs and the front door is closed. Into the kitchen, turn the dials, open the doors and let the room fill with the pungent aroma of gas. Back up the stairs, climb the bannister post, heave up into the loft, onto her feet and stand with hands on knees while panting hard.

'Shoes?'

'No shoes,' she shakes her head, 'ready?'

'I am and so are they,' he says without turning from the hatch, 'whoa you little sod,' he fires once and leans forward to watch the body slump down amidst the legs of its brethren.

'No choice,' she says moving to the last loft hatch closest to the firewall, 'we get down and out the back...then run...got it?'

'I have and again so will they,' he says pointedly.

'Roy, we don't have a great deal of choice.'

'I understand that but the second I move away from here they'll be coming up and chasing us.'

'Well we can't stay here.'

'I also understand that but like I said, they're going to charge after us...what's that smell?'

'Gas.'

'Gas? You turned the gas on? I'm bloody firing a gun here!'

'Yeah yeah, come on...hatch is open and...' she leans down to check the underside, 'it's clear, ready?'

Roy stares down to the bodies cramming into the hallway, his finger pressed lightly on the trigger as he waits for the next one to try and make the leap. Then they change. A flutter of something that passes through them and those immediately underneath the loft hole drop to the ground. Roy frowns, watching intently with morbid interest as more infected bodies pile onto those already lying down. A wide base that narrows as more and more fling themselves down to form a pyramid that rises in height towards the ceiling.

'GO!' With an electric pulse of understanding he races down the joists and through the boxes to Paula waiting by the last loft hatch, 'go down...they're coming...'

She drops down onto the hallway and moves aside to take the assault rifles passed down then moves to the top of the stairs as Roy drops nimbly into the carpeted floor. Down the stairs and a hard left turn to charge down the narrow hallway and into the kitchen and already above them they can hear the footsteps of the undead bounding across the loft space. She pauses to flip the dials and open the oven doors while Roy gets the back door open and moves out into the bright sunshine.

'Paula,' he hisses, 'now...go now...'

'Oh Christ,' she mutters as the first one falls heavily through the loft to land with a whump on the hallway above her head. To the back door she runs after Roy and side by side they sprint towards the fence at the bottom of the garden.

'Go,' he pauses to form a cup in his hands which Paula uses to get a boost to reach the six foot high fence. He drops to one knee, lifts the weapon to aim and twitches to point into the windows of the next house along. The magazine is emptied. The windows imploding from the high velocity bullets whipping to strike the walls and cupboards within the kitchen but not one of the strikes anything to cause a spark.

With a muttered curse he backs away from the fence to gain a run up and sprints to vault and gain purchase on the top edge and flip himself over and land next to Paula.

'Didn't ignite,' he says quickly as they both start running straight out away from the houses towards a copse of trees on the other side of the field. The fence behind them shatters down with the force of the bodies flinging themselves through it. A splintering wrenching noise that only adds to the howls and screeches of the deranged infected so desperate to reach their quarry.

The field is hard going. Once ploughed and the divots and dips are treacherous underfoot. Dried out mud, cracked from the incessant blistering heat of the summer and the sweat cakes their faces.

Two people running from a thick line of undead that pay no heed to the trip hazards beneath them and the houses behind them continue to fill with gas as they run desperately away.

CHAPTER TWENTY

'Fuck,' Cookey whispers.

'Car park, remember?' Nick says at seeing the swirling lines so perfectly moving together as the square fills with undead. The four lads stare from the window down into the open ground and already the path to the Saxon is cut off. The speed of the infected is incredible. They sprint flat out to blend seamlessly with each other in long snaking lines that seem to blur into one huge coiling entity.

They see it instantly. The dire threat now faced as their group is divided into four smaller teams. No way of getting to the others and no chance of reaching the Saxon.

'We've gotta go,' Nick says urgently.

'Not the front,' Blowers runs from the window and round the littered dining table to reach the kitchen window on the other side of the room where he yanks the net curtains down and stares out, 'this way,' he climbs the kitchen surface and with a foot in the sink he gets one window open to peer down.

THE UNDEAD DAY SEVENTEEN

'Incoming,' Cookey pushes away from the window to slam the door closed, 'get the table over.'

Nick and Mo Mo rush to tip the table over onto its side, the dinner bowls and food smashing onto the floor. They work quickly, barricading the door with anything they can grab while the undead gain entry to the front door below and start the thunderous charge. Noise everywhere. Gunfire and Meredith barking. Snarling voices that screech with fury and the door bangs hard as they reach the other side.

'Can we get down?' Nick shouts across to Blowers leaning out the window.

'Yeah, flat roof below…must be a store room at the back of the shop…'

'What about the dog?' Nick asks running over to join him.

'Curtains,' Mo Mo shouts and yanks the thick material hanging by the side of the window free from the fixings, 'we can lower her.'

'Quick,' Blowers shouts, 'Cookey hold that door.'

'Yeah right,' Cookey throws his weight into the barricade while holding his assault rifle clutched in his hands, 'fucking hold the door he says.'

'Done it?' Blowers looks over at Nick and Mo Mo wrapping the middle of the curtain under Meredith's stomach.

'Have to do, come on,' clicking his tongue Nick guides the growling dog to the window, 'go down and I'll lower her.'

'Mate, you can't hold her, she's way too fucking heavy. Mo, grab one side with Nick.'

'Yup,' Mo jumps onto the kitchen side and waits while Blowers pushes through the frame and lowers himself down until hanging by his fingertips with his assault rifle slung across his back. He lets go and thuds down onto the hot surface of the flat roof.

'Ain't long enough,' Mo Mo leans out to stare down, 'curtains ain't long enough.'

'Fucking go!' Cookey strains to push against the barricade being slowly forced back.

'Have to do,' Nick clambers up while keeping a firm grip on the two lengths of curtain. Passing one end to Mo Mo they heave Meredith up and start manhandling her to the open window.

Meredith lets the first lift happen. The things are coming and they must fight. The pack must be defended and there might be little ones near here that have to be protected. The things must die. The pack is strong. They should fight. Her paws start to scrabble to find purchase. Her claws skittering across the draining board and her panic starts to rise. Still barking with hackles up she fights to face the door Cookey is holding closed while Nick and Mo Mo curse and grunt to get through the window. Her back legs find the insides window sill and she powers away as though ready to bound free.

'Higher,' Nick grunts and gets one knee under her chest to help lift her up. She goes ungainly, undignified and clearly unhappy but she goes and swings out into the air with a very worried looking Blowers staring up at her legs thrashing in the air.

The two lads start lowering her, inching closer to lean out of the open window until they're on their stomachs straining to hold her immense weight. Blowers underneath making soft noises the sooth the dog. He reaches up to grab her paws, 'bit more,' he says, 'she's too high.'

'No....more....' Mo Mo grimaces.

'Now,' Nick says and lets go of the curtain. With Mo

Mo still holding his end the dog slides down the material to land with a soft thump on the roof where she bounds to the side with her tail high and teeth showing, 'thank fuck,' Nick sighs.

'Er...we going or what?' Cookey shouts.

'Go,' Nick slides aside to let Mo Mo drop down. 'Cookey...on three,' Nick shouts and moves round to edge backward out of the window, 'one...he lowers himself down, 'two...' he shuffles his legs down while clinging onto the sill, 'three!' He lets go and lands heavily. All three of them move back and away with rifles up and aimed at the window as Cookey appears, twists round and drops lightly to hang for a split second by his hands before dropping down.

A loud crash of furniture being smashed aside and the room fills with noise. The first undead through catches sight of Cookey going through the window and surges across to launch himself head first after the disappearing lad and into a hail of bullets fired by three waiting assault rifles.

Blowers turns and runs to the edge, scanning the ground all around for a route to take. This block backs onto the village with the lanes that run to the blocks of cottages and buildings nestled into the countryside. In an instant he knows they've scored the best chance of retreat with more houses, walls and places of escape to use and fire from. The other three will have open countryside to run into. A sickening sensation of being separated, that the hunger they all faced made them make a bad decision but when Mr Howie said to split up they all figured it would be okay. The village was deserted.

'Come on,' he drops onto his backside, flips over and snakes his way down over the edge to land on the ground proper. Cookey next, copying his actions. Nick gets Meredith over and pauses while thinking how to do this. She has a better idea and breaks free to run to the far end and she bounds down onto the top of a large wheelie bin and then onto the ground.

'Didn't you see that bin then?' Nick asks with a quick smirk.

'Did you?'

'Course,' Nick runs to copy the dog as Mo Mo fires a sustained burst into the faces appearing at the open window. 'Mo,' he calls, 'come on...Mo Mo...MO MO...GO NOW,' Nick bellows at the sight of Mo Mo standing his ground to kill the undead as they appear coming through the window of the kitchen.

'GET HIM,' Blowers points at the youth.

Nick runs back and grabs Mo Mo's arms. The youngest lad turns with a snarl and wild fury etched on his face, 'go,' Nick drags him away, 'get down there.'

Mo Mo goes but his eyes stay fixed on the undead dragging their own kind free of the window so they can get through.

All four on the ground and Blowers takes point. They cross the enclosed courtyard to the high gate. Bolts are drawn back and the gate pushed open as Nick and Cookey fire back up into the window and the infected crossing the flat roof.

They have no choice but to run and flee. The ferocity of the assault is overwhelming in speed and dynamics. All four of them harrying the big German Shepherd to keep going knowing she'll go back to take the lot of them on. Escaping but fleeing. Saving themselves but at what cost? Mr Howie can fight but he's on his own with Marcy. Dave and Clarence will be okay but Paula and Roy?

'Why's we running?' Mo Mo demands, 'stand and fight.'

'Just fucking go,' Blowers orders

Glances are exchanged. Blowers to Cookey and Nick. All three of them worried about running from the fight and keeping a close on Mo Mo who seems hell bent on standing his ground.

A narrow tree bordered lane. Beautiful and picturesque with a sun dappled old tarmac surface. Wild flowers border the sides, protected from the worse of the harsh sun by the thick canopy meeting overhead.

Harsh breathing as they race with feet pounding the road and the dull chink and rattle of assault rifles rubbing against clothes. Meredith's claws scraping lightly as she bounds easily ahead to scout the ground with a desire to turn and kill but a knowledge that the pack know what they are doing. There is a clear hierarchy within the pack and the hard faced dark haired man takes the lead when the others aren't with them.

Frequent looks over shoulders tell them they are being chased. Thick lines that still stream from the window to fall down onto the flat roof and down again onto the ground. Nothing stops them. Nothing makes them slow down. They are relentless in nature and redesigned by a virus to move faster, to feel no pain and drive on.

'Count to five....' Blowers snatches breath, 'turn and fire...all of us...be ready...' He catches a quick look behind and then ahead to the curve in the lane. 'One...two...three...' he slows down and checks his weapon is ready to go, 'four....FIVE!'

As one they stop and as one they turn and drop to a steadying knee and four assault rifles are fired on single shots with repeated tugs on the triggers as they make each shot count. One after the other is shot down to spin away and trip those behind. Nick reaches a hand out to grab

Meredith's neck, a brief pause between shots and still holding the dog he continues to empty his magazine.

A devastating effect that shreds many. Crawlers are formed but many are killed outright with good shots aimed despite heaving chests.

'Up...GO...' On their feet with a running magazine change. Old ones out to be tucked away. New ones dragged from pockets that are rammed up and bolts slid back. They build up to a sprint, stretching their strides to make the most of the delay caused to those pursuing them. The curvature to the left is followed and still they gain speed with grimacing smiles and tears being whipped from eyes. A chance to gain distance and get out of sight. To choose a fighting ground or hide somewhere to double back to the others.

The lane is long with the high trees still giving thankful shade. Cookey slows, pukes the food so recently taken in and steps up to keep running with a face flushed from the heat.

'Ahead,' Blowers pants the word at the sight of the wall glimpsed in the distance and the promise of a building or a house.

Nick pukes next. The meal they took in churning too much with the heat and the frantic motion of running. It burns his throat and the thick tears sting his eyes. A hand on his arm keeps him steady and he glimpses Mo Mo guiding him with quick furtive looks back down the lane.

'Keep going,' Mo Mo breathes easy, his lighter body and years spent running through the estate standing him in good stead, 'you's alright...keep going.'

'Dig in, Nick,' Blowers calls out and spits at the vomit threatening to push up from his own stomach.

The wall gets closer but it takes forever to reach. Roofs

behind it. Houses and street lights. Cars parked up on driveways and greater signs of the outbreak and storm start showing.

A huge tree ripped from the roots lays thick across the road. The foliage of the branches only just starting the turn as they die slowly and morph from glorious green to brittle brown.

'Fire…' Blowers spits again to clear his mouth, 'fire point…tree…'

'Yep,' Cookey nods once and all four fix their eyes on the thick trunk and the promise of being able to stop and rest.

Under, over and round they go to the other side and they drop down onto knees with shaking hands bringing their rifles to bear.

'Water?' Nick asks between ragged breathing. Heads shake as they pant and heave. Blowers swallows the sick down with a look of furious determination. Mo Mo glaring with longing at the curve in the lane and his rifle up and raised ready to be fired.

'Pick your shots,' Blowers says. The distance is quite long from here to the curvature in the lane and their ammunition is valuable. Which is ironic considering just how much they've got stacked in the Saxon. The GPMG would be perfect here, Blowers shakes his head and snaps his thoughts to the now, 'make ready…single shots…who's got Meredith?'

'With me,' Nick replies with one hand on the back of the dog's neck. She pants hard with a long tongue lolling from the side of her mouth but her eyes are as fixed as the others.

'Here,' Cookey whispers as the first one bursts into sight as she roars down the lane towards them. A wild look of pure hatred on her face. Hair patchy on her mottled head. Red eyes blazing but her motion is fluid with knees high and arms pumping to gain momentum and keep balance. 'Nice tits,' Cookey remarks at the sight of the boobs under her filthy blood soaked t shirt bouncing in a crazy circular motion.

'You're fucking sick,' Nick says, 'that...is minging.'

'You would,' Cookey says.

'Not with yours,' Nick says.

'See those, Blowers,' Cookey says quietly, 'they're called boobs...women have them and it's what makes them sexy.'

'Funny fucker, shut up and focus.'

Four lads watch two boobs that develop a motion and fluidity of their own. Seemingly possessed and they try to break free from the undead woman to run free and live a new life. The right goes up and to the left but the left goes down and to the right. Independent motion and mesmerising until a single shot takes her head off with a sudden boom.

'Who did that?' Cookey blinks as the woman flies back to lie prone on the ground.

'Yep,' Mo Mo claims the shot, 'she was minging.'

'Shot mate,' Blowers calls down, 'fair distance that was.'

'Call of Duty, sniping...'

'Preferred Battlefield,' Nick says.

'Yeah?' Mo Mo looks across in surprise, 'I played it.'

'Give you a game sometime,' Nick says.

'You two finished speed dating we got incoming,' Cookey fires at the infected running into view, 'I played Call of Duty,' he adds between shots, 'Blowers didn't, 'he played with men.'

'Dick,' Blowers fires, adjusts his aim and fires again and

bends double as the vomit spews without warning from his mouth.

'Mate, you alright?' Cookey shouts in alarm, 'Blowers?'

'I'm fine, just that fucking food you made.'

'Not my food you twat it's the bloody running.'

'Poisoned us,' Blowers wipes his mouth and blinks to clear his vision before firing once again.

'That bowl you used,' Cookey shouts, 'I rimmed it.'

'I rimmed yours,' Mo Mo calls down.

'Argh Nick, the bloody dog is eating my puke,' Blowers groans, 'I thought you had hold of her.'

'I did, she was lying down...don't let her eat your puke.'

'Meredith no! Stop it...Meredith I said no...' Blowers shoos her away, 'you dirty girl,' he admonishes gently with a tut.

'Clear,' Cookey shoots the last one down and scrabbles back to look over at Blowers staring disgustingly down at his half eaten mound of vomit, 'that's fucking gross.'

'Telling me,' Blowers says, 'ready? Move out.'

They stand slowly, still breathing hard and the sweat gleaming on their faces. Magazines are changed and dry lips licked in a vain effort to draw moisture.

Meredith sniffs the vomit and goes to start eating it again until her ears pick up the sound of drumming feet. Her head whips up and the low growl alerts the others that the fight isn't over. They turn to watch, readying weapons and expecting a few stragglers when the first thick rank appears at the head of a dense crowd moving as one.

'Fuck,' Cookey takes a step forward and stares hard, 'look at that...'

'Move out...we're going,' Blowers says at the sight. Bigger built undead at the front. Obese. Fat. Large. Big boned. Dense bodies that can absorb the firepower of the assault rifles and so give protection to those behind.

The four start running, building once again to a sprint as they get past the wall and rows of cottages so like the ones back in the square. Stone built with tiled roofs. Blocks of several in a row. A small access lane and more to the left and right. The village laid out in a haphazard wonderfully eccentric way of old England in its glory.

A village pub under a thatched roof. A post office further down. Benches at the sides of the lanes and more rows of cottages. An idyllic place to live and grow old, where everyone knew everyone else and the gossip of the day was to be shared over a pint of ale in the pub of an evening.

Mo Mo stares, taking it in. In reality this town is but a couple of hours from his old estate but a different world. A gentle place seen in old black and white films. No crime rate. No immigration issues. No underperforming schools refusing admissions to the most desperate of children in an effort to please the inspectors. No job centre where you signed on. No cars burnt out and left for weeks by a council too hard up to get it moved.

The effect isn't lost on the other three. All of them from town centres that were filled with betting shops, second hand stores, charity shops, payday loan shops and take away food places. Towns filled with traffic lights and sign posts that ordered you what to do and where not to park.

They take the twists and turns of the lanes and avenues. Lefts and rights that loop through tree lined roads to yet more rows of cottages. Snaking, confusing and they push on following the gentle inclines up and the relieving declines down. No brick built alleys here. No barbed wire or high walls with camera's fixed behind dark globes on long posts.

Footpaths instead that have been maintained and looked after. Pavements in good repair. Road surfaces smooth and not covered in pot holes or utility company patchwork bumps.

They become hotter. Thirsty. Breathing hard and all the time the snarls of the undead push them further away from their team and deeper into the village.

The lane splits in two. The main road to the left and a smaller, narrower lane to the right. Instinct says to go left and stick with the wider road but Nick thinks fast under pressure and pulls an empty magazine from his pocket which he throws down the main road and motions they should take the smaller one.

No words are needed. The decision is made and they run on hoping the chasing horde will follow the bigger road.

Denser thickets on both sides of the lane. Forests that stretch back to dark depths overgrown with thickly sprouting saplings, ferns and bushes. They get a good distance down then vault the fence and move into the forest, moving fast, pushing on, making distance.

Only after several long minutes of being whipped in the face by low branches and getting feet snagged on roots does Blowers allow them to slow and ease the frantic pace.

They don't speak but listen intently, staring round into the surrounding undergrowth and constantly watching Meredith for signs she can hear or smell them. She snuffles the ground ahead and pants hard but shows no discernible signs.

'Down,' Blowers waves his hand up and down, signalling them to go low and rest. Finding thick trees to lean against they slump down and crane necks to stare back to the road.

Hot and humid and the sweat is wiped away so much it

makes the skin on their foreheads sore. Cookey swallows noisily, his throat parched. Eyes flitting left and right, breathing through mouths.

Nick looks over at Blowers. They share a glance. Nick nods, *we're safe*. Blowers nods back, *agreed*.

'Come on,' he speaks low and hoarse, urging them onto their feet so they can thread carefully through the forest and away from the immediate point of danger.

'Plan?' Cookey asks once the four have grouped together to walk as a unit.

'Keep going and find somewhere to wait,' Blowers says, 'get water and hope to fuck they kept going down that other road...'

'We going back for the others?' Mo Mo asks.

'Definitely but we've killed a few and taken a few more away,' Blowers explains, 'let them fuck off and we can go back.'

The others nod but show the worry clear on their faces, 'listen up,' Blowers takes a breath and exhales slowly, 'Mr Howie can fight like a bastard...we've all seen him do it right? So he'll be okay. Nothing on this fucking planet can touch Dave or Clarence and Paula can outthink them easy... they'll get together and slaughter the lot before we even get back then we'll get a massive bollocking for taking so long and it'll all be alright.'

Cookey snorts dry humour. Nick smiles a tight smile and Mo Mo hangs on every word.

'Fuck I'm thirsty,' Blowers says after a few minutes, 'puking has dried my throat out.'

'At least we're in the shade,' Nick says after another few minutes of silent walking, 'cooler in here.'

'Mo, you okay?' Cookey's turn to break the heavy silence.

'Good,' Mo Mo says not used to people asking him if he is okay all the time. Only Jagger used to ask him that and that wasn't very often. They didn't need to ask each other.

Twigs snap underfoot. Branches snag and muttered curses sound out and with as much stealth as a herd of foraging pigs they stomp, swear and trip through the forest while all the time believing they are being as stealthy as a stoat.

Meredith finds the new smells gloriously different after a lifetime within the habitats of humans. The smells here are strong and natural. They cling to the ground like colours and speak of beasts both male and female that use winding paths. Rotten vegetation and old droppings give her an urge to drop and roll to coat herself in the scent. Something else was here recently too. Humans.

Stomp. Swear. Trip. Snag. Rattle.

They stop and look down at the loud foreign noise.

'What was that?' Nick whispers. A loud rattling noise coming from both sides. Metallic and distinct.

'Tin cans,' Mo Mo says, 'like…filled with stones…there, over there, see?'

'Fucking trip wire,' Cookey looks down at the fishing line pressing against his right ankle. He pushes it out and the line pulls hard as the tins cans rattle again.

'Don't keep doing it then you dick,' Nick says, 'stay still,' he edges over and follows the fishing line through a pair of saplings to a tin can held off the ground, 'old tin of beans filled with stones,' he calls out.

'Same other side,' Blowers says, 'who the fuck has done that?'

'Can I move now?' Cookey asks.

'Step over the wire,' Blowers says, 'Nick, you've got good eyes, go on point.'

'On it.'

'Why has he got good eyes?' Cookey asks, 'what's wrong with my eyes?'

'You snagged the wire.'

'We weren't looking for a wire then.'

'Still snagged it cockface.'

'Nick!' Blowers snaps at the loud rattling sounding out from the sides, 'don't just keep going you twat…'

'Not me,' Nick plants his feet to examine the ground in front, 'Meredith,' he groans at the dog trying to pull her foot free from a tangle of fishing wire. Tin cans rattle and bang noisily as the dog gets increasingly frustrated, yanking her back legs up and down while twisting round to try and see what's catching her.

'Good girl,' Mo Mo drops down at her sides, his assault rifle laid on the ground and he starts pulling the wire from her leg, 'you's a good girl.'

She whines softly and gives his cheek a big lick that makes him grin widely. The other three stare round with confused looks, shrugging at each other.

She bounds free from the wires and pushes on with nose down and tail up following a new scent trail. People. People who came here a few days ago. More than one. They came from one direction and went back the same way. The scents are similar in a way that her amazing sense of smell can discern age, weight and gender of the species.

'Fuck!' Cookey hits another trip wire and curses loud into the air.

'Fucking blind,' Blowers tuts disdainfully then sets one off himself, 'cock it.'

'Twat!' Nick is next, his own foot pushing the thin wire.

'How many!?' Cookey snags another.

Meredith follows the scents to the points of the cans.

She sniffs the tin and detects the faint aroma of the previous contents. Baked beans in tomato sauce. Washing up liquid. The pebbles now in them have been brought from somewhere else and they still hold the smells of the sweat from the hands of those that carried them.

'FUCK!' Nick hits another one.

Meredith runs side to side in delight at having a puzzle to follow. The smells are glorious. Rabbits, badgers, fox shit that makes her want to roll over. Birds and insects. A fat worm wiggling under a broad leaf. Rats, voles, mice. There, the people went this way. She noses the ground and jumps lightly over the wire.

'Oh my god,' Blowers trips over a tight wire, 'who fucking did this?'

One of them ate food here. Chocolate. She sniffs round and finds the crumbs spilled on the earth. They sat down for a while. The scent is strong. They gathered together. A pack. A new pack but a different pack. She looks back and pants at Blowers picking himself up from the ground and Mo Mo laughing while Nick shouts at being caught again and Cookey kicking out at something in front of him. She loves these ones from her pack. They are younger and have a playful energy.

This way she rotates on the spot with her tail wagging, a high pitched yap and she thrusts her nose down to lead the path through the trees.

'I'm gonna punch them,' Blowers seethes, 'when I find them I'll fucking punch them...in the face...really hard...'

'Just lift your feet,' Mo Mo laughs at the sight of the three blundering through the wires. They're so competent, so experienced and always know what to do and the sight only serves to humanise them more.

'Yeah,' Cookey points at Blowers, 'just lift your feet.'

'Right in the mouth,' Blowers nods firmly, 'gonna smash 'em in the fucking mouth for putting stupid fucking wires everywhere and...I mean...utter cunts...complete utter cunts.'

They push on. Snagging wires that set the rattling tins off that make them swear. Blundering stomping feet lifting high like Mo Mo. Moon men defying gravity and the sight sets Mo off even more until tears are streaming down his face.

'Right in the chops,' Blowers mutters, 'in the chops...'

Close now. The scent trail is stronger and the smell of the new pack hangs in the faint breeze coming through the trees.

'Aye up,' Cookey holds a hand up, 'ahead.'

'Bout fucking time,' Blowers mutters again, 'really will punch them in the face.'

'Yeah you said,' Nick says peering through the trees.

'I will,' Blowers says emphatically, 'really will.'

The tree line ends. Open sky beyond and they edge forward slowly until the huge roof of the building comes into view. Different to the houses they saw. Bigger. Longer and wider with higher bits and lower sections.

'What is that?' Cookey asks quietly.

'Like a...big house?' Nick says. The view opens gradually and not knowing what they're going into makes them slow down and use the cover of trees to check each step.

A vast open ground beyond the trees. A huge house set in gardens with playing fields on all sides fitted with football goal posts, rugby goal posts. Tennis courts, netball courts and hard hockey surfaces.

They drop down in the ferns at the edge of the tree line and stare hard. Sweeping eyes over the deserted grounds to the house.

'No cars,' Nick whispers.

'Coach,' Mo Mo nods at the single vehicle parked in the car park to the front of the house, 'sign board...see it?'

'Yeah,' Blowers strains his eyes at the big square sign board erected in front of the house. 'See anyone?' He asks in a muted voice.

'Nope,' Cookey wipes his sore forehead again, 'people in that house though.'

'Really?' Blowers asks, 'do you think?'

'Sarcastic prick,' Cookey tuts, 'who do you think put the wires up?'

'Really? Do you think?' Blowers asks again in a forced light tone, 'what else have you deduced Poirot?'

'Er, that your mum is fat.'

'Fact, right...we'll go down...spread out in a line.'

They edge sideways to create distance between each and slowly emerge from the undergrowth. Rifles held ready, eyes scanning. Four sweat stained young men with hard faces and lean bodies that step with sweeping strides. Four young men watched by many pairs of eyes from within the house.

CHAPTER TWENTY-ONE

Shots off to the side. A sustained burst of firing. Clarence looks quickly to Dave who nods and the new direction is taken without words being needed. A thick line of undead behind them and they veer off to aim for the sounds of their team fighting.

'Paula and Roy,' Clarence works out the direction and who it would be, 'Dave...call out...'

'**HERE,**' the voice booms into the air so loud it forces an instant yelp from the still terrified Reginald.

Hard ground underfoot. A field that was once ploughed and it saps energy to keep the pace high. Reginald sweats profusely with his heart rate thundering up. Unused to such exercise and he can hardly generate coherent thought but stays doggedly behind Dave.

Clarence risks a turn to view the horde coming behind them. They're gaining. The undulations of the ankle snapping ground not causing them such a concern. This ground is too open. No cover. They'll catch them within minutes.

'Dave...got...got to...cut them down...' Clarence heaves the words out.

'Keep going,' Dave stops dead, turns and raises the assault rifle to aim at the horde. As Reginald passes him the first shot booms clear into the air. A head shot that bursts the skull clean off with a pink mist hanging in the air. Second shot and another skull bursts. Third, fourth. They start to weave side to side but he fixes aim, tracks and fires. One by one they are killed outright. They weave faster but the effect is the same. Dave doesn't miss. Dave doesn't get tired and once the front section is dropped he turns and runs after Clarence, passing him and Reginald with ease as he gains the front once again.

The back of their row of buildings is passed and they turn with the contour to get level with the back of the next row and the distinct sight of Paula and Roy sprinting flat out from a huge line of infected charging after them. The danger is obvious, the horde are gaining as Roy stays with Paula to urge her on.

Paula turns with a frantic look and tries with every ounce of effort to drive power into her legs. It's no good. The infected are too fast, too pumped up and relentless. The tiny nuances of concern that the ground is so bumpy it risks tripping over and that sole thought takes the edge of their speed and saps the strength from their legs. A tree line in the distance but even that won't help them. It breaks the ground up but doesn't offer any defensible point.

Shots from the side and they snatch a view to see Dave sprinting flat out with the rifle aimed and firing into the horde so close behind Paula and Roy. Head shot after head shot takes them down but it's not enough.

'FIRE ON THEM,' Dave calculates the danger and can see the other two will be overrun within seconds. They have to fire and cull the numbers, 'PAULA...FIRE ON THEM...'

The two come to a sudden stop and trusting Dave implicitly they turn and start firing straight into the ranks coming after them. Gunfire from both sides. Clarence shooting as he runs. Dave firing. Paula picking her shots. Roy giving burst fire.

Dave lowers his rifle, the magazine empty. He locks eyes on the very front of the horde and drops back to hand his weapon to a panting terrified Reginald. Then he runs. Opening his stride while drawing the knives from his belt. Feet brushing the surface of the ground.

'I AM DAVE...I WILL KILL YOU,' he roars with fury at being separated from Mr Howie and the trickle of fear coursing his veins, 'FIGHT ME...I AM DAVE...' at the last second before impact he calculates the kills to be done. That big man coming towards him will be sliced with his right hand then the woman behind him on the follow through. The two behind them will be done in succession, twist and a gap will form and he can take the old lady and the young man.

'PAULA...FIRE ON THOSE BEHIND CLARENCE...'

The impact is almighty. The big man has his throat cut. The woman behind him drops on the follow through. Two more sliced and dead and into the gap where the old lady is cut from behind and the young man has the artery in his groin opened. Amongst them now he plays to his advantage of densely packed bodies unable to turn and react fast enough. Slice and kill. Spin into a gap planned three kills ago. Go low and stab up, go up and leap, slice at the throat as he comes down.

The three remaining guns turn on the horde behind Clarence. Withering fire that cuts them down. Magazines are changed while Reginald gibbers and holds the assault rifle given to him by Dave clutched to his chest. Heaving for air. His mind panicking with the intense danger. Blinking as he watches Dave slaughter them one after the other. Watching the horde behind being cut down by the high velocity rounds tearing through them.

'GO,' Dave drops the last one and spots the fresh hordes streaming from the houses. Too many to kill and not enough ammunition to do the job. They have to run and gain a defensible position or a bottleneck that will force them into single or double file attack.

'Dave…' Clarence shouts the warning as he spots another huge horde running free from a tree line at the end of the meadow.

Three distinct thick hordes now. From the houses immediately behind them. From the side where they ran from and from the tree line.

'We're being shepherded,' Paula states, 'can we fight them here?'

'Not a chance,' Clarence says, 'run…go for the other tree line and we'll work back to the village and find the lads… Paula on point but for fuck's sake run.'

Dave growls with intense fury. Forced to run away when he knows he could get through them with ease. He could simply run through the horde and kill those that get in his way and find Mr Howie but the team are running out of ammunition and without him they'll die. Mr Howie will be displeased if he leaves them. His face shows a rare look of emotion at the conflict within his soul.

So they run. Shepherded and forced into a route chosen for them.

Gunfire in the far distance. Four rifles firing together. The lads are alive and fighting from the direction they are running towards. That gives them hope. Find the lads, regroup and get back for Mr Howie.

They all feel it. Unvoiced and unspoken. If the infected are so pumped they have forced this reaction from everyone else, how the hell will the boss cope on his own with Marcy?

To them, Howie is immortal. Nothing can touch him. A supermarket manager driven with an ethereal ability to kill vast opposition without hesitation. His speed matches Dave. His ferocity is greater than an angry Clarence. He is immune. Special. Chosen. Howie will fix this. He is the one to make this better.

But still. One man on his own? Against something like this? The thought is too dreadful to be considered on a conscious level. The consequences are too awful. Without Howie there is no future.

So they run. Shepherded and forced and with pain in their hearts and legs they run.

CHAPTER TWENTY-TWO

'Fucktown Sports Academy,' Cookey reads the sign.
From the tree line they worked slowly down the bank and into the grounds skirting the old mansion house until reaching the front of the building.

'Doesn't actually say that,' Blowers says reading the sign then looking around in a slow turning circle.

'Finkton Sports Academy,' Nick reads the words slowly, 'is that right? Finkton?'

'Yep,' Blowers says.

'Anyone for tennis?' Cookey asks, 'or football, or rugby, or netball or hockey or badminton or table tennis...table tennis? What the fuck is table tennis doing on there?'

'It's a sport,' Nick says walking a few steps further down the driveway to stare back towards the wide entrance and the road beyond.

'Are you suggesting ping pong is a sport?' Cookey asks.

'Yeah I am suggesting it.'

'Suggestering? That's not a word like ping pong isn't a sport...they might as well put dominos on here.'

'Dominos? Have they got a Dominos?'

'Not the pizza place you dick, the game...'

'Well my suggestion,' Blowers interrupts them, 'is we get inside, get some water and then head back to the others.'

'I suggest that is a good plan,' Cookey says.

'I suggest we do that,' Nick says.

'The suggestion is a good one,' Mo Mo joins in.

'Blowers makes a good suggesterer,' Cookey says.

'I am the nominated suggestee,' Blowers says almost absent minded as he scans the grounds and turns slowly back to face the building. 'Okay, I'll call out...try and look non-threatening,' Blowers makes a point of lowering his rifle while lifting his chin, 'HELLO? ANYONE HOME?'

They wait quietly in the near silence only broken by the odd insect buzzing past, 'HELLO?' Blowers calls again, 'WE'RE NOT A THREAT...WE JUST...'

'Shush,' Nick says urgently, 'what if they're near here...'

'Fuck good point mate,' Blowers winces at the lack of thought.

'Let's go in,' Cookey leads off towards the entrance. A set of wide double wooden front doors complete with pinned notices and posters of the sports training on offer. 'Open,' he pushes one door and waits while it swings in.

'Go in,' Blowers says from the rear.

'Hello?' Cookey calls out, not loud but clear enough to announce their arrival, his tone easy and gentle, 'we're not a threat...we just need some water...can we get a drink please?'

They gather in the cool lobby feeling the relief of the shade. High vaulted with doors leading off and a wide staircase on the right side. Notice boards set back into a reception area with lists and dates printed on.

'Anyone here?' Cookey calls out again, 'really we mean

no harm…we're just thirsty and need a drink…do you mind if we get a drink and then go?'

'Tell 'em we're with Mr Howie,' Nick whispers.

'We're with Mr Howie from the fort,' Cookey calls out, 'we're not bandits or anything like that.'

'Bandits?' Blowers asks, 'fucking bandits?'

'What? I just thought it?'

'Don't say bandits, we're not highway men or bloody smugglers.'

'S'what I said, we're *not* bandits…well we're not,' Cookey motions to Nick and Mo Mo as Blowers starts to groan, 'you are…'

'Don't start.'

'What? I never said it.'

'You're going to say it.'

'Nah I won't.'

'Oh thank fuck for that.'

'Arse bandit.'

'Such a twat!'

'Well, I had to say it,' Cookey says proudly.

'Say we're from the army,' Nick urges.

'Er…We're from the army,' Cookey calls out, 'listen, we'll just get some water and then go. Is that okay? Our dog is really thirsty too…so….thanks!' He adds and shrugs at Blowers, 'they don't want to say anything.'

'Fair enough,' Blowers mutters, 'would you speak to us?'

'Not a fucking chance,' Nick says. 'Where's the kitchen?'

They head off through the left doors into a large lounge area complete with sofas, bookcases and easy chairs. Tables adorn the sides with computers fixed atop with more signs indicating Wifi is accessible with a code from the instructors but restricted to fifteen minutes per person per evening.

Into a dining room laid like a school refectory with big tables designed to seat ten people so the students are forced to mingle and eat together. Rows of hooks on the sides and even more signs that muddy boots and shoes will be removed prior to eating.

'Look,' Mo Mo nods at the rows of yellow and red tabbards hanging from the hooks, each with a number and some with letters etched on them, 'people here then.'

'Kitchen must be down there,' Blowers indicates the next set of doors.

Meredith runs ahead with her nose to the ground and her tail up and wagging. This is the den of the new pack. This is where they live. They are hiding because they are afraid of the new pack coming in. She wags her tail to show she is no threat.

They head through the next set of doors into the vast kitchen of stainless steel tables, sinks, cupboards and walk in fridges. Shelves stacked with pots and pans. Knives held to magnetic strips on the wall and each one numbered.

'Smell that?' Nick asks, 'coffee, can you smell it?'

'Yeah,' Cookey says in a low voice, 'someone been in here, oh my god...what's that?' He walks forward with his nose in the air, 'wow, can you smell it? That's bread...'

'Yeah,' Mo Mo joins him sniffing the air, 'someone making bread...'

'Old stove,' Nick heads to the huge appliance recessed in the wall with a wide air filter above it, 'fuel stove...wow haven't seen one of these for years. You can run them on wood, oil...fucking anything that burns really...oh that bread smells nice.'

Blowers pulls a pan from the wall and pushes it under the cold tap to fill with water as Meredith snuffles through the kitchen. Cups are found and the lads gather to quench their thirst as the pan is put down for the dog to lap.

'Mind out,' Cookey gets to the tap and thrusts his head under the flow of cooling water, 'oh man that's nice,' he rubs his hands through his hair and face then stands up to let the water drip down his neck and back. Mo Mo goes next, his own jet black hair glistening with the water. Blowers and Nick follow suit, rinsing off the sweat. Cup after cup is drank down to rid the taste of being sick and replenish the fluids lost.

Eyes flicking constantly to the oven and the tempting aroma of freshly baking bread, 'imagine eating fresh bread,' Nick says, 'with butter.'

'We can't take it,' Blowers says.

'I'm not suggesting that,' Nick says defensively, 'I wouldn't eat someone else's bread, mate.'

'Sorry,' Blowers says with a dip of his head, 'I didn't need to say that.'

'Mo Mo would,' Nick says with a slow grin, 'he'd pinch it.' He looks to Mo Mo to make sure the joke is taken as intended and stops dead at the intense look on the younger lad's face. 'Mo? What's up?'

Mo's nostrils flare, his eyes narrow and the hair on the back of Nick's hair prickles to stand on end. A low growl from Meredith who stares fixed towards the front of the house. All conversation stops and the water dripping from their sodden heads drips to land on the hard tiled floor.

'Found us,' Mo Mo whispers.

Blowers stares quickly to the oven and the signs of habitation. People living here. Surviving and trying their best to survive and the sensation of guilt at leading the undead to them ripples through his insides, 'we can't bring them in here,' he rushes the words out, 'ain't fair…'

'Agreed,' Cookey says following the same train of thought, 'out the front then...so they see us yeah?'

'Yeah,' Blowers downs his water and lets the hardness of battle settle on his face. His own dark eyes nearly match the brooding gaze of Howie, thin pursed lips and a determination to the do the right thing, 'that's not our way,' he murmurs and glances to Nick.

'Not our way,' Nick nods, 'we'll draw them away.'

'Get four,' Blowers looks past Nick to Mo Mo reaching out to the big blades held in place on the magnetic strip. Ranging in size from paring knives up to meat cleavers the size of which Lani would be proud to wield. The sight of it only hardens the resolve within the corporal of the team.

Mo Mo takes the four largest blades. High tensile steel with curved handles. One each and they're handed round in an almost symbolic gesture that the fighting will be done now. They've led the horde from the square and could keep running but then the horde will sweep through and kill whoever lives here, and anyone nice enough to make bread is nice enough to fight for.

'Go,' Blowers leads the way. Four young men with hard faces and determined steps that clutch their rifles and slide their newly acquired blades into their belts ready to be drawn and used. 'Nick...when it comes to it...you and Mo go...me and Cookey will...'

'Get fucked,' Nick snaps.

'We're immune,' Blowers snaps back, 'it makes sense.'

'He's right, Nick,' Cookey says without humour now, 'you two get back to Mr Howie.'

'Mo?' Nick asks fuming from the suggestion, 'fancy that? Running away while our mates get fucked over?'

'No.'

'Nick, I am ordering you to...'

'I'll always follow what you say but don't ever fucking ask me that again,' Nick says, 'not ever...'

'Nick!' Cookey implores.

'You came back for me in that fucking house...think of all the shit we been through and you asking me to fucking do one and run? Fuck off.'

Through the dining room into the lounge, angry words said with emotion and honest intent.

'We alright?' Nick asks with a hard glance to Blowers after a minutes of charged silence.

'Yeah, mate,' Blowers nods back, 'had to ask.'

'We stay together,' Nick says, 'team right.'

'Team,' Blowers says.

'Team right?' Nick says to Cookey.

'Team,' Cookey repeats it back. In the lobby they stand and already the distant howls drift on the heavy hot air through the open front doors.

'Mo,' Nick looks across, 'team right?'

Mo Mo looks back, his soft brown eyes lingering on Nick then Cookey and finally Blowers. A sudden feeling of belonging, of being part of something and that bond between them extends to envelope him. In truth the invite has always been there, but now, with the loss of Jagger so heavy in his heart, he starts to understand what has kept them alive this long, 'team,' Mo Mo says softly, 'yeah...yeah team...always.' They're all scared. He knows that now. The fear is real but that fear can be taken and turned into something else. An intrinsic instinct that knows what the right thing is. To hold that honour and know when to run but when to stand and fight. Mo smelled the bread baking and the house has the feeling of being lived in. People living here. It ain't right that the infected should be brought in here but they have to keep them from going back to the square too. No choice then. They fight them outside to the last man standing.

'Ready,' Blowers looks to his small team and feels the burden of leadership solid on his shoulders. Nods come back. Hard eyes from killers that will not flee. 'Pick your shots until the ammunition runs out...then we go back to back and fight out...let Meredith do what she can and hope to fuck we're harder than they are.'

'Fuck 'em,' Mo says, 'we'll win.'

All eyes snap to stare at him. Innocent words spoken but the lad has no idea of the effect or the history attached to those words, 'what?' Mo shrugs.

'Move out,' Blowers goes first. Solid strides that cross the threshold and pace out from the front of the house to the edge of the driveway. Snarls and howls permeate the air as the raging horde work up the main road towards the gate.

The others form a line either side and walk side by side up the driveway until they're a decent distance from the house.

They drop down onto one knee and start pulling the last remaining magazines from pockets to lay ready to be taken up. Rifles are checked. Magazines ejected, tested and pushed back in. Bolts are drawn back. Single shots selected.

From end to end, Mo Mo, Cookey, Blowers and Nick with his hand resting gently on Meredith's neck. She knows now to wait until she can attack. She growls. Warning the pack of the coming danger. She lifts her hackles to make herself bigger.

They breach the gate and there they are. Monstrous, fetid and charging with discipline. Lips pulled back to show teeth. Hands clawing into weapons. Heads fixed and staring. The bigger ones at the front to protect those behind and the slower pace has preserved their energy levels.

She gives voice and tells them who she is. She tells them this is her pack and the pack fight and they have to stop or they will die. She has killed them before and will kill them again. Stop. Go back. Do not come here. Do not attack us for we are pack and we will fight you to the end.

Snarls show. Blowers top lip lifts at one corner. Cookey's right eye twitches as he lets the anger flood his system. Nick spits and glares cold and dispassionate. Mo Mo sees the things that killed his friend and he'll be fucked if his new friends will die before he does. Five against many.

'TAKE AIM,' Blowers roars the order to show defiance and allow a vent for the wild energy pounding through his body.

Four rifles are raised. Nick lets go of Meredith but she waits now. She holds position next to the pack and she tells them the final warning is being given and that to follow this course of conduct will end their lives. They are things. They smell wrong. They move wrong. They tried to hurt her little one and for that she will never forgive them and never stop killing. Her head low. Eyes of a wolf. Teeth huge and gleaming white. Every muscle quivering in anticipation.

We are human, Blowers lets the thought whirl through his mind, *we have discipline and command and we will go out in a show of respect to the things taught to us by Mr Howie, Dave, Clarence and the team.* 'ON MY COMMAND...WE WILL COMMENCE FIRING.'

Cookey feels the thrill of Blowers calling out the order. Showing the infection that despite the overwhelming mass of the enemy coming at them they retain order and focus.

'**FIRE.**'

An order given. Structure and discipline and it serves to ease the tremble and focus the aim. The gunshots ring out loud and true as the first four bullets spin with deadly aim to whip through the bodies of those at the front. Each firer acknowledges the strike of the first round and adjusts tiny increments to aim better. Head shots are scored. One after the other. Some strike bodies or necks. Some miss but strike those behind. Some go straight through to kill two in one shot.

Structure and order is maintained. Four young men that fire with calm ruthless precision. Picking targets and plucking the shots. Picking another target and plucking the shot.

'MAGAZINE,' Blowers is the first to change and in seconds the procedure is done and the rifle brought back up.

'MAGAZINE,' Nick goes next.

Still they come. So many of them. Thick and charging the distance but not flat out. Energy being preserved. The infection can see they are alone. The infection knows where every member of the team is. These have no help coming. They are isolated. Divide and conquer. The dog will be slaughtered. These youths will be slaughtered and the losses inflicted by this group will end today.

'LAST ONE,' Blowers rams the last magazine up, slides the bolt, takes aim and makes every bullet count. He counts them off in his head. From thirty down to twenty down to ten. He snorts a dry laugh when only five shots remain. Seventeen days of slaughtering them. Seventeen days of causing carnage and he wouldn't change a second of it. Not for anything in the world. To die now is honourable and worthy. This horde is huge and every one brought down here is one less to go after the others.

Five. Four. Three. Two. Last bullet and with a grin he sights the head of a big hippie looking male and takes pleasure in seeing the skull burst apart. Rifle discarded. On his feet. Knife drawn and he waits with that top lip pulling back.

Cookey drops his rifle. On his feet. Knife drawn and he waits. Mo Mo discards. On his feet. Knife drawn and not an inch of fear is shown, only desire to be there now, to charge now, to fight now.

Nick. Rifle down. Up. Knife out. He looks across at the others and nods. They look back and nod. He turns to look down at Meredith, 'go.'

She's away. Bounding and unleashed. The warnings given and right behind her the pack charge with absolute hatred bursting through every pore of their bodies.

I warned you. I told you to go back. You paid no heed and now this is it. She leaps and those paws strike the chest, the neck extends, the teeth grip and she drops, rags and the death is given. She whips round and grabs an ankle to wrench the next one down so she can reach the throat.

Back to back was the order but that is forgotten as the bloodlust of battle takes over. Close and intimate without the range of axes to be used. Knives that stab and slice. Face to face with those that seek to end their kind.

Nick stabs into the chest and drives his forehead into the nose of the woman lunging at him. Heedless of the risk of blood transference for this is the time to fight like a bastard. He roars with the power of his strong arms that deliver the slices and stabs and the strong legs that drive him forward.

Mo Mo whips with incredible speed. Dancing left and right on the balls of his feet. Never staying in one place long enough to get caught. Slicing and driving the point into neck after neck. One drops. The next one drops. The third goes down.

Immune and Blowers was trained as a boxer so the knife

is gripped in his right hand while his left punches out with solid blows that drive them back enough for the stab to be given. The pent up aggression unleashed and without realising it, without conscious thought given, he fights slowly towards Cookey as though the instinct to be near him dictates his actions.

Cookey for his part glowers with consuming passion to slice and protect his mates. Stabbing deep into the neck and his thumb drives in to pop an eye. He bites, punches, kicks and gouges and the laughing lad is serious in his business. They are dirty so he fights dirty.

The initial rush abates and they do fall to reform back to back. Encircled and flanked on all sides and they know, deep in their hearts they know that without the combined strength of the team, without the axes and without the passion of Mr Howie to lead they will die here. This is the end.

Meredith senses it. She knows they are too many. The pack is reduced and split but that doesn't mean the fight ends. It means you fight harder. So she does. She gets faster. Ragging and biting until her mouth drips blood and her paws are coated in the fluids of the fallen.

Engulfed. Encircled. Four men and one dog against a foe that numbers so many. They give losses but not enough and on the seventeenth day since the outbreak started, they prepare to die.

Tiring now. Arms growing heavier and the roars they gave become grunts of exertion but the other side show no sign of weakening. They don't regret it. As long as Mr Howie survives then the chance to fix this remains and for that chance they will fight to the last.

A screech joins the noise of the fight. More join in. Wild screeches that are fresh and wild.

Meredith gains the first view and takes it in within a split second before she goes back to the killing.

Blowers snatches a glance and blinks but there isn't time to do anything other than kill the thing in front of him and then the next one and the next one. One by one the lads see the source of the screeching.

Multi-coloured figures that pour from the house. Bulky with leg guards, arm guards and helmets with face plates worn. Thick gloves on their hands and they are led from the front with the leader lifting the weapon into the air with a screech that tells those four lads they have help coming.

A solid line of bulky bodies that race with voices howling as they charge into the fight. The infection spots the new threat and sends host bodies to intercept.

The new attackers are prepared and suddenly they run low with their hockey sticks held ready. The first undead aims for the middle to take the leader who waits until the last second before deftly side stepping past and hammering a blow into the neck with the curved part of the hockey stick. The blades fitted to the stick slice the skin open and it drops bleeding out.

The air glints from the sunlight reflected of the blades attached down the shafts and curves of the sticks. Faceless fighters hidden behind masks and the protective goal clothing gives them a confidence to get close.

Into the fray now. Sticks striking with unbelievable power. The speed they display is stunning. Years of training to run flat out then stop and spin on the spot. Never losing balance, never overstretching.

With fresh energy Blowers leads his team out to fight harder. The instant threat of death they faced now abates and they can fight on. They can inflict losses and reduce the numbers that could harm Mr Howie and the others.

The hockey players run deep into the opposing team and use the curved hook to trip and snag the ankles so they can be driven down and a killing blow delivered. They are not natural killers and the first one is taken down by a wild charge of a heavy male. Pummelled and killed within seconds but the others fight on. Another player goes down but the kills they give are worth the losses.

The players heard the wires being pulled as those wires in the forest were connected to longer wires that stretched all the way to the house. With the warning heard they scrambled to gather and wait quietly until the strange looking four young men came from the trees. They tracked their movements as they reached the front of the house and heard the conversations taking place with eyebrows raised as they discussed Dominos pizza. They watched and heard them enter the house and drink water. They heard the discipline and respect within their speaking and mannerisms. Then, as they became aware of the infected coming, they chose to go out and fight and thereby protect the unseen and unknown people within the house. That was honour and honour was a thing that had to be worked to achieve.

'Suit up,' Charlie said after a brief discussion and a vote held. Charlie was the leader and on Charlie they formed to be led out and join the fight.

The adapted hockey sticks worked well. Hockey is a violent, aggression led tactical team sport using a long stick and a high level of fitness to drive a solid object at the opponent's goal that was protected by someone wearing highly developed clothing and equipment designed to withstand the most fearsome of strikes.

Hard fighting. Dirty fighting. Blood spilt and bodies ruined. Players killed but slowly the tide of battle is turned and the numbers thinned out.

THE UNDEAD DAY SEVENTEEN

The lads feel it. They see it. Meredith detects the enemy are fewer. Nick breaks free from the group and snatches a fallen hockey stick up. A range weapon like an axe and he relishes the chance to fight like he was shown. Battering and slicing now and the kills he gains double in rate and speed.

'BLOWERS,' Nick hooks another on the tip of his toes and flicks it high for Blowers to snatch and wield.

'Oh yes,' Blowers grins evilly and steps out to increase his range of attack. Cookey casts about and spots a player running towards him. The player bends to snatch a stick up and passes it over quickly.

Cookey nods, takes the weapon, drops his knife and charges out. Mo Mo takes Cookey's fallen knife and using two he slashes and cuts deep with a wild snarling grimace etched onto his face.

Many down to a few but still they charge and charge hard. The lads dance out to dodge and hack. The remaining players work hard to attack. Running through the ranks of undead as they snag ankles and hack legs to inflict deep wounds that drop the infected to the ground.

Then it's over and the ground is awash with a sea of dead bodies that bleed and fill the air with the metallic tang of blood. Blowers hacks down at his last one and staggers back with his chest heaving.

Nick already swaying amidst a mound of broken bodies. Cookey has two coming and makes light work with vicious strikes left and right as he weaves round and through them.

Mo Mo runs past his last one then stops to vault high onto its back and he drives the points down into the neck and lets his body fall with the corpse. On his feet and his chest heaves but the fire still blazes in his eyes as he scours for more to kill.

The players slow down and work through the crawlers to finish them off with nasty strikes down into throats.

Meredith pants with blood pouring from her mouth. Not her blood but the blood she took from them. Her coat matted and glistening and she paces like the wolf from crawler to crawler and ends them with a snarl and a bite. Her pack have survived. This pack. This small pack took the fight and won. She looks round to Blowers to Cookey to Nick to Mo Mo. They still stand and they still live.

The four stand breathing hard with filthy faces and hands covered in blood and gore. Arms coated in grime. Eyes stinging from sweat and mouths parched so dry they can't spit.

'We,' Blowers coughs to clear his throat, 'we gotta go back now...' his words cut off as Charlie walks through the devastation and finds four hard faces looking over with an intense ferocity.

Nick inclines his head, too tired to speak but offering thanks all the same. Cookey lifts a tired hand.

'Thanks,' Blowers says hoarsely.

The hockey player says something but the voice that comes back is as gruff and thirsty as his own and the words are lost and Charlie stares through the mesh grid at the blank faces.

The gloves come off first. Tugged and eased until the fingers can waggle in the soothing air so many degrees cooler than inside the padded material. The helmet is next but the fingers are sweaty and can't grasp the buckle under the chin. Charlie huffs and drops the hockey stick cursing muffled at the slippery clasp.

'Want a hand, mate?' Cookey asks at watching the man floundering to get the helmet off. He gets a thumbs up and the arms drop to the sides as Cookey walks over, 'tilt your head back...done it...'

'Thanks,' the hoarse voice says.

'Cheers for the help, mate,' Cookey says and smiles tiredly at the sweat soaked hands slipping over the smooth sides of the helmet, 'here,' he motions for the head to drop and grasps the sides, 'I'll hold it you pull back.'

Charlie steps back and finally gets free of the helmet. Having never played in goal the equipment is strange and foreign.

'Oh that's better,' she stands straight and pushes her fingers into her long brown hair to ease it away from her face, 'so hot in that,' she says and coughs loudly to clear her dry throat, 'thanks for that,' she says to a stunned Cookey and three more equally stunned young men stood behind him, 'I'm Charlie.'

CHAPTER TWENTY-THREE

This has happened before. The surreal awareness that comes when your body and mind sink into the belief that these are your last few seconds of life. Everything becomes so clear, like my vision has sudden and incredible clarity.

In the bathroom and I look round at the sodden floor and the water spraying from the burst pipe that glints and reflects the particles of sunlight coming through the window. Like a waterfall in a beautiful forest glade. The smashed up shower cubicle, by contrast, is jagged and full of right angles. The dead body of the huge infected man that ragged me senseless just looks like wet organic material. His bald head so round and smooth and the blood all washed away. The walls are soaked with rivers of water that stream down in never ending races to join the puddles at the bottom. The thick wooden door is being inched open by the weight of those behind it in a surging rhythm that makes me think of old castle invaders using a log to batter down the portcullis.

The absurd sight of our feet almost makes me chuckle.

THE UNDEAD DAY SEVENTEEN

My right foot at the bottom then her left foot then my left foot then her right foot. Her feet are a lot smaller than mine so it just looks funny. Like two people are standing on the door and having a conversation in some weird position. She does have nice legs though. Very shapely. Not thin but muscled nicely and I know it's her strong thighs keeping them out as my legs have become weaker by the second.

Other senses come to life. Every noise is separated and uniquely distinct. A snarl from a female outside, sort of lighter pitched and feminine. A much deeper bass growl. A strange scratching noise that must come from nails raking at the door. The shuffle of feet outside. The wheezing breaths they take and the grunts of exertion. Bangs and thumps. Marcy's rapid breathing as she gulps at the air in terror of the situation, in pain at our positions and from the focus needed to keep her legs locked out.

I can see every strand of her hair. It looks black when you glance at it but it's not black. Dark brown but with lighter strands. The wet strands hang down her shoulders and neck. The warmth of her body is there too. I can feel it. I can feel the breath exhaled by her on my cheek. Her eyes are closed and she looks serene with golden tanned skin and dusky pink full lips.

Her right arm stretches *over* me. Protective and reassuring. I'm wet but warm and held in an enveloping womb-like embrace. Her left hand clings to mine that clutches the pistol. Like being in the womb I know something bad is coming and I don't want to go. I want to stay here. Warm, wet and safe.

The thumb of my left hand strokes her cheek, smudging the grime and water and I can't help but let it drift down to her mouth with a sudden desire to feel the softness of her lips. So gently I touch, so gently I feel. Her eyes squeeze tighter closed and she shifts position trying to be closer to me. Fear on her face, pain too but the touch reassures her. She opens her eyes, so red and bloodshot but not so bad to look at now and not as bad as they were before. Her pupils retract from going dark to light. Dishpans that become pinpricks. She swallows and I can feel the movement of her throat on my hand holding the gun. The tip of her tongue flicks out to wet the middle of her lips and her breath quavers with a tremble that hurts me more than anything else.

What she did was beyond awful. The death she gave. The torture and agony that was given with pleasure. The hunting and seeking those so terrified they begged and wept for mercy. But it wasn't her. It wasn't this person. It was the thing inside. The infection that was given to her by Darren. I can feel the terror she must have felt at being taken by him. The pure heart stopping horror at being bitten and knowing she will die and come back and all the time being held by a crazed strange man. Priests give absolution but there is no absolution to be given for she is not the sinner. I cannot give her absolution or forgiveness. I cannot take the pain away or make this better, but I can give some small comfort. I move closer with the edge of my thumb under her chin that tilts her head up a fraction of an inch. She blinks in surprise and the breath catches in her throat. Yearning eyes that seek peace, that this is another foul trick to be snatched away by a harsh comment designed to hurt her soul in the last few seconds of her life. Her eyes widen and a tear falls from the corner.

'Don't cry,' I whisper and my lips touch hers. Instantly she responds, pushing up and into me as though desperate for the sanctity of the touch of another human being showing love and being hungry for a sensation other than pain or deep regret. Everything feels okay now. We're safe and not here. Our lips stay touching in an eternal kiss and the second that contact was made I knew I had wanted to kiss her since the first time I saw her. No Lani. No infected undead. No death or pain but a simple kiss and one given with love.

My tongue darts out to touch her lips. An act done to show I do not fear being infected by her and I am not appalled by her or the person she is. But more than that, I do it because I want to, because I need to. Tighter still she holds me and our tongues meet in the most erotic kiss I have ever known and it soars my heart into heaven and makes me want life. This. This is the thing we yearn for. This is the reason for living and being. For this feeling now. To be with someone you love and care for. To feel that thrill of contact and knowing the other person shares with you as you share with them.

It strengthens me. It gives me hope but more than that it gives me the purity of thought that I want Cookey, Blowers, Nick and Mo Mo to have this feeling. I want Clarence to feel peace of mind and for Paula and Roy to live on. I have tasted this and had this. They must have this. Our kind must have this. The kiss goes on and it floods me with energy and purpose. The good of it seeps into my heart while the sadness of the future tells me what is destined if this ends now. Like in the dream when Marcy kissed me and made me go back to fight in the munitions factory. Her. Marcy. That connection is this. That she gives me hope because she did the foulest of deeds yet no longer does she desire those acts but seeks to amend the wrongs and only through me can they be amended. Only through us. Through the team. The few that have come together to make a stand and defy that which seeks to eradicate us.

My legs stiffen. My body stiffens. My feet planted on the door and the rigidity of my body forces the power from my shoulder wedged into the toilet down to those feet. She stiffens too with the same power. Our eyes snap open while we kiss and hold that kiss. Forcing our bodies to go strong with every nerve and sinew straining to do what must be done. Not one can do this. Not one can achieve this. Two can do this. A combined strength that works in the harmony given by the kiss we share. A circle formed from my feet, up my legs through my back and through my mouth and into her body and down to her feet and when our tongues meet so soft and gentle so that power grows and that door is pushed away and against the infected.

Then it hits. The realisation that the team haven't come because they've been unable to come. Dave hasn't come because he'd know to stay with them if they were in danger and the risk must be real and immediate to keep him away from me. Gunshots in the distance. Sustained bursts of fire and single shots taken. More further away. Multiple weapons being fired. The Saxon is in the middle and we've each only got the magazines in our pockets and no hand weapons.

It happens without conscious thought or planning. On my feet with the pistol in one hand while I wrench the fucking door open and face the beasts while the cleanest, purist, most sterile form of rage I have ever known pulses through my body. I meet them coming through. I meet them head on with the pistol firing into brains that burst apart with grey matter spraying out. Everything slows. I pick the shots. The hallway beyond the bathroom door is narrow and only a few could fit there and I blast them away faster than they can charge in towards me.

THE UNDEAD DAY SEVENTEEN

Marcy screaming. Gunshots. Howls and snarls and my own voice roaring.

Fear me. Fear what I am. Fear what I can do to you. I fight for Marcy. I fight for my friends so they may experience what I just did. So they may savour the love of a person that loves them. I fight for Dave who stays with the team and ignores every instinct in his head to turn and run to me.

The pistol empties. I cast it aside and drop down to pick the knife up and as I rise I surge out and into them with the point driving up through a throat. I stab and stab until the neck is flapping ragged skin that pours blood. I stab one to the right while my left hand draws the one on the left into me so I can sink my teeth into the side of his neck. I bite deep and feel the gushing blood pumping out, spraying me in hot metallic crimson arterial blood. He goes down and I twist the knife in the neck of the other one before yanking it clear. A boot to the chest of one reaching the top of the stairs and she goes flying back to crash into those behind.

It's not enough. I need more. I want more. I launch myself from the top step and sail down into them and the darkness of my eyes makes them wilt and stagger back.

Frenzied stabbing. Biting and clawing. I hack at anything near me with such speed that it makes them feel as slow as they were in the daytime when this first began. They fear me. They wilt back and I can see the conflict of the urges given to them by the infection inside. They attack but wilt. They flay out but are killed in a dirty close quarters fight that has entrails and body parts falling with ease. I get bit, punched, kicked, gouged and shoved but what I give back is worse.

I stab into groins and slit stomachs open. I bite noses off and relish in the destruction I am able to give. An ear comes away in my mouth but it's not enough so I stab the earless thing in the face through the eye socket. A hand claws my face so I bite down on the thumb and rip it free with the ragging motion that Meredith does. I am an animal. I am Meredith. I am Dave with the speed I use. I am Clarence with awesome strength. I smile and laugh like Cookey. I have passion like Blowers and I am as fierce and loyal as Nick. At the bottom of the stairs I trip and slip over dead bodies and laugh a maniacal laugh as I fight dirtier than I have ever fought before.

Marcy at the top staring down. I fight for Marcy. I fight for them all. A big man takes me down with his body weight but I get the knife up into his gut and saw it sideways to spill the innards while I clamp my mouth on his cheek and tear the flesh away. Nothing is beyond me. I spit the flesh aside and heave him off before scrambling to my feet and lurching out the open front door and somewhere behind the raging mask of bloodlust my mind makes the connection that they've thinned out and that thought sends a shiver of fear that they've split the team and gone after them.

In two strides that thought process is complete. I can make the Saxon and get to the GPMG or my axe. I can do this. I run fast in a straight line and they charge to converge in a head on rushing howl. I can make it. I can get there. They've thinned out and reduced their numbers to go after the others. My stride lengthens and my eyes remain fixed on the broad side of the vehicle. Feet pounding the earth, arms pumping and I give it everything I've got to run through them in the pure held belief I will get there.

I don't get there.

I get taken out from the side and swept up high off my feet by an undead that looks eerily like Jimmy Carr with a high forehead and gleaming white teeth. He's naked though, Jimmy Carr that is. Naked and pumped up and snarling to show me the gleaming white teeth while ripping me off my feet and into the horde coming from the other way. I go down in a tangle of limbs, the air whacked from my lungs by naked Jimmy Carr landing on me with his bollocks far too close to my face for comfort. I could bite them but biting Jimmy Carr's testicles just seems wrong.

More add to the scrum. The weight of them bearing down, pinning me in place. Bodies over my legs and torso. I can't breathe or see anything. Darkness and the close up stench of filthy decaying bodies covered in shit and gore. Still they come, flinging themselves onto the mound like lemmings from a cliff. I writhe and buck and get twatted round the face by Jimmy Carr's testicles. I try and headbutt up but knock gently against the saggy sack which makes me gag more than anything else so far. The weight above drives him down and soon his naked groin is smothering my face with his anus far too close to my mouth. I want to scream but I can't breathe and the air is being pressed further from my lungs.

Something hot and wet dribbles across my chin and the downwards force applied is not only crushing the life from me but the shit from Jimmy Carr's bowels that oozes from his arse. The smell makes me gag and I try and twist my head away but manage an inch at the best. Another wet squirt and more pushes out. My mouth clamped shut but I can feel it hit my chin and dribble down my neck and cheeks. Whimpering in my throat, preening like a baby but there is nowhere to go and nothing I can do to stop it. Flashes of light in my eyes now as the oxygen is cut from my brain. A dull thunder of blood roaring through my ears. Another noise joins the tricks of sensations as I sink into unconsciousness. Bangs. Sharp retorts from close by and several sound out before I recognise the sound of gunfire. A single weapon being fired then something else. A drumming noise that I can feel through the ground that gets faster and closer. The weapon fires again and the drumming impacts the mound on top of me with a shuddering jarring sensation but the weight is less now and I snatch air from the split second relief on my chest. It hurts like hell but it's enough to keep me alive for another few seconds.

The drumming fades then stops but starts again. Gaining faster and closer and again I can feel the vibrations through the ground. Something so familiar but I can't make the connection. It almost makes me scared, like a primeval sound ingrained to strike fear. The second impact shudders the bodies again and more are whipped off. The weapon fires dull and close. The drum fades, stops and comes back and the weapon fires. The third impact and I can start to buck and thrash at them. My body heaving with a frantic motion to get out and away. I kick and twist and beat the things on top of me and I realise my hand still grips the knife. I stab up and into anything that the blade can bite. I stab and thrust and twist side to side and amidst that frenzy so the drumming comes again.

Daylight above me. Enough bodies shifted to let light into the press. I fight harder, stabbing faster and the blood and shit spills over my body. A noise, animalistic and strange. Gunfire. I surge up, swimming and fighting against the writhing once human forms that groan and snarl.

My head breaks through them, my shoulders pushing to get up. My legs kicking to find purchase and all the time stabbing and punching. I grasp the long greasy hair of a woman and drive the point of the knife into her throat and saw until she goes limp enough to stop fighting.

In my peripheral vision I see something huge looming. A shadow that blots the sun and it rears up on back legs to pummel out with hard hooves that smash the skull of a fully grown man to pieces. It drops and rears up again, fast as lighting and kicking out. Whinnying but a harder whinny from a horse I have never heard. An angry sound, aggressive and baleful. With the sun behind it I can't see details, just the size and shape that drops, turns and lifts. The man on the back holding an assault rifle and gripping the reins one handed. The death it gives out is staggering. Clarence is strong but he has nothing compared to this beast. It takes them down with a simple turn that drives its back end into their shoulders with enough force to send them flying metres to the side.

Mesmerising and wonderful in a way only nature can be. Then it runs off and the connection to the drumming sound is made. Heavy hooves that thunder on the hard earth. It stops, turns and comes back with a head that thrashes side to side and eyes that glare without fear but pure stubborn aggression. It heads straight for the mound I am still emerging from and I watch as the infected lunge to intercept it only to get knocked flat and trampled one after the other without the blink of an eye. The realisation hits as the rider waves his assault rifle at me in wild panic. He has no control of the direction or steerage and waves frantically for me to get down, get up, run or do something because he can't bloody stop.

I scream and with new found strength in my limbs I surge up and dive free as the horse leaps to jump the mound but purposefully kicks down and uses the bodies as a ramp with bone breaking force. I'm screaming. The rider is screaming and the horse is killing zombies while we gibber in fright.

It lands from the mound and rears straight back up and then back down to break the spine of a man. Stamping down on the body it turns with ruthless precision while the rider hangs on for dear life. As it turns we lock eyes for a second then the horse canters off to gain space and speed for the return.

A scream behind me. Not me. Is it me? Am I still screaming? Marcy! Everyone is crammed into the space between me and the front door to the house while the rest of the square is now empty. Dead bodies are thick on the ground, mangled and bloodied. Some from being stabbed, others from being shot but most from the horse trampling and kicking down and without the crazed bloodlust driving me on the going is suddenly very hard. Tripping on limbs, slipping on blood and getting snagged by entrails.

Into the house and Marcy in the kitchen stabbing out to a cluster of undead males converging on her. A hastily grabbed kitchen knife but it's a serrated blade and not up to the job. Three of them. All rangy and thin with decaying skin and sickening grey pallor. She backs into the kitchen cupboards as I charge into the side of them with a yell. A tangle of limbs as we crash through into the alcove of the back door. Stabbing down and stamping as they thrash to get past me.

Arms wrap round my neck and for a second I think it's Marcy either trying to pull me away or attacking from behind. They grip tighter, squeezing hard to crush my throat. I jerk up and away while spinning round and grasping to pull the arms away. What I grip are the tiny wrists of a child. Then the tiny teeth of the child bite into the back of my shoulder and I howl with pain while trying to prise its grip off my neck. It clings on and two little legs wrap round my waist like a limpet. Another child flies past my head and on the turn I see Marcy fending off another trio of small bodies whipping about trying to attack her. Children everywhere. Under my feet, round my legs and Marcy flailing trying to knock them away. The noises are the worst thing, like children trying to be monsters but with clawed hands and wild bloodshot eyes.

'Get it off,' I hiss the words out while spinning on the spot and trying to pull the little shit's arms from my throat and all the time being bitten in the shoulder, 'Marcy...'

'Busy!'

'Fuck's sake,' I go to kick an undead child away but it dodges and I overextend with the thrust and get pulled down backwards from the extra weight on my shoulders. The landing kills it. Crushed and broken from my heavy body impacting hard and I can feel the small bones cracking and a sense of enormous guilt floods through me. I've killed children before, loads of them but this act sickens me to the core.

The rest stop attacking and stare fixed at me with a weird, intense expression. Then one of them bursts into tears. A small girl that once had long black hair. She cries and sobs with real tears coursing down her grey face. The rest follow suit with faces screwing up in expressions of abject pity and their tiny voices wailing sorrowfully. Marcy reels away aghast at the sight and my shock is visible. The infection playing tricks. The infection detecting the guilt I felt and instantly using the advantage.

'Mummy,' a single world stuttered between sobs and it makes my stomach churn with terror at what we've just done. Children, small children with tiny hands and thin legs and long hair. Crying and standing pitifully sad with arms hanging limp.

'Mummy...' another one plays the trick and wraps her own arms round her body as though cold and afraid, she snivels and shudders with fright and looks up at me with huge terrified eyes.

'Marcy...' I say in a whisper, '...Marcy...'

'Go,' she says and backs into me. Facing the children she pushes me backwards towards the rear door, 'go...'

'Mummy!' One of the girls holds her arms out for a hug and we both scream and turn to fight through the dead bodies and wrench the back door open so we can run into the garden.

'Please mummy...' It follows us out with those arms raised and begging to be hugged. The others behind her, 'mummy...please mummy...' they copy the first and walk slowly begging to be hugged with hands held out in front.

'You're sick,' I shout in disgust, 'fucking sick...'

'Mummy please...'

'Stop doing that...it's sick,' I back away pointing the knife at the lead child.

'I'm sorry mummy.'

'Oh you cunt.'

'Howie!'

'What? It's not a real child.'

'Don't be angry at me, Howie,' the child speaks with a hoarse rattling voice that just makes the effect even worse.

'Don't use my name you evil fucker,' I rage at the infection within the dead child stalking us down the garden.

'I'm sorry, Howie.'

'Oh you fucker...you bloody wait...'

'I'm better now, Howie. Really I am.'

'Try this on Dave and see what happens.'

'We're better now,' the child gargles the words out, the rest of the children out in a wide line behind her.

'Argh,' I dart forward with the knife but stop mid swing and jump about in temper instead. The thought is there now. The mere suggestion that this is a child and not a monster. So small and weak with her arms held out and adopting a sad expression, 'oh you little sod,' I shout, 'Marcy...you do it.'

'Me?' She looks at me like I just offered to shit in her mouth.

'Yeah you, you've killed kids before.'

'What?!'

'Well you have, kill it...'

'I can't believe you just said that,' she says glaring at me.

'Just kill it,' I nod eagerly at the child, 'go on...get it.'

'I'm not Meredith,' she snaps, 'don't tell me to *get it*...'

'Eh?' I look from the child to her, 'what? I just meant...'

'And you've killed enough kids by now...'

'Yeah but...'

'You squashed one in the kitchen about thirty seconds ago.'

'It was on my back and I fell!'

'You stilled killed it.'

'Yeah but...so yeah I did one so you do this one.'

'Oh for the love of God! Give me that knife...right,' she grips the handle then screws her face up in disgust, 'it's filthy...' she swaps the knife from her right hand to the left and stares down at her right palm, 'Howie,' she admonishes me, 'this is disgusting.'

'What? I was bloody using it.'

'Bloody isn't the word...what's that smell? That's...' she sniffs her hand once then again, 'that's shit!'

'Er...'

'Howie, there is shit on the knife handle.'

'Forget that...just kill that bloody child!'

'How did you get shit on the handle? Oh my god...what is that?'

'What?'

'On your chin? Is that shit?'

'Eh?' I reach up to touch the smearing goo at the same time the stench hits me, 'oh,' I say dumbly, 'Jimmy Carr shit on my chin.'

She blanches, blinking a few times and staring at me in utter confusion, 'I'm so sorry,' she says politely, 'what did you say?'

'Jimmy Carr, he was naked and shit on my chin,' I nod as though it's the most normal explanation ever given, 'what? He did! He's right out there getting trampled by the fucking great big horse.'

'A horse? What horse? Jimmy Carr? You've lost it.'

'Lost it? I haven't bloody lost anything. Jimmy Carr was naked and landed on top of me and shit on my chin then the horse came and squashed him. WHAT?! That happened… it happened…stop looking at me like that.'

'Of course it did,' she rolls her eyes and looks away, 'right,' she fixes her gaze on the child.

'It bloody happened!'

'Of course it did,' she repeats without looking at me and takes a tentative grip of the handle on the knife, 'this is gross.'

'Blame Jimmy Carr.'

'Of course and I suppose Bernard Matthews was shoving the handle up his backside.'

'Bernard Matthews?'

'I meant Manning!'

'You said Matthews.'

'I meant Manning.'

'Bernard Matthews did the turkey stuff.'

'I know who Bernard Matthews is.'

'Anyway, they're both dead.'

'So is Jimmy Carr apparently, by a big unicorn that just happened to appear.'

'Horse,' I say quietly, 'it was a horse not a unicorn. Can you please just stab that child.'

'I AM!'

'Well do it then!'

'I WILL!'

'GO ON THEN!'

'STOP SHOUTING AT ME!'

'YOU'RE SHOUTING....okay, okay fine...I'm not shouting...now please will you stab that freaky fucking child.'

'Please, Marcy,' the child bleats.

'SHUT UP,' we both roar at the child.

'Are you stabbing it or...'

'I can't,' she turns to me with a wince, 'you'll have to do it.'

'Oh for fuck's sake, listen why don't we just leg it.'

'Yeah, let's do that,' she says eagerly.

'SHIT!' We both run as the child launches itself at Marcy's legs and perhaps it wasn't the best idea to give the plan away. We sprint down the garden and leap high to gain the top of the fence with the mini horde of mini zombies charging after us. Both of us get halfway over and both of us get little teeth biting into our ankles. We kick out, cursing and flailing until enough of our weight gets over the edge and we fall tumbling down the other side clutching sore ankles.

'Bit me,' Marcy groans, 'right on the ankle bone.'

'Did it break the skin?'

'Duh,' she says with a withering look, 'I'm already infected.'

'Alright I bloody forgot.'

'How can you forget something like that?'

'I can't keep track of everyone bitten and immune, Marcy.'

'What you mean Blowers, Cookey, Reginald, Me and you? Five?'

'Sod off my ankle hurts.'

'Did it bite the bone?'

'No the fleshy bit.'

'Then you don't know what pain is.'

'*I* don't know what pain is? I got bit on the shoulder... and the arm...and the thigh...'

'Okay, hero. *Sorry,*' she says sarcastically.

'And Jimmy Carr shit on my chin.'

'Of course he did.'

'He did!'

'Yep, sure. And you're just leaving it there for what reason exactly?'

'What? I don't have any water. Do you have any water?'

'Spit, Howie. Spit on your hand and wipe it off.'

'It'll smear everywhere.'

'So you're just going to leave it there?'

'You spit and wipe it.'

'No way. I'm not wiping my hand on your shitty chin.'

'Well I'm not doing it either.'

'Your top is still wet, use that.'

'Eh?' I look down at my still sodden top, 'it's covered in shit too.'

'Oh my g....use the other side then you idiot.'

'I'll use yours if you don't stop yelling at me.'

'You will not.'

'I bloody will,' I stand up with a wince.

'Really,' she stands to glare at me, 'you will not.'

'Yours is clean,' I point out, 'because I was out there fighting to save you and…'

'I was inside fighting the ones you left while you were outside pissing about.'

'Oh the children? Sorry I left you a small child to fend off.'

'Please clean your chin, I can't look at you,' she turns away in disgust.

'Give me your clean top then.'

'Not a chance.'

'Let me use the back, that's wet and clean…'

'You are not wiping your shit on my top.'

'Jimmy Carrs shit not mine…'

We both stop to stare at the sound of hooves drumming across the ground and the sight of the horse appearing at the end of the row of fences. A strangled yell coming from the rider clinging onto the reins and a look of pure panic on his face. They thunder past heading further into the meadow and the thicket of trees at the far end.

Silence between us. Not a word uttered. I cough then cough again when she doesn't say anything.

'Horse,' I say, 'that was a horse.'

'I saw it,' she replies stiffly.

'Yep, a horse…so?'

'So what?'

'Apologise then.'

'Yeah right. I'm a woman, Howie. I don't do apologies.'

'Oh you…'

'What?' She smiles a dazzling grin, 'what was that honey?'

'Don't you honey me.'

'There there,' she smiles sweetly, 'wipe the shit off your chin and we can move along.'

'Fine,' I tug my filthy top off and use the back to scrub at the drying faeces on my face as the first child drops down from the fence. We both start running. The killers of hundreds that have done the most terrible things since this began and we flee from a few children after getting the thought lodged into our minds that they're real children.

'Fuck!' I cry out as more undead drop from the backs of the fences we're alongside off. Forced to veer off into the meadow we run with me holding my filthy top and Marcy clutching the shit smeared knife, 'give me the knife,' I hold my hand out and take the hilt from her while risking a glance backwards. Still loads of them and they show no signs of slowing down. The children are at the front, running flat out with little arms pumping furiously and remarkably serious expressions on their faces. I trip, snagging the tip of my toes on a hole in the hard compacted earth. With a yelp I go down hard with the knife flying off to be lost in the long grass.

She drops back, gripping my hand to tug me up onto my feet. No time to go for the knife so we run with feet lifting higher than normal to avoid the dips and rises of the rough ground. Taxing and hard work and we gasp for air as the sound of drumming comes from the left side and the horse bursting from the thicket of trees.

The speed of the beast covers the ground in seconds. The rider still clearly having no hope of controlling the horses direction or speed but hanging on with the same terrified look. A slight variance of direction and the horse swishes past us with the man on the back screaming out. The noise of bodies being slammed into comes from behind. We both turn and see the children we were so afraid of getting flung and trampled as the horse goes straight through them and runs on towards the square.

We need the same direction but if we change now the horde behind will cut us off. With no choice we run on, hoping to drawn them out and away from the buildings enough so we can turn and somehow get back to the Saxon.

The change comes quickly. The sunlight fades into shade and so abruptly I cast my eyes up to see the unnoticed thick clouds filling the sky. Dark and grey. Loaded and ready to open.

'Rain,' I get the word out but Marcy focusses on running, straining from the hard ground, the heat and the energy sapping constant action.

The first few drops are gorgeous. Fat dollops of water that hit the top of my head and provide an instant cooling effect. More follow until a light shower works to soothe the heat in our faces. Perfect and timed just right to give us the boost we need. Legs working hard, burning from the pain of having to hold that door shut but the rain gives us enough to keep going. Then it gets harder. Falling heavier and the view in front becomes a blur of grey and a billion drops of water spatter the ground on all sides.

We're rinsed clean and I use my hands to rub my face as we sprint on. Open mouths turned up and mine fills quickly to quench my parched mouth and throat. It tastes perfect. Wondrously clean and fresh, warm but cooler than the air we've been used to.

Still it gets heavier. A shower into a downpour into an all-out deluge from the heavens above. The compacted earth can't keep up and soon the puddles form which make the going even harder. Our view is restricted to a few feet ahead at best. Marcy gasps with water pouring from the point of her chin. I blink and wipe my eyes trying to keep them clear. A deluge that increases second by second. The noise becomes so loud. A cacophony of drums beating all around us.

Water being kicked up by our feet and it makes the running harder, more effort is needed on each lift of each foot with an increase of friction and weight. Blinding rain that hammers down to sting our heads and exposed skin. A monsoon of a tropical storm and streams are formed in the dips of the ground. We wade through, tripping and slipping. I go down first and get coated in mud. Marcy helps me up and within seconds she slips and lands heavy. We cling to each other, guiding and pulling on. Glances back but nothing to be seen in the few feet of vision we have. They won't stop. This rain won't slow them down but it does slow us down.

The horse came from the left and went on to the right towards the square. I can hope we've stayed in a forward straight direction and with the opportunity of not being seen I guide Marcy on a hard right angle.

All direction is lost from the lack of features to use to gain a bearing. No sounds other than the rain and our feet splodging through the increasingly slippery mud.

Holding hands and I can feel the energy draining from her. Feet landing heavily. Her head drooping and the limpness of her arm all point to exhaustion and fatigue.

'Keep going,' I urge her on. She nods and stays silent but I can see the determination in her face.

So we run. We run on slowly and with every stride now an effort in focus and purpose and all we can do is hope we find the square before they find us.

CHAPTER TWENTY-FOUR

Paula in front with Roy right behind her, urging her to keep going. Clarence behind them forcing Reginald to stay the pace and Dave bringing up the rear. Intensely worried but the hordes converging from all three sides behind them force them to run. Ammunition dangerously low. No hand weapons other than the knives held by Dave. Reginald wheezing from the effort. Roy glancing back in worry at the thick lines forcing then onwards. Clarence ignoring his own pain to reach out a steadying hand to Reginald at his side.

Dave calculates and plans. Always planning. Always thinking. He can stop and fight but they'll pour past him to keep driving the others away from Mr Howie. If he knew they would focus on him he would turn back. The gunfire in the distance ahead is the unmistakable sound of SA80 assault rifles being fired on single shot. Four of them and the gaps between each shot tell him they are picking their targets with care. That also means the lads are facing a big group and are down to the last of their ammunition.

A hope that he would hear the GPMG coming from the

square that would signify Mr Howie getting to the Saxon. Nothing. Just the snarling fury of the things chasing them away. That's what they're doing. Chasing. Making them flee. Dave understands a tactical withdrawal and understands a strategy of drawing the enemy to an advantage point but running away? Dave doesn't run away. Dave runs towards. But he can't run towards so he has to run away. Not right. Not right at all.

The village is close and from the field they crash through a hedge onto a lane and find instant relief from a hardtop to run along. Speed can be gained and they push on, working into the shade given by the tree tops overhead. Sweat pouring down all but one face. Dave detects the humidity increasing and first looks up at the sky then back at the sound of gunfire coming from the square. His head cocks at the noise, eyes as sharp as Meredith.

'What's that?' Clarence looks back with the same expression.

'Colt M4 Carbine,' Dave says, 'with a folding stock.'

'How the hell can you tell if...never mind...who's firing it?'

'I don't...'

'It was a rhetorical question, Dave.'

'Actually,' Reginald wheezes, 'a rhetorical question is a figure of speech used in the manner of asking a question but one done to enforce a point rather than to actually get an answer.'

'That's what I said.'

'You asked a question,' Reginald gasps for air between words, 'not a rhetorical question but just a question and if I may say so a rather stupid question.'

'Focus on running,' Clarence snaps.

A new weapon being fired. An American weapon

issued to American troops but the M4 carbine with a folding stock is not the average issue weapon for American soldiers. A weapon like that is issued to Special Forces, or at least it was until they upgraded and started using a wider range of tactical weapons. That would mean the firer is not a current serving US Special Forces but someone who managed to obtain a weapon. He listens to the fire rate. Single shots then a sustained burst followed by sporadic bursts, untimed, rushed and not belonging to any trained discipline.

The anxiety increases and a desperate urge to turn round and run back but the horde behind them are crashing through the hedge now and far too great in number.

The lane winds through the village and past the local pub and Roy takes the same route as the one used by the lads earlier. Sharp turns into avenues and wide paths.

A worried glance from Clarence at Reginald's face that has gone from bright red to blotchy and pale. A sign that fatigue is threatening to drop him any second. They have to get somewhere, find something or hide. The desperation increases. Legs burning and chests heaving for air. The sound of the infected behind only serves to tell them what will happen if they stop or slow down.

'Keep going,' Clarence's hand shoots out to guide the faltering steps.

'I...'

'You can and you will,' Clarence injects force into his voice, 'you will run or they will tear you apart in seconds and the rest of us too.'

Reginald shoots a terrified look up at the broad glaring face of Clarence. The pain is indescribable but the indignity is worse. Being forced to get hot and sweaty when he is a man of learning and culture, not a common thug who goes galloping around streets being chased.

Into another lane and they flow down with ragged breaths and heavy feet pounding the surface.

'Ahead,' Roy gets to the bend and spots the first dead bodies. Dave sprints through ready to fight and instantly spots the tell-tale signs of gunshots wounds. Good strikes and the lads aim is getting better. Heads blown apart and far fewer missed shoulder and torso shots. He spots the fallen tree and instantly feels a sense of pride at Blowers finding a hard cover firing position. Spent shells litter the ground, a full magazine fired by each lad and a pile of half-eaten puke already drying out. He spots beans and ravioli and knows they took too much food on without consideration of the consequences. A mental note to give advice on the size of meals to be taken.

The others catch up and wheeze their way round the tree before they keep plodding on down the road and past the houses. It gets worse. Drained and exhausted and every glance back shows they are inching closer. Prickles of fear in Clarence and Roy. Paula too focussed on running and keeping moving to think anything. Reginald missing Marcy. Dave fretting about Mr Howie. On they go. Stitches form. Chests tighten. They reach a junction and take the main road. The first drops of rain fall as every pair of eyes flicks down to a single magazine lying on the tarmac.

CHAPTER TWENTY-FIVE

Silence only broken by the sound of tearing flesh as Meredith tugs at the arm of the dead body.

A second hockey player pulls her helmet off to reveal another mane of long hair tumbling free. A third follows suit with slender fingers that sweep the loose strands free from her forehead. The fourth and last stands watching Meredith tugging backwards with her arse in the air and her mouth clamped on the arm that finally breaks free with strands of skin stretching out like spaghetti and instantly heaves to bend over and puke at the sight. A strangled noise and she works with frantic movements to undo the clasp before the inside of the helmet fills with vomit. It gets thrown aside and she drops to puke again as Meredith detaches the arm and wanders over holding the limb to show the kneeling woman.

Cookey blinks and stares at Charlie. Nick grins, chuckling quietly with a slow shake of his head as Blowers and Mo Mo copy Cookey and just stare.

'Are you okay?' Charlie bends slightly forward with a look of worry.

'Huh?' Cookey bleats.

Charlie lifts her eyebrows and looks to the others. One slightly smaller with darker skin and younger in years, she heard them call him Mo. Nick, the one chuckling and Blowers their leader staring as dumbly as Cookey.

Cookey finally pulls his gaze away to look at the other two standing hockey players but not seeing the fourth kneeling over to vomit, 'girls,' he says, 'oh my god...oh my actual fucking god...an actual hockey team...like...like an actual girls hockey team...' his mind in overdrive and gibbering in wonder, blinking and shuffling on the spot, 'an actual girls hockey team....' He repeats and shakes his head, 'here,' he says quickly, 'have you got a coach driver called Bert?'

'Bert?' Charlie asks as Nick bursts out with a snort of laughter, 'there *was* a coach driver but I don't know his name,' Charlie says with a slight smile at the absurd and surreal nature of the situation. Standing amidst a sea of broken bodies, blood and gore everywhere.

'Are you here looking for our coach driver?' a confused Charlie asks, 'I thought you just wanted water...'

'He wanted Bert,' Cookey points quickly at Blowers.

'No,' Blowers sighs, 'I did not want Bert.'

'Er, he left on the first night,' Charlie says softly, 'he er, he never came back. I am so sorry if he was your father or...'

'Oh poor Blowers,' Cookey smirks, 'you've missed Bert.'

'Such a dick,' Blowers groans, 'we don't want the coach driver or anyone called Bert.'

'But he said you were looking for Bert,' Charlie says pointing at Cookey.

'Poor Bert,' Cookey says.

'There was no Bert!' Blowers snaps as Nick wipes the tears from his face.

'Blinky,' Charlie calls out to the kneeling girl still heaving her guts up, 'what was the coach driver called?'

'Oh my god,' Blowers groans again, 'Cookey you are such a twat.'

'He was Polish,' the kneeling girl says between heaves, 'Mario or Marius? Something...' she cuts off to puke again.

'Oh he was wasn't he,' Charlie says, 'yes, yes he was Polish. Lovely man though, er...so no, we haven't seen Bert.'

'There was no Bert,' Blowers repeats.

'No, that's right we never had a Bert,' Charlie confirms, 'unless he was a groundsman or...'

'Groundsman Bert,' Cookey laughs, 'will that do you, Blowers?'

'Blinky,' Charlie calls out again, 'do you know the names of any of the groundsmen?'

'No I...' Blinky heaves a final effort and wipes the back of her hand across her mouth, 'don't think so,' she says with a belch and stands up, 'did you know your dog has an arm in his mouth?'

'It's a her,' Nick says with an effort to stop laughing, 'and yeah she does that.'

'Does what?'

'Er...gets arms,' Nick says.

'Why?'

'Why? I don't know,' Nick says with the smile frozen on his face.

'Bit strange isn't it,' Blinky states, red haired with a blaze of freckles across her nose and a glare only broken by the constant blinking.

'Blinky,' Charlie says, 'don't be rude. So no chaps, sorry we don't know anyone called Bert. There might be some records in the main office or something if that helps?'

'Chaps?' Cookey grins with delight, 'so are you a hockey team then?'

Charlie stares, Blinky blinks. Mo Mo shakes his head and Nick snorts a snort of laughter again while Blowers groans. The first fat dollop of rain falls from the sky to land with a plonk on Charlie's helmet on the ground.

'Ignore him,' Blowers steps forward, 'he's got issues. I'm Blowers, that's...'

'Cookey,' Charlie points to Cookey, 'Nick...Mo and I think I heard them call you Blowers?'

Blowers shows surprise then glances back to the house as the rain starts drumming on the ground, 'you heard us then?'

Charlie nods, 'we heard you coming through the forest...'

'Those bloody cans,' Blowers says quickly, 'was that you?'

'Yes,' Charlie says with a firm nod, 'our early detection warning system. Blinky had the idea.'

'Oh,' Blowers says, 'er...good warning system.'

'Gonna punch 'em straight in the chops,' Cookey adopts a low gruff tone speaking into his hand.

'Pardon?' Charlie asks.

'Nothing,' Cookey says innocently, 'it's raining,' he adds knowledgably at the now heavy rain coming down.

Heavy rain sheets from the grey clouds and for a second all else is forgotten as faces are turned up to feel the relief given. Refreshing cooling water that rinses the sweat and gore. Soaking hair, cleansing faces, quenching thirst. Only Blinky doesn't look up but stares fixed at the dog trotting about with the arm in her mouth.

Charlie sighs heavily. Her long brown hair glistens down her back and the tone of her skin hints at a mixed ethnicity background. An open pleasant face and hazel eyes that stay closed to let the rain cascade down her face. An effect not lost on Cookey who stares mesmerised until spotting the accusing glare from Blinky then quickly looks away.

'**STAND TO…INCOMING…**'

'GROUND LITTERED,' Blowers roars back without a second of hesitation, 'fall back in a line here,' Blowers snaps the order as he paces back from the line of mangled corpses, 'Mo Mo, get those hockey sticks ready to hand out… Nick, hold the dog,' he turns to the hockey players, 'get behind our line, helmets back on.'

The change is instant and seamless. From warriors to joking lads and back to switched on keen eyed soldiers within a few minutes.

'Mine's covered in vomit,' Blinky calls out.

'Discard it and get back here,' Cookey replies, 'do it now, please.'

'Charlie,' Blowers gets her attention, 'where in the house can we use as a defensive point? A long corridor that will force them to bottleneck or…'

'Who? What?' Charlie snaps back through the driving rain now stinging their exposed skin.

'Our team is coming and they've got the fuckers right behind.'

'How can you…'

'No time. Answer the question. Where in the house can we use for defence? Nick,' Blowers turns away from the woman, 'get inside and find somewhere we can use.'

'On it.'

'Wait,' Blinky shouts, 'upstairs corridor is long and narrower than the stairs, will that do?'

'Perfect, we lead them in the house and up the

stairs....WE'RE READY,' Blowers shouts through the rain, 'HOW MANY?'

'TOO BLOODY MANY,' Clarence's voice booms through the grey blur of rain, the shout of a Viking giant that fills the air, 'ARE YOU EMPTY?'

'YES, HAND WEAPONS READY TO USE AND A DEFENSIVE POINT.'

Two figures loom first through the pouring monsoon. A man and a woman, both slightly older and looking strained from the effort of running. Behind them a small man wearing a shirt and tie with a giant holding a steadying hand on his shoulder. Huge, broad and bald headed. He sweeps his eyes over the ground then back to the lads and finally the hockey players, 'good work,' he nods once, 'defensive point?'

'Through the house and up the stairs,' Blowers replies, 'upstairs corridor is narrow.'

'It'll do,' Clarence says pushing Reginald through the line, 'get to the back and rest, Paula stay with him. Roy at the front with us.'

Authority handed over. The dark haired youth passes an invisible torch to the giant who assumes control with instant ease, 'weapons?'

'Here,' Mo Mo hands out the bladed hockey sticks, 'not great but...'

'They'll do,' Clarence passes one to Roy, 'you four,' he points at the hockey players, 'can you fight?'

'They can,' Blowers replies, 'wild, untrained but protected.'

'Oi,' Blinky snaps.

'You four will form a guard on those two,' Clarence points to Reginald and Paula kneeling on the ground, 'we'll lead them back to the front door first,' he adds pointing to the entrance to the house, 'where are the stairs?'

'Inside to the right,' Blowers says.

'On the right inside,' Blinky says at the same time.

'I AM DAVE…'

'What the…' Blinky blinks and stares through the blur to see a small man walking slowly backwards. A knife in each hand, stepping slow and careful but with the grace of a ballet dancer. In front of him a frightening looming rank of people staying close side by side and moving in perfect timing. Not running now but stalking. Forcing the small man back.

'I AM DAVE,' the small man booms an incredible voice, **'FIGHT ME.'**

Meredith growls, teeth showing as Dave walks back to the line and takes his place beside Clarence, 'don't eat so much and you won't vomit next time.'

'Sorry, Dave,' Cookey says instantly.

'Sorry,' Blowers says.

Charlie watches with stunned fascination at the fluid movements and exchanges between them.

'I need a weapon,' Paula says pushing into the line.

'Paula you should,' Clarence starts to say.

'Weapon!'

'Paula,' Mo Mo hands the last hockey stick down the line.

She takes it, examines the blades strapped firmly in place and nods, 'jolly hockey sticks,' she says and grips the shaft, 'come on then you bastards,' she growls, 'making me run…I hate running…'

'Are these carbon composite?' Roy asks politely leaning from the line to look down at the hockey players.

'Yes,' Blinky says firmly.

'Nice to meet you,' he nods amiably, 'I'm Roy.'

'Not now, Roy,' Paula says staring at the coming horde.

'I'm trying to be friendly and polite!'

'Not now, Roy,' Paula says loudly.

'Roy, where's your shoes?' Cookey looks down at the bare feet.

'Didn't have time to put them back on,' Roy says.

'Back on? Why did you take them off?'

'When we had sex,' Roy says.

'Roy!' Paula snaps.

'Oh,' Cookey nods, 'makes sense.'

'Unbelievable,' Paula shakes her head.

'I mean who has sex with their shoes on?' Cookey shrugs.

'Switch on...' Clarence calls out in a low voice, 'any sign of the boss?'

'None, you?' Blowers asks.

'Nothing,' Clarence says, 'we heard an M4 firing in the square but couldn't get back.'

'With a folding stock,' Dave says.

'M4?' Blowers asks, 'American?'

'Must be,' Clarence replies, 'we'll sort these and head back.'

Sort these and head back? Who are these people? Charlie takes in the confidence and absolute certainty of not getting killed. Outnumbered, vastly outnumbered and armed only with knives and hockey sticks.

'Are you from the army?' She asks quickly before the slowly encroaching horde get too close.

'No,' Clarence replies, 'not really...we're with Mr Howie from the fort.'

'Oh,' Charlie says as though it makes perfect sense.

'What are you doing here?' Paula asks without taking her eyes from the front rank of the infected.

'Selections,' Blinky states, 'for the England under twenty-ones hockey team.'

'A fucking hockey team,' Cookey sighs, 'best day ever.'

'Oh really?' Roy asks.

Charlie nods, 'first day here when it happened. Er, why aren't they charging at us?'

'We're being held,' Clarence rumbles, 'so they have time to get Mr Howie and Marcy...but if they're still trying to keep us here then it means they haven't actually got the boss yet...HAVE YOU?' He roars at the undead, 'ALL OF YOU CANNOT TAKE ONE MAN...'

'That's done it,' Nick remarks and his hand lifts from the neck of Meredith as she strides out at the now charging horde. An incredible noise of howling infected and the roars from the team as they step forward, brace and start the fight.

'Sod this,' Blinky starts to move towards the fight but gets a hand clutching the protective pad on her arm.

'They said to stay with him,' Charlie says with a nod at Reginald.

'Stay with him then,' Blinky tugs free, 'I'm not missing this, we should have done this days ago' she turns and runs to the end of the line to fight next to Nick. Bodies dropping one after the other. Clarence smashing away with pent up fury at being forced to run away. Dave slaughtering with incredible ease.

Charlie looks at the last two girls, Kazzer and Shell. The others now dead in amongst those bodies, bitten to be turned only to have their throats ripped out by the dog pacing through them.

Everyone else fled. Running away back to their homes or families throughout the country. None of the girls knew each other and had no allegiances or loyalties and it was only the first day of the selection trials so no bonds had been created. Only those with nothing to run back to stayed.

'FLANKED,' a voice shouting the alarm. Charlie whips round to see the main battle being held at the line of the newly arrived people but lines of the infected have peeled off from the back and taken advantage of the reduced visibility to go wide and come in hard from the sides in an effort to loop round the back of the fight. She hadn't put her helmet back on, didn't even think about it and doesn't have time now as the fight is upon her. Through the driving rain they come with faces twisted in pure wild violent intent. Only time to lift the hockey stick, feint left but dodge right and back to sweep the hook into the neck of the first one. With a grunt she fells it down and swings back up into the face of the next.

'FALL BACK,' the voice of the big man shouts the order.

'Go,' Charlie has no idea why the little tie wearing man has to be protected but she does it while he whimpers and scurries towards the front door. The living collapse into a tight ball with Reginald held securely behind them. Fighting out against an enemy so determined to keep driving them back and away from the square.

'Kazz...' the warning is too late and the girl is taken down from the side as she fights against one to the front. The girl screams as her flesh is torn apart by teeth gnashing to shred through her cheek. Her mouth fills with blood and is sprayed out. She flails and bucks but the damage is done. Shell drives her stick down onto the head of the male biting down on Kazzer. The blade cuts but is too blunt from lack of care and the superficial wound only warns the infected male of the second attack. He surges up with incredible speed and lunges for the helmeted head. Another jumps onto Shell's back. Charlie rushes forward but is beaten straight back by another three working to cut her off. The hockey stick, so familiar in her grasp, swings out with strength that has built up over years of constant play and training. Game after game. Working every week to get faster, harder and nimble to trap the ball, run to dodge and weave and strike for the goal. A body hardened to withstand the impact of players smashing into her from the sides. She whips out to break the jaw of the first, steps and backswings into the neck of the next. The third she trips with a hook to the ankle and a hard jerk to the left. It goes down and she stamps her foot on the face while beating furiously at the other two.

Shell screams as the fingers clamp firmly into her arms, legs and neck. Strong and fast but caught out and she cannot withstand the violence being applied. A fraction of a difference from her mind-set to that of Charlie and Blinky. This is still a game, there are rules of movements and what the other player can do and an over reliance on the protective clothing the goal defenders wear. A fatal mistake as the rancid hands shred the clothes apart and find the seams, joins and gaps to get through and at her soft skin underneath.

A filth encrusted fingernail slashes at her exposed neck, a sliver of a wound that, under normal circumstances, could be washed and would heal within a few days. The infection on the nail passes into her bloodstream which is taken through to her heart. Within two minutes the work is done. Her stomach grips with intense pain. Heart slowing. Vision blurring, sounds gone. She dies. Shell dies on the sodden ground from a single nick caused by a nail.

What comes back is instant and charged. Chemicals that surge from glands into her bloodstream. Her eyes red bloodshot and her own mind-set now completely absorbed by the hive mind of the infected driving her on. These must be killed. Images of tearing them apart flood through her mind. Pulsing sensations ramped well beyond that of a psychotic killer or a mentally deranged patient intent on causing harm. The end goal is not to cause pain but to end them and please the infection. Do what is ordered. Join the group. Be part of the base state of being in this new world. Belonging, loyalty, intense hatred, rage and the tiniest glimmer of individuality so she can move independently to take advantage of gaps and openings.

Back through the door they go, Reginald first then Paula. Blinky fights with battle lust coursing through her veins. A hard player with a penchant for violence. She wasn't as pretty as some girls and lacked the social grace of so many others. She was direct, forthright, doesn't suffer fools and loved the hard tackling of the game. She also knew she was being monitored closely by the selections squad. They needed players who would show no fear but not players that would get sent off or disqualified for excessive violence, so she held it back on the pitch when so many times she just wanted to smash the fucking stick into the face of the other player. Now she can. So she does. She smashes and kills while a tiny voice at the back of her head still suggests meekly that this is wrong and she'll get sent off.

'Go,' Nick motions her quickly to fall back, 'GO...'

She wants to stay and fight. She doesn't want to turn but Blinky also knows team sports and when to do something for the benefit of the team so she drops back and gets through the door and curses as she realises Charlie and the others are still out there, which means she was the first through, which is a show of weakness.

Charlie comes next as Nick checks his side and yanks

her back to get through the door as the team fights into a tighter ball.

Blinky didn't puke earlier from the sight of the dog tearing the arm from the body. She puked because she always puked after a game. She played with such ferocity and aggression that vomiting post-game was normal.

'Shell?' She pants at Charlie heaving with a face full of shock, 'Kazzer?'

Charlie shakes her head once, 'dead.'

Blinky shrugs and spits to the side, life is cheap, 'you okay?'

'Fine,' Charlie turns the head shake into a head nod, 'you?'

'Loving it,' Blinky grins evilly, something else she did after every game and normally after being reprimanded by the referee.

'Move back,' Nick gets through followed by a rapid influx of Cookey, Blowers, Roy and Clarence until Dave remains in the doorway holding the entirety of the horde back.

'Love him,' Blinky says with a nod at Dave, 'I want his babies.'

'I thought you were gay,' Charlie says.

'Not anymore,' Blinky says with the evil grin and blinks heavily. She always blinked like that when she wasn't on the pitch playing. The aggression didn't go away so it manifested in her eye lids, forcing them to blink more than normal.

'Stairs,' Clarence pushes through the group, stopping only to bend over and scoop Reginald up onto his feet, 'up you get...you okay?'

'Really I am not okay,' Reginald bursts in a rapid voice, 'I am assuredly not okay.'

'Good stuff,' Clarence cajoles him up the stairs, 'everyone up, who's got some fight left in 'em?' He asks the assembled gasping group.

The four lads step forward instantly, Roy a split second later. Blinky widens her eyes and takes the step, desperate to be picked for the team.

'Who are you?' Clarence glares at the woman.

'Blinky,' Blinky glares back.

'I like you,' Clarence growls in compliment at her spirit.

'I like him,' Blinky points at Dave in the doorway.

'I'm central,' Clarence plants his feet on the first step, ' I need one either side...we let Dave get through and up and we work a fighting retreat up the stairs...which side is the narrow corridor?'

'That side,' Blinky points to the right side at the top of the stairs.

'You lead us,' Clarence points at her.

'She leads I fight,' Blinky points at Charlie.

'I'll lead you,' Charlie says.

'I'll help Charlie lead,' Cookey says.

'Nick and Blowers then, either side of me...Roy and Cookey be ready to take over behind them.'

'And me,' Blinky says.

'Everyone get up....Paula, you okay?'

'Fine, stop asking me. I'm not feeble.'

'Sorry, just asking. Dave...we're ready when you are,' he calls out and braces with the hockey stick looking tiny in his hands. Nick and Blowers either side of his, ready to fight and hold the stairs.

Dave drops without warning. Simply turning and running across the hallway and up the stairs through the gap left. The horde waste no time but pour through the doors, tripping over the bodies cut down by Dave.

THE UNDEAD DAY SEVENTEEN

'Who has knives?' Dave asks at getting up the stairs.

'I got two,' Mo Mo says.

'Mine are blunt,' Dave says and takes the ones from Mo Mo.

'I got no weapons now,' Mo Mo says.

'You got me,' Dave nods and turns back to face down the stairs.

'You can get to the kitchen from the backstairs,' Charlie says quickly.

'Clarence, can you hold them?' Dave asks.

'Not forever,' Clarence grunts mid swing as they each step up the stairs to give ground.

'Mo Mo and Cookey on me...' Dave points them out, 'you,' Dave points at Charlie, 'does the kitchen lead to the other side of that door?' He points without looking down into the hallway and the door to the lounge area.

'Yes!' Blinky steps in front of Charlie, 'are you going to attack them from that side?'

'I am.'

'I'll show you,' she nods eagerly.

'Go,' Dave snaps a final look at the three holding the stairs and runs after the bulky clothing wearing woman as she runs up the stairs and through a myriad of corridors and doors until they reach a back service staircase.

Down into more corridors and finally into a store room connected to the back of the kitchen.

'Who are you?' Blinky asks while running.

'Dave,' Dave says.

'Blinky.'

'What is?'

'I am.'

'You are?'

'Yes.'

'Okay.'

The four get to the knives on the magnetic strip and give way while Dave pulls them down one after the other. 'Yours,' Dave hands one to Mo Mo, 'Alex,' he hands another one to Cookey.

'Got the stick, Dave,' Cookey says politely and *still* managing to make the word Dave sound like Sarge.

'Yours then,' Dave hands it to Blinky.

'Got a stick,' Blinky says.

'Dave,' Cookey whispers, 'say, Dave.'

'Got a stick, Dave,' Blinky says knowing she is in the company of a master.

'Mine,' Dave selects two equally sized knives and spins them over the back of his hands to test the weight and balance point, 'lead,' he orders Blinky.

She leads them back through the dining room and lounge where Dave signals for her to drop back and finds Meredith pushing past him. She'd got through the door and remembered the pan of water in the kitchen so ran that direction to quench her raging thirst. Then scuttled to a corner to take a desperate piss as Dave led the others through.

'We charge and divert their forces,' Dave says in his dull deadpan voice, 'draw them back to this doorway.'

'Got it,' Cookey says.

'Yep,' Mo Mo confirms the order.

'Yes, Dave,' Blinky copies the others.

They charge through and out into a line as Meredith once more leaps into the fray. The flanking movement done by the living this time and the first few kills are glorious and quick but the host bodies they fight ramp up a level with increasing savagery. A dirty fight. A filthy dirty sordid scrap and the infection pits the many against the few.

On the stairs they give ground, forced back step after step until Charlie and Paula join the front rank as they hack down at the never ending surge of bodies throwing themselves without any sign of weakening.

Dave spins through the ranks slicing and killing but the battle is pitted against them. Mo Mo stabbing but he slips on the wet floor and just manages to avoid the instant lunge taken on sight of the mishap. Voices shouting, giving warnings to each other but drowned out by the howling undead.

Clarence knows they can't hold the line. The hockey sticks give range but the blades are poor and no match for the axes they are so used to fighting with. His fury builds up as he prepares for the final onslaught and the soldiers mind is already working, knowing he and a couple of the lads can hold them back while the two young girls and Paula get away. Sexist. Misogynist but there's no point in everyone dying when some can get away and he knows the lads won't step away from the fight, probably not Paula either but he can scream an order for her to go with the girls and maybe she'll see the sense.

A wave of pressure sweeps through the infected. A new charge that drives them wild with fury and harder they push to get through that door. Harder they drive into the old house. Something pushing them. Eyes flick up to the wide doorway and a strange change in the action taking place. Mo Mo beaten back towards the lounge doors, flanked and encircled by a closing group. Cookey screaming as he batters and swipes. Dave slicing into anything he can stab. Blinky overextends and fights deep into the lines with strong arms that yield the stick and strong legs that drive her on. She takes hits and swipes but the protective clothing absorbs the impacts and only serves to give a false of security.

By the door now, too far from the others and she slips on the tiles but without the dexterity of Mo Mo and weighed down by the clothing she staggers, tries to find balance and falls hard to the ground. On her back and a head drops onto her chest. Dave snaps round, his eyes fixed on the door and a rare smile shows on his otherwise expressionless face. Nick on the stairs finds fresh energy surging into his arms. Cookey and Blowers get a pulse of strength and suddenly the fatigue is gone. The infected ramped up but the team matches that level. Blinky, on her back with a detached head on her chest stares in horror at the old woman lunging towards her. Slow motion now, the final seconds of death and her body dumps endorphins and hormones into her system, slowing everything down, speeding her mind up, greater strength, greater speed but frozen in fear of the final act. The old woman's teeth are bared. Her eyes ablaze with a terrible red bloodshot appearance. Hands ready with jagged broken nails that will slice Blinky's skin open. Gravity and thrust working to drive the old woman over and down onto the hockey player. A foot slams into the side of the woman's head and knocks her clear to the side. A roaring voice filling the air, louder than all the others. A man's face glaring down at her with eyes so dark and filled with such death that it sends more terror into Blinky's heart than anything she has ever known. Dark hair dripping wet and plastered to his scalp and lips curled back in such primeval rage that it seers the memory of that view into her brain. A double bladed axe rises over him, held tight on the shaft by knuckles showing white from the pressure. Heads lunging towards her. Hands outstretched to rake and claw. The man closer now, smiling an evil grin as he glides through the air and that slowness ends as abruptly as the world began and he swings the axe into everything and everything is taken away. Nothing can withstand him. He steps easily over her and into the battle and she snaps her view with eyes wide to see them wilt from his presence. Blinky has seen it before. On the field at play when her aggression sends an instinctive impulse into the opposing players and they can't help but fall back from the onslaught of absolute hatred bolstered by an unwavering certainty of victory. That's what it is. There is no doubt to be had for this man drives an energy before him that sends electric pulses through her body.

'Get up,' A voice breaks through the static charged air, a hand on her arm tugging her to rise, 'get up!' the woman urges and tugs harder. A beautiful woman holding a machine gun, 'GET UP,' the woman shouts and fires the weapon into the face of a monster bearing down.

Blinky rises, her feet scuffing to gain purchase and she gets pushed roughly back against the wall by the beautiful woman who steps in front to shield Blinky from the still raging infected bodies.

Against the wall she stares in rapture at the battle taking place in front of her and the man with an axe moving faster than any man has a right to move. The others rally on him. Fighting with an intensity that sends her heart soaring with incredible beats per minute. Dave at his side and that grace defies the executions he administers. Blowers from the stairs to the side of Cookey and with snarling faces they bear down with unrelenting force. Mo Mo on his feet whipping left and right to fell those that encircled him. The giant discarding his weapon to hammer fists into faces that break necks. She watches him bend with a speed that defies his size and rip a full grown man from the ground by his ankles and use that living form to batter at the helpless undead. Round and round he spins and the body bloodies into a pulp but it's not enough, it's never enough. The violence in him explodes and a berserker he becomes. Smashing, stomping, snapping and downing them with horrendous blows. Nick like a demon that smiles wryly as if he knows something they don't. That they can't be beaten. That they will never be beaten and the huge dog matches him kill for kill and without Nick knowing it, the dog chooses and protects her partner within the battle. Paula flaying with a wildness and always watched by Roy and there, in amongst them and snarling with the pulsing energy that drives them on is Charlie. The captain of the team. The leader that saw them through the dark days when the world was falling. Charlie snarling and raging with hair flying out as she scythes left to right. That energy catches. It extends from the group to flow into her. Blinky feels it. Deep inside. A real thing that drives and makes her launch from the wall and attack. Attack anything that gets in her way. Slaughter them for that man with the axe leads and everyone must follow. The beautiful woman fires the weapon into the crowd then slams the butt of the gun into a face that looms too close and always, like the others, her eyes flick to the man with the axe.

He gets faster still and like a ghost the dark brooding man whips through them with Dave forever at his side. Between them they kill more than the rest combined. Death after death is given out but it's clean and pure and the exact opposite of the tainted touch of death so threatened by these things.

Then it's over and a single solitary infected man stands stock still amidst the bodies of his kind that lie broken and forever dead on the tiled floor. The fighting ends. Chests heaving, eyes dark and fixed. The brooding man turns and stares across to the single undead. Dave adjusts the grip on his knife, ready to flick it out and across that short distance, always watching, always scanning. The dog drops her head and moves out to the side of the brooding man, her lips pulled back to show the teeth that wait. The speed is stunning. From one side of the room the brooding man crosses until his hand clutches the undead by the throat.

'He is coming,' the infected man chokes the words out.

'Bring him,' the man with the axe hisses.

'One race…'

'MY RACE,' the brooding man rallies the words back without a flicker of hesitation, 'and we win this day,' with a vicious twist he sends the undead down onto his knees and into the open lunging jaws of the dog that snaps and rags and the last one dies a terrible death.

CHAPTER TWENTY-SIX

'Where are we?'

'No idea, I thought we were heading towards the square but...' I look round at the featureless view of sheet rain greying everything out. Our feet splodging through the field becoming heavier with mud that clings to our feet, 'listen,' I reach out to place a gentle hand on her arm, 'hear that?'

She stares at me than down at the ground while straining to hear. The rain is a blast of noise that strikes the ground in varying rhythms of water on water and water on mud, but it's steady and almost formulaic. Something else. A harder sound of water being poured or a hose turned on a concrete path.

'Hear it?'

She nods and bites her bottom lip while turning slowly, 'this way,' she reaches back to take my hand.

'Sure?'

'Definitely,' she tugs me on but doesn't let go of my hand. 'Water from a roof,' she turns back to smile and the sight of her catches the breath in my throat. Soaked with wet hair plastered over her scalp with strands across her forehead and down her cheeks. A day of action, of movement, tension, fright, fear and it's put a rosy hue into the golden skin of her cheeks.

It gets like this. A weird sense of hysteria, of a good mood and happy endorphins that get released when you survive something so dangerous and deadly. So close to dying and being hurt but we survived. We ran and survived, fought and survived. I grin back and jog a fast step to fall in beside her.

The different sound matches the description she gave and I can hear the intense pouring from an overflowing drainpipe as it falls the distance from roof to ground. The shape comes slowly. Indistinct and more a suggestion of structure, of something lurking and waiting. Approaching from an angle and we're dead on towards the gap between two of the rows of buildings, but which ones I wouldn't be able to say. The fences of the rear gardens show stark now and we slow down, dropping our profiles into a loping crouch so we can edge forward. The rain is so intense it masks any noise we make, but what masks our noise also masks the noises of others. We stop frequently, listening, waiting then another few feet we go. Between the buildings and the broken drainpipe cascades a water fall from the tiled roof down onto the ground. Marcy shivers but whether from a chill or fear I know not.

Open ground ahead of us but the rain is so intense I've got no idea if the Saxon is still there or not. Only a few corpses here which must mean we're on the other side of the square, opposite to where we fought. For all I know there could be a hundred more undead gathered round the Saxon waiting for us. They might be inside it or hiding underneath.

I lean over to place my mouth into Marcy's ear, 'wait here.'

She shakes her head vehemently and grabs my arm, 'no way.'

'They might be there.'

'Together,' she mouths back and fixes me and angry stare to enforce her point.

'We have no weapons,' I try and give an angry stare back but I'm sure the water running down my face makes me look more comical than otherwise.

'We have you,' she mouths and nods for me to go on.

Her confidence is inspiring but very misplaced. Without a weapon I can't fight my way out of a paper bag.

Fuck it. In for a penny and all that. We stand up, lean out from the building line then burst into a flat out run. Splashing through deep puddles and without the cover of the buildings the rain pelts us hard in the face.

There it is. Broad sided with those huge wheels and mighty engine block standing proud. We get to the side and drop down to a crouch before I ease forward and peer up through the passenger side window. Nothing obvious. Grimacing in anticipation of the consequences I crack the door and slowly open it. Inch by inch. Nothing. No snarls or howling decaying faces that charge from the back. I dart forward and snatch a view of the back which is exactly as we left it with boxes of ammunition and our hand weapons left in situ.

I waste no time and clamber into the vehicle, over the seats and get my beloved axe back. One of the spare assault rifles is next, checked, loaded and ready. There are two rifles and a pistol back in that house and those are weapons we can ill afford to lose.

'Here,' back outside I hand the assault rifle over, 'safety is off. Listen, we left our rifles and the pistol in the house...'

'You want to go back for them?'

'We can't lose weapons,' I wince as though expecting a harsh rebuke but a look of determination crosses her face and she shoulders the weapon.

'Ready?'

'Guess so,' she swallows at the thought of going back in, 'what have you got?'

'Axe,' I lift it to show her.

'Okay,' she pushes the air out between her cheeks and nods, 'let's go.'

'You've done well today,' I say quickly, 'really well.'

'Aw thanks,' she shoots me a wide humourless grin followed by a roll of her eyes, 'you can thank me later but right now I'm soaked and getting cold.'

'So ungrateful,' I add my own tut and stand up.

'Bloody should show some gratitude,' she mutters.

'Shush now,' I wave my hand at her and step round the back of the Saxon to ignore the string of expletives being muttered.

We tread slow and careful, heading in a direct line towards the house and the weight of the axe held ready in my hands feels really bloody nice. Like I'm complete again. The rain is incredible and the sheer weight of water is already covering the flat ground in a huge shallow lake.

The bodies come into view first. Singles then more until the ghastly mound of bodies killed by the horse is right in front of us. It looks worse than ever. The rain has washed the blood away and left glistening exposed bodies that look like something from a wax works museum. Gnarled faces still twisted with expressions of utter hatred. Some stare open eyed with red bloodshot glazed looks to the sky. The wounds are clear without the blood. Hoof marks and broken limbs. Shattered skulls and knife wounds from my relentless stabbing. A bare arse catches my attention and I stop to point down, 'Jimmy Carr,' I call back softly with an emphatic nod.

'That,' she replies, 'is not Jimmy Carr.'

'It so is, look...look at him.'

'I can bloody see and that is not Jimmy Carr.'

'You can't see! You can only see his arse...turn him over and...'

'Howie I am soaking wet and am not turning bodies over to see which one looks like Jimmy Carr. Can we please just go.'

Her tone leaves no room for negotiation so with a huff I move on towards the house. Which turns out to be empty, apart from the bodies that is. No living undead. No snarling furious attacks. What we find is the kitchen ceiling hanging down and a waterfall pouring from the burst pipe in the bathroom above.

We find the assault rifles and I head upstairs to the bathroom and look down at the sagging floor. Bodies everywhere. Some are slowly sliding down the hole in the broken floor, others have already gone through and still the pipe pumps water into the room.

'There,' Marcy scoops it up from underneath the head of the corpse and passes it over.

'You got the holster,' I say and pass it back.

'Smart arse,' she shoves it down into the holster, 'will it still work?'

'No idea, water isn't good for them but...Dave can strip and clean it.'

'What about these rifles in the rain? Will they work?'

'Er...'

THE UNDEAD DAY SEVENTEEN

'Say if you don't know.'

'It's not that…'

'Do you know?'

'No. No I don't know.'

'You don't know if your weapons work in the rain?'

'It hasn't rained that much,' I say weakly, 'so er…it never really came up in conversation.'

'Yeah but still, you'd ask right? If they worked in the rain?'

'Um. Maybe Dave mentioned but…'

'Okay.'

'No, no it's a valid point and I should have asked Dave or Clarence.'

'It doesn't matter,' she says politely, 'you can't remember everything.'

'It just hasn't rained that much, you know…like been really hot and…'

'Seventeen days though?' She says with a questioning tilt of her head, 'and you didn't ask if they worked in the rain?'

'Yeah but…'

'And the fort is next to the sea…so water everywhere… you know….just saying.'

'No it's fine, it's a good point.'

'Have I hurt your feelings?' She asks, 'sorry, I was a bit blunt then.'

'No no, really, it was a good point and…'

'No listen, I was out of order, sorry, Howie. I shouldn't have been so blunt.'

I toe the head of a corpse and shrug, 'yeah you know, been a lot going on.'

'Course, yeah I totally understand.'

303

The eye from the head plops out, 'I mean, you know... we haven't done *that* badly considering.'

'Oh you've done really well,' she places a reassuring hand on my arm while I gently tap the hanging eye back and forth, 'like *so* well and...it's one thing, rifles and rain and you're right, it hasn't rained so...'

'Yeah but I should have checked.'

'Hey,' she says softly, 'come on, I'm sorry okay. I shouldn't have asked so harshly.'

'Okay,' I shrug and blink as the strand holding the hanging eye snaps and the ball plops down onto the wet floor to roll away. Red and bloodshot and without thinking I bend down and pick it up to stare hard. 'Yours aren't that bad anymore,' I look from the disconnected eye to Marcy's eyes.

'No?' She says leaning over to look at the eyeball.

'Not as bad as this one anyway.'

'I can't see my own eyes.'

'True, take my word for it...or I'll keep it so you can compare...okay I won't keep it then.'

'Don't keep it.'

'I'm not. I've put it down. Right, let's go.'

We head back down and out into the now very unpleasant sensation of the driving rain. Head down we move fast back to the Saxon and quickly check the back before getting round and up into the front.

The rifles are both dry so I swap for fresh magazines and place them close at hand. The pistol I leave in Marcy's holster for Dave or Clarence to check later. That stops me in my tracks. An assumption that we will see them later. Not *if* we see them later but *when*. That feeling. Deep inside. A tangible thing that is separate to my own feelings but as soon as I try and focus on it the feeling fades away.

'You okay?' Marcy twists from the front passenger seat.

'Huh? Yeah...yeah fine,' I clamber over back into the front and start the engine. They're alive. I don't how I know but I do.

'Which way?'

'Fuck knows,' I move off and head down the only road available which leads towards the village. Clothes soaking and I shift uncomfortably from the squelching material clinging to my skin.

Following the road we head into a shute with high trees touching overhead and the rhythm of the rain changes again as the water pours from the branches and leaves. Water everywhere and lying deep across the surface of the road.

Through the village and we scout round looking for signs but see nothing. There could be trample marks in the verges or grass but the rain hides any signs of recent passage.

Then we see the bodies and my heart swells. Clear gunshot wounds from a firing position of a fallen tree. We stay silent, scanning the view ahead and to the sides into the depths of the trees while the Saxon bumps easily over the corpses strewn in the road. We have to go round the branches end of the downed tree and let the weight and force of the vehicle bust through the mostly dead wood.

More houses, rows of cottages so like the ones back in the square then a junction with a narrow road leading off. I stay on the main road ahead going steady but not fast. A long country lane but then all of these roads are long country lanes.

'Howie,' Marcy spots the two big stone pillars through the squalling rain.

'Finkton...what does that say?' I wipe the condensation from the driver's window.

'Sports Academy,' she reads over my shoulder.

I roll forward and steer in towards the wide gap between the pillars and the sea of dead bodies coming into view, 'I think we've found them,' I say quietly then floor the accelerator as that same sensation sends a harsh jolt through my insides. In there. In that house that looms from the rain. A horde fighting to get inside the entrance doors. Over dead bodies we drive with increasing speed and I slew the vehicle round to a stop and I'm out the door with axe in hand without conscious thought.

'BEHIND YOU,' I run into the fray with a glimpse of the team inside being beaten back by these filthy dirty bastards and the thing I longed for happens now. Into that zone and the axe becomes a part of my body. They slow down to become painfully sluggish. I promised the team a day off. I promised them a meal and a rest and another day has been spent running from the hatred they have for us. That single fact becomes the focus point for a rage that has the axe sweeping them away. I batter them down at the door and clear the way through. A girl with red hair falling to the floor. Bulky clothing like an ice hockey player and the axe removes the head of the one bearing down to bite. An old woman lunging next and the axe is still on the upswing so I boot the fetid bitch aside and glance down to see a pair of brown eyes staring up wide and terrified.

'GET HER UP,' I shout back for Marcy behind me and roar my challenge into the room with a wild swing that drives them back from the fallen girl.

The team rallies and we fight. Dave smiling. Blowers leaping from the stairs to get next to Cookey and they go at it. We all do. Meredith next to Nick. Mo Mo slicing them down. Roy and Paula and another girl dressed in hockey gear. Clarence goes berserk with an explosion of temper and then Dave is at my side and we speed up, we get fast.

Faster than ever before. He smiles and I smile back. Kill for kill we become a thing that cannot be stopped and every step I take is the step I needed to take. Every swing is correct with the right amount of force applied. They wilt and drop back but the infection pushes them on and then it's over.

I'm facing back towards the team when I see Meredith's head drop as she fixes sight on something behind me. I turn. One single adult male remains and as we did with Lani, so the dog gets to my side as we stalk towards it but the lust for kills is too high so I move quick to grab the thing by the throat before Meredith can do it.

'He is coming,' the infection spits the words out while I choke the air from the host's throat.

'Bring him,' I pull him in closer and stare into the red eyes to the thing within.

'One race...'

'MY RACE,' I scream back, 'and we win this day,' then I fling him down for the dog to eat and show the infection what teeth can really do.

CHAPTER TWENTY-SEVEN

'So,' I turn round and ask cheerily, 'nice day off?'
'Did it have a folding stock?'
'Did what have a folding stock?'
'No it's a bloody awful day off.'
'Noted, Clarence.'
'Hey, Marcy.'
'Hey, Clarence. Reginald still with you?'
'Up here.'
'You can come down now, Reggie.'
'I'm not going down there! My legs hurt and my feet are wet and I am simply strained to the point of exhaustion.'
'Did it have a folding stock?'
'What? What's a folding stock?'
'It's been a really bad day off.'
'Noted, Clarence.'
'Was it an M4 with a folding stock?'
'I don't know what that is.'
'I think Paula and Roy had a nice day off.'
'Alex!'
'Sorry, Paula.'

'Did you all get something to eat?'

'We did but then we puked it back up and Meredith ate Blowers' puke.'

'Nice, Cookey...who cooked for you lot?'

'I did.'

'Not surprised he puked up then.'

'The worst day off in years.'

'Still noted, Clarence.'

'M4 with a fold...'

'Dave, what's an M4?'

'American military issue assault rifle but that one had a folding stock.'

'What one had a folding stock?'

'That one.'

'What one?'

'The one with the folding stock.'

'What's a folding a stock?'

'A stock that folds.'

'Of course it is.'

'We heard firing and we both,' Clarence shoots Dave a dark look, 'worked out it was an M4.'

'With a folding stock.'

'Oh the bloke on the horse.'

'Horse?' Paula asks.

'What horse?' Clarence asks.

'The bloke that had the other gun.'

'With a folding stock.'

'I don't know if it had a folding stock.'

'It did.'

'Okay, but I didn't see the stock folding or unfolding.'

'How big was it?'

'I dunno,' I shrug, 'like huge...' I hold my hand over my head, 'up here somewhere.'

'The M4 not the horse.'

'I didn't see, I was busy getting Jimmy Carr's shit off my chin.'

'You did that later,' Marcy says, 'and only when I pointed it out.'

'Whoa!' Cookey holds a hand out, 'Jimmy Carr?'

'Yeah.'

'Jimmy Carr shit on your chin?'

'Yeah.'

'The comedian Jimmy Carr shit on your chin?'

'Allegedly.'

'Yes,' I say with a look at Marcy, 'and he was naked.'

'Whoa!' Cookey holds his hand back out, 'Jimmy Carr was naked and shit on your chin?'

'Moving on,' Paula sighs, 'what happened?'

'Well,' I say with a nod, 'I was outside and Jimmy Carr was naked and running at me then I got pulled to the ground and...'

'I mean today not with Jimmy Carr.'

'Oh. Sorry. Er...lots of zombies came and we all ran away and er...oh we had some food...and there was a bloke on a horse.'

'With an M4,' Dave says.

'With an M4,' I say to Paula, 'that may or may not have had a folding stock.'

'Oh my god,' Paula shakes her head, 'Marcy, fancy a coffee?'

'Yes, yes I would,' Marcy replies heavily.

I interrupt before they can move off, 'not here, we've still got infected out there somewhere. We gave them the slip but they'll know we're here. Everyone get fresh magazines and hand weapons. Do it now and be ready to go.'

I spot the looks of uncertainty pass between the two

girls and move over closer to them with Marcy at my side and I'm thankful Paula and Clarence have the presence of mind to stay with us.

'This is Mr Howie,' Paula says with a nod at me, 'this is Charlie and er...Blinky?'

'Yes,' the blinking girl says abruptly.

'Under 21's England hockey team,' Paula adds.

'Wow,' I say with genuine admiration, 'Howie, nice to meet you both. Charlie?' I hold my hand out to the mixed race girl, pretty with long brown hair and hazel eyes. She's tall and swamped in the bulky hockey goalie clothes.

'Hi,' she greets me with a strong confident voice trying to mask the utter terror they just faced but there's no trembling when we shake hands.

'Hi, er...Blinky?' I switch to the next girl. Red haired with a blaze of freckles across her nose, shorter than Charlie but her frame looks bigger.

'I blink,' she says abruptly, 'a lot.'

'Right,' I nod as Clarence coughs into his hand and glances away.

'It's not nerves,' she says in that same tone of rushing the words out, 'the therapist said it was aggression that manifests in blinking when I'm not playing...'

'Okay.'

'I don't do it when I play.'

'Blink you mean?'

'Yes. I don't blink when I play. Hockey. Play hockey.'

'Right...'

'And I puke after most games but it's not cos I'm scared but cos I get so worked up and...'

'I see.'

'I'm aggressive.'

'Aggressive,' I say back, more at a loss of what else to say, 'er...this is Marcy and...'

'I'm Paula,' Paula says then looks at me, 'we only just arrived before they did,' she motions to the bodies on the floor, 'the lads we're here before us.'

'The lads?' I ask with a lift of my eyebrows, 'in here? With a ladies hockey team? Christ, I bet they thought this was the best day ever.'

'We're they polite?' Clarence asks.

'Very,' Charlie says looking up at him, 'we hid...they came in and got water then left.'

'Left? How did you all end up fighting together then?' I ask.

'The er...those things came when they were leaving...we thought they'd run off but er...' she shoots a look at Blinky, 'but they said they couldn't let them attack the people in the house but,' she stops to sweep her hair from her face, 'but they hadn't seen us and didn't know who was in here...I...I mean we think they smelled the bread we were cooking and...'

'They said anyone nice enough to make bread is nice enough to fight for,' Blinky says.

'Words to that effect,' Charlie carries on as I lean closer to listen. All of us in rapt attention. 'There was only four of them...and the dog...and they only had a few bullets but... they stood there calm as day and faced them down,' she pauses for a second and I swallow the lump of pride in my throat and glance at the strange look on Clarence's face, 'there were so many,' she stares at me unblinking in the memory, 'four...just four,' she whispers as though to herself, 'and...then,' she lifts her head higher, 'and then their guns ran out of bullets and they stood up and they charged, Mr Howie. They ran *at* them with knives...'

Tears stream down Paula's face. Clarence looking choked and I feel my own breath quavering with emotion at the visual image created. Even Marcy looks down with a heavy sigh.

'So yes, yes they were polite,' Charlie says to Clarence then looks back at me, 'and that's when we went out to help them.'

'Mr Howie, Dave sent us back in to get some wat…' Blowers leads the three lads back inside, dodging bodies and they stop dead at the stares being given, 'what?' Blowers asks.

'I didn't do it,' Cookey says quickly, 'it was Nick,' he adds pointing at Nick.

'It was Mo Mo,' Nick points to Mo.

'Wasn't me,' Mo Mo says.

'I thought they trapped you here,' Clarence says in a hoarse whisper, 'you went out against them?'

'Yeah,' Blowers says quietly.

'Seemed the right thing to do,' Nick adds.

'The four of you went against them?' Clarence asks again, 'how many magazines did you have left?'

'One each,' Blowers answers, 'and we had Meredith,' he looks down and away at the intense scrutiny, 'we couldn't…'

'…Let them get in here,' Cookey finished the sentence, 'we all decided…Blowers didn't order us to…'

'Not angry,' I say thickly.

'Thank fuck for that,' Nick mutters with relief.

Words cannot do justice to the swell of pride I feel and anything said by me now would be trite and serve an injustice to what they just did.

'Christ,' Clarence growls the word out and crosses the ground in two big strides before scooping all four shocked lads into an uncomfortable bear hug. A big man with a big heart and the pride shines from the tears in his eyes.

When he releases he turns quickly away and heads out into the pouring rain without saying a word.

The surprise at being hugged by Clarence only continues when Paula moves to Blowers and kisses him gently on the cheek. Next to Cookey and she grips his face between her hands as though examining his eyes, 'you little sod,' she half laughs and half cries, 'I can't leave you lot.' She moves to Nick and pulls him in for a hug, 'you're incredible, all of you,' she finishes with Mo Mo, 'and you,' she says softly with a kiss to his forehead like a mother to son, 'all of you,' she whispers and draws a deep steadying breath '...I'll be outside.'

Blowers shuffles with a deep blush spreading through his cheeks. Cookey grinning at the attention. Nick looking slightly perplexed while Mo Mo looks stunned to the core.

'Marcy?' Cookey asks with a cheeky grin, 'aren't you hugging us too?'

'Sods,' she laughs and grabs him for a hug, 'that better?'

'Yeah,' Cookey sighs theatrically in the warm embrace.

'You did well,' I nod at Blowers and the simple words are enough to lift him inches from the ground.

'Cheers,' he half grunts, 'we'll get the water then?'

'Yeah, yeah do that.'

'Are they coming with us, Mr Howie?' Cookey asks as they traipse past.

'We're getting to that bit,' I reply and look back at the two girls, 'we can't stay here, the...those things know we're here and will send more so...'

'How will they know?' Charlie asks.

'Hive mind,' Marcy replies, 'they are all connected to each other. What one sees they all see.'

Blinky blinks and stares after the boys heading through the doors, 'can I go with them please?'

'Er, yeah sure,' I reply.

'Thanks, Mr Howie,' she runs off behind them, 'we've got bread you can eat!' She calls out.

'Blinky!' Charlie calls, 'we've got to decide what we're...'

'You're the captain you decide,' she shouts back then disappears through the doors.

'Captain?' I ask.

'I was going to be trialled as the team captain,' Charlie says.

'Bloody hell, so...listen I'm sorry to rush you but staying here isn't safe. You should come with us. Is it just the two of you?'

'We had more,' she says, her eyes flick past me to the bodies on the ground and I don't need to turn and see what she's looking at, 'just the two of us now...Blinky and I.'

'Come with us,' Marcy says softly, 'I know we all probably look very strange but you'll be safe with us, I promise.'

It strikes me then that the girl doesn't stare at Marcy's eyes. I glance over and can see they don't really look any worse than Paula's a minute ago, like she's been crying recently or they've been irritated by something.

'Safe? I hardly think that is the correct way of...'

'Reggie, go outside with the others,' Marcy says gently without turning to look at him trudging mournfully down the stairs and staring at the bodies with distaste.

'Charlie?' I ask, 'we really need to be gone from here.'

'We'll come,' she says quickly, 'can I tell Blinky and get changed?'

'Sure,' I reply, 'just be quick.'

'Get the lads,' Marcy says, 'I'll stay with the girls.'

A fluid interchange of suggestion and counter suggestion. Marcy, a member of the team as much as any other now and she follows Charlie through the doors with the assault rifle slung over her shoulder.

On my own I look round at the bodies and blood soaked walls then out the door to the sheet rain hammering down. Figures by the Saxon. Clarence up top covering the GPMG saying something to Roy and Paula hugging her own body but standing with her face turned up towards the sky.

Time ticks on and the day isn't over yet. With a sigh I pat my pockets down for a smoke then with a tut I head through the doors to find Nick.

CHAPTER TWENTY-EIGHT

Crates of ammunition, assault rifles, axes, kit everywhere, a big dog and thirteen soaking wet people crammed into one vehicle. The Saxon can take it, the weight of it all I mean. This thing would pull a herd of stubborn rhino's.

Clarence up front to give the others some space and with the wet weather cover over the hole for the GPMG they're sealed in snug and tight, with steam coming off clothes and hair and everyone squashed into the seats.

'We're going to need a bigger vehicle at this rate,' Clarence says twisted round in his seat to look at the sardines in the back.

'Nah,' I say lightly, 'be alright.'

'Have you seen them?' He asks.

'Nah,' I say just as lightly to a low chuckle from him.

I pull the vehicle round the driveway and head back up towards the gates, bumping and bouncing over the corpses littering the ground. Blinky wasn't fazed one bit at leaving the house. Quite the opposite in fact. She couldn't get changed and ready fast enough to get back to the lads.

Charlie was a bit more pensive but I think she knew their time there was over and although they've done a brilliant job of staying hidden it couldn't stay like that forever. There was no time to ask if they wanted to go anywhere as the priority was to get loaded and get gone.

'Marcy,' I call out in a loud voice.

'Yes,' she replies in a low voice from right behind me that makes me jump a foot from the seat.

'What the fuck...'

'Made you jump,' she laughs, 'no room to sit down so I'm standing up...right behind you...watching you,' she adds in a sinister voice.

'Lads, someone give Marcy a seat,' Clarence booms out.

'We offered...' Cookey starts to say.

'They did offer,' Marcy says, 'I'm soaked though and can't stand sitting down in wet clothes. Besides...I'm watching Howie,' she adds in that sinister voice.

'Get Dave or Clarence to check your pistol,' I say with a chuckle.

'Why? What's up with it?' Clarence asks.

'It was submerged in water for a few minutes,' I say, 'and will these rifles still work in this wet weather?'

'Pistol will be fine,' Clarence says, 'just shake the water from it so the moisture doesn't build up inside...here, I'll check it.' She hands it over and he goes to work stripping the pistol down with deft movements, 'as for the SA80,' he says, 'the first lot back in the day would have fallen apart by now.'

'Really?' I ask.

'Oh yes, first gulf war they were falling apart in our hands, bloody awful things. Then we got them upgraded...' he speaks while working, taking parts of the pistol to dry and shake out, 'much better now and as long as they're cleaned, greased and kept maintained they'll work...no electrical parts or anything like that, just the moving parts that need proper care.'

'So we can stand out in the rain and fire then?'

'Yes, you might get the odd misfire when the round gets jammed in the chamber but that can be cleared in a second and Dave has drilled the lads on how to do that...'

'Yeah he did back in Salisbury,' I say.

'Quite rare now though,' Clarence continues, 'the upgrade made them one of the most reliable weapons in the world, apart from the AK that is, those things can be shoved up an elephants arse and still fire. Here,' he hands the pistol back, 'it's fine.'

'What about the GPMG?' I ask.

'Covered now,' he replies, 'so it's not getting wet but as long as we clean and maintain it there won't be a problem.'

At the top of the drive we take a right and head away from the village but the going is slow. Visibility is down to a few metres at best. Everything outside is grey and the road is already covered in a deepening layer of water coming off the hard packed fields too dry to absorb the rain.

'Roy,' I call back, 'we need clothes, kit...bags, outdoors gear...do you know anywhere?'

'Hang on,' yelps sound out as he mooches about trying to find a map, 'where are we?'

'Fucktown...'

'Finkton,' someone else says.

'I'm sure it said fucktown,' Cookey says.

'Finkton....Finkton...' Roy says the name while he searches the map, 'where is it near? It's not on this map...no I've got it, yes here it is...right so we're heading this direction...there's a town a few miles along. I don't know anywhere near here but I guess the town will have shops?'

'I'd prefer some distance from here,' I reply, 'everyone okay if we drive on a bit?'

'Not too far,' Marcy says quietly behind me, 'everyone's drenched to the bone.'

'Okay,' I nod and keep the vehicle driving steadily through the pouring rain. The noise of the water striking the metal body is soothing and slows the frantic state we were in down to a tired silence. Two new people in the vehicle and I'd be expecting the lads to be messing about but they're soaked, probably exhausted and crammed in.

It takes time but the distance is made and the miles fall behind. Clarence's head falls back as he drops into a doze. Marcy's hand on the back of the seat and I can feel her move her fingers every now and then.

I bump the back of my head against her hand to gain her attention, 'you okay?'

'Ssshh,' she drops down and leans forward with her head next to mine, 'they're all sleeping.'

'All of them?'

'Apart from Dave, yes.'

'Dave never sleeps, he's a machine.'

'So who was the man on the horse?' She asks.

'No idea, didn't see where he came from or where he went after.'

'He wasn't a good rider,' she whispers, 'he was only just about hanging on to that horse.'

'Bloody big horse though.'

'Hanoverian,' she says, 'they're used by the police, might be a mix breed.'

'How do you know?'

'Where do you think I got my strong legs from?'

'So vain,' I say half-jokingly.

'Don't hate me cos I'm beautiful.'

I burst out with a snort of laughter that earns me a sideways glance from Clarence.

'Ssshh,' she whispers.

From the country road to an A road to a slip road to a motorway and the view ahead opens up with the wide flat ground. Speed is gained and the distance increases. I let two junctions go by then gently ease off the next junction and through the connecting service roads. Power lines overhead with pylons in the fields so we must be close to a town.

'Okay, wake them up,' I nudge Marcy's arm with my head again, 'we're getting close to...'

'Wake up,' Dave barks the order, 'Mr Howie said we're getting close to a town.'

Groans and stretches from behind, Meredith panting in the wet warmth of being stuck in a tin can with so many bodies.

'Check your weapons and carry extra magazines,' Dave orders, 'have hand weapons ready. Eyes up and alert. We got caught out and it will not happen again.'

'Yes, Dave,' a chorus of voices sound back as magazines are checked and axes tugged free of the boxes.

Ubiquitous Britain and another plodding dull layout of a town done by council officials that copy what everyone else is doing. Roads bordered by houses. Houses burnt out and damaged. Cars littering the road and pavements. Bodies being washed clean by the rain. We pass petrol stations and entrances to industrial estates. Drains bubble as they visibly struggle to cope with the sheer amount of water hitting the ground.

Into the town centre and through to the High Street complete with signs telling us the area is not for vehicular traffic Monday to Friday 8am to 5pm. A glass fronted vestibule sticks out from the building line with wide entrances that lead to an enclosed shopping centre and sign boards indicating the array of stores within.

'Perfect,' I point to the glass front and look at Clarence.

'Go for it,' he says.

'Listen in,' I call out, 'we're going for this shopping centre. Blowers on perimeter, Roy work with Blowers and his team. Paula and Marcy stay with the two girls and Reggie in the middle...'

'Reginald.'

'Stay with Reginald in the middle, Dave on point with me and Clarence...Everyone understand?'

'Yep.'

'Got it.'

Voices call back clear with affirmation.

'Like Dave said, we got caught out. Magazines to be carried *and* hand weapons at all times and I want everyone carrying magazines...Reginald, Charlie and Blinky too.'

Order, structure and discipline.

'Do we take our hand weapons?' Blinky shouts, 'our hockey sticks?'

'Yes,' Dave answers, 'until we find you better weapons and once trained with rifles you'll be with Simon's team.'

'Simon?' Blinky asks, 'which one is Simon?'

'I'm Simon,' Blowers replies as Clarence and I share a shrugging glance at Dave already working the teams out.

'What is your real name?' I hear Dave ask.

'Blinky....Patricia,' she says after a brief pause that I can assume was filled by a glare from Dave.

'You?'

'Charlotte,' Charlie says.

'Okay,' I call out as I bring the Saxon to a slow crawl over the last few metres, 'everyone out and eyes up.'

'Cookey with me on the right, Nick and Mo on the left, Roy you check dead ahead at the doorways and windows.'

Doors open and we climb down and out with weapons raised and ready. Every doorway and window is checked and scanned. Blowers and Cookey go out to the right side and stand solidly in the pouring rain. Nick and Mo on the other side. Roy checking the shops opposite. Marcy and Paula with rifles held ready shepherding Reginald and the two girls holding hockey sticks to the front of the Saxon and both dressed in sports gear of tracksuits, trainers and hooded tops.

'Looks clear,' Clarence calls from the front and steps through the busted doors into the dry interior of the shopping centre. Meredith gets through and nose to the ground she runs ahead while we watch and wait.

'She seems happy,' I say after watching her run to the side and squat down for a piss, 'we're going in...Blowers bring the rear up.'

'He's good at that,' Cookey shouts to a low groan of chuckles and Paula rolling her eyes.

Dave, Clarence and I take the front and walk slowly past the first few shop entrances. Shoe shops and juice bars. A mobile phone store. Some protected by pulled down mesh fronts padlocked to the floor. Some have been opened before us with looting evident. A dead body slumped beside a row of benches in the centre of the main aisle gets a low growl from Meredith who tells us the body was infected.

Fashion stores with mannequins wearing skinny jeans and tight t shirts. Indie clothing stores and a high end clothing shop that has ball gowns and dummies wearing full suits. Potted plants wilting from the high heat and lack of water. Dark in here, gloomy from the lack of light coming in and it takes a few seconds for our eyes to adjust. The first entrance aisle leads to a wide circular middle section with sets of escalators going down to a food hall and up to more shops on the upper level. An information desk to one side and the circular perimeter has store front after store front ranged round.

I peer over the safety railing to the seats and open plan bars below. Counters covered with chiller cabinets and shelves with bottles. Notice and display boards give prices and menus. The floor is tiled and still quite clean. Only a few smears of blood here and there and a couple of bodies lie amongst the overturned chairs down in the food section.

'Blowers, work left and we'll go right,' I call out softly and get a thumbs up from the corporal of the team.

He heads to the left and starts moving round the perimeter of the circle while we go right. Every store that is open is checked by taking a few steps into it and scanning for noise or signs of debris. There will be storerooms and back offices everywhere but that will take more time than we have. We meet at the other side.

'Up next, we can see down into the food hall, same again we get to the top.'

Blowers nods and keeps his team facing out, indicating with hand movements for Mo Mo to look away and not back at the group.

We head up the broad steps of the escalator with Dave at the front. At the top are more stores in a replica layout of the main floor we came from. We head right and Blowers takes the left side. Paula bringing the girls and Reginald behind us. I glance back and notice Blinky staring longingly at the lads as they work their side but Charlie looks alert and serious. Checking every doorway that we pass and moving to peer down into the food hall below. Not leaving her care to others but accepting the responsibility for her own welfare. She doesn't grip the hockey stick as though ready to strike but holds it down to one side, relaxed but ready.

After the day we've already had the tension is high with expectation of something utterly shit happening again. We meet at the opposite point then head back as one group to the escalators and down to the middle floor, swap stairs and then down into the bottom section.

The food hall has seen action. Desperate people searching for food and desperate infected searching for people to infect. More bodies at the sides that we didn't see from above but they look old and already decaying. The smell isn't pleasant but it's something we've got used to now. Well most of us have, Charlie doesn't look too impressed and Blinky just stares at the lads and blinks a lot.

'Seen that,' I nudge Clarence and nod back to Blinky.

'Yeah,' he smiles, 'she hasn't taken her eyes off them. I think I know who she wants to work with.'

'You reckon?' I ask with a smile. We spread out and check the various outlets, behind counters and every nook and cranny we can find.

'Howie,' Marcy calls out and I turn to see her pointing to the entrance to the toilets, 'can we use them?'

'Yeah, we'll check first.' We lead on into the recess that splits left and right for the male and female toilets. Rifles up we check every cubicle within the toilets and the sight of ourselves in the mirrors above the sinks is a sight to see. Bedraggled. Soaked. Filthy with dirt ground into clothes despite the pelting rain. My face is bearded now from days of growth and I can't remember the last time I had a shave. Clarence is the same, his head bald but his chin thick with dark stubble.

'Clear,' outside the main entrance to the toilets we meet

back together, 'who needs to go?' Nearly every arm raises apart from Dave. 'Dave, you staying out here?'

'Yes, Mr Howie.'

The boys traipse into the gents and the ladies take the other side. Eight of us that head to the urinals and prop hand weapons and assault rifles against the wall before we choose our position and yank flies down to a chorus of relieving groans and eight streams of piss that strike the porcelain bowls.

We wee in silence until Cookey slowly turns to face Blowers, 'alright mate,' he asks casually.

'Get fucked.'

'What?'

'Just fuck off. You're going to make some crap joke about me being in a toilet with other men...'

'Who me?' Cookey asks so innocently that the rest of us can't help but burst out laughing, 'an actual girls hockey team,' he says down the line of men urinating, 'like...an actual girls hockey team...can't believe it.'

'Cookey was joking that we needed to find a netball or hockey team that needed moisturising,' Nick explains, 'about half an hour later and we actually bloody find one.'

'No way?' I lean forward to look down to Cookey, 'is that real?'

'Yeah,' he nods eagerly,' I said it while doing the food... an actual hockey team.'

'Fuck,' I rock back on my heels, 'weird.'

'Then most of them got killed,' Cookey tuts, 'which is the story of my life seeing as Dave chopped the head off my one true love...'

'Alex!'

'Sorry, Dave,' Cookey calls back then drops his voice, 'how can he hear that?'

'I hear everything, Alex.'

'Yes, Dave. Sorry, Dave.'

We finish off, zip up and move automatically to the long line of sinks. Hands squish the soap out and we push the tops of the taps down to get the five seconds of water flow.

'They seem nice,' Nick says while rubbing his hands, 'they staying with us?'

'I don't know, mate,' I reply, 'we'll have a chat in a minute and find out…but it seems Dave has already selected who they're working with,' I look down at Blowers, 'you alright with that?'

'Me? Yeah sure,' he nods.

'You're getting a bigger team,' Clarence says, 'but you can handle it. Dave wouldn't have said it if he didn't think you could.'

'Okay,' Blowers says dully, clearly uncomfortable at being the centre of attention again.

'Oh god,' Cookey tuts, 'he's head will get even bigger now…er,' he leans forward and suddenly looks worried, 'are they gay?'

'Eh?' I ask.

'What?' Clarence says equally as stunned as me.

'Can I still make the jokes?' He asks, 'I'd better stop,' he nods to himself, 'I'll stop for a bit.'

'Might be a good idea,' I say.

'Charlie is really pretty,' he blurts in a whisper, 'like proper hot.'

'They're both very nice,' Clarence says stiffly, 'and you'll be a gentleman at all times.'

'Yeah course.'

'Won't you,' Clarence stares down at him.

'Yeah course,' he says again, 'promise.'

'Good lad,' Clarence nods with a grin, 'they'll be scared and worried so take it easy for a bit.'

'I don't think Blinky is worried,' I say after a second's pause, 'er...quite the opposite in fact.'

'True,' Clarence says, 'Reggie, you okay?'

'Decidedly not,' he says as stiffly as Clarence a second ago, 'I am wet and tired...'

'I know mate,' Clarence says, 'bad day all round...but you kept up so...that's a good thing.'

'And despite my moaning I am eternally grateful for both you and David saving me. Truly I am. I am just not used to all...' he looks down over at the weapons, 'all of this.'

'Dave,' Dave calls out.

'My apologies,' Reginald says instantly.

'Did you see that shop,' I ask casually, 'on the way in.'

'Which one?' Clarence asks, 'the one with the suits?'

'Yeah, looked good. We should head back there and see what they've got.'

'Sounds good,' Clarence says.

'Nice ties in there,' Nick gets the hint and joins in, 'clean shirts and trousers too.'

We all stand back and start shaking our hands off while Reginald looks sheepishly touched but smiles all the same, 'thank you but perhaps I should adopt some more suitable clothing from now on.'

'You wear whatever you're comfortable with,' Clarence says.

'Can Blowers wear a dress then?' Cookey asks.

'What are you lot doing in there?' Paula calls out, 'hurry up.'

'We we're having an important boys meeting,' Cookey says as we head back out, 'are either of you gay?' He asks the girls.

'Alex!' Paula snaps.

'Cookey,' Clarence groans.

'Not now, mate,' I say firmly.

'What? Why?' Charlie asks with a firm look.

'That was completely out of order,' Paula says with a glare, 'we've talked about this.'

'Sorry,' Cookey sags on the spot from the shaking head and tuts.

'You do not have to answer that,' Paula says to Charlie and Blinky, 'and the reason Alex asked that question is not because we're homophobic but because he makes jokes about Blowers being gay which is childish and immature.'

Cookey reels from the rebuke, looking crestfallen he blushes deeply.

'Are you?' Blinky asks Blowers.

'No, Cookey doesn't mean any harm though,' he adds quickly.

'I'm gay,' Blinky says in that abrupt tone which makes Cookey look like he wants the ground to open up.

'And that is something we all respect,' Paula replies.

'Ease up,' I cut in, 'Cookey keeps our spirits up when otherwise we'd fall over and bloody cry. He isn't homophobic or anything like that.'

'He ain't,' Mo Mo comes to the defence of his team mate, 'and he ain't racist either, none of them are.'

'The lads take the piss out of each other all the time,' I say.

'Yes but making fun because of sexual orientation is not something we can condone.'

'We don't,' I say to Paula, 'Cookey only does it to Blowers and Nick and that's because he knows them. 'Look at what they did back there, Paula...'

'Yes but asking people if they are gay to find out if he is safe to continue making jokes is not okay.'

'And we don't live in a perfect world anymore,' I say back, 'and at least he asked.'

'I don't care,' Blinky says with a shrug, 'I don't give a shit if Cookey makes jokes.'

'Yes but you have only just joined us,' Paula says, 'and no doubt you're both scared and not wanting to say anything that will upset anyone...we're all armed and you've just seen us killing...'

'So?' Blinky says, 'everyone takes the piss out of everyone. Don't give a shit.'

'She's being honest,' Charlie says quickly, 'Blinky er... has a very strong sense of humour.'

'I'm gay,' Blinky shrugs, 'but I want his babies,' she points at Dave who blinks in surprise.

'Right,' I says firmly, 'Cookey don't ask stupid questions like that in future.'

'Yes, Mr Howie.'

'And if Cookey says anything that offends anyone then just say because he would never want to offend anyone. We need clothes, bags, boots...'

'I was thinking about this,' Paula says and quickly reaches out to squeeze Cookey's arm, 'we should each have a personal equipment bag with water, torches, batteries, tools and a first aid kit.'

'Good idea. Anything else?' I look round at the group, 'we got fucked up this morning...my knife got us out of the shit...but getting caught out like that was awful. We only had a couple of magazines because we were wearing normal clothes and didn't have anywhere to put the extras. Find clothes with pockets, strong boots...wet weather gear, jackets and trousers...spare tops...Dave?'

'Dry socks and foot powder,' he says.

'Underwear,' Clarence adds, 'and waterproof torches will be best. Multi tools are a good idea,' he nods to Paula, 'and first aid kits yes, but be careful we don't get weighed down by heavy kit.'

'Paula, can you take Charlie and Blinky and find them suitable clothes to wear.'

'Will do,' she says, 'Marcy, you coming with us?'

'A shopping date?' She laughs, 'wouldn't miss that for anything.'

'There was a couple of outdoor shops on the top floor,' Roy says, 'Blacks and Trespass.'

'To infinity and beyond then,' I say with a grin and stare round at the blank faces and the tumbleweed rolling across the ground, 'no? Anyone? No sense of humour you lot,' I tut and walk off towards the escalator.

Thirteen of us and we head up the stairs to the top floor and find the two outdoor shops at the end separated by a lingerie shop in the middle. I look across to Cookey expecting to see his face lighting up but he looks down at the ground and still crestfallen at being told off so severely. I drop back a few paces and get Paula's attention then nod to Cookey. She looks back at him then over the lingerie shop and gives me a quick wink.

'Ladies, look what I can see,' she says in a clear voice, 'crotchless panties anyone? Nipple tassles?'

I keep my eye on Cookey snapping his head up to stare over at the window.

'I knew someone who wore crotchless knickers,' Marcy says brightly, 'her name was April...'

'Oh my god she never did?' Cookey bursts out, 'no way? Really? Did she really?'

'No you daft plank,' Marcy laughs, 'stopped you sulking though.'

'Oh April,' Cookey sighs, 'she wore them for me you know.'

I snort with laughter and get another wink from Paula.

'She did,' Marcy says, 'she told me...'

'Fact,' Cookey says, 'Blowers, you getting any then?' A test joke. A tentative step to see if anyone will yell at him.

'For you, mate,' Blowers says and the world moves on. Blinky laughing, Charlie smiling and the tension eases. Clarence smiling ruefully and Meredith taking a dump on the floor that she turns round to sniff before trotting off happily.

'I might get a dildo,' Blinky announces to a mix of shocked faces and others bursting out laughing.

'Ladies with me,' Paula leads her group into Blacks while we head for the cheaper Trespass.

Both stores have already been broken into, so gaining entry is a simple matter of stepping across the threshold. Trespass was never as good as Blacks and lacked the top brands like Berghaus and Peter Storm. The rucksacks look the part but the clasps are flimsy and the straps thinner than they should be. Same with the boots, they look the part but the glue securing the top to the bottom is visible and poorly applied. Three weeks ago and none of that would have bothered me, but now, knowing our lives will depend on the quality of the kit we use and suddenly those things matter.

Every day is now life and death. Every decision matters. If we have to run we'll either be running to save our own lives or running to save someone else's so the last thing we'll need are bags that will fall apart or boots flapping about with soles coming off. We need hard stuff that is made to last or designed for people intending to climb mountains or hike through jungles. Not weekend day trippers that will piss about in the local woods.

The technical equipment might not be up to the job, but the socks, tops and trousers are suitable. We empty the shelves of socks, taking everything with us and what we can't wear now we'll stuff in the ever filling Saxon.

Torches on the counter but they're cheap and flimsy. The best ones are behind a glass case behind the counter and Nick makes light work by tapping the glass out with the butt of his rifle. We grab rucksacks and fill them with everything we can find. Torches, first aid kits, belt pouches, multi-tools, even survival whistles get thrown in. Bright orange things that claim to be at 108 decibels when used, they could have been used today when we got separated. Loaded up with full bags we head outside.

'You decent?' I call out through the busted open entrance.

'We're not changing here,' Paula shouts back, 'we'll do it downstairs.'

'Same,' I say as we walk in. The store is bigger with less room used for back areas and more given over to shop floor space.

'Getting much?' I ask at the sight of several full bags of gear stacked up by the girls.

'Everything,' Marcy says with a smile, 'do you want us in black or bright clothes?' She asks.

I walk over and stand watching Charlie holding a pair of trousers against her legs.

Should we look the same? Like a uniform of sorts? We did that before when we got kit from the army stores and it made everyone think we were from the army. I look round at the clothing on offer in every colour imaginable, including plenty in black. Twelve other people in the store and if the girls stay with us then that makes it a big team. Meredith brushes past me to nose around the bags the girls have already filled and I watch the black sides of her coat and her broad black head. It's not just her size that is intimidating, it's the colouring of her coat. Rottweilers and Dobermans are the same. Special Forces wear black, police SWAT teams are in black too. It doesn't just look professional but it helps hide the individuality of each person.

'Howie?' Marcy asks, 'black or…'

'Black,' I say, 'everyone in black so we look the same.'

The right decision seems to have been made and they get to work with purpose. Nick and Roy head to the counter rifling the head torches, hand held torches and every other bit of equipment on display.

We empty the store and with everyone carrying rucksacks filled with gear, plus assault rifles and hand weapons we start the journey back down to the escalators to the food hall.

'Can we go there?' Paula nods to the Marks and Spencer on the middle floor as we get from the first escalator, 'hair bands.'

'God yes,' Marcy says, 'good idea, and facial wipes.'

'Toothbrushes,' Paula says, 'and paste and I haven't shaved my legs in days.'

'Tampons,' Blinky announces, 'my period is due.'

'Argh gross,' Cookey says.

'I can just bleed on the floor if you'd prefer,' Blinky says to him.

'Argh even more gross,' he says and leads the way round the circular walk way to the store doors.

More stuff is taken. Wipes of all manner and type and just about every hair band in the store is removed and bagged up. Razors, shaving gel, anti-bacterial soaps and sprays. We load up with toothbrushes, pastes and even hand towels from a display stand. Foot powders, deodorants, shampoos, hair brushes…everything we can carry or that can be stuffed into bags. Finally, and now completely loaded down with gear, we take the final escalator and down into the food hall where everything gets dumped in one central place.

'Plan?' Paula asks me, 'or can I go ahead and organise it?'

'You can fill your boots,' I say with a grin, 'everyone listen in…Paula is now in charge as the personnel manager and I am relieved of duty for a bit.'

'Nooooo,' Cookey says in a low voice.

'Boys, grab a towel and some soap…razors and get washed and shaved dried and changed. Ladies the same and once we're cleaned we'll start organising the bags but nobody…and I repeat, Alex Cookey…nobody is to go through these bags until I'm back and can do it properly. Understood?'

'Bliss,' I sigh theatrically.

'Mr Howie, will you be shaving today?' Paula asks me pointedly.

'Er…yes?' I venture the answer.

'Good, then we look to cutting some hair too.'

'Eh?'

'Have you seen yourselves?' Marcy asks, 'you're all hairy and dirty looking.'

'But…'

'You said I was in charge so in charge I shall be,' Paula grins evilly, 'right, get to it,' she claps her hands like the tyrant she is and makes a point of handing each of us a towel, razor, toothbrush and paste and telling us to get our new clothes to take down with us now, and then telling us not to put them on the wet floor, and also telling us not to spend the time pissing about and she expects us back out within ten minutes.

We get shooed away with Marcy laughing in delight at the sight of a dominating Paula. Grumbling and feeling henpecked we do as bid and head back to the same sinks we used earlier.

Toothbrushes are taken from packets and it feels nice to clean our mouths. The air fills with minty smells as the paste gets handed from one to the other down the line. Nine heads bent towards the sinks and nine blokes spitting into the bowls. We soak our faces with water then wait for the shaving gel to get handed down the line. Even Mo takes his turn despite the four or five hairs sticking out from his chin. Clarence spots him watching the older lads and smiles wryly to himself.

'Shaving,' he announces to the room, 'is done like this...' he glares down the line in a way that does not invite flippancy from the lads. 'rub the gel into a lather so it's nice and thick...wet the razor head...' he pauses until everyone has wetted the head of their razor, 'and we press the head to the skin and bring it smoothly down,' he starts next to his ear and smoothly pulls the razor down his face to his jaw line, 'then we rinse the blade and do the next strip...' he pauses again letting everyone catch up. Even Reginald, Dave and I do as we're told just so Mo Mo doesn't feel left out. Uniform shaving. From one cheek to the next with careful instruction applied to the top lip and the skin at either sides of the mouth. Clarence explains the pluses of shaving with the directional growth of hair and also going against the flow. We work our chins and jaws, and onto the throats.

'Good lads,' Clarence booms, 'now get washed...tops off, armpits cleaned thoroughly and we make sure anywhere that can harbour bacteria is cleansed thoroughly. That means our penises, bollocks and arse...Cookey...

'Didn't say a word, Clarence,' Cookey says, 'er...we doing it all together?'

'No we are not,' Clarence says, 'we shall all turn around and take it in turns to preserve the dignity of our comrades...'

'Thank fuck for that,' Cookey says.

'About turn,' he snaps the order then stares down the line to Mo, 'not you, Mo Mo, you go first.'

The lad turns about and sets to it.

'Pull the skin of your penis back and clean it thoroughly,' Clarence says while we all face the wall on the other side, 'clean your arse crack and make sure everything is dried properly.'

'Okay,' Mo Mo says. I smile to myself and offer a prayer of thanks that someone like Clarence is with us. One by one we take turns and make use of the privacy of a few minutes to clean thoroughly and Paula was right, the floor does become soaking wet within a few minutes.

Clothes are sorted, boots handed round and socks paired up. We get dried and dressed with clean dry clothes and freshly shaven chins and it makes a difference. Black cargo trousers, lightweight but water repellent. Sturdy boots and black quick dry wicking tops that cling to our frames.

Nine bedraggled blokes entered the washroom, filthy with ill-fitting clothes and stubbly chins. What comes out is a team of nine men wearing fitted clothing suited to purpose and all matching. Even Reginald decided to try the clothes on the promise we'd still get him some new shirts and ties from the suit shop on the way out. We walk taller, prouder, backs straight and striding like men.

We aim for the middle and wait for Nick to pass the

smokes out, muted conversations and I can't help but sweep my eyes over them. Blowers growing into his role as corporal but with a deft touch that takes him from one of the lads to leader with ease. Cookey, with his blond hair looking handsome with his freshly shaved chin. Nick, tall and smiling as he shares a joke with Mo Mo who looks so different now. Younger than the rest but he stands proud now, not skulking or hiding at the back. His dark features match the black clothing perfectly and you can tell he feels more included now they all look the same. Roy and Clarence tutting with disgust at everyone else smoking. Both of them standing at ease with legs planted apart and arms folded. Dave is Dave and the black clothes make him look even more deadly than before. Especially when he threads the knife scabbards through the belt to hang one on each hip and another two more in the small of his back.

'You use knives,' Dave walks to Mo Mo and states the question as fact rather than asking.

'Yeah,' Mo Mo nods, 'axe is too heavy for me.'

'Take your belt off,' Dave orders and waits for Mo to unclasp his belt and pull it free, 'carry four,' Dave drops to one knee with four scabbards to thread through Mo's belt. 'They're modern and lightweight, one on each hip and two more at the back...put it back on. I've watched you fight. Don't use two knives from now on. Use one in your right hand until you are good enough to fight with two. Understand?'

'Yeah sure.'

'Like this,' Dave moves to stand beside Mo and drops into a crouch before drawing one knife in his right hand. Mo Mo copies him and flips the knife so the blade is reversed up against his forearm.

'Stab,' Dave thrusts forward with the knife, 'slash,' he

slices the knife cleanly at throat height, 'backstab,' he drives the knife to an imaginary foe behind him. 'Now you...stab, slash, backstab...Roy stand there please, Clarence go behind Mohammed...use them to aim for...stab into the stomach and twist then draw back. When you cut the throat you apply force to open the skin down to the artery...the backstab is done to buy time so you can turn and use a killing blow but when you get good the backstab can be used to open an artery in the groin...now practise.'

We watch Mo Mo getting drilled as Dave uses all of us to position round Mo so he can move from person to person and be guided on the best angle of attack for each. Nick has his throat cut from behind while Blowers is backstabbed in the stomach, shouldered back and stabbed through the neck. Clarence's height makes him a hard target for a cut throat so Dave guides on where to aim for the groin, the wrists and the legs.

'Plan ahead...the one you kill now was planned three kills ago...you know where they will fall, which way they will move, where they will lunge and you use that space against them...do it again.'

Mo Mo is put through his paces and I wonder if he knows how much Dave must like him to be getting such attention and training.

'Well now,' a voice call out from behind us, 'there's some very handsome men in here,' Marcy calls out. We all turn and a mutual admiration society is formed as four black clad women take in the sight of nine black clad men.

They look fantastic and in them I see us reflected back. The clothing is good, not black like paramilitary but professional looking and strong. Paula in the lead and you can tell she's been doing this for a while by the way she carries herself now. Head high and a natural air of confidence about everything she does. Charlie looks great, tall and strong and the clothing fits perfectly. Blinky too, she looks tough like a soldier. Her squatter frame is strong but lithe and very athletic. Wet hair pulled back from foreheads into ponytails held securely by the bands.

'You look better,' Paula smiles at the lads then drifts to Roy, 'all clean shaven,' she kisses him on the cheek, 'much better.'

'Everything okay?' I ask Charlie and Blinky.

'Fine, thank you,' Charlie says.

'Are we staying with you?' Blinky asks.

'Good question,' I reply, 'everyone grab a chair and come in close, we need to talk.'

'Drinks behind that counter, Mr Howie,' Nick says, 'bottles of Coke.'

'Bring them over mate.'

Chairs are pulled up round the tables until we're all together with a table full of coke bottles. I look round and smile again at the sight of everyone looking the same. Some faces I have become so used to seeing, others new and unfamiliar.

'We're going to have a conversation,' I say as a way of starting, 'about who we are and what we've done,' I look over at Charlie and Blinky, 'we'll be completely open and honest...nothing will be hidden from you,' I look to Marcy who nods seriously.

'We'll be honest,' she says with look at Reginald.

'Then, if you decide you want to stay with us we'll be honoured to have you. If you want to go anywhere else we'll make sure you get there safely. If you want to simply walk off and leave we'll give you what we can to protect you...is that fair?'

'Completely,' Charlie replies.

'Once we've done that, we'll decide what we're doing next, everyone okay with that?' I look round the table.

'Question,' Nick tilts his head up.

'Yes you can smoke, there's plenty of space in here... right...where the fuck do I start?'

CHAPTER TWENTY-NINE

Day Seventeen

That blasted horse has the devil in her. That damned blasted violently deranged psychotic lunatic bloody horse. Look at her now! Eating oats like nothing happened. Softly munching and snorting in her bucket while just a short time ago she was attacking them! Attacking them I tell you.

I ventured out from the stable block late in the morning and, feeling decidedly brave, which is not something I am feeling now, I made the stupid decision to go back to that town in an effort to try and find out why they were massing in one place.

. . .

My thought process was that I am a scientist and uncovering facts with a view to determining outcomes is what scientists are meant to do. I had Jess, who at that time, I believed would carry me swiftly away from any dangers.

We went at a steady pace and I kept a high awareness of my immediate surroundings and the view further out. We stuck to open fields and I chose a route that afforded me an ability to turn about and flee should the need arise. I was terrified but the act of taking a pro-active decision did adorn me with a feeling of being brave and I figured that doing something brave might actually lead to courage. After all, isn't it said that the courage comes after the act of fear?

Be that as it may, we cantered the distance and started to skirt the town where we had previously seen the massed infected host bodies. I couldn't see them and Jess was showing no immediate signs of them being close so we headed closer to the town. Still nothing to be seen and a silence so profound it was foreboding. Not a bird was singing. Not a flitter of a breeze. A void of emptiness that, in view of the sheer numbers of host bodies that were here before, was decidedly worrying.

The route we had taken to the town had provided opportunities of height, meaning that we had crested hills and inclines that gave me a view to the sides. I deduced that the hosts had not gone towards the direction I had come from, nor had they taken immediate routes to the *sides as otherwise I felt sure I would see signs of their transit.*

Indeed, the only viable route was away from the direction I had come from. I came from the north so they were heading south. What was in the south?

My map of the area showed me this town was bordered by open fields, pasture land, farms, farmland, grazing land, open land and, well, land in general. The next centre of habitation was a small village called Finkton, which is a place I have never heard of and by God I hope to never hear of it again.

It was quite possible they were not heading to Finkton in the sense of Finkton being the end objective but rather it was most likely, or so I thought at that time, that Finkton was merely on the way to wherever the end objective was. However, with no other information to hand, it was towards Finkton we went. BIG MISTAKE. Damn that horse.

The twenty five miles was covered easily by Jess, and in retrospect I can see she wholeheartedly enjoyed the ride. It was good firm ground, gently undulating with valleys and hills and wide plains that enabled her to gain speed. We even stopped at a small brook from which Jess took on water before we proceeded. We were following the main road from the town to Finkton but at a safe distance to the side of it and it was on the crest of one aforementioned hillocks that I first spied the host bodies and the sight held me fixed with stunned disbelief at what I was seeing.

. . .

THE UNDEAD DAY SEVENTEEN

Hundreds of them. Human bodies running in perfect order down the main road. Perfectly ranked and perfectly spaced and even from the distance we were at I could hear the solid crunch as a hundred and more right feet struck the ground followed by the left. It was incredible, truly mesmerising. It was both frightening and eerily wonderful. It was an army of soldiers speed marching to a destination, but not human. Human's, despite the best training in the world, cannot maintain such perfect spacing and pace of movement. This was exact and precise and I would suggest it was precise down to a millimetre. What struck me was that, having such things on movies and in documentaries of the armed forces of communist countries goose-stepping past their leader, that my eyes demanded to see fit young men all of a size and body type. What I was seeing in reality were people of all ages and body types, from fit young men and women to children and elderly, obese and large down to emaciated frames.

We were too close for comfort and Jess was reacting to their presence with snorts and by throwing her head up and pawing one front foot at the ground. Forgive me if the terminology of a horse stomping on the ground is not "pawing" but I am not versed in equine procedures. Could it be hooving the ground? Hoofing? Raking the ground? Hmmm, this is irritating not knowing the correct term.

We moved away but stayed the course and gained the forward direction towards Finkton. There was a delay caused by coming against a high hedge that was thick with spiky brambles and seemed to go on miles. Jess, I am sure, would have liked to jump the *hedge. I did not want to jump the hedge and was quite content to find a gate through which we could traverse.*

We found a gate then had to move back to the intended course and seek the road on which we had viewed the host bodies. By this time we were very close to Finkton and I could see the buildings in the distance. Slate roofs nestled into a picturesque spot surrounded by open countryside.

At that time, I was still of the mind that Finkton was not the objective but a way-point, so I was content to keep a safe distance from which to monitor the passage in an effort to understand the final destination. My intention was to see which direction they took after Finkton, and then establish the most likely destination and race ahead to warn whoever may be at that location.

Now. Explaining what I then saw will be hard and I will try to lay it out in a logical manner.

The army of host bodies reached the village edge. Ahead of them lay the village square and it was only at this point that I viewed an army vehicle in the centre of the square. A big squat thing with large wheels and what looked like a machine gun fitted on the roof.

Approximately two hundred metres from the square, the host bodies did something remarkable. They split into four lines. Two of the lines moved ahead to skirt the centre. The third line moved off at a tangent and the last line slowed down. Each line appeared to be assigned a corner to aim for. There were four rows of buildings within the square with space between each building. Each line moved to the assigned corner and, with perfect execution, they poured into the square from all corners at the same second.

That was impressive on its own. That so many people could be split so fluidly to move independently but with synchronisation to the other lines.

As the four lines ran into the square so they all howled into the air. At the same as doing this, each line then split into several more lines so that as each line entered the square from their corner, they split until four or five lines that were running. From each corner, those four to five lines then ran either clockwise or counter-clockwise around the square. This meant that up to twenty or so lines of people were running with and against each other at full speed.

I had a position of height, and although I was at a distance, not one mistake did I see. Further, those twenty lines seemed to increase until there were countless lines flowing in a sickening circle within the square. Again it was not human. It was not something humans can do without weeks of intense training. Stage shows, such as Irish dancing, achieve such things but those dancers and actors are drilled like soldiers for months to get it right. These hosts did this instantaneous, without hesitation and without mistake.

I struggled to watch everything but what I did see was

lines of hosts then break from the main swirling mass to attack a specific point of each building row. I could hear the howling voices, although somewhat muted due to my distance. I then heard the distinct pops of gunfire, but again I could not place which side they were coming from.

It appeared that as each point of attack was pressed, so more host bodies were sent to re-enforce certain points. Lines peeled off to join the attack. It was then that I viewed more hosts running to the rear gardens of the buildings and climbing fences to get within those gardens.

The gunfire continued. People ran from the backs of houses. On the row with the back direct to me I saw the hosts attacking one end of the row, and a time later, a man and woman ran from the other end. Another side I could see three people running from the back. One was a very large man while the other two were very much smaller.

The row of buildings with the back towards the village I could not see, although I gathered there were people also escaping from the rear due to the numbers of hosts pouring through a single door at the ground level.

. . .

By far the greatest numbers were attacking the last side but I did not see anyone escaping into the rear. Instead it appeared that the hosts ran into the building until no more could fit and then formed a solid group at the front door all trying to get inside.

Those that escaped from the rears were then chased by thick groups out into the open fields. I saw those escapers stop and fire back with weapons and to me, it looked desperate and doomed. They were outnumbered by many to one. I willed them to run faster but it was clear they were tiring and slowing down.

Between watching them, I watched the house of the largest attack taking place and couldn't help but wonder what was in that house that prompted so much attention.

The man and woman, and the three men (the big man and the two smaller ones) then joined together and I watched as one of the small figures attacked the host bodies. He charged into them and I fully expected it to be over. They would be killed outright. Instead though, the small man killed them. The distance was too great to see anything of detail but I did see body after body simply falling down as though the small man was pushing them over. Those people then ran off with a combined force of many numbers of hosts giving chase. From the village I could hear sustained gunfire and even, amongst that noise and spectacle, what I took to be the sound of a dog barking.

I then saw, and I confess I was so rocked with coursing emotions that my exact flow of events may not be correct, but I saw a man run from the house that had previously been besieged. One man. On his own. Running into many. He had dark hair and was sprinting towards the army vehicle in the middle.

It was at that point that everything went terribly, terribly wrong because without warning, and at the second the dark haired man appeared, Jess went from standing still to galloping. Not galloping. Galloping is the wrong word as it suggests a controlled manner of movement and this was not controlled. Jess ran towards the square with a pace that increased with every stride of her legs. She was charging and somewhere amidst the screams I was emitting I became aware that we were running towards lots of infected hosts that appeared to be very angry indeed.

The dark haired man was targeted by every host body within that area. They swarmed him with such numbers that he disappeared under a growing mound of bodies that flung themselves bodily onto the growing heap. One of them was naked and looked remarkably like a comedian I had seen on television but whose name now escapes me.

It was that mound that Jess was aiming for and such was the fright that took over me I somehow, God knows how, managed to get my assault rifle free and was firing into them as we charged. I do not know how I held the weapon, aimed, fired and held onto the horse and it is highly likely that I did not aim at all.

The mound of bodies was already high by the time Jess reached it. I say Jess reached it as I was not part of this but an unwilling and screaming passenger. Jess vaulted the mound and in so doing she viciously stamped down and used the mound of human forms to propel her forward. The effect was incredible. Bodies were crushed and scattered from the top of the mound to be flung aside. There were host bodies now flinging themselves into our path and Jess swatted them aside with her bulk. She stopped, turned and despite my protests, decided to have another run at the mound. Again she skimmed the top and used the crest of the heap to propel us harder from the other side. She reared up and used her front feet to batter them down. She trampled them underfoot and swung round to use her substantial rump to knock them down. She was fighting them. There is no doubt. It has been some time since it happened and the memory is a blur of events, of seeing hosts decaying and snarling being killed outright by a herd animal that should be gentle in nature. Indeed, everything Jess did goes against my knowledge of what her species of animal should do. They give flight from danger and run away. They do not run into danger and take on people intent on doing her harm.

Several times we went for that mound and each time saw it wither in size until the dark haired man appeared from the tangle of limbs and torsos. All I remember is going up as Jess reared then going down as she dropped and going round in circles as we skittered back and forth. She killed many.

. . .

There was one view that remains in my mind. A distinct view seared into my memory and it was gained as we reared up high into the air and the dark haired man pushed himself free. We locked eyes and never before have I seen a man with such an intensity within his expression. There was not an ounce of fear within him and the second he was free of the press of bodies he was stabbing a knife into the neck of a host female. He was consumed with intensity and drive. Then we were off and Jess galloped to the side, spun round, shook her head and again either pawed or hooved the ground before once again charging at the mound.

I screamed a warning to the dark haired man who scrabbled to break free and dive to the side as Jess used her weight to pummel the remaining mound to a pulp. The dark haired man went back into the house at which point Jess decided that fighting people was old news and ran off in a different direction and galloped about the area for a bit. Nothing I could do would stop that horse. I shouted and yanked once or twice on the reins but it was made clear to me that yanking on the reins would be an action that resulted in being thrown from her back. In the end I clung on and prayed that it would end soon.

At some point in the ensuing time period we abruptly changed course and ran back towards the rear of the houses and passed the dark haired man and a very attractive woman who were by now, standing on the outside of the rear garden fence clutching their ankles in what appeared to be the middle of an argument. What possessed Jess to do this I have no idea. Truly I *have no idea why the horse reacted in such a way. Jess took us to a thicket of trees and whinnied noisily to draw the attention of host bodies within that thicket. She then enticed them to come after us and ran away when they gave chase.*

I do not know what happened to the dark haired man after that, nor any of the other occupants of the village. It started raining and soon the whole of the vista about us was consumed with driving rain that obscured everything from view.

We became lost, or rather, I became lost and had to once again give Jess the control of our direction. She led us back to our stables from where we had set out. Straight here without error or seeming concern of the route.

Now she eats oats while I once again come down from the anxiety of the recent events and commit my thoughts to paper.

We set out this day to seek answers but have only gained yet more questions.

Why were the host bodies so intent on targeting the dark haired man? He would have been bitten and scratched within that mound of bodies so he must be immune. Which one on my list is he? Or is he an unknown entity? At what rate is the virus evolving to organise such perfection of movement so soon after the event began? Why did Jess charge in that manner? There was an immediate reaction caused on seeing the dark haired man *that caused the horse to charge? Was she seeking to protect him, or was there something else happening?*

Who is the dark haired man?

The rain is coming down hard and I suspect it will remain so for some time now. The going will be harder and I can only hope the water seeks to protect those that have survived so far.

I will rest tonight and stay here. I am exhausted, terrified to the core but also now very intrigued.

NB

CHAPTER THIRTY

Day Six

He sits in the dark of the house. Quiet. Pensive. The boy sleeps in his room upstairs and the Albanian stares into the darkness of the kitchen.

Everything is wrong. Nothing is right. All rules have gone. No structure. No orders. No hierarchy. No overseers waiting to find out how the mission went.

His heart rate increases but without reason to increase. Anxiety forming but so foreign to him and it feels like his body is preparing to fight or run, but there is nothing to fight and no reason to run.

He shifts position and drums his fingers lightly on the table top on which his arm rests. He blinks and swallows, fidgets and drums his fingers. A deep sigh, an exhalation of air but it does nothing to ease the troubles building within.

Streams of worry in his mind. Streams that all come

from different directions and carrying their own flotsam and together they form a raging river full of debris. His past, the way he lived his life. Killing as a job. Taking life on the orders of another person. His childhood given away to pay a debt. The years of solitude and training, the beatings, the harsh regime, the skills tortured into him. The world ending. Dead people rising up with an infection. Having no structure or knowledge of what to do next.

The boy.

The boy is a worry enough despite all the other things hammering through his head like a swirling vortex of images, sensations, feelings and emotions repressed and stunted for so many years.

The boy was killing the thirty in the garden. An acceptable thing as the boy needs to know how to survive in this world. The infected are dead anyway and they don't feel pain and each one killed is a good thing. Gregori knows this and is at ease with that knowledge.

Sit. Open your legs. Bend over. Give me your arm. Stand there. Lean forward. Orders given by the boy and they complied but the boy got annoyed that the others were all moving away in a slow shuffle towards Gregori. So he told them to stop.

Stop.

One word and every single remaining infected person stopped moving and stood still and that, that very thing is what drives the deepest sense of unease through Gregori.

Not the word used but the meaning and the message given. Over twenty were still on their feet and the boy simply said *stop,* but he did not specify who was to stop. The boy did not look at any given person nor point at them in turn. The boy said *stop* and they stopped. All of them.

Gregori has spent a lifetime studying the fine nuances

of human behaviour under intense stress and at the point of fearing for their life. He has stood over fully grown hardened men and told them to do something and watched as they did it. They gave up and became submissive. Gregori was the *ugly man* and they knew they were already dead so they complied with a deep instinct that the only hope left was to somehow please the monster and hope it goes away.

It was not the word used that made them comply. It was the boy that made them comply. It was what the boy *wanted*. The connection from the boy to them.

Again his heart rate ramps with such a sudden surge that his hand clutches his chest with fright at the suggestion of a heart attack. That fear increases the heart rate. Adrenalin is released. His foot starts tapping. His head beads with sweat. His fingers drum on the table and his breathing becomes faster.

Kill the boy. What he is doing is wrong. Kill him. Go upstairs, open the door and fire the pistol into his head then burn him so there can be no way back. Decimate the body. Kill him.

Both his feet tapping now. His fingers drumming harder. Gasping as though he's running and the sweat coursing to drip from his chin. The hand on the table reaches out and grips the pistol. On his feet and he's halfway up the stairs before the realisation hits him.

Do it. The urge is overwhelming. Do it. Kill the boy.

Not a sound he makes as he climbs those stairs and at the top he pauses outside the closed door to the boy's room as his face screws up in a struggle of mind over reason.

KILL THE BOY.

His hand twists the door knob, slowly, gently but gripping so hard his hand aches from the exertion. The door opens, a gap forming that widens inch by inch. His eyes wide with fear and hurt. The sweat pouring now. His heart booming with such ferocity it makes him want to drop down and cry.

The boy. Standing in his room staring out into the hallway at Gregori. His arms hanging down at his sides. Eyes open and staring. Chin tilted up. Small, defenceless, puny, weak, feeble but that pistol doesn't lift and Gregori doesn't move as the minutes tick slowly by. Determination against fear and something unknown, something Gregori has not the emotional depth to understand makes it impossible to kill the boy.

'Night, Gregoreeee,' the boy wins and watches unblinking as the Albanian closes the door.

CHAPTER THIRTY-ONE

From the beginning to the end everything out in the open and not only does it let Charlie and Blinky know exactly who we are, but it also brings everything back into perspective for the rest of us. Of what we've been through, what we've done and that includes the things Marcy did.

Terrible things. Awful things. Things that mean she should be shot through the head and killed outright while we rip Reginald limb from limb in front of her dying eyes. Except all that we are is what we are now, and we're formed by the paths and journeys we took to get here.

If Marcy had not been turned by Darren she would never have come to the fort that day and saved us. It would have ended right there outside the fort. We were beaten that day and we knew it.

If we had fallen that day the fort would have been lost. Maddox would never have come. We'd never have found the doctors or teamed with Paula and Roy. We'd never have got the ammunition or saved the children in that stately home that Nick went to. Lilly and her brother would have been killed by now. Milly would be eating shit and living in filth.

Every step, every second, every decision made, right or wrong, has made this moment possible and I know, with everything I am I know that Marcy would do anything to take away those few days of her life. Like I said before, it's not my job to give absolution or forgiveness but show me a saint and I'll show you the devil in disguise.

In a nameless town, in an empty shopping centre in an empty food hall with dead bodies at the sides we seek to know who we are now and in doing so, we make an unconscious decision that the past is gone and only the future lies ahead.

Blinky zoned out in less than three minutes of talking. She started with rapt attention then gave way to fidgeting, then started staring about and finally glazed over and sunk into a dream where no doubt she and the lads ran through hordes of zombies chopping them down with razor sharp hockey sticks.

Charlie stayed the course though, listening, asking questions to clarify things, Mo Mo asking questions too about things that happened before he joined us. Paula and Roy telling us the things they had seen and done. Marcy taking her turn and forcing herself to relive the memories so etched into her mind. What gets me for a second is that Lani is just a name to Charlie and Blinky. They never knew her and never will. She is someone who, to them, simply never existed as a real person.

That helps bring some perspective to my own troubled thoughts. The guilt, the raging screaming wailing guilt at flirting with Marcy when just a few hours ago I was looking down at Lani's charred body – that guilt eases into a dull roar. I am human and I am flawed. What things I do to get through the day and the pain of this life is down to me and never done with malicious intent. If seeking solace in the arms of a woman at the point of believing we were about to die, and sharing a kiss to feel the touch of love, if they are bad things then I am a bad man, but I wouldn't deny that hope to anyone in the same circumstance.

'So,' I exhale a long breath from puffed out cheeks and sink into my chair, 'there you go.'

Charlie nods thoughtfully while Blinky stares up at the ceiling way above our heads.

'What about you?' Marcy asks gently, 'family?'

'Huh?' Blinky blinks at realising a question was aimed at her, 'what's that?'

'Do you have family?' Marcy asks again.

'Wankers,' Blinky replies, 'hate 'em.'

'Okay, so do you...' Marcy starts to say.

'Hope they got chomped by the zombies,' Blinky says, 'and then...and then...dunno, fuck 'em...wankers.'

'That's...' Marcy trails off.

'Honest,' Paula says nodding to keep the flow going, 'it's honest.'

'Yes, very honest,' Marcy rallies.

'So,' Nick leans forward to look down at Blinky, 'you want to go and find them then?'

'No!' Blinky scoffs, 'wankers.'

'So you do want to find them then?' Cookey asks.

'No I bloody do not.'

'Okay, we've got to find Blinky's family,' Blowers says.

'Who's family?' Nick asks.

'Blinky wants to find her family,' Cookey says.

'Oh okay.'

'Twats,' Blinky says with a snort of laughter, 'no fucking

chance...only if we can shoot them,' she says with sudden hope, 'can we go and shoot them?' She looks at me.

'Charlie,' I turn quickly to the other girl, 'what about you?'

'No one,' she says with a shake of her head.

'Sure? No family, friends? Anyone that might be alive and...'

'No one,' she says with a finality that ends the conversation then seems to realise the force she used in her tone, 'I mean...we only stayed behind because there was nowhere else to go...otherwise we would have gone...'

'Fair enough,' I say, 'what do you want to do now? We'd love to have you with us...I think I speak for everyone when I say that?' I look round at the others questioningly.

'It's hard,' Paula says, 'harder than anything you've ever done.'

'In what way?' Charlie asks.

'What we did today, in your house...that's *every* day for us...and it will probably get worse.'

'Why worse?' Charlie asks.

'Can I say?' Paula looks to me.

'We left the fort to go after them...today was not the plan as we got caught out but...the plan is to find them, inflict losses and then move on somewhere else and keep doing it. They want us, well you saw that for yourself, so instead of running we're going to fight back.'

'I'm in,' Blinky states, 'so in...do I get a gun?'

'Weapon not a gun,' Clarence says.

'Do I get a weapon?'

'Yes you'll get a weapon and you'll be trained how to use it,' I say, 'and be expected to work with the team and follow orders...'

She cuts me off with a hand held up, 'I was trialling for

the England team,' she says, 'so like...team work is easy and...I can work with a team...and...I can follow orders can't I Charlie...'

'Yes she does.'

'See,' she nods at me, 'so can I join?'

'Charlie, what about you?'

'I'm in,' she says instantly, 'same as Blinky.'

'Yay!' Cookey on his feet as the rest of us clamber up to shake hands with them in turn.

'One thing though,' I cut through the noise, 'you can stop any time you want...that goes for everyone,' I look round at the faces and let my eyes rest first on Roy then on Paula, 'none of you have to stay if you don't want to...'

'I know,' Paula says to me then glances over at Roy, 'Roy?' She asks, 'what do you want to do?'

We all go quiet and listen respectfully, 'I wouldn't stay here,' Roy says, 'if it was just me. I don't like other people and prefer to be on my own.'

'I get that, mate,' I say back, 'but we like you being with us.'

'Oh I like you all,' he says, 'most of the time, but...I don't need other people the way other people need other people... does that make sense?'

'It does.'

'Some people need others to validate them, I don't. I worry and have anxieties and get worked up over stupid, stupid things and I then hate myself for not being able to get over that way of thinking and...well, it's been with me for years and I can't see it ever being any better...' he stops and looks round at everyone, 'so I didn't socialise for a long time and got out of the habit of being with other people, which means I say stupid things and offend people...'

'Ah, Roy,' Cookey says, 'you don't offend us.'

'I offend Blowers quite a lot,' Roy says honestly.

'Fair one,' Blowers nods, 'doesn't matter though mate, it's a big team and we ain't always going to get on like best mates with each other.'

'Anyway, if it wasn't for Paula I would leave and yes, Paula and I have talked about leaving the group but...'

'Paula?' Cookey asks suddenly, 'you're leaving?'

'Listen,' Roy says with a huff.

'Sorry, Roy.'

'We talked about leaving the group but I can see how attached Paula is so...well, not to sound overly dramatic but if Paula wants to stay then I will stay.'

'I do want to stay,' Paula says earnestly, 'look at what the lads did today...I can't leave them...'

'I know you can't and I'd never ask you to,' Roy says, 'so if you want to stay then we'll stay but we'll have to re-think it if you're pregn...'

'Roy!' Paula snaps.

'Pregnant?' Clarence booms, 'are you?'

'No way?' Cookey's eyes go like dishpans.

'No I am not!' Paula snaps, 'Roy,' she says with a groan shaking her head.

'Are we having a baby?' Cookey asks, 'are we? Can I be uncle Cookey?'

'No I am not but...if I was then yes you can be uncle Cookey but I am not...right, just shush now, I said to Roy earlier that I *might* get pregnant as we haven't...well...you know...'

'Used a condom?' Cookey asks with delight.

'Yes, Cookey,' Paula laughs, 'we haven't used a condom or anything else.'

'Is that wise?' Marcy asks, 'taking that risk?'

'Probably not but we never really planned it like that,'

Paula says, 'I cannot believe I am even having this discussion.'

'I cannot believe we are having this discussion either,' Reginald says tightly, 'is nothing sacred within this group?'

'Apparently not,' Paula says, 'right look...we're getting off track. Roy, I want to stay but if you really want to leave then I will go with you.'

'Stay, Roy,' Nick says, 'Roy...stay with us, Roy...Roy... Roy...stay, Roy...'

'Roy,' Blowers joins in, 'Roy...don't go, Roy...Roy...Roy...'

'You's staying Roy? Roy,' Mo Mo chuckles, 'Roy you's stayin or what, Roy?'

'You can't take my Paula,' Cookey goes for a serious expression and deep voice, 'she looks after us and makes us wear clean pants...' he looks round at the laughing, 'we'd be left with Clarence telling us to do that stuff...'

'Yeah don't go, Paula,' Clarence says with deep chuckle, 'or take me with you.'

'You're not leaving me on my own with them,' Marcy says, 'if I've got to stay then you should too.'

'Okay okay,' Paula relents from the barrage, 'Roy, I want to stay,' she says with an apologetic look at him.

'We'll stay,' he says simply, 'as long as you want.'

'FUCK YES!' Cookey yells 'nice one, Roy.' He holds his hand out to Roy with a wide grin on his face.

'Cheers, Roy,' Nick pushes in and clasps Roy on the shoulder. Even Blowers steps forward with a grin and handshake.

I turn round to see Marcy hugging Paula and murmuring *thank you* into her ear. It's funny really. Clarence has his strength, Dave has his ability, the lads have the heart and I lead but Paula dominates us in a way only a woman can. She brings common sense to our world, a voice of reason and thought. The feminine against our masculine. We got by before she joined but it's far better with her here and I breathe my own sigh of relief while the others shake hands and take it in turns hugging Paula. She smiles warmly to each of them, and I notice she doesn't exclude the two new-comers either. She gives warmth and something else, she gives assent that what we're doing is right. Blinky would stay with us no matter what, that's obvious. Charlie however is clearly a lot more complicated and she looked to Paula as though seeking knowledge that we're safe to be with. Marcy too, she looks to Paula for advice and kinship.

'Paula,' I nod in formal greeting when she steps away from the group over to where I'm standing.

'Mr Howie,' she nods back formally.

'Glad you're with us,' I say, 'I couldn't do this without you, you know that, right?'

'Yeah,' she grins wryly, 'I know that. So I'm still the personnel manager then?'

'Yes,' I laugh, 'I'll lead, Clarence and Dave will train but everything else is all yours.'

'Sounds good but I want a pay rise, my own office, weekends off and a company car.'

'I can give you a rifle,' I say with a shrug, 'crap food, probably no sleep...a bigger team to look after and a whole heap of shit to go with it.'

'Fine,' she snaps, 'I'll take it. You and Marcy okay?'

'Yeah,' I lean round to look over at Marcy laughing with Clarence and Charlie at Blinky making a beeline for the lads, 'yeah I think so...we almost lost back there, in that house...'

'Yeah?'

I nod, serious now, 'she came through though, was right behind me the whole time...we got stuck behind a door and just about kept them out with our legs. I'd got knocked senseless by some animal but she kept them out while I recovered.'

'Really?' Paula says turning to look at Marcy, 'she's genuine then.'

'Yes,' I give the reply instantly, 'yes she is...' I think back to the kiss we shared as we prepared to die and the outpouring of grief she gave, and how she tried to get me to leave while she held them out, 'no doubts,' I say to Paula.

'I like her,' Paula says quietly. The sixth sense of being watched prickles Marcy who turns and offers us a puzzled grin at the way we're looking at her, 'she's stunning too.'

'Is she?' I ask lightly, 'can't say as I noticed...'

'You fibbing...'

'Right,' I call out quickly, 'we're moving out to find somewhere for the night. Get your kit, get the bags Paula assigned and be ready in five. The light will be fading before too long and we don't want to be here when it does.'

'I haven't done the bags yet,' Paula says, 'we got talking right after getting cleaned up. Give me five minutes. Nick and Roy, get the torches and batteries into one pile. Marcy and Charlie, can you make sure each bag is assigned antibacterial cleansing wipes, a first aid kit and spare socks, make sure Clarence's bag gets the big socks...Cookey, water bottles...Reginald, we've got safety whistles on lanyards, can you make sure everyone gets one please and make sure they're wearing them...'

'Once we get back to the Saxon I want everyone loading their bags with ammunition and rifle cleaning kits...' I add to her orders.

Organised chaos ensues with everyone moving between the bags of pilfered goods to get what they want but there's method to the madness. Reginald has to join in and sort through the whistles which means he doesn't get to stay on the outside. Blinky works with Cookey getting the water bottles sorted while Charlie and Marcy go through the wipes and first aid kits.

'Can everyone listen for a sec,' Nick calls out holding a strap in his hand, 'this is a head torch, it goes on your head…'

'Really?'

'Fuck off, Cookey. Turn on,' Nick pressed a button at the top, 'turn off,' he switches it off, 'batteries last for ages but there's spares in the bags, 'these are normal LED torches,' he flicks the hand held torch on and off, 'very bright… very fucking bright.'

'Can everyone listen for a sec,' Cookey stands up holding a water bottle, 'this is a water bottle,' he plays to his audience with a straight face, 'inside will be water…to access the water you flip the lid and…'

'Such a cunt,' Nick laughs.

'On with it,' Paula calls through the bedlam.

'Wipes and first aid kit in each bag.'

'Thanks, Charlie,' Paula says, 'Cookey are those water bottles getting themselves into those bags?'

'Yes, Paula…I mean no, Paula…I mean I…fuck me, we've got a Dave a Clarence *and a* Paula now,' he groans, 'can I take it back about you going?'

'No,' Paula says.

'Marcy, will you stay nice or you gonna be all bossy like them?' Cookey asks.

'Thank you, Alex.'

'Sorry, Dave.'

'Whistle, Mr Howie,' Reginald appears in front of me holding out a bright orange whistle on a lanyard.

'Cheers, mate,' I tug it over my head and feed the whistle under my top, 'you okay?'

'Yes yes, of course, thank you, Mr Howie.'

'Reginald,' I call him back as he goes to walk off, 'you don't sound very convincing.'

'I simply have no skills to offer this group, Mr Howie,' he says stiffly, 'everyone else can fight. I cannot fight. Everyone else can run. I cannot run. Everyone has a part, Mr Howie but I am unable to provide any essential needs. Forgive me if I sound ungrateful because I am eternally grateful for the heroic endeavours of Clarence and Dave, especially Clarence, but I fear I will hold you up should something happen...'

'It will happen, mate,' I say, 'it's not a case of if but when. You and Marcy are integral to this. You were both infected *and* unlike Lani you were fully turned...but you aren't now...'

'That is what I am and not what I can do. I can do nothing to assist your team.'

'Have you seen your eyes?'

'They are lessening, yes I saw in the washroom. Again, Mr Howie, and I say it with the greatest of respect but I am terrified out of my wits and my fear is not something that can be trained away. The mere thought of picking up a weapon fills me with as much dread as being eaten alive or...oh my word, I cannot express the fear that grips me...and I am wearing black. Black. I am wearing clothing designed for outdoors when I detest the outdoors...'

'Okay, what can you do?'

'Nothing, I cannot do a thing. I have no transferable skills. There is nothing I can bring to this group.'

'There will be,' I say with a firm nod, 'wait and see.'

'Your confidence is inspiring and yes, I will admit that after seeing you in action as it were today, yes I see why you lead and why they follow but truly I fear I will get in the way and cause you delays and trouble.'

'I don't know what to say, mate but everything we're doing seems to be for a reason so...stick with it and see how it pans out.'

'Indeed,' he turns away and stops briefly, 'and may I ask, politely of course, that we do not stop and undertake an embarrassing situation of getting shirts and ties on the way out. It would be patronising and...'

'Course,' I cut him off but feel the sting of his words as he walks away.

'We're ready,' Paula says, 'your bag, Sir.'

'Cheers,' I take the rucksack and push my arms through and start adjusting the straps so it cinches tight enough for the axe to slide down and be held in place, 'perfect.'

'Can't carry the world, Howie,' Marcy says quietly. I look up to see her smiling softly and nodding towards Reginald, 'he'll be okay.'

'Christ, you got the hearing of a bat or something?'

'Maybe,' she laughs, 'but I didn't need to hear it, I know Reggie and can guess what he said.'

'Aye,' I shrug and pick my assault rifle up, 'he's lost in the size of the team.'

'Aren't we all? So what were you and Paula discussing earlier that warranted such interesting stares?'

'I was telling her how mean you were today.'

'Mean?'

'Yep, how you shoved spam in my mouth and then bragged about your boobs and legs.'

'Really?' She arches an eyebrow at me and hefts her rifle up, 'we're doing that again?'

'Maybe,' I take in the sight of her wearing the black

clothes and carrying an assault rifle and her hair pulled back in a ponytail, 'suits you.'

'I know,' she quips.

'So vain!'

'I was joking.'

'You were not joking...'

'I was joking...but seriously? Does my bum look big in this?'

'Oh my god,' I start walking off towards Dave.

'Seriously, Howie, does my bum look big in this?' She calls out as everyone else looks over and starts laughing at her turning on the spot trying to see her own arse, 'does it? Mr Howie...does it?'

'Dave, would you please get them formed up and ready.'

'Oh that's below the belt,' Marcy gets in quick before Dave barks the order.

'Form up and be ready to move out, bags on, weapons ready, eyes up. They are ready, Mr Howie.'

'Thanks, Dave. Right, let's get the fuck out of dodge... Dave on point with me...everyone stay together.'

We load up with the left over goods from the stores and head up the escalators and round the circular walkway to the main aisle back down to the entrance. I ignore the suit shop and hear a few comments behind me offering for Reginald to get new shirts and ties but he replies stiffly and makes it clear he doesn't want anything.

Time to switch on and the banter ends. Eyes up scanning the entrance, the others slowing down on signal from Dave who moves out to view both sides with Meredith sniffing the ground. The rain is still heaving down in a torrential downpour that sounds an orchestra of drums and pings into the air.

'Straight in,' I open the rear doors to the Saxon and

move out to provide cover while the rest run from the shopping centre and into the back. More bags, more kit, more things that fill the limited space and we need to organise and find a way of storing it all, but not now and not here.

I'm drenched in seconds, we all are but the clothing does the job and doesn't soak the water up like before. I climb into the driver's seat with Clarence up front and we pull away moving down the High Street and away from the town centre.

Early evening but it seems later with heavy clouds lying low in the sky. The end of the High Street is already submerged from a natural dip in the ground that stores the run off from the pavements and gutters.

'It looks weird,' Nick says from behind the front seats, 'like normal.'

'Normal?'

'Yeah, like...when it was raining like this before... everyone would be at home anyway, so it looks normal now.'

'Shit,' I realise he's right. The scene is normal. Like the rain has taken everyone off the streets. The blood smears and stains are hidden from view and the few bodies we see are already partially obscured by the deep puddles and water rushing along the gutters. For a minute I feel a deep pang of homesickness. A desperate desire to be at home watching the rain from the window and drinking tea, or at work watching the soaked shoppers coming into the store. Everything is gone. Everything is changed. Even if the infected all dropped down dead right now we'd never be able to return to what it was before. Families, friends and people we knew. Gone. Then it hits me even harder at how Reginald must feel. At least we've got each other but he must feel desperately alone now with a self-perceived image that he can't bring anything to the table.

THE UNDEAD DAY SEVENTEEN

I shake it off and focus on the task at hand, which is driving out of the town and finding somewhere to stay for the night.

'We cannot stay like this,' Paula huffs from behind, 'we can't move and Meredith hasn't got any space.'

'We'll tidy up and sort it out when we stop for the night,' I call back.

'Won't do any good,' Marcy says, 'all the cupboards are full...it's the ammunition boxes taking up the room.'

'I don't know what you want me to do.'

'Can't we find a bigger one of these?' Paula asks.

'They don't come bigger,' Clarence turns round to join the conversation, 'in fact they made them smaller after these...we'd need a lorry or something but they're not armoured, the next ones up are tracked and...'

'Tracked?' Someone asks.

'Like a tank, with tracks,' Clarence explains, 'the fuel consumption is terrible and the speed is nothing like these things.'

'Poor Nick is standing up and the girls are wedged in at the end,' Marcy says.

'I don't mind standing,' Nick says.

'We could try and find another Saxon?' I call back, 'or something else.'

'I had a van before this,' Roy says adding to the clamour of voices, 'we could get another van.'

'No protection,' Clarence says, 'thin body, the tyres will blow...no, they'd have that in seconds if they saw you in it.'

'So we try and find another Saxon then,' Blowers says, 'but they stopped making these and most of the vehicles were deployed overseas.'

'We can look for a training vehicle like this one,' I suggest, 'but it'll take time.'

'Howie, have you seen how bad it is back here?' Marcy says.

I try and twist round to look and struggle keeping a straight line until Clarence reaches out to grab the wheel, 'go on,' he says, 'I'll hold her steady.'

Turning round I look down and can't help but laugh at the sorry sight. Ammunition boxes stacked everywhere, bags and rucksacks jammed into any space available. Rifles, axes, people, a dog, legs stretched out or tucked up and everyone staring back at me with red faces from the build-up of heat.

'Okay,' I take control of the wheel again, 'we'll find something...dunno what but we will.'

Through the rain we drive. Monsoon conditions but no wind. Just water falling straight from the sky and adding yet another worry to the many we've already got. One thing at a time though. One task at a time. Find somewhere to stay.

Easier said than done.

CHAPTER THIRTY-TWO

Day Seven

'PARK!' The boy bounces on the seat clapping his hands, 'look, Gregoreeee...look...a park, Gregoreee...canwego? Canwego?'

'What park?'

'That park!' The boy squeals pointing to the right and the play park beyond the brightly coloured looped metal fencing.

'No park,' Gregori grunts.

'THERE IS,' the boy works quickly to unclasp his seatbelt and stand up from the seat close to the windscreen, 'that park...there it is...'

Gregori looks round, looks up, looks left and right at everything apart from the park, he grunts disdainful and nonchalant, 'no park.'

'Gregoreeee,' the boy laughs, 'there...stop and I'll show you.'

'Stop? Stop where?"

'Stop here.'

'Where? There?'

'No here!'

'I stop over there.'

'Noooo, Gregoreeee, stop now we're going past the park....stop...'

The van stops and both doors open, one faster than the other as the boy drops down to sprint flat out over the road and down the fence line searching for the gate, 'here,' he shouts back and pushes through.

Gregori walks slowly with his hands at his sides. Sniffing the air, scanning every window and door of the surrounding houses. Turning to check entry points, escape routes, the distance from the park to the van, trip hazards and parked cars. Into the park he goes, pushing through the gate and taking in springy rubberised matting at the base of each piece of equipment. A roundabout, slide, swings, ropes, climbing frames, seesaws and an area set aside with benches for picnics complete with corpses rotting in the hot sun. Swarms of flies lift from the several bodies strewn about the benches and a wide dried pool of blood writhing with fat white maggots.

'Push me,' the boy on a swing kicking his legs to and fro, 'push me, Gregoreee.'

The Albanian heads over and moves round behind the boy. Placing his hands on the back edge of the swing he pushes out to glide the boy forward.

One of the chains rubs against the fitting. A squeak that sounds with each swing. The boy laughs and demands to be pushed harder. Gregori pushes and stares round at the park, at the houses, at the street, at the area they are in. Back to the boy and he pushes out, taking steps back to let the boy swing further on the reverse.

Everything so clean and nice. The rubber floor laid down to protect the children who played here. The metal fencing designed to entrap the children and stop them running into the road but painted in different primary colours so it blends with the environment of play and fun.

Mothers with children came here. Fathers too. Families that laughed and loved. The houses nearby are nicely fronted with clean windows and pretty little gardens full of flowers. The cars left in situ are shiny and new.

'Push me harder...'

Gregori pushes harder with that growing sense of unease spreading through his mind. Houses. A play park, nice cars, nice everything. Why aren't the infected things attacking the boy? Why couldn't he kill the boy last night?

'Harder!'

He pushes harder and the boy sails forward to rise on the swing with his legs kicking out and his small hands gripping the chains as the funny sensation in his stomach lifts and sinks.

The squeak. Again and again. The boy laughing. The houses so nice and clean. The bodies writhing with maggots and a big black bird that falls from a tree to land in the pool of dried blood to feast on the fat maggots.

'Again!'

The chain squeaks, the boy laughs with delight. Gregori tenses, his face showing emotions that bubble from the core. Of a life denied and a life lived.

What he never had. What he could never have. What he would never have. Nice houses and families laughing. Shiny new cars. Kill the boy. A play park with coloured fences. His breathing gets harder, his frown showing and the corner of his mouth twitches. The bird pecks at the maggots and feasts on the death. Why couldn't he kill the boy?

What he never had and what he was. Life and death. The bodies are what he was. He gave that death and made the flies swarm to lay their filthy eggs so the maggots would feast and grow. He did that. Hundreds maybe more. Men. Women. Children. All cut down by his hand and yet he cannot do what must be done.

The chain squeaks and rubs. The boy laughs and the nihilism settles in Gregori with a plunging sinking sensation. It drives him down into despair the like of which he has never felt. Gregori never felt anything. He was a machine that gave death. Emotions course through his body, his hands shake and tremble and tears prick the backs of his eyes. He opens his mouth, stretching the jaw in an attempt to rid the feeling.

The boy laughs and the chain squeaks while the maggots writhe and the bodies rot in the blazing sun. It's too hot. Gregori sweats. That damned chain squeaks too much. Those bodies are dead. Torn apart and they would have been running, fleeing, hiding, fighting to live. Just like every victim did when Gregori came. The *ugly man* who appeared like a ghost in the middle of houses and streets. The *ugly man* who never ran but walked with a steady pace, who never flinched from the bullets sent his way and never missed with the bullets he sent back.

His parents gave him up. A debt settled with a human life. The ultimate rejection. Beaten. Starved. Tortured and trained.

The tears stream down his face as the twisting emotions grip his gut. Despair, depression into anxiety that everything was for nothing. There was no purpose. There is no purpose. Nothing has purpose.

'Harder, Gregoreeeeeee.'

The chain rubs and squeaks and Gregori wipes the back of his hands across his pock-marked cheeks to dry the salty tears. His bottom lip trembles so he clenches his jaw and feels a surge of fear from the emotions so new to him.

Everything for nothing. There is no point. Kill the boy then kill yourself. Two bullets bang bang and it's all done. Sleep forever and pray there is no god waiting for a reason for there was no reason. There is no reason. The bird hops away too full and fat to take instant flight. Blood. Bone showing through the ragged flesh.

A groan to the side and a body shuffling from an open door to a house. The head lolling to the side. Another further up, more further down. Red eyed, useless, slow, cumbersome and ungainly. More men and more women and more children to be cut open and sliced to death.

Why go on? Why? For what? There is no home. No place to go. No lessons to be learnt or forgiveness to be given.

Kill the boy. End it. Kill yourself. Die. Be nothing because you are nothing. You were given up as a debt and used as a tool. The boy doesn't love you. This world doesn't love you. This world hates you for what you are. End the life of the boy. End yourself and fall down so the fat maggots can writhe in your corpse.

Staggering away from the swing he sways and lurches to the fence, falling and tripping from the exact profound knowledge that there is nothing. Die. Die now and be done with it. There is no reason for being here. There is nowhere else to go.

His chest tightens, constricts and breathing is hard.

Gasping for breath he tries to walk but the fence blocks his way. He slides and falls, gets up and staggers on while the boy twists round and laughs in delight. A cackle that fills the air. A wild sound of no humour and of no love. He doesn't love you. He hates you. You are nothing. All you have given is suffering and death.

A pistol in hand. How did it get there? He has no recollection of drawing it but the signals from brain to hand are so versed it required no conscious thought. Aiming now. Aiming at a boy swinging back and forth on a chain that squeaks. He tracks. He sways and tenses to lock the bead. His breath pushing from his nose while the other hand splays out with fingers wide on his chest.

'Hahahaha,' the boy mocks and taunts, he knows no fear or regret but only to cause pain, 'hahahahaha,' laughing at him, laughing at the sad man with no life who points a pistol with the promise of giving yet more death. Left to right he tracks the boy and knows with everything he is that if he pulls the trigger the boys head will be blown apart. He is Gregori and Gregori never misses. They trained him well and they beat him hard to cement those lessons into his mind.

Without inertia applied the swing slows through the pendulum and another wave of absolute despair pulls Gregori down to his knees. He whimpers, rallies and lifts then growls at the desire to be dead.

'I GREGORI,' he screams to the world, to the bodies and the fat bird, 'I GREGORI…' he is the Ugly Man. The Albanian. The bringer of death and the exacter of vengeance but he weeps now like a child. Tears pouring down his face. Tears that course from the bulging eyes and slide over the dented, pitted skin to the corners of his cruel thin lips.

THE UNDEAD DAY SEVENTEEN

One shot. Two shot. Three shots and the bodies are blown away. Spinning on the spot he takes wild plucks of the trigger at the infected shuffling down the street but even his wildest shots with tears blurring his eyes are direct hits.

Why now? A sudden deep and creeping realisation that there is a reason, a conspiracy. He was led to this. He was brought here to suffer this very thing. It's been coming for a long time and now it's here. Happening. What's happening?

'I GREGORI,' he bellows with spittle flying from his lips and the boy slides off the swing to skip gaily over.

'I GREGORI,' the boy copies the man, bending from the waist and clutching his chest while staggering round in tight lurching circles.

Gregori's eyes widen at the mocking, at the cruelty of the boy. At how he laughs and copies the pain the Albanian feels. Away, he must get away from the boy and return to the...go back to...

He runs, slamming into the gate and taking seconds through the fog of confusion to realise it must be pulled and not pushed. Wrenched open and into the street, pistol in hand, one hand on his chest and he weeps and cries. Behind him the boy lurches in exaggerated steps with his own hand clutching his chest and half laughing half crying to copy the man.

Away from the van they run. Further up the street which is now filled with the walking corpses that should have died decently. He aims but loses heart to kill anymore and drops the pistol on the ground.

'I GREGORI,' the boy grabs the pistol and aims it at the staggering forms ahead. The trigger is pulled which sends the firing pin into the cartridge which ignites the primer to send the bullet flying from the barrel and the boy flying back off his feet onto his arse with a stunned look on his face.

Gregori pays no heed and runs, he runs staggering and lurching but he runs. He slams into a slow moving creature who bares teeth and lunges at the last second but Gregori has instinct and that instinct drops a shoulder into the chest that sends the woman sprawling away. Gregori spins from the impact into the path of another and whips out a vicious open handed slap that drives the drooling man to the ground. Round and round he goes. Feet not knowing direction. Eyes not seeing. Ears not hearing but still he fights them and still he wins.

The boy, on his feet and still clutching the pistol, charges after Gregori. Calling his name, calling him again and again but the Albanian doesn't hear it. The Albanian is feeling every repressed emotion from a most horrid life. The guilt from every death is present. The pity for his own childhood taken from him. The pain he suffered from the physical beatings and the deeper pain of rejection from a family that used him to pay a debt. His whole world crumbling in an instant and within that conscious stream of whirling thoughts he knows he was fine just a few minutes ago but now he is not fine and will never be fine again.

The world is cruel but he is crueller still. Existence is suffering. Existence is futile. Everything is futile. End it now. Lie down and die. Let the maggots feast on your bloated corpse and feel not these emotions.

He stops. Sudden and staring without blinking, without breathing. His hands fall to his sides and he drops painfully to his knees that sends a jarring crunch through his body. Surrounded by red bloodshot eyes. Surrounded by death and he welcomes it. He welcomes it as he can no longer breathe the air of this world. He slumps to the side and closes his eyes, waiting, longing to feel the teeth sink into his flesh and deliver the deadly virus that will end his life. It's what you deserve. It's what you are. You will come back as a drooling thing that has no mind.

The sun is hot and beats down. Insects buzz in the charged air. Seconds become minutes that stretch and very slowly, so very slowly, Gregori becomes aware that nothing has happened. The tightness in his chest eases. His breathing recovers to a normal state and his eyes open to take in the tiny valleys and peaks of the tarmac beneath his face.

'Gregoreee, can we go back to the park now.'

He rolls onto his front and up onto his knees to twist round and look at the boy sitting cross legged a few feet away with the pistol in his lap, 'we didn't go on the slide,' the boy says, 'do you like the slide, Gregoreee?'

The bulging eyes blink and look round. He was down for a while, long minutes of self-pity that gave time for slow feet to shuffle and get closer. They did get closer. They all got closer and stopped.

A street filled with them. Adults and children, elderly and young and every single one stands still and facing away from Gregori and the boy. Not a few, not tens but hundreds. Hundreds of them that fill the street in both directions and stand unmoving while the boy sits with his legs crossed and his chin cupped in one hand.

Gregori's heart was racing when his mind fractured and now it races again. Thundering in his chest as he springs to his feet and moves like lightning to snatch the pistol from the boys lap at the same time as drawing the second pistol from his waistband. Arms stretched, pistols aimed and he moves round the boy.

'Do you? Do you like the slide, Gregoreee? I like the slide…and then we can go on the roundabout and then we can go on the seesaw…haha, seesaw majory door…do you know that rhyme, Gregoreee? Can we have a puppy?'

The adrenalin released into his body demands usage lest he be left shaking and trembling. Force is needed and force is applied as he pistol whips the closest body with a dull crack to the back of her skull.

'Don't hit Sarah,' the boys tone is low and accusing, his eyes squinting up petulant and sulky.

'Sarah? Who Sarah? This Sarah?' Gregori spits the questions out while his mind loses its grip on reality.

'And that's Thomas and that's Derek and…' the boy points to the drooling bodies standing so close, 'on his feet and he starts skipping and pointing them out, 'John and Sundip and Mandy and Ishmail and…'

Name after name is given and suddenly the boy stops in front of an obese woman, a giant staring down at a child that stares up with wide eyes, 'she's so fat,' he mouths in awe, 'and that's Carl and that's Jennifer and…'

'STOP,' Gregori roars at the boy, 'boy you stop, stop now…I KILL YOU,' he lifts the pistol and aims at the boy who laughs and dodges swiftly back to hide behind the fat woman's legs.

The gun booms, the bullet flies and the fat woman drops with a thud to the floor leaving the boy staring down at the brains scattered on the ground, 'you made her brains come out,' he says quietly, 'oh wow…Gregoreee, do all the brains look the same?'

'How you do this?' Gregoree paces towards the boy

THE UNDEAD DAY SEVENTEEN

with the pistol held ready, 'how? How you do this? You tell me.'

'Why are they grey? There was a book and it had pink brains but all the brains you make come out are grey not pink...'

'How?' Gregoree seethes with fear of something he can't understand and can't comprehend, 'tell me, Boy...how you do this?'

'Are the brains...' the words are cut off as his feet leave the floor. Gregori lifts the boy with one hand gripped to his upper arm, 'GET OFF ME,' the boy erupts in instant temper.

'HOW?'

'GETOFFME.'

'How, Boy? You tell me how?' Gregori shakes hard, heaving the boy back and forth while digging his fingers into the soft flesh of the boys arm, 'tell me...tell me...'

'GETOFF,' the boy thrashes and kicks, his face flushing bright red from temper.

'You tell me...I kill you now...I KILL YOU, BOY...'

The boy screams in fury, bucking harder, kicking wildly and not heeding the pain that must be shooting through his body.

A hand raises, the time is right and Gregori knows the will of the child must be subdued. Again the boy spots it and lifts his head daring the man to strike, his small blue eyes so cold and taunting.

A single open handed slap delivered across the cheek and boy's head snaps to the side but what snaps back is fury so wild it makes Gregori hesitate before striking again.

The boy growls and the infected growl with him. Hundreds of voices growling low in their throats and turning slowly on the spot to glare with wide eyes at the man holding the child.

'This wrong,' Gregori says in a hoarse whisper and glares round at the bodies ranged all about them, 'come...we go.'

He drags the boy back down the street to the van. The boy huffs, bucks, tries to pull away but then gives in and runs along at the side of the man. The boy is lifted into the van and makes no attempt to run off when Gregori slams the doors and moves round to the driver's side. The engine is started, the van backs away and uses a junction to turn before heading back down the road and away from the still turning undead all staring after the boy.

CHAPTER THIRTY-THREE

'FIRE...down and fire...up and fire...forward stop fire...down...get up run forward...fire...Nicholas you have a misfire...clear it....clear it...now fire.'

I hate golf, always have.

'Marcy you have a misfire, clear it...take the magazine out...back in...out...in...out...IN...OUT...down and fire...blockage, clear the weapon....'

A golf hotel was a lucky find though. A nice squat building in the middle of a massive golf course, couldn't get a better place to lay up for the night really.

'Simon, Patricia, Charlotte, Mohammed, Marcy, Paula you are team alpha, go back to the wall now. Alex, Nicholas, Roy, Clarence, Reginald and Mr Howie, you are team bravo...go to the other wall...team alpha will step forward and fire as one on my command....FIRE....Team bravo will step forward and fire on Clarence's command...'

'Team bravo...FIRE...'

'Alpha...FIRE...'

'Bravo FIRE.'

A nice big restaurant, big kitchens and a shop full of

shiny golf clubs. Breaking in was easy. Clarence was going to batter the doors open until Mo Mo shimmied up a drain pipe, cracked a sky light, dropped down and opened the door from the inside. He's got some useful skills that lad.

'Bravo you all have blockages…clear those weapons.'

'Alpha, magazine change…'

The restaurant tables and chairs were cleared away, stacked to the sides so we had space to do this.

'ALPHA DOWN…'

'BRAVO UP…'

Get drilled. Drilled and drilled. Dry firing weapons. Changing magazines. Misfires and clearing the misfires. Running up, staggered firing lines, firing from our stomachs, on our knees, running, walking, turning. Dave and Clarence drilling with basic skills to help Charlie, Blinky, Marcy and Reginald all get used to the assault rifles.

It is basic. Basic drills but that's all we've got time for. Learn to shoot and learn to change the magazine and clear a misfire. Blowers and the lads help the others and I didn't need to do this, being the leader I could have slouched on a chair and watched everyone else. That didn't seem right though and all skills are good skills.

'Alpha and bravo you have run out of ammunition…you will sling the weapons and draw knives…DRAW…'

Knives are pulled out and again we go through the basic killing movements. Stab, slash, backstab. Knives away, knives out, knives away, knives out. Getting used to the position of the scabbard and then ditching the knives to pull the weapons back round.

Everyone works, including Reginald, especially Reginald. He focusses hard and mutters to himself when he gets things wrong, which he does frequently. He sweats hard and his face flushes and although there is a determination within him it's obvious he's not cut out for this type of work.

A long day already and we're all exhausted but I notice that Charlie and Blinky are absurdly fit and take to the drills with ease. The way they move, the confidence in their own physical forms and how to twist, drop, get up and run, and they don't moan about the weight of the weapons either. Blinky loves it, you can tell instantly.

'Room clearance,' Dave announces, 'everyone to reception...go go go...'

We run out to the main reception to gather by the desk and stare down the corridor leading to the hotel rooms.

'Pistols,' Dave strides ahead of us and draws his pistol, 'are held in a double handed grip...'

Room clearance with pistols. Room clearance with assault rifles. Room clearance done on our own, in twos and threes. Room clearance done with hand weapons. Most of them are done by kicking the doors in until Mo Mo has his turn.

'Mohammed,' Dave says pointing at the next door and I swear there is a glimmer in those dull eyes.

Mo Mo steps forward, sizes the door open and looks round with a slightly worried expression before producing a laminated card from a pocket. He slides the thing between the door and the frame, wriggles it back and forth while trying the handle then pops the door open to a brief stunned silence followed by a raucous cheer.

'Show the team the method you deployed,' Dave says stepping back as they all clamour in to watch Mo Mo close the door and start again.

'You bloody knew,' I say quietly to Dave at the back.

'What, Mr Howie?'

'You knew he would do that.'

'Yes.'

'Seriously?' I stare at Dave with pure shock on my face, 'you're giving a straight answer?'

'Yes, Mr Howie,' he says dully.

'An actual straight answer.'

'Yes, Mr Howie.'

'So I asked you if you knew he would do that and you said yes, that you did know he would do that. Is that right?'

'Yes, Mr Howie.'

'Fuck me...' I mutter quietly.

'No thank you, Mr Howie,' the bugger then moves off back into the group to watch Mo Mo open the door and leaves me standing with a mouth wide open.

Room clearance is continued, up and down the corridors of the hotel. Dave doesn't overcomplicate the instruction but keeps everything basic. The only downside is that we can't risk the noise of firing live weapons. That will have to wait until tomorrow.

An exhausted group finishes the last room and heads wearily down the corridor, through the main room and into the kitchens.

'No gas,' Nick says twisting the dials on the various appliances, 'no power either...probably a generator somewhere I can jack up.'

'Tuna, baked beans and more fucking pasta,' Cookey comes out of the store room holding big catering size tins of food and bags of dried pasta.

'You ain't cooking,' Blowers says in alarm, 'he isn't cooking,' he repeats to the group.

'What? I'm a good cook,' Cookey scoffs.

'I puked up from your meal.'

'No, you puked up from running after eating,' Cookey replies.

'I puked up from eating that abomination you bloody made.'

'Abomination? What like that snowman?'

'Abominable you dick,' Blowers says trying to wrestle the tins from his mate, 'you ain't cooking, Cookey.'

'Lads,' Paula calls out in a tired voice, 'long day...'

'Can't we just start a fire on the floor?' Marcy asks, 'the room is big enough and those metal shelves can be dragged over it...we can use them to heat pans for water and make coffee...'

'Coffee?' I perk up immediately, 'someone say coffee?'

'We need fire,' Marcy says.

Furniture is broken up and brought in and paper taken from the office is used to ignite a fire that is gently brought to life until we have a nice bonfire blazing away on the tiled floor of the kitchen. Pans are filled with water and set to boil using the metal shelving dragged over. It's crude but it bloody works. One pan to cook pasta and one for water for coffee. Everyone does something. Finding bowls, plates, cutlery. Getting mugs for coffee, finding the coffee, sugar, milk portions. The pasta is loaded into the boiling water and takes ages to cook. Tins of tuna are opened, baked beans and tinned tomatoes. Meredith gets fed a huge bowl of food and still snuffles round looking for more.

We eat in turns. The pasta is drained and placed in a bowl while we work down the line of tins adding what we want. A comradery builds, a sense of team work and people chatting. Suggestions and counter suggestions and slowly that bond starts reaching out to take in the new people in our group.

A few minutes later and we're pulling chairs up round a few tables and easing tired legs and backs down to rest and drink coffee. Nick hands the cigarettes round and the few of us that smoke light up and inhale pleasurably. Meredith moves round the table searching for the last morsel of food and finally flops down beside Nick to commence a very noisy cleaning session complete with much licking and sucking noises.

'Tomorrow?' Clarence asks in his deep rumbling voice.

'Is another day,' I reply, 'but,' I pause to sip my coffee, 'we're all bad motherfuckers now so...'

'What?' Marcy spits her coffee to a response of chuckles, 'we're what?'

'Bad motherfuckers,' I say with a firm nod, 's'wot we are.'

'Are we?' She asks while mopping the coffee from her legs.

'Yep, we'll find somewhere to fire the weapons so you two can get some practise,' I say with a nod to the girls, 'you both okay?'

'Yeah,' Blinky scoffs with a grin, 'this is fucking awesome.'

I laugh and look to Charlie, quieter and more pensive than her friend, 'Charlie? You okay?'

'Fine, thank you,' she says politely.

'Okay so tomorrow is another day but we've got tonight to get through first,' I say to the group, 'my thoughts are that we'll all sleep in here so everyone is together in case something happens. Agreed?'

'Makes sense,' Clarence says, 'unless Paula and Roy want some privacy.'

'Use a condom though...'

'Alex!'

'Alex...'

'Sorry, Dave, Sorry, Paula.'

'We'll be fine in here with everyone else,' Paula says.

'Will we?' Roy asks.

'Yes, Roy. We will.'

'Apparently we will,' he mutters.

'Lookouts,' I say, 'we'll need lookouts for the night… there will be no arguments about this but some of you are exhausted and need a solid sleep. I'll take first watch, Clarence after me then Dave…everyone else sleep…I said no arguments!' I cut through the voices and stare at the exhausted faces.

'Mr Howie,' Roy says politely, 'I'm fine and can take my turn.'

'Clarence, if you feel tired wake Roy up…everyone else is to sleep and get rest. We've been non-stop for too long and you'll burn out if we're not careful.'

A sullen silence envelopes the room but I can see even the lads look drained with bags under their tired eyes, 'listen' I say in a softer tone, 'I'm asking a lot from all of you…I know that and I also know we're going to be very bloody busy for the next few days so we'll get what rest we can…if we don't get rumbled tonight we can sleep in and take our time in the morning. We're not at the fort now so we can do what we want when we want. Right, go get the bedding and get some rest.'

They head off into the hotel rooms to drag back mattresses, blankets, pillows and covers. The blinds on the windows are closed against the night sky and the pelting rain driving against the glass. Candles from behind the bar are brought out and a few lit to give some light and the room takes on a cosy feeling.

I watch the dynamics of the group with interest and notice the way the lads make camp further down the dining room and draw Blinky and Charlie with them. Clarence, Reginald and the older ones set up at the other end and I can't help but chuckle at the sight. I feel bad for Charlie, she's quiet and withdrawn but then anyone would be in a group like this, but I also know that being with the easy banter of the lads will be the best thing for her. They'll be respectful and gentle and slowly bring her into the group.

Meredith is funny too, running from bed to bed sniffing and wagging her tail with every stroke and fuss of her head. She takes ages to decide but I already knew she'd head back to the younger ones and after getting more fuss she finally settles down on Charlie's bedding and flops down on her side.

'She likes you,' Nick says with a smile.

'She's lovely,' Charlie says pushing her hand through the thick fur and getting a contented grumble in response.

Boots are eased off and they settle into low chat and laughs as Cookey plays expertly to his audience. Whatever they talk about I don't know but this is their time to relax. They're so young and need to have these stolen minutes to be young. Soft candle light, muted voices and the atmosphere blends to a relaxed warm environment.

Paula and Roy slightly off to the side and I smile softy at the sight of them cuddling up on the big mattress, both of them already asleep with Roy's arm held protectively over her. Words cannot explain how relieved I am that Paula is staying, the strength she brings to the team is something we all need. A natural organiser and driven to find solutions in any situation.

Clarence stretches out on his back with his hands behind his head chatting quietly to Reginald. That the big man likes Reginald is obvious. Dave waited until my bedding was put down before putting his own between me and the main entrance. Now he sleeps or rather he lies down with his eyes closed. Does Dave sleep? Does he know how much we rely on his abilities and instincts?

Sitting on a chair away from the group I light a smoke and look from person to person. How are we all together? Dave and Clarence in one place is an incredible thing, but to add Paula into that team then Roy too. The man is gifted with his abilities with a bow and arrow and even now those weapons are beside him on the floor. Then the lads, the central core to the group. Blowers, Cookey and Nick and now Mo Mo. I can't understand it and truthfully I know there must be a reason for it. A dog that can smell them and kill with ease. Some of us are immune and a strong suspicion that most of us probably are.

I can't grasp it. I can't understand it but it's a real thing. When we were separated earlier it felt wrong, like a part of me was missing. They all felt the same and the primary objective was to get back together as soon as possible and that feeling, that feeling when I burst into the room and the battle was underway. That energy between us at being together and fighting as one. It surged like a real thing, like a drug pumped into our veins.

Ah fuck it. It's late and the soft flickering candle light is making me think too deeply. I need to move because as much as I keep looking at the people in our team, I also keep looking at Marcy. The way her hair sweeps back from her head onto the white pillow. The contour of her body from shoulder down to waist and the flare of her hips. Her golden skin and plump lips. I look away, forcing myself to look somewhere else but within seconds my eyes are back on her and on those lips that I kissed earlier. The warmth of her body as we lay on a sodden bathroom floor clutching each other, holding onto each other.

Lani died last night. The guilt sweeps through me and I

force myself to stand and walk away. The assault rifle slung across my back and my beloved axe held at my side. I head out into the near perfect darkness of the reception and let my eyes adjust to the night until I can make out the squat form of the Saxon outside.

Christ I feel like an utter prick. Lani died last night but I can't shake Marcy from my head. Marcy. Always bloody Marcy since the first time I saw her. I pace up and down and light another cigarette.

Back to the matter at hand. Tomorrow. Tomorrow we will go after them and start our guerrilla campaign. Yep, we'll work out a way of hunting them down and killing them

But did you see her when she came out of those toilets all dressed in black? My god she looked incredible.

We'll find a new van for Roy so we can take some of the shit out of the Saxon. Things to do, tasks to be done.

She held that bloody door closed though. Any doubts I had about her vanished at that point. She was real, the emotions in her were real. The remorse, the guilt, the abject misery of what she'd done but then the flirting and when she was feeding me in the kitchen.

Ah, stop it. We've got to find a new van and...and...and kill zombies, find radios. Go places and do things.

'Want some company?'

'Huh?' I turn round guiltily and hope to hell the darkness hides the blush on my face, 'dunno,' I say stupidly.

'Pardon?'

'Er yeah, yeah course, can't sleep?'

She walks in and lets the door close quietly behind her and stepping wide to make sure her rifle doesn't knock on the frame.

'Not yet,' she says, 'you were deep in thought.'

'Er, yeah, yeah you know…lot to think about.'

'Such as?' She stops and leans back against the reception desk and I wish she wouldn't because the poor light from outside captures her too well, 'Howie?'

'Huh?'

'What's got into you?'

'Nothing,' I shrug and casually move to lean on the desk beside her then worry that I was too casual so I stand up and then lean back against the desk.

'Just relax,' she chuckles, 'I didn't come out to get you.'

'I'm fine,' I announce bluntly, 'you?'

'Me what?'

'Er, you er…you okay?'

'You asked me that.'

'Did I?'

'So,' she looks at me full on, 'I have a question,' I swallow and wait, 'does my bum look big in this? You never answered.'

'So vain,' I tut and roll my eyes.

'If you've got it….flaunt it…'

'Oh my god did you really just say that?'

'What?'

'It's just…you're so…'

'Chilled you out a bit though,' she says with a quick grin.

I chuckle and concede the point, 'fair one.'

'What a day,' she says after a pause and letting the tension release from the air.

'Get used to it, always the same.'

'Really?'

'Really.'

'What do you want with me?'

'Eh?'

'Relax,' she tuts, 'I meant why are me and Reggie with you?'

'You know why. Because...'

'So that's the reason? To find scientists and figure out why you're immune and we turned but came back?'

'Er, yeah.'

'Nothing else?'

'Fishing.'

'I'm not, I just want to know.'

'You're fishing.'

'Just be honest.'

'So vain.'

'Not vanity, Howie. I want to know the reasons.'

'How the hell do I know?'

'You know everything, you're Howie...'

'Ah piss off.'

'Apart from if your weapons work in the rain.'

'I found that out.'

'Only after it started raining.'

'But I still found out.'

'Okay.'

'Okay what?'

'Nothing. Just okay.'

'Fine.'

'So,' she says, 'we're just going to ignore it then.'

'Yep, don't know what you're talking about.'

'Okay,' she sighs, 'you're in charge.'

'Yep, still don't know what you're talking about.'

'Hold my hand,' she holds her hand out and I don't hesitate but entwine my fingers in hers, 'that's nice.'

'What is?'

'You're a dick, hang on,' she lets go of my hand and pulls

herself up to sit on the desk. I do the same and sit beside her and make a point of holding my hand out.

'What's that for?' She asks staring at it.

'Fuck you then...'

'Joking, give it here,' she grabs my withdrawing hand and pushes her fingers between mine holding tight, 'and stop swearing at me.'

'You called me a dick!'

'Oh yes, I did didn't I? Okay, no swearing at me from now on.'

'Okay, Marcy.'

'Okay, Howie.'

We sit in the dark watching the front and the rain on the windows. Holding hands. Sitting in the dark and that guilt I had a minute ago is gone. Completely gone. There is only the now and every path we took led us to this point and if this is wrong then I am wrong and, like before, I will take that judgement on the chin.

For now though, I'll sit in the dark holding hands with a beautiful woman who offered her own life so I may live. I'll take that comfort and even edge closer so our bodies touch and even when her head leans over to rest on my shoulder I won't move or flinch.

I'll see this day out and wait for the next and all the shit that comes with it because all that we are, all that we were and all we will ever be is now, in this moment.

ALSO BY RR HAYWOOD

EXTRACTED SERIES
EXTRACTED
EXECUTED
EXTINCT
Block-buster Time-Travel

#1 Amazon US

#1 Amazon UK

#1 Audible US & UK

Top 3 Amazon Australia

Washington Post Best-seller

In 2061, a young scientist invents a time machine to fix a tragedy in his past. But his good intentions turn catastrophic when an early test reveals something unexpected: the end of the world.

A desperate plan is formed. Recruit three heroes, ordinary humans capable of extraordinary things, and change the future.

Safa Patel is an elite police officer, on duty when Downing Street comes under terrorist attack. As armed men storm through the breach, she dispatches them all.

'Mad' Harry Madden is a legend of the Second World War. Not only did he complete an impossible

mission—to plant charges on a heavily defended submarine base—but he also escaped with his life.

Ben Ryder is just an insurance investigator. But as a young man he witnessed a gang assaulting a woman and her child. He went to their rescue, and killed all five.

Can these three heroes, extracted from their timelines at the point of death, save the world?

THE WORLDSHIP HUMILITY

#1 Audible bestselling smash hit narrated by Colin Morgan

Available Amazon May 2019

Sam, an airlock operative, is bored. Living in space should be full of adventure, except it isn't, and he fills his time hacking 3-D movie posters.

Petty thief Yasmine Dufont grew up in the lawless lower levels of the ship, surrounded by violence and squalor, and now she wants out. She wants to escape to the luxury of the Ab-Spa, where they eat real food instead of rats and synth cubes.

Meanwhile, the sleek-hulled, unmanned Gagarin has come back from the ever-continuing search for a new home. Nearly all hope is lost that a new planet will ever be found, until the Gagarin returns with a code of information that suggests a habitable planet has been found. This news should be shared with the whole fleet, but a few rogue captains want to colonise it for themselves.

When Yasmine inadvertently steals the code, she and Sam become caught up in a dangerous game of murder, corruption, political wrangling and…porridge, with sex-addicted Detective Zhang Woo hot on their heels, his own life at risk if he fails to get the code back.

ALSO BY RR HAYWOOD

THE UNDEAD SERIES

THE UK's #1 Horror Series

"The Best Series Ever…"

rrhaywood.com

Printed in Great Britain
by Amazon